The Mysterious
Doctor Cornelius
3. The Rochester Bridge Catastrophe

The Mysterious Doctor Cornelius
3. The Rochester Bridge Catastrophe

by
Gustave Le Rouge

translated, annotated and introduced by
Brian Stableford

A Black Coat Press Book

Visit our website at www.blackcoatpress.com

ISBN 978-1-61227-245-0. First Printing. February 2014. Published by Black
Coat Press, an imprint of Hollywood Comics.com, LLC, P.O. Box 17270, Enci-
no, CA 91416. All rights reserved. Except for review purposes, no part of this
book may be reproduced or transmitted in any form or by any means, electronic
or mechanical, including photocopying, recording, or by any information storage
and retrieval system, without permission in writing from the publisher. The
stories and characters depicted in this novel are entirely fictional. Printed in the
United States of America.

TABLE OF CONTENTS

The Story So Far

When a series of mysterious murders imperils the future of Jorgell City in the U.S.A., its founder, the billionaire Fred Jorgell, teams up with Harry Dorgan, the son of another billionaire, who is in love with his daughter Isidora, to set a trap for the murderer. The guilty party turns out to be Fred Jorgell's son Baruch, who flees the country when he is found out. Although the role played by his two accomplices, the plastic surgeon Cornelius Kramm and his brother Fritz, an art dealer, remains undiscovered, they also leave the city, relocating to New York.

After being robbed and left for dead in Brittany, Baruch Jorgell is taken in by a Chemist, Gaston de Maubreuil, who lives with his daughter Andrée and another stray he has taken in, the young hunchback Oscar Tournesol. Maubreuil's nearest neighbor is another scientific genius, the naturalist Prosper Bondonnat, who resides in a little artificial Eden with his daughter Fréderique and two laboratory assistants, Antoine Paganot and Roger Ravenel. When Maubreuil succeeds in realizing his long-held dream of synthesizing diamonds, Baruch cannot resist temptation, and murders him in order to steal the gems, fleeing once again.

Back in New York, Baruch seeks help from his old allies, Cornelius and Fritz Kramm, who conceive a daring plan to make use of him, by remodeling him as a duplicate of Harry Dorgan's brother, Joe. In order to make the substitution, they have Joe kidnapped by a gang led by Slug, a key member of the criminal organization they have long been building up, the Red Hand. Cornelius completes the identity exchange by remolding Joe into the physical image of Baruch, and then deliberately inducing brain damage, the effects of which include amnesia. While Baruch takes Joe's place, Joe is arrested as Baruch, tried, but found to be insane, and committed to Greenway Lunatic Asylum.

Cornelius, Fritz and Baruch—now established as the third Lord of the Red Hand—provoke a financial war between Joe's father, William Dorgan, and Fred Jorgell, in spite of Harry's attempts to prevent the conflict. With Isidora's help, Harry prevents Fred Jorgell's complete ruination, but William Dorgan nevertheless ends up with complete control of a Trust monopolizing American production of cotton and corn. In order to improve the yields of the two crops, Baruch attempts to imitate a technology developed by Prosper Bondonnat, and when it fails, the Lords decide to kidnap Bondonnat and force him to work on their behalf.

One of Cornelius Kramm's many secret projects involves the "resurrection" of criminals condemned to death whose executions, thanks to interference by the Red Hand, have been botched. Until they can be provided with new identities and brought back to the U.S.A., the supposed "dead men" are accommodated on an island in the northern Pacific bought from the US government by Fritz Kramm, which becomes the Red Hand's secret base, known to its residents as "The Island of Hanged Men." That is where Bondonnat is imprisoned after his abduction, and also where an eccentric millionaire, Lord Burydan, and an Indian named Kloum, are cast away after a shipwreck, and similarly kept prisoner.

The Lords of the Red Hand are now within sight of obtaining William Dorgan's billions, but, in reaching that position, they have acquired more adversaries than Harry Dorgan. Lord Burydan and Kloum escape from the Island of Hanged Men with Bondonnat's dog Pistolet, although Bondonnat fails to get away with them. After recovering from an injury sustained during Bondonnat's abduction, Oscar Tournesol travels to America, soon followed by Andrée de Maubreuil and Frédérique Bondonnat, with their fiancés Antoine Paganot and Roger Ravenel. Thanks to Oscar, who has made contact with Fred Jorgell, the Red Hand's first attempt to get rid of these new adversaries, using a contingent of the Red Hand known as "the Knights of Chloroform," goes awry, and the contest begins to heat up.

The Red Hand's attempt to murder Harry Dorgan by infecting him with green leprosy is thwarted by Antoine Paganot, and their second plan to kill the French party is sidelined because Baruch has become infatuated with Andrée and does not want Cornelius and Fritz to kill her. The Lords fare better in trying to thwart Lord Burydan's quest for revenge after escaping, because he is arrested after killing a member of the Red Hand that he recognizes. His cousin, Matthew Fless, a miser eager to take possession of his estates, has profited from his death, and collaborates in having him declared to be an impostor.

Unfortunately for the Red Hand, Lord Burydan ends up in Greenway Lunatic Asylum, from which Oscar Tournesol and Burydan's former secretary, Agénor Marmousier, set out to rescue him, with the aid of a monkey costume borrowed from a circus troupe known as the Gorilla Club, with whom Oscar has been in training. In the course of the flamboyant escape, Oscar, Burydan and Kloum also free another inmate: the supposed Baruch Jorgell, actually the amnesiac Joe Dorgan. Lord Burydan takes Joe with him to Canada, where he succeeds in reclaiming his estates, also spoiling a plot by the Red Hand to steal his wealth by having Slug murder Matthew Fless.

All of the Red Hand's enemies now converge on San Francisco, where Fred Jorgell is building a yacht, the *Revenge*, with a view to sending it to the Island of Hanged Men to free Bondonnat. An attempt by the Red Hand to misdirect the search goes awry, thwarted by the intelligence and ingenuity of Pistolet, who also thwarts an attempt by Baruch to kidnap Andrée. The Red Hand are, however, more successful in corrupting Fred Jorgell's concierge, Edward Edmond, exploiting his infatuation with a gypsy dancer, Dorypha, and have a stroke of luck when Edmond is given the job of recruiting a crew for the *Revenge*.

Fritz Kramm has a further stroke of luck when he is commissioned by an eccentric art collector, Balthazar Buxton, to acquire a portrait of Lucretia Borgia owned by William Dorgan. He employs a brilliant artist, over whom he had acquired empire by means of cunning blackmail, Lois Grivard, to produce a copy that he can switch for the original. That plan goes awry too because Fritz becomes infatuated with the woman who loves Grivard, the "healer of pearls" Lorenza. Fritz ends up murdering Buxton, but gets away with that crime and the financial proceeds of the deal.

With Edmond's help, the Lords of the Red Hand manage to place dozens of their own men in the crew of the *Revenge*, including Slug, who becomes its captain. Unfortunately for Slug, the first mate he takes on to assist with the actual navigation, a pirate named Christian Knox, has ambitions of his own for the *Revenge*, and before Slug can succeed in murdering the passengers, he has to cope with a mutiny, further complicated the fact that the dancer Dorypha, taken aboard as Andrée's chambermaid, switches sides and persuades her new lover, a Flemish mariner named Pierre Gilkin, to become the leader of a fourth party aboard the ship. Slug agrees to set his adversaries ashore, but covertly steers the ship toward the Island of Hanged Men.

The *Revenge* is not the only ship heading for the Island of Hanged Men, because Lord Burydan has commissioned a vessel of his own, the *Ariel*, and has hired Oscar's old friends in the Gorilla Club to assist in his assault. The *Ariel* launches an attack on the island, assisted by the fact that a contingent of the Hanged Men have made their own bid for independence using another ship strayed on to its shore, which has left behind on the island a party of refugees from a Russian prison camp, including a Cossack named Rapopoff.

Not only is the *Ariel*'s attack successful, but Lord Burydan is then able to set a trap for the *Revenge*, which results in the capture of all the crewmen belonging to the Red Hand, except for Slug. Unfortunately, by the time the island is captured, Bondonnat has already escaped with Rapopoff, leaving behind an embalmed body that has been surgically modified into his double in the course of one Cornelius Kramm's experiments. The rescuers who have come to free him therefore believe, erroneously, that he is dead.

Now read on.

13. THE FLOWER OF SLEEP

I. The Invisible Thief

The quays of the little port of Basan were subject to a hectic animation that morning. Japanese, Tagal, Chinese and Malayan coolies were busy unloading a huge junk with a gilded poop and sails of woven bamboo, whose cargo consisted of porcelain from the great island of Nippon, swifts' nests harvested from the caves of Sumatra, holothuria, crystallized ginger, bamboo shoots pickled in vinegar and other exclusively Asiatic aliments.

The arrival of the junk, which had stimulated the interest of all the traders in the small town, was not the only thing that had excited the curiosity of the idlers. Shortly after the junk, a large fishing boat had come into the port. It was manned by four men: two Eskimos; a Cossack or Kalmuck of a very emphatic Tatar type; and a European, who was assumed to be English of French and whose physiognomy, framed by long snow-white hair and large side-whiskers, expressed mildness and intelligence.

The old man, who was doubtless the owner of the boat, was luxuriously dressed in an overcoat lined with blue fox fur and coifed in a hat of the same fur. He had numerous items of baggage with him, which the three servants hastened to take out of the boat and deposit on the quay.

They had scarcely finished when the governor of the port, a Japanese named Noghi, advanced in the midst of a large crowd of curiosity-seekers to ask the stranger to explain himself. Pretentious dressed in a check suit of American manufacture, Mr. Noghi spoke English fluently; it was in that language that the conversation took place.

The new arrival immediately furnished the most satisfactory explanations. His name was Prosper Bondonnat. He was a French scientist known throughout the world for his work in meteorology, botany and medicine. He declared that, while traveling from San Francisco to Vancouver, he had been the victim of a shipwreck, from which he had only been able to save his most precious papers, some scientific instruments and a sum of money.

At the request of the Japanese, Monsieur Bondonnat showed him several documents that left no doubt as to his identity.

Once this point was settled, the governor obligingly put himself at the old scientist's disposal with regard to any information he might require. "The island of Basan," he explained, "is one of the most southerly Japanese possessions. Completely isolated in the Pacific, it is hundreds of leagues from any other inhabited land, between the Philippines and the Hawaiian islands."

"That's regrettable," said Monsieur Bondonnat. "As you can imagine, my keenest desire is to return to France as soon as possible."

"You will not have long to wait. In three weeks, you will be able to take the American steamer that operates a regular service between Shanghai and San Francisco."

"That reassures me slightly. I'll go immediately to telegraph my children, who must be very anxious about me."

The Japanese smiled ambiguously, uncovering his pointed teeth and emphasizing the angle of his oblique eyebrows. "Unfortunately," he said, "the island of Basan is not yet linked to Japan by the electric cable."

"Too bad!" murmured the scientist, whose physiognomy expressed deep disappointment. Since that's the case, Monsieur le Gouverneur, I'll count on your kindness to indicate a means of finding comfortable lodgings."

"As to that, nothing is easier. On the outskirts of our little town, there are several villas to rent, fully furnished and surrounded by beautiful gardens."

"I won't quibble about the price, provided that the habitation is comfortable, for I won't hide it from you that, following the distress of the shipwreck and several nights spent at sea, I need rest. I'm no longer young, alas."

"You will see that you'll be very comfortable, and the forced vacation will permit you to visit our country, which, though very little known in Europe, certainly merits the attention of a scientist like yourself in several respects. The flora and fauna are very various and have not been much studied to date. Finally, you will find picturesque scenery everywhere, and in the interior, ruined Buddhist temples that are true marvels of their kind."

Monsieur Bondonnat, who had only expected to encounter savages in that remote island, declared that he was delighted by the governor's courtesy. After half a hour, they were the best of friends; after an hour, the scientist had become, in return for the sum of twenty-five dollars, the tenant of a delightful habitation surrounded by a vast garden.

Once that business matter was concluded, he returned to the quay where the boat was moored, and on his instruction, the Eskimos and the Cossack loaded the bag on to their shoulders in order to transport them to his new dwelling.

All four of them went through the narrow streets of the small town, still accompanied by Governor Noghi, who had appointed himself the Frenchman's obliging cicerone.

"Thanks to its particular situation between Asia and Oceania," he explained, "the island of Basan is inhabited by a very various population. There are seven or eight different races here: first of all the Japanese, who are the masters of the country and fulfill the political functions; then the former inhabitants, who belong to the Malay or Chinese race; and finally, emigrants from various points of Oceania—Kanaks, Tahitians, Papuans. Maoris and Fijians."

"It only required myself and my servants," said Monsieur Bondonnat, "to complete the ethnological collection."

Their conversation was abruptly interrupted by a series of moans and plaintive cries that went up from the other end of the narrow street they were in the process of traversing. They hastened their steps and suddenly found themselves in the presence of an Oceanian, already old, who was holding an almost-inanimate bronze-skinned girl in his arms, presumably his daughter. He was the one uttering the lamentable moans that they had heard.

"What's the matter?" the Japanese governor asked the indigene, urgently.

The man raised his arms to the skies in despair. "My daughter!" he cried. "My dear Hatouara! Dead! Lost! She's just been bitten by a red-crested viper! There's no remedy!"

Monsieur Bondonnat came forward. "My arrival is truly providential," he said. "By an extraordinary stroke of luck, I have a few phials of Dr. Yersin's antidote to snake-bite in my luggage."[1] He turned to the Cossack. "Quickly, Rapopoff," he ordered, in Russian. "My medical kit and bag number one—that's where the serum is."

---

[1] The reference is to the Swiss biologist Alexandre Yersin (1863-1943), who worked extensively in the Far East from the 1890s onwards; he is most famous for his work contributing to the discovery of the bacillus responsible for Bubonic plague.

The Cossack hastened to obey.

"Save my daughter," murmured the indigene, "and everything I have is yours."

Without replying, Bondonnat set to work immediately. With the aid of a Pravaz syringe he made a few injections of the serum; then he enlarged the wound in the arm where the girl had been bitten, and made a crucial incision with his scalpel. He made the wound bleed, and then cauterized it with a few drops of calcium hypochlorite.

He had carried out all these operations with a swiftness that one would not have expected in a man of his age.

"Yes," he said, "now I think we can considered this charming child as almost out of danger. Is it a long time since she was bitten?"

"Only ten minutes, Doctor," the indigene replied, in poorly-enunciated English, so bewildered by joy that he was stunned.

"Farewell, my friend," said Bondonnat. "Put the patient to bed and give her warm effusions. Unless my serum has spoiled—which sometimes happens, alas—I believe she'll recover."

Leaving the two indigenes still in the grip of the violent emotion they had just experienced, Bondonnat continued walking with Governor Noghi, who accompanied him to the threshold of his dwelling, thanking him profusely for his kindness and presence of mind. They separated on the best of terms.

Japanese houses are generally constructed out of bamboo and light planks, and the interior walls are usually formed by sheets of paper extended in frames. They do not have any serious form of heating. Fortunately, the house that Bondonnat had rented was more solid. It had been built some years earlier by an Englishman, and the walls were brick. The roof was covered with green and yellow tiles, producing a verity picturesque effect, and, to Bondonnat's great pleasure, it was equipped with doors with locks.

It only had four rooms: two on the ground floor, separated by a corridor that led to the garden; and two on the first floor. The furniture had remained as its original owner had left it. The comfortable chairs were made of bamboo or rattan. The larger items of furniture were made of the pink camphor-wood abundant in the region. The bedroom, equipped with a dressing-room with a sink, had a bed with an iron and brass frame, protected by a mosquito-net.

In sum, Bondonnat could not have hoped for anything better. The garden, in particular, delighted him with its luxuriant vegetation, surrounded by a bamboo palisade. There were beautiful collections of lilies and chrysanthemums, cycads and banana-trees, flowering cherry trees, palm trees, orange trees and superb coconut palms laden with fruit. In the center a pool ornamented with rocks was filled with Chinese dorados and fish with huge mouths, some of which had little silver rings passed through their gills.

Bondonnat unpacked joyfully. He arranged his papers in the little camphor-wood chest of drawers in his bedroom, and also deposited there an apparatus that served to register the presence of ultra-violet radiation, which he had invented during his imprisonment on the Island of Hanged Men. That exceedingly sensitive apparatus was enclosed in a case.

But for the impatience he experienced at the thought of spending another three weeks before sending news to his daughters, the old scientist would have been quite happy. He would be able, at any rate, to bring back some curious documents from his sojourn on Basan, which had not been studied by any scientist, and perhaps—who could tell?—an unknown plant or animal. After having made the usual "proprietor's tour" Bondonnat summoned Rapopoff and instructed him to procure provisions.

Rapopoff hastened to obey, taking the two Eskimos with him. He came back and hour later, sagging under the weight of victuals of all kinds; the Japanese and Tagal merchants had abused the Cossack's naivety by persuading him to buy all kinds of exotic comestibles. He brought back foodstuffs so bizarre that they even puzzled Bondonnat. There were shark-fins pickled in brine; earthenware pots containing stillborn puppies preserved in honey—which are considered a great delicacy by mandarins; rice wine in bottles wrapped in violet silk; silkworm cocoons from which, it appears, delicious creams can be made; and finally, earthworms pickled in kava alcohol in a calabash, and seaweed marmalade. We shall skip over the corned beef from Chicago, German pickles and a host of other European items, the list of which would be interminable.

Fortunately, Bondonnat perceived in the midst of this indigestible medley a beautiful crayfish and magnificent fruits: pineapples, guavas, Japanese medlars, coconuts, mangos, cream-apples, and evens voluminous breadfruits, which it is sufficient to cook briefly in an oven to have a delicious cake.

"So many things!" exclaimed the scientist. "But you're crazy, my poor Cossack. There's enough here to open a shop. We'll never be able to eat all this."

"They'll take charge of that, Little Father," replied the Cossack, pointing at the Eskimos, who were laughing blissfully, with exceedingly broad smiles."

Bondonnat was in such a good mood that he had no intention of reprimanding Rapopoff. "You're right," he said. "These two brave Eskimos, thanks to whom, after all, we owe our liberty, will be putting to sea tomorrow to return to the Island of Hanged Men; it's only just that we give them a feast before saying goodbye."

The Cossack suddenly became pensive. "I'd prefer it," he said, "if they didn't go back to that accursed island. I'm sure that they'll get a very poor welcome there."

"No," said Bondonnat, "if I thought that they'd come to any harm, I'd keep them with me, but they won't. When they go fishing they sometimes remain at sea for several days, simply by virtue of being drawn away by contrary winds. Since my supposed cadaver will have been discovered, no one will think of troubling them."

The Eskimos surpassed Bondonnat's hopes. They found everything delicious, including puppies, earthworms and shark-fins; they devoured everything. Their bellies were visibly rounded out, and Bondonnat secretly feared that they might burst. Fortunately, that did not happen. The two fishermen, whose stomachs were doubtless as strong as those of boa constrictors, serpent a peaceful night, and the following morning, fit and well, they came to bid the scientist farewell.

Bondonnat allowed them to take away the remains of the Oriental dinner by way of provisions for the voyage, and—which gave them even more pleasure—he gave the each a hundred dollars in silver.

Rapopoff went back to their boat with them, and came back with a satisfied expression to tell his master that the Eskimos had put out to sea, favored by an excellent south-westerly breeze that ought to take them home rapidly.

The next day and the following ones were employed by the naturalist in settling into his villa, with which he was increasingly content, and visiting the town, an incoherent aggregation in which palaces of colored brick were mingled with huts covered with palm-leaves and houses of bamboo and paper, as pretty and frail as dolls' houses.

The old scientist no longer attracted anyone's curiosity. Since it was known that he was on good terms with Governor Noghi, everyone treated him with the most amiable kindness.

In the course of his strolls the old man was able to convince himself that Mr. Noghi had not exaggerated in describing the picturesque charms of the island. Located far away from the highways of civilization, that corner of the earth had retained all its originality and color. Furthermore, the climate, hot but tempered by the Pacific breeze, made it a veritable Eden in which all the plants of Japan grew alongside the greater number of those of Java and the Polynesian islands. The air was delightfully embalmed with a light and subtle perfume that blended musk, amber and lemon-flowers. In that enchanted atmosphere, the mere fact of existence was a veritable joy.

Undermined by the perfidious climate, Bondonnat lost his energy and let himself relax into long reveries, spending entire hours in idleness in his garden, as bushy as a forest clearing, or on the shore, where the eternal song of the wind in the foliage of the filao trees and coconut palms resounded noisily.

While paying a visit to Governor Noghi, the scientist had learned with pleasure that the young indigene Hatouara was as well as could be expected, but he heard no further mention of her or her father thereafter.

A week went by in that fashion without the old scientist being bored for a moment. He was agreeably surprised one morning on seeing the young invalid at his house, accompanied by her father, who had thought it appropriate for such an important visit to but on a brightly-colored check suit that looked as if it might have been borrowed from the wardrobe of a clown. A coconut-fiber hat imitative of a Panama hat completed the worldly disguise.

Hatouara, whether by virtue of natural good taste or pecuniary impossibility, had not thought it appropriate to have recourse to European fashions in her adornment; her slightly curly blue-tinted black hair had been put up in the Japanese fashion, retained by coral pins, and her only garment was a light silk kimono decorated with arabesques of flowers and foliage, which left her arms bare to the elbows.

The adolescent had a bright coppery complexion and a straight and delicately-formed nose. Her slightly fleshy lips and languid dark eyes gave her a primitive grace with which our pale beauties have nothing to compare. Hatouara was admirably formed, and a sculptor would have found nothing to criticize in her entire person, from her small breasts whose points were outlined by the light cloth to her already-opulent hips. Her beautiful body had the purity of design of a Greek vase or a slender flower. She also had a vivacity of movement, a frankness of gaze and gesture, and an almost animal charm, which added to her other seductions.

Hatouara was carrying a net woven from raffia, filled with the most magnificent fruits. They were a present that she had brought her savior, which she promised to renew frequently. Rapopoff put that tasty gift, which embalmed the entire dining room, in a basket. Bondonnat refreshed his visitors with an excellent cup of yellow tea, accompanied by dry cakes and jam, and they chatted.

Amalu, Hatoura's father, had amassed a certain amount of money trading in the Polynesian islands in a small schooner that he owned. Now, with his savings securely deposited in a bank in Yokohama, he lived quietly on his income, and his only concern as fining his daughter a suitable husband.

He plied Bondonnat with questions about Europe, France and Paris, and the old scientist answered them with his customary patience and generosity. Hatouara remained silent, contemplating the dining room furniture admiringly. Then she went to visit the garden, and came back just as Amalu was trying to persuade the doctor to accept a few English gold coins by way of an honorarium. Bondonnat refused energetically, to the worthy man's great chagrin.

"What, then, can I do to be agreeable to you?" he asked the scientist.

"Well, when you arrived I was planning to go fishing. Come with me, and you can show me the best places."

"I'll leave you my little Hatouara. She's a very skillful fisherwoman, and will be very happy to go with you."

"I accept with great pleasure. Come on, Rapopoff, bring the lines and the basket."

Ten minutes later, the three of them went down to the shore, which was only a few paces from the garden wall, and installed themselves in a little cove, which Hatouara declared to be full of fish.

The sky and the sea were an admirable azure and the waves were almost caressing the roots of the coconut palms and tamarinds with bright green foliage. The water was so calm that they could see the white branches of coral in the depths, above which jellyfish scintillating with all the colors of the rainbow were swaying. From time to time, shoals of pink, lilac and golden yellow fish threaded their way between the green algae, to the holdfasts of which sky-blue holothuria and green and violet sea-urchins were attached.

Beneath the crystal of transparent water there was a series of fantastic landscapes, whose rich hues were almost unreal in their brightness.

Bondonnat cast his line, armed with a few marine worms, and had soon brought back bright red gurnards and an eel with a velvety black body constellated with golden spots. Hatouara watched him do it with a pitying smile.

Truly, she thought, the venerable stranger who had saved her life knew nothing at all about fishing; it was necessary to give him a lesson. Without saying a word, she picked up the landing-net—and English item found by Rapopoff in a shop in the town—and caught some tiny fish, which she deposited in a rock-pool beside her. When she had enough of them, she put them in her mouth. Then, casting off her garment with a single gesture, she dived boldly into the sea.

Bondonnat, somewhat at a loss, watched her streak like a siren between the corals and multicolored wrack. She soon reappeared at the surface, smiling and holding in her hands two huge silver-bellied dorados.

"I am little savage," she explained, in her awkward English. "Very young, I learn to fish that way."

"How do you do it?" asked Bondonnat, highly amused.

"Not difficult. I let out little fish one by one, and when big one comes close, I kill it with bite on top of head."

"I confess," said Bondonnat, with a paternal smile, "that I'd be quite incapable of doing as much. My line is sufficient for me."

Now that she had demonstrated her talents to the doctor, without shame and without coquetry, Hatouara lay down on the rock to dry her beautiful body. She moved back and forth, as lively and petulant as a bird, picking flowers, collecting coconuts fallen from the trees or chasing butterflies and other insects.

Bondonnat was delighted by the gentility of his young comrade, and when they parted, he insisted that she take half the fish that they had caught together. She promised to come back to the villa the next day with more presents.

From then on not a day went past without Bondonnat receiving a visit from her. Sometimes she brought fruits, sometimes beautiful seashells or fish that she had caught.

Occupied with walking and studying, the old scientist saw the days go by without experiencing the slightest ennui. He promised himself that he would return one day with his two children, his daughter Frédérique and his adoptive daughter Andrée, so that they could visit the enchanted island.

Basan was decidedly a faultless country. The inhabitants, almost all Buddhists, were very mild, benevolent and obliging. Governor Nighi had warned Bondonnat that thieves were very numerous on the island, and amazingly skillful, but thus far the scientist had not had to complain about anyone. As a measure of prudence, however, he made the faithful Rapopoff sleep on a mat in front of his bedroom door; having taken that precaution, he slept as peacefully in his brass bed as if he were not on a remote island two or three thousand leagues from his homeland.

One morning, Bondonnat observed that the drawers of the little chest had been left open, and soon perceived that his papers had been searched, disturbed as if by an impatient hand.

"That's strange!" he exclaimed.

He went to see Rapopoff, who was busy dusting. "Did you go out last night?"

"No, Little Father."

"You didn't leave your post?"

"I didn't budge from the threshold of your door. I only dozed lightly."

"You're not a sleepwalker?"

The Cossack opened his eyes wide. It took a quarter of an hour to explain to him what a sleepwalker was, and when he understood, he declared that he was utterly unafflicted by that singular infirmity.

"That's quite extraordinary. Perhaps, after all, it's me who is the sleepwalker." Bondonnat was joking; for his nerves had always been perfectly equilibrated and he had never suffered anything of the sort.

Somewhat preoccupied, he started setting his notes and papers in order. He had not yet finished when the Cossack asked him for some money in order to buy supplies.

Bondonnat took the little key that opened one of the drawers in the chest, which he had locked himself the previous evening, and found to his profound astonishment that that drawer too was open. The wallet that contained the banknotes was still there, but it seemed somewhat deflated.

Intrigued, he counted the banknotes that he had once been given by the Lords of the Red Hand. Ten were missing.

He was amazed. This time, his perspicacity was found wanting. It was impossible for anyone to have entered the room without waking the Cossack, but, on the other hand, he could not suspect the worthy Rapopoff, who had given him so much proof of devotion, and who had always professed a profound scorn for money.

Bondonnat examined the window. It was one of those windows found in all English colonies, known in France as *guillotines*, which open vertically. The interior bolt was in place. It was not by that route that the thief had entered.

It was the same with the ground floor windows, and as for the two doors—the one that let out into the road and the one giving access to the garden—the scientist found them in the same state as the previous evening, locked with a key.

It was incomprehensible.

Bondonnat considered the wildest hypotheses, without finding one that was plausible. In despair, he went so far as to sound the walls with taps of a hammer to see whether they might contain some secret issue; everywhere, they ran true, and in any case, they were not thick enough to conceal any hidden doorway.

The old scientist spent much of the morning trying to solve the enigma, but could not do it. In the end he gave up, trying to persuade himself that he had been the victim of a hallucination or a sudden fit of amnesia—but he was far from being convinced.

"Decidedly," he said, shaking his head, "I'd rather believe that I'm dealing with an invisible thief."

II. The Bare Foot

That day, Bondonnat ate lunch in his garden in the midst of the flowers and exotic plants that were, to him, like friends, all of whose species and varieties he could name.

In truth, he said to himself, philosophically, after having drunk his coffee, *I ought not to get too upset regarding this theft. Whoever committed it ought to be satisfied and doubtless won't return. Besides which, they must be relatively honest; they could have taken everything. Let's not think about it anymore and go for a walk.*

The scientist immediately put this plan into action. He put on a light rattan hat, equipped himself with a large paper parasol and went down to the shore, stopping from time to time to contemplate the play of the seagulls and cormorants, or to examine some flower or stone.

He went slowly along the coast in the shade of superb coconut palms in which squirrels and palm-rats were playing, dawdling. Then he followed a path that led down to the beach, and walked over the sand covered with a profusion of nacreous seashells. He had never felt the joys and charms of walking and meditation so forcefully. How sweet it was to stroll in this fashion, through one of the most beautiful landscapes in the world, after so many months of harsh captivity!

Lulled by his reverie, Bondonnat did not notice how far he had gone. Eventually, he found himself in a veritably grandiose location that was completely unfamiliar to him. He had not previously ventured so far from his house.

Above a forest in which all the species native to tropical regions were mingled, he perceived gilded cupolas and slender turrets: an entire elegant and complex architecture that made him think of the castles inhabited by genies that were found in the pages of the Arabian Nights.

He would have liked to visit the magnificent edifice, but he was separated from it by inextricable thickets of thorny plants, in the midst of which it would not have been prudent to risk himself, because they might serve as shelter for a great many snakes. The naturalist therefore resigned himself to continuing to follow the coast, and soon emerged into a profound bay, a kind of fjord that extended into the heart of the forest. In the depths of the bay, which was bordered by a steep cliff, there were numerous caves produced by the incessant and patient action of the waves.

He walked in that direction, but suddenly uttered a exclamation of surprise on finding himself unexpectedly in the presence of a wretchedly-dressed man with a hirsute beard, who was sitting on the sand in the shadow of the cliff eating a few bivalve mollusks similar to clams, opening them with a knife and then throwing away the shells.

As he drew closer, Bondonnat remarked with surprise that the seemingly-distracted man was white, doubtless a European, perhaps even a Frenchman like himself, for his unkempt hair and beard were ardently blond.

The scientist thought at first that he was in the presence of some naval deserter, and he drew closer, moved by curiosity and also by pity, for the poor fellow was in a lamentable state.

At the sight of Bondonnat, the solitary man made as if to run away, but, on recognizing that he was dealing with a man of his own race, he stayed where he was, and a smile was sketched on his distressed features.

Bondonnat thought it appropriate to strike up a conversation and asked for directions as to the best way to return to the port. Without thinking about it, he had expressed himself in French. It was with an inexpressible pleasure that he heard the stranger reply in the same language.

"You only have to follow the shore, Monsieur. It's impossible to go astray. There is a shorter path, which cuts through the woods, passing by the Buddhist temple, but you might get lost. It's more prudent to go along the seashore."

"I see with pleasure that I'm in the presence of a compatriot. You're French?"

"Yes," the man replied, somberly.

"Have you been here a long time?"

"I don't know exactly…a month, perhaps more."

Bondonnat perceived that his questions displeased the man, whose features had resumed their distraught expression. "If I'm interrogating you," he said, "it's not, believe me, to satisfy a vain curiosity. It's to discover whether I can be useful to you in any way."

"I don't need anything."

"You don't seem very fortunate, though. If a sum of money…"

"I don't want anything," the man replied, with a muted anger. "I'm quite all right as I am. I don't want anyone to take an interest in me, or pay any attention to me."

Bondonnat was profoundly puzzled. "You must have experienced some great misfortune," he said, "but there are very few that are completely irreparable." As the man remained silent, the naturalist's suppositions took another direction. "Perhaps you've been the victim of some unfortunate impulse and committed a crime?" he suggested.

This hypothesis extracted the stranger from his apathy. "Monsieur," he said, "I don't know you, but you seem to me to be full of benevolence, and I wouldn't want you to mistake me for a malefactor..."

"My name is Prosper Bondonnat."

"The famous naturalist?"

"The same."

"My dear compatriot, I can tell you my story in a few words, but you'll see that the catastrophe of which I've been the victim is irreparable, and that it would be best to leave me to my chagrin and sadness."

"I'm listening," said the scientist, sitting down on the sand.

"My name is Louis Grivard," he young man continued, "and it might not be completely unknown to you, for I've organized several exhibitions of paintings in France and America that had a certain success. It was in New York that I met the woman who was to become my wife, my dear Lorenza..."

At the mention of that name, the artist dissolved in tears, and was only able to continue his story after an interval of a few minutes.

"We were perfectly happy. We had loved one another since the day we met. There was a marvelous union between us, such a perfect harmony that we never had a different opinion about anything, even without prior discussion. We understood one another with a glance. It was a happiness beyond the simply human, and it's not extraordinary that it didn't last and ended tragically.

"We had only been married a few weeks when someone made us a very advantageous proposal. It's necessary to tell you that my dear Lorenza possessed the strange power of restoring all the brightness and luster to dead pearls. Several times, sovereigns had summoned her in order to confide their jewels to her."

"I've heard mention of that phenomenon," said Bondonnat.

"That tells you that Lorenza knew a great deal about pearls. A jewel merchant whose acquaintance we had made was looking for someone trustworthy to travel to Ceylon, Timor and Oceania to purchase considerable quantities of pearls. He thought that Lorenza was perfectly qualified for that delicate mission, and he proposed that we undertake, at his expense, in the most agreeable conditions, a voyage around the world. As I hesitated, he dangled before my eyes the potential I would have, in contemplating exotic landscapes, to introduce new and original notes into my work. Had not Paul Gauguin gone to Tahiti and Albert Besnard to India? And would it not be the most marvelous honeymoon voyage?

"We allowed ourselves to be persuaded and departed. The first weeks of our excursion were ideal. I could almost have died after being as happy as I was during those few days. Furthermore, our business affairs went well. In Ceylon and Timor we concluded very advantageous bargains on behalf of our employer. It was then that I had the fatal idea of spending a little time on this island of Basan, whose perfidious charm had seduced me, and which is the meeting-place of a large number of pearl fishermen and traders.

"We rented a small house on the outskirts of the town and, without neglecting the serious side of our mission, began our excursions through these marvelous landscapes. It was then that the first catastrophe fell upon us, in the midst of that tranquility and happiness, like a bolt from the blue.

"One morning, we perceived that all our pearls, which were the property of our employer and represented an enormous sum, had disappeared; the iron safe that contained them had not even been forced. It was ruination for us, and even dishonor; no one would ever have believed that we had allowed ourselves to be robbed so naively.

"I complained to Noghi, the governor. With a great deal of zeal—apparently, at least—he began an investigation. It produced no result, and, although I can't be sure, I've always thought that that cunning Japanese was in league with my robbers.

"We did not lose heart, though. I was considered to have talent; Lorenza, for her part, earned a great deal of money thanks to the marvelous faculty she possessed. We resolved to set to work and amass a sum of money sufficient to reimburse the cost of the pearls. Our love held us together; we loved one another so much that no misfortune was capable of overwhelming us.

"Is there any need to tell you that we resolved to quit this accursed island as soon as possible? It was then that the supreme catastrophe occurred..."

The artist began to tremble; a sob caught in his throat.

"Two days before our departure," he stammered, "Lorenza disappeared in the same mysterious fashion as my pearls! Yes, Monsieur, it's frightful but it's true. One morning, when I woke up, I found that she was no longer by my side—and the most terrible thing of all is that there was no trace of a break-in, no vestige, no clue! I was in despair...

"I went back to the governor. I begged, I implored, and I threatened. As before, he pretended to yield to my insistence; he even had a few inhabitants on whom suspicion weighed arrested, but in the end, he obtained no result, and eventually no longer paid any heed to the matter."

Bondonnat was profoundly troubled. Thinking about the theft of which he had been the victim, he wondered what mysterious malefactors he might be dealing with. They were doubtless the same ones that had taken possession of the pearls and abducted Lorenza.

"Go on," he said to the artist, who now seemed to have fallen into dejection again. "I need to know the slightest details of this adventure."

"I've told you the essence of it," the artist said. "I've been mad for several days, wandering through the woods and along the seashore without wanting to take any nourishment. I was looking for Lorenza; that was my obsession. I'm still searching. I'm convinced that she's still alive. Why would she have been killed? If I were certain that she was dead, I wouldn't survive her by a minute. The hope of finding her again is the only thing that gives me the courage not to die..."

"That is certainly a strange story," murmured Monsieur Bondonnat, sincerely compassionate. "But why haven't you gone to Japan to register a formal complaint with the French consulate? It seems to me that that's what I would have done in your situation."

Louis Grivard laughed bitterly. "You're forgetting, my dear compatriot, that I was devoid of money, completely ruined, my baggage sold to pay for the rent of our house and the expenses of the first futile search. But that's not the real reason. I might perhaps, by signing on as a seaman, have got back to Yokohama, but the mere thought of leaving the place where my Lorenza certainly remains overwhelms me. Besides, am I not better off here? In the eyes of my employer, the eyes of French law, am I not a thief? Perhaps, as I set foot on the quay of any civilized port, policemen would seize me by the collar. My description might have been circulated everywhere..."

Bondonnat took the hand of the unfortunate artist and squeezed it effusively. "My poor friend," he said, "it's not in vain that you've told me your story. I promise you that I'll do everything humanly possible to clarify this frightful mystery and recover your wife. But I have many things to tell you myself.

Bondonnat told him about his imprisonment on the Island of Hanged Men by the bandits of the Red Hand and the extraordinary manner in which he had escaped. He concluded his story by explaining how he too, the previous night, had been the victim of a theft whose circumstances were exactly similar to the one by means of which the artist had been robbed.

"They're obviously the same bandits," Louis Grivard replied, "and I tremble to think that some misfortune might overwhelm you too."

"Don't worry," replied Bondonnat, energetically. "I'll take precautions—and I won't hide it from you that this mystery impassions me. My self-esteem as a scientist is at stake."

The artist shook his head sadly. "I strongly doubt that you'll succeed," he said.

"I've discovered more difficult things, damn it! Let me reflect, formulate a plan, a stratagem, and we'll see…but let's leave that for the moment. You aren't, I suppose, going to continue living like a werewolf in those rags. I'm taking you with me; there's room for you in my house."

"I'm sincerely touched by your generosity, but I refuse. I can't sleep under a roof, in a room closed on all sides. I'd wake up with a start every five minutes, believing that I sensed invisible malefactors nearby. Come with me—I'll show you where I lodge."

Louis Grivard went as far as the entrance to one of the caves in the depths of the bay, beneath a large arch of madreporic origin. Bondonnat perceived a bed of palm leaves and large seashells that served the hermit as bowls. A little stream flowed down the cliff and as lost in the sands. Above the rocks was the forest, with its inextricable lianas and majestic verdure.

"This is my lair," said Louis Grivard, with a melancholy smile. This is where I sleep for much of the day, only going out to procure fruits and mollusks. I spend all night wandering around the island, though, and roaming the streets of the town, listening to conversations, watching and observing everything that goes on. With a bleak expression, the unfortunate fellow added: "Who knows? Perhaps one word would suffice to put me on the right track. In the morning, I come back, exhausted by fatigue, and I sleep. That's my life."

In spite of Bondonnat's persistence, Louis Grivard refused energetically to come to reside in the villa, but it was agreed that the scientist would visit him frequently and inform him of anything that happened that might be of interest.

As he was about to leave, the naturalist noticed that the walls of the grotto were sculpted into monstrous idols, with long almond-shaped eyes and thick smiling lips. He thought that the place might perhaps, before the arrival on the island of Buddhism, have been a temple consecrated to idols, to the evil spirits in the existence of which all Oceanian savages believe.

A circumstance that supported his opinion was that, five or six meters from the entrance, the cave was blocked by rockfalls; and he remembered having seen similar crypts ornamented by gigantic statues in India.

Bondonnat went home slowly, prey to an urgent preoccupation. Louis Grivard's confidences had forced him to think again about the previous night's theft. He had sworn that he would get the unfortunate fellow out of his sad situation, but no matter how hard he searched and racked his brains, he could not discover the good idea, the victorious ruse, that would allow him to get his hands on the invisible malefactors.

That evening, he ate very little. His heart was aching, and even Rapopoff was struck by his sadness. He went back to his room very anxious, but before going to bed, he instructed Rapopoff to lay down a long rattan mat between the door and the camphor-wood chest of drawers that was set against the far wall. He had him bring some rice flour, and, with the aid of a sieve, he spread a perfectly even layer over the entire surface of the mat.

"That way," he said, "if my robbers aren't pure spirits, they'll have to leave a few traces of their passage, assuming that they come back. I can't quite believe that they will."

He took another precaution, which was to place the wallet containing the remainder of his banknotes under his pillow. Then, satisfied with that idea, he went to bed.

Wearied by his long excursion, Bondonnat fell profoundly asleep almost immediately after going to bed, and slept straight through until the morning.

When he leapt out of bed his first concern was to look at the mat; the rice flour bore the perfectly clear traces of a small bare foot, the foot of a woman or a child.

Bondonnat looked round. As on the first occasion, all the furniture had been disturbed, and the papers were still in disorder in the open drawers.

"This time," the scientist exclaimed, "it's too much!"

He slid his hand under his pillow. The wallet was still there, but again it had diminished in volume. The thieves, emboldened by their first success, had taken twenty thousand-dollar banknotes.

Even when chance had put him on the track of astonishing discoveries, Bondonnat had never been so astonished. He tugged his white side-whiskers in order to convince himself that he was not asleep.

"Come on," he said, "this is insane. These indigenes aren't sorcerers, damn it, and we're no longer in the Middle Ages."

He opened the door of his room, which was locked, as on the previous occasions, and woke Rapopoff, who was still asleep, snoring like an organ-pipe, on the mat extended across the doorway.

Like his master, the Cossack had slept through the night and had not been woken up buy any suspicious noise.

The enigma remained insoluble.

"Any yet," said Bondonnat, profoundly intrigued, "I'd really like to know who that pretty naked foot belongs to!"

III. The Apparition

For the rest of the morning Bondonnat was prey to a strange mental malaise; he had the sensation of being caught in the gears of an invisible mechanism. All his reading about cases of suggestion and hauntings came back to his memory, and he now felt certain that the mysterious burglars would not stop there. In fact, he divined that the incomprehensible events of which his dwelling was the theater would continue to unfold with an inflexible and bizarre logic.

He was somewhat distracted from his cares by the visit of the amiable Hatouara, very proud of a brand new blue silk dress, pretty slippers embroidered in gold and a beautiful coral necklace, of which her father had made her a present that morning. She brought a basket of spiny crabs, eccentrically formed like Japanese monsters, and large tropical crayfish known as "carracks," which were as long as a man's hand.

"I bring you good news, Doctor," she said, in her awkward English. "The American steamboat not expected for twelve days more be here tonight."

"Who told you that?"

"Everyone on the quay. The steamer has been seen at sea by the fishermen."

"Thank you, my child," the scientist murmured, having abruptly become thoughtful.

"Then you go leave us?" asked Hatouara, with a genuine sadness in her voice.

"I don't know yet," he replied, "but go and play in the garden with Rapopoff. I need to think."

Bondonnat was perplexed. In spite of his keen desire to re-embark for France, it would cost him enormously to leave the island without having discovered the thieves. He had a heavy heart at the thought of abandoning the unfortunate Grivard to his despair, to whom, drawn by his natural generosity, he had made such fine and perhaps somewhat imprudent promises.

I believe, he thought, *that it will be necessary for me to remain for a while longer on this diabolical island. I know there'll be another steamer in a fortnight. The delay won't be enormous, and I can always give someone aboard the ship a telegram addressed to my daughter, in order to reassure her. And yet, do I have the right to make my poor Frédérique wait like that?*

Bondonnat was prey to the most cruel indecision. He could not make up his mind, either way, and concluded that it might be better to let himself be guided by events. He promised himself, moreover, to do everything in his power to hasten the solution of the enigma and the denouement of the drama. The more he reflected, however, the more he realized that that might be very little.

Nervous and indecisive, agitated by discontent, the scientist did not go out that day. He spent the whole afternoon sitting in his garden in the shade of a cycad, thinking and riffling through a few books in English that he had found in a Japanese paper-shop in Basan.

Hatouara had not deceived him. Shortly after sunset, Rapopoff came to tell him that a large steamship was moored in the harbor. From one of the first floor windows, Bondonnat was able to see the elongated hull of a steamer of medium tonnage anchored about two kilometers from the coast, already surrounded by a host of junks, sampans and boats laden with fruits and local merchandise.

The old scientist had definitely lost his appetite; that evening, as on the previous one, he scarcely touched the excellent meal that his Cossack had prepared for him.

As the latter was clearing the table, Bondonnat said to him, abruptly: "Rapopoff, you know that I'm being robbed every night?"

"Yes, Little Father."

"Well, it's necessary that you help me to discover the thieves. Tonight, you'll lie down on your mat but you won't sleep, and if anyone comes, you must seize them and call me."

Trained since childhood to passive obedience, the Cossack did not raise the slightest objection to this plan. He lay down on his mat as he did every evening, across the doorway, with the firm resolution not to close an eye all night.

On Bondonnat's advice, he had placed a large Japanese saber and a revolver on the floor within arm's reach.

Once he was in his room, the naturalist put out his lamp, and lay down fully dressed on the bed after having taken care to put his wallet in the inside pocket of his jacket. He too had resolved firmly to remain awake until dawn.

The night was very hot; the air was embalmed by the voluptuous breath of the gardens and woods. Bondonnat opened the window wide, and breathed in the air charged with languorous odors with delight.

It seemed to him that the night wind had never been charged with such heady aromas. He only had to let his eyelids droop to be transported into a field of tuberoses and narcissi, from which scents of overwhelming voluptuousness rose.

Soon, his eyes closed completely and he fell asleep.

It was broad daylight when he woke up, and at first he had great difficulty restoring order to his ideas. It was only after several minutes of effort that he remembered that he had promised himself not to fall asleep, but he soon reconciled himself to that negligence.

"Bah!" he said "I've disobeyed orders. Too bad! Rapopoff will doubtless have been more vigilant than me."

He leapt down from his bed, and his first concern was to dart a glance at the flour-covered mat that he had taken the precaution of disposing in the same fashion as the previous evening.

The tracks of little bare feet were clearly displayed there.

"This is beyond the bounds of the permissible!" cried the naturalist. "It's making a mockery of everything! And that imbecile Rapopoff has gone to sleep in spite of my prohibition! I'll have something to say about that!"

While talking to himself in this fashion, Bondonnat had put his hand mechanically to the pocket where his wallet was. He was more irritated than surprised this time to observe that it had been lightened by a further twenty bills. Of the hundred banknotes that the Lords of the Red Hand had once given him, only forty remained.

Suddenly, Bondonnat became genuinely angry. "This is becoming intolerable!" he cried. "It's stupid! It's nerve-racking, this manner of proceeding, of only removing a small number of bills at each expedition. I'd almost rather they'd taken them all at once. At least I wouldn't have to think about it!"

Genuinely exasperated, the scientist opened his bedroom door, firmly intent on roundly reprimanding the Cossack's negligence and idleness.

Rapopoff had disappeared.

His boots, his fur hat, his Japanese saber and his revolver were in their places beside the mat, but their owner was no longer there.

In vain, Bondonnat searched the other rooms of the villa and the garden; Rapopoff had vanished without leaving a trace, like the queen in the three-card trick.

This time, the circumstance was amazing, not to say terrifying. Anyone other than Bondonnat would have been gripped by panic and would doubtless have taken refuge on the American steamer, determined not to spend another minute on an island where such things occurred.

Not for a moment did Bondonnat think of giving in to his invisible enemies, however. The disappearance—or perhaps the murder—of his faithful Cossack irritated and pained him profoundly. He only took the time to tidy himself up before going to Governor Noghi.

The shrewd Japanese received him, as usual, very amiably. He listened to his story without blinking, agreeing with him in deploring that such crimes were possible in a civilized country dependent on the scepter of the Mikado and, finally, assuring him formally that he would put the entire local police force on campaign.

"I'm very sorry about what has happened to you," he concluded, "but as I told you when you arrived, these inexplicable thefts are very frequent on the island of Basan, and thus far, it has been impossible to discover the perpetrators. In any case, I promise you that we'll do everything n our power."

Bondonnat withdrew, not very hopeful about seeing the unfortunate Cossack again. He realized that the island was the seat of a formidable hidden power against which nothing could be done. He was furious and distressed, unable to see any resolution on which he could settle and profoundly humiliated by the observation of his own impotence.

He went home, ate a few fruits hastily by way of lunch, and then had the idea of going to relate his misfortunes to Louis Grivard. He therefore went to the cave that served as the artist's dwelling.

There was no one there.

Everything was definitely turning against him.

He spent the rest of the day prey to a feverish agitation, coming and going from one of the villa's rooms to another, and, without admitting it to himself, penetrated by a secret terror at the thought of the approaching night.

He thought about going to find Amalu and obtaining, via the intermediary of the indigene, some robust men to guard him, but after considerable hesitation, he renounced the idea. He was reluctant to put any confidence whatsoever in his fears, and told himself that the means of discovering the key to the mystery as not to frighten off the singular malefactors who were robbing him.

The result of his reflections was that he did not appeal to anyone, and mounted guard himself.

He took all possible measures not to be surprised by sleep, drinking several cups of strong coffee, equipped himself with a revolver and, leaving the door to the garden open, sat down under a bamboo bush, getting up from time to time in order not to allow himself to be numbed by the delicious atmosphere escaping from the dew-moistened foliage.

The air was crystalline in its purity. Hundreds of nightingales were chirping in the neighboring gardens, and large fruit-bats were passing silently in front of the moon on their velvet wings.

But Bondonnat was insensible to the glamour of tropical nature. He had but one thought in his head—to catch his thief *in flagrante delicto*—and through the gap in the garden door he watched the other door, the one that led to the street and was at the far end of the ground floor corridor.

It was almost one o'clock in the morning, and the naturalist was beginning to get irritated when he thought he heard a slight grating in the lock of the exterior door.

Soon, the door opened silently; a form was outlined in the gloom of the corridor, and from his hiding place Bondonnat saw a strange apparition.

It was a young woman, entirely naked except for a scrap of cloth that scarcely covered her loins, and from which a silken bag was suspended. What intrigued him mist, however, was that the young woman, whose slender bronze torso was illuminated by a ray of moonlight, was wearing one of those ancient Japanese helmets that are nowadays the joy of antiquarians, which are made of flakes of tortoiseshell or horn. Amazingly, the helmet had no holes in the position of the eyes; two thick plaques of horn blacked them completely. The person wearing it must necessarily be blind.

The apparition, which was holding a think bouquet of pale flowers in its right hand, with a penetrating odor simultaneously reminiscent of tuberoses and narcissi, stopped directly in front of the door that led to the garden and began to climb the stairs to the first floor.

Monsieur Bondonnat experienced a violent emotion. He felt that he finally had the first link in the chain that would lead him to the discovery of the truth.

Evidently, he thought, *that phantom is going to rob me again, but too bad—I have my banknotes in my pocket. They won't be taken again. Doubtless she won't take long to come back down. Then we'll see!*

He was not mistaken. After five minutes, the young woman in the helmet reappeared. She was still holding her bouquet and waving it mechanically, but Bondonnat perceived, stuck in her loincloth a wad of papers and the case containing the apparatus designed to measure the intensity of ultraviolet radiation, which he had carefully locked away, the previous evening, in the camphor-wood chest of drawers.

The naturalist was prodigiously interested in what he saw. All his suppositions had been surpassed; he seemed to be on the threshold of a strange world, and he could not repress a shiver on thinking about what he was doubtless about to discover.

Gliding almost soundlessly over the tiled floor of the corridor, the apparition had arrived at the door to the street. She opened it with a key that she took from the little silk bag hanging from her loincloth and went out, leaving the penetrating odor of her bouquet behind her, like a perfumed wake.

Bondonnat went out a minute later, and followed her, his heart beating rapidly

To his great surprise, she did not head in the direction of the town of Basan, presently plunged in sleep. She took the path that led into the forest.

At a steady pace, her bare feet trod on the moss, as thick and soft as velvet. Phosphorescent flies came to settle on her black helmet, further enhancing the fantastic quality of her silhouette.

Bondonnat could not help comparing himself to an old magician attracted by a female demon toward some infernal gulf.

A quarter of an hour, and then half an hour, went by. They were still walking through the woods, full of nocturnal rumors: dead branches breaking, the sighs of rutting beasts; the slithering of snakes; the stirring of insects, or birds in their nests. It also seemed to the naturalist that voices were whispering in his ears, telling him to turn back.

Bondonnat was brave. Gradually, however, he felt himself overtaken by a strange emotion. His composure gradually abandoned him, and twice he stumbled over twisted roots that barred the path, like nests of interlaced serpents.

Finally, he breathed more easily. Still on the heels of his mysterious guide, he had just entered a large avenue bordered with plane trees, with trunks that were pale gray in the moonlight. Their foliage formed a majestic and placid vault, from the height of which slender lianas fell, swaying at the slightest gust of breeze.

At the far end of the avenue there was a high wall, above which the trees of a garden were visible. Beyond the trees there were the sparkling cupolas of the Buddhist temple.

The entire landscape seemed to be painted on a silver background, with pinks, pale grays, blue and violets of an ineffable softness. It was a truly dreamlike décor. In spite of his preoccupations, Bondonnat could not help admiring it.

Suddenly, the apparition veered to the left and went into an avenue narrower than the first but much darker. The foliage was so dense there that the moon's rays could not get through it.

Soon, the old scientist observed that the avenue was narrowing further; a time came when it was no more than a path, only sufficient for the passage of a single person. The path went down a steep slope, and as it was bordered to the left and the right by thorny bushes, it required great attention not to be scratched as one went along.

The apparition did not seem to pay any heed to such obstacles; it was still moving at the same steady and rapid pace. Bondonnat had great difficulty in following it, and his fingers were bloodied several times in the darkness by the sharp thorns of the plants.

They descended in that fashion for a quarter of an hour, and then became to climb again. The path gradually widened, and Bondonnat was surprised to find himself on the other side of the garden wall; that thorny hedge, which must have continued through an underground passage, was an invention well worthy of the complications of a Chinese or Japanese brain.

The naturalist looked around. At a fairly considerable distance he could see the majestic buildings of the monastery, brightly lit by the moon. In front of him extended a Japanese garden as complicated as a labyrinth, with its tortuous side-paths, its little stone bridges, its pools of water and its tormented and deformed trees.

In the center, a vast stone Buddha overlooked the entire landscape with is benevolent smile and gilded aureole.

The garden must have been filled with magnificent flowers, and Bondonnat breathed in the perfume they emitted voluptuously. He had never known anything as troubling; and, in trying to analyze it, he found the same scents of tuberose and narcissus that had struck his nostrils when the apparition had passed close to him.

It's obviously in this garden, he thought, *that she must have collected her bouquet.*

He had slowed his pace. He started walking more rapidly again when he saw that his guide was heading toward the Buddha. Suddenly, however, she disappeared from view, as rapidly as if she had vanished in a puff of smoke.

The naturalist was profoundly disappointed. He went all the way to the pedestal of the god, uselessly, and then retraced his steps.

He went astray in the complicated network of pathways and bushes; he tried to figure out where he was, but it was impossible.

Eventually he found himself next to a bed of large pale flowers with broad corollas—the same flowers as those in the bouquet, and breathed in the perfume once again with pleasure; but half an minute had not gone by when he felt his head spinning and his thoughts becoming blurred.

He closed his eyes and fell down, inanimate, almost as suddenly attained as if he had been struck in the heart by a bullet.

Above the fantastic garden, the Buddha with the golden aureole was smiling enigmatically.

Amalu and his daughter Hatouara had got up early in order to bring Monsieur Bondonnat some beautiful pineapples and watermelons. They were quite astonished, on arriving at the villa, to find the door open and the house empty.

"Perhaps the doctor hasn't got up yet," said the young woman. "Let's go up to his bedroom. He won't hold it against us if we wake him."

Amalu found that proposal quite natural. With the naivety and simplicity of mores that is the charm of certain Oceanian peoples, neither the father nor the daughter thought that it might be committing an indiscretion to wish their friend good morning in his bedroom.

They went upstairs, surprised not to encounter Rapopoff. The bedroom door was open. Monsieur Bondonnat was lying on his bed, fully dressed, but he was so pale that Amalu and Hatourara thought he was dead.

"How pale he is!" cried the girl, hurrying to the inanimate body of the old scientist. "His heart is no longer beating!" The poor child's eyes were moist with tears.

"You're mistaken," said Amalu, after a more attentive examination. "The heart is still beating, very faintly—but what a strange odor there is in the room."

He hastened to open the window.

As he came back to the bed, his foot slipped on something, and he almost stumbled.

"What's this?" he said, bending down to pick up the object that had nearly caused him to fall.

Between his fingers he was holding a flower petal. He bought it closer to his nostrils and then threw it away with a kind of horror.

Hatouara watched him do it, surprised.

"I know now why the doctor is ill," said Amalu. "Someone has tried to poison him. It's fortunate that I had the idea of coming to see him this morning, for I'm perhaps the only man on the island of Basan who knows the remedy for his illness."

"He saved me," the adolescent said. "How glad I would be if we were able to do the same for him. Do you think, Father, that we can cure him?"

"Yes, my love—but there's no time to lose."

Amalu ran into the garden. He picked half a dozen different flowers and roots, pulverized them with a grater that he found in the kitchen and expressed the juice into a glass, which he topped up with pure water. Seconded by Hatouara, he succeeded on unclenching the invalid's teeth with his knife, and, raising his head, forced him to absorb the contents of the glass, a little at a time.

The effect of the medication was immediate. Bondonnat opened his eyes; his cheeks colored slightly and he darted fearful glances around him.

"Yes," he said, in a faint voice, "the Buddha...with its golden aureole...the garden...but I'm at home...and the woman with the black helmet...what's become of her?"

Amalu and his daughter understood that the old man was delirious. He did not take long to regain his faculties, however; he recognized his friends and wished them good morning.

"I'm very glad to see you," he murmured. "Strange and terrible things have happened to me in recent days..."

Amalu interrupted him. "Go play in the garden," he ordered his daughter. "I need to have a serious talk with the doctor."

Hatouara obeyed this paternal injunction, but not without pulling a face that demonstrated how disappointed she was in her curiosity.

As soon as she had gone out, the indigene lowered his voice. "You almost died, doctor! I succeeded in waking you up, but it was just in time. You must avoid any recurrence of the misfortune. Firstly, I must ask you to tell me frankly what has happened to you. I think you trust me?"

"Entirely. I'll tell you everything."

Bondonnat told the story in full, beginning with the successive thefts of which he had been the victim, and then his expedition to the gardens of the temple. Naturally, his story concluded at the moment when he had lost consciousness. He was unable to explain how he had found himself lying on his bed in his house, and wondered whether he had been the victim of a hallucination.

"Everything you have seen really happened," said Amalu, gravely. "It was the bonzes that brought you home. The fact that you're a European doubtless made them fear some repercussions, especially given that this isn't the first time something of the sort has happened..."

"But why did I fall unconscious so rapidly?" asked the naturalist, anxiously.

"You breathed in the flower of sleep."

"The flower of sleep?" queried the naturalist, surprised. "That must be the flower with the large white corollas, whose perfume is delicious?"

"Yes," said Amalu, looking round as if he were afraid of being overheard. "The perfume is so penetrating that it puts all those who breathe it in to sleep, and if they breathe it for a long time, they die. Once, before the Japanese occupation, many crimes were committed thanks to that flower. When they arrived here, the Japanese had all the plants that produced it destroyed, and if a few rootstocks remain, they're probably deep in the virgin forest. That, at least, is the official version."

"But I've seen entire beds of them with my own eyes, in the garden of the Buddhist temples—almost fields!"

"You're doubtless right, but it wouldn't be prudent to advertise that discovery too loudly."

"Obviously. I can figure it out now. The bonzes have reserved the monopoly of these mysterious crimes that always go unpunished." Bondonnat became indignant, and continued: "However, if the governor knew that they were cultivating these venomous plants in such large quantity..."

"He probably knows it as well as you and me, but he wouldn't dare and wouldn't want to order them to be destroyed. No one imagines that a priest of Buddha can commit an evil action." With a sigh, the old indigene added: "Oh, our old idols were better than their Buddha!"

Bondonnat remained silent. Fundamentally, he was satisfied. Hazard and his courage had permitted him to lift a corner of the veil of mystery. It would not take long to discover the entire secret.

"At any rate," he said, "you know the antidote to the flower of sleep, my brave Amalu?"

"I'll gladly show you the plants that serve to make up the beverage that I made you drink. It's a recipe that I got from my father, who got them from his own forefathers, along with others of the same sort—but that's not what it's most vital to know. At the most, it's useful, as in your case, for recalling to life those who've breathed too much of the fatal flower.

"What do you mean?"

"Simply that the bonzes must possess a means of resisting the effects of the asphyxiating perfume."

"Undoubtedly," exclaimed the scientist, for whom that response was a flash of enlightenment, "the young thief who robbed me must know that means! I've got it—it's the helmet. That must contain the antidote."

"Perhaps," said Amalu, "but why are the eyes blindfolded?"

"That's not difficult to explain. The young woman who came into my house must have been in a hypnotic trance; she probably doesn't even know what role she as playing. She's put to sleep; she's given orders; she obeys. I'm beginning to see the business clearly. A few skeleton keys, which are easy to fabricate, have done the rest."

"It might be more complicated than you think," said Amalu, whose face expressed a deep preoccupation.

Bondonnat was not listening to him; he was following his train of thought. "I can put it together quite well," he said. "Rapopoff, sent to sleep first, was unable to prevent her from opening the door to my room, and I immediately fell victim to the subtle perfume, which must be much more active in a limited space like a bedroom."

"The power of the flower is so great that insects fall unconscious into the depths of its cup-shaped corolla and birds that approach it too closely flutter their wings and fall. Snakes have often been found dead because they had the imprudence to coil around its root.

"I must procure a few specimens of his bizarre plant, at all costs," said Bondonnat. Then, suddenly passing on to another idea, he said: "My dear Amalu, what do you think they've done with poor Rapopoff? I hope they haven't killed him."

"No, the Buddhists have a horror of bloodshed. It's almost unprecedented for them to commit a murder, and when they do, it's in a very indirect fashion."

"As in my case, for instance?"

"Exactly. The Cossack must be imprisoned in some crypt. I wouldn't be surprised if, like many of his compatriots, he belongs, or has belonged, to the Buddhist religion."

At that moment, Hatouara burst into the room with her habitual vivacity.

"Well," she exclaimed, "is it over, all this mystery?"

"Yes, my child," said Amalu.

Bondonnat remained silent. He could not take his eyes off the little native, who, as insouciant as ever, had left her beautiful embroidered slippers in the garden and ha just jumped with both feet on to the mat, which was still covered with rice flour.

The old man was suffocated by the discovery he had just made.

"Go back and play in the garden," he said to the young woman, in a voice that was completely changed.

Hatouara obeyed, but with a sulky smile.

"What is it?" asked Amalu, who had observed the scientist's astonished gaze.

"Need I say? It's poor little Hatouara that has served as the bonzes' instrument."

Amalu's brown faces went the gray color of ashes. The poor devil was distressed. "Oh, Doctor," he stammered, "if I ever thought that my daughter..."

"Don't worry—I'm not accusing her. She certainly has no idea what she's done. She's only introduced herself into my home while plunged in the unhealthy trance whose cause and result I've explained to you."

"But how were you able to discover that?"

"Look!"

Bondonnat showed Hatouara's father the identity of the old imprints left on the mat and those that the little feet of the young woman had made in the rice flour a few moments ago.

"That's terrible!" murmured the native, sincerely consternated. "I'll call my daughter!"

"Refrain from saying a single word about what I've just confided to you! It's necessary that she knows nothing. You'd cause her grief without getting us any further forward. The poor girl is very fond of me, I know."

"What do you advise me to do?"

"Say nothing. Tonight, if Hatouara gets up, you need to follow her. I'm sure, myself, that she'll come directly here."

"I'll do as you say," said Amalu, bowing respectfully. "But I beg you, don't hold any grudge against the poor girl for the harm she's caused you."

"On the contrary," said Bondonnat, who had recovered his good humor. She'll be rendering me a great service. I'm on the track of a very curious discovery, and I'll owe you my gratitude."

After some final detailed instructions, Bondonnat bade farewell to the father and daughter, not without having fed them some dry cakes and a glass of rice wine.

The scientist was radiant. "Definitely," he murmured to himself, "all is going well. It would have been stupid for a man like me to be rolled over by savages!"

After that reflection, which testified to a measure of vanity, Bondonnat ate lunch with a hearty appetite—which led him to think that as well as its narcotic effect, the flower of sleep might also possess appetite-enhancing properties. Now that he believed that Rapopoff had not been murdered, he felt relieved of an immense burden.

As soon as he had finished his coffee, which he made himself, the scientist armed himself with his paper parasol and set out for the cave of his friend Grivard. This time, however, instead of following the shore, he went through the woods. The path he had taken led him along the façade of the Buddhist temple. Its appearance was majestic. A monumental stairway, ornamented by admirable bronze monsters with the bodies of reptiles and the heads of dogs ended at a peristyle supported by elegant columns of granite ringed with copper.

In front of it extended a semicircular courtyard, in which bamboo huts were installed from whom incense-sticks, little ivory idols and all kinds of curiosities and religious articles were sold.

Bondonnat paused for some time at the entrance to that courtyard, but he did not do so merely to admire the work of art; he tried to obtain an exact idea of the constitution of the buildings and their layout. The façade that he could see, he knew, must be situated at the extremity of the gardens into which he had penetrated the previous night, and that was an important reference-point.

Rested by that halt, Bondonnat continued his walk. He soon arrived at the bay that served as Louis Grivard's retreat. The artist was eating a meal of coconuts, from which he first sucked the milk and then smashed the shells in order to extract the flesh.

"You have no idea how much good your visit did me," Grivard said. "I'm completely cured of my melancholy; I've rediscovered all my energy, and am sure now that I shall recover Lorenza."

"For my part, I have interesting things to tell you."

For the second time, Bondonnat told the story of his fabulous adventures of the preceding night.

The artist listened until the end, his gaze burning with fever and his features contracted. When the story was concluded he got to his feet abruptly. "My dear friend," he said. "I promise you that tomorrow, it will be me who has something new to tell you."

"What are you going to do?"

"I can't tell you anything. I only ask one thing of you, which is to lend me an iron bar and a good revolver. That's indispensable for what I've decided to do."

"I have what you're requesting at the villa. You can collect the whenever you wish."

"Right away! But as I don't want to be seen, we'll go along the shore."

Bondonnat was intrigued, but he understood that it would be futile to question Grivard. They both set out, therefore, going placidly along the beach and talking about trivial matters.

V. The Living Idol

Bondonnat spent the rest of the day writing a long letter to his daughter and drafting a telegram that was also addressed to her. After much hesitation he had decided to let the steamer depart without taking passage on it. With the particular obstinacy of scientists, he did not want to leave the island of Basan before having found the solution to the problem of which he thought that he already had the principal elements. He would be able to take the next steamship, and his daughter Frédérique and his ward Andrée de Marbreuil, reassured by the telegram that he had sent them, would await his return without anxiety.

After the evening meal, he removed the mat covered with rice flour, which was now unnecessary, from his bedroom and he waited, with a curiosity mingled with impatience, for the nocturnal events that would doubtless not take long to unfold.

As on the previous evening, he installed himself in the garden, leaving the door ajar. There was no reason why that stratagem, which had been so successful before, should not be successful a second time.

He had not anticipated the arrival of the apparition—which is to say, the amiable Hatouara—before the middle of the night, but a surprise was in store for him. It was only a little after ten o'clock when someone rang the bell at the exterior door. Bondonnat hastened to open it, thinking that it might be Rapopoff, who had succeeded in escaping. As he was about to turn the key in the lock, however, he reflected that at such an hour it might not be prudent to open the door without knowing more.

"Who's there?" he asked.

"It's me, Amalu. Open up, quickly."

The scientist hastened to light a lamp and took his guest into the dining room. Amalu seemed distraught.

"You were right," he stammered. "Hatouara, who was sleeping peacefully on her mat, has just got up, and I perceived that she was under the influence of some evil spirit. Her eyes were fixed, her movements abrupt and jerky, and even though I stood directly in front of her, she didn't see me. She was like a dead woman who had been forced to emerge from her tomb."

"She was in a hypnotic trance," the naturalist explained. "I hope you didn't wake her?"

"I was careful not to do that. I remembered your instructions. I contented myself with observing everything she did. First she went into a room that no one ever enters, where all sorts of objects are stored seashells, old chests, porcelain and ancient suits of armor. I was amazed to see her emerge from there with the eyeless helmet that you had described."

"She has no need to see, since she's asleep."

"Then she went out of the house at a slow, almost mechanical pace that had something frightful about it. She went through the streets of the sleeping town and headed out into the country."

"Did she go to the Buddhist temple?"

"Yes, but I dared not follow her to the other side of the garden wall. I was afraid, and in haste to come back and warn you."

"Well, sit down there and wait calmly. I'll wager anything you like that she'll be here within an hour."

At that moment, the faint noise of a key in the lock of the exterior door was heard.

"There she is!" exclaimed Bondonnat, excitedly.

"What should I do?"

"Nothing at all. I'll act alone."

He went to station himself at the garden door, which he opened wide. When Hatouara passed in front of him, he snatched the bouquet of flowers of sleep from her hand, abruptly, and threw them far away into the garden.

Deprived of her bouquet, the young woman had made a bizarre gesture, but she continued to keep her hand closed, as if the flowers were still between her fingers.

"Come quickly," said the naturalist to the old indigene. "You'll have to light my way."

Amalu picked up the lamp; they both climbed the stairs behind Hatouara. The young woman, still walking like a phantom, went straight to the camphor-wood chest and started ferreting through the drawers.

"This is the propitious moment!" exclaimed Bondonnat.

He drew nearer to her, deftly unfastened the clasps that were securing the helmet, behind the head, and removed it.

Hatouara did not seem to perceive it. Her eyes half-closed, she continued searching the drawer, picking up papers at random and wedging them into her loincloth.

Bondonnat examined the helmet attentively. He observed that it was lined inside with a fine mat woven from herbs that gave off a bitter aroma. Breathable air could only arrived at the nostrils and mouth after having passed through that mat, doubtless soaked in powerful antidotes. Without hesitation, Bondonnat put the helmet on, which, much too large for the young woman, fitted him marvelously.

He fastened it, took it off, and fastened it again several times, to make perfectly sure of the functioning of the clasps.

"What are you going to do?" asked the indigene, who was watching the scene curiously. "Do you want me to go with you?"

"No—I can only do it alone. All I ask is that you take poor Hatouara home with you and don't do anything else."

Bondonnat studied the helmet carefully. It was, by virtue of its curious design, a veritable museum piece.

Swiftly, he took a number of tools out of a drawer. To Amalu's great amazement, he prized loose the two disks of horn that were covering the eye-holes and replaced them with two convex glass lenses borrowed from a pair of protective goggles that he used in certain dangerous experiments. Fortunately, the lenses had the same diameter as the disks. The naturalist fitted them solidly in place with the aid of some wax.

While he was engaged in this task Hatouara went to feel under the pillow on the bed and, not finding the wallet there, returned to the chest of drawers, which she resumed searching. She seemed irritated, like someone unable to find what they are searching for. She went back to the bed, then returned to the chest of drawers, repeating the sequence several times with all the signs of a manifest ill humor.

After instructing Amaklu not to let the young woman out of his sight, Bondonnat went down to the garden and, putting on the helmet, had no difficulty recovering the bouquet of flowers of sleep. As he was about to go back up he found himself face to face with Hatouara, who was coming out. Without hesitation, he approached the bouquet to her nostrils.

The young woman uttered a profound sigh, and suddenly collapsed. Bondonnat jut had time to catch her in his arms, getting rid of the dangerous bouquet again, which might have been harmful to Amalu.

At a signal from the naturalist, the latter took Hatouara, whom he could carry without difficulty, with her head over his shoulder, for she was little more than a child.

The door closed behind them, and Bondonnat, wearing the helmet, remained alone in the house.

"There!" he murmured. "A good beginning. Now I have to return to the Buddhist temple. Should I take the bouquet? I'll find enough of those strange flowers out there."

After a moment's reflection, Bondonnat decided to take the bouquet, which might serve as a defensive weapon. He also equipped himself with a revolver and a sturdy knife.

Having made these arrangements, he set forth, and took the same route that he had taken the previous evening, following the native girl. He found the broad avenue of plane trees easily enough, and then the path bordered by thorny bushes, whose dark slope he followed. He admired the artistry with which those who had constructed the passage had been able to extend the hedge underneath the walls.

Finally, his heart beating with emotion, he found himself in the magical garden dominated by the giant statue of Buddha with the golden aureole.

This time, he took great care to mark the exact spot where the subterranean passage began, with several broken branches and a large stone. Walking slowly, in order not to go astray in the labyrinth of pathways, Bondonnat headed for the statue of Buddha.

On the way, he passed alongside the immense bed where the flower of sleep grew, and observed with great satisfaction that the delightful odor simultaneously reminiscent of tuberose and narcissus no longer reached his nostrils. His anticipations had been correct. The helmet he was wearing did indeed contain the antidote that permitted the mortal odor to be confronted.

He paused momentarily to consider the plant that produced it. The leaves were large and dark, similar to those of an acanthus; the stems, very straight, bore two or three calices and their extremity, which terminated in six large petals of an immaculate whiteness.

That, he said to himself, *is certainly a plant that does not figure in any classification system and has not yet been studied by anyone. It's absolutely necessary that I take a few rootstocks and seeds back to France. That way, my sojourn on the island of Basan won't have been wasted.*

Extracting himself from his scientific considerations, Bondonnat soon arrived at a kind of cloister supported by columns whose capitals were ornamented with lotus flowers, on to which several doors opened.

He opened one at random and found himself in a long corridor, which he followed for some time.

A shadow loomed up in front of him. A bonze clad in an ash-gray robe barred his way. The naturalist reached out and applied his bouquet to the nostrils of the priest, who immediately collapsed to the floor. Bondonnat was able to continue on his way.

He opened another door and found himself in a vast hall with majestic vaults. He realized that this was the temple, properly speaking.

The floor was covered with slabs of yellow marble, covered with mats woven with a metallic thread as shiny as gold.

At the back of the sanctuary stood three effigies of the Buddha, entirely gilded, and a gigantic statue. The old scientist glimpsed all of that by the glow of large paper lanterns that hung down from the vault and cast a strange red and green gleam over everything.

Facing the altar, separated from the principal nave by a balustrade, there were large bouquets of flowers in silver vases, and incense smoke was emerging from symmetrically-disposed cassolettes.

Bondonnat was about to traverse the temple when three bonzes he had not noticed, who were praying in front of the altar, rose to their feet and advanced toward him with menacing expressions.

The naturalist went straight ahead to meet them. He knew that with his bouquet, he was invincible, and he had seen at a glance that his three adversaries were unarmed. There was also a certain hesitation and terror in their movements, which caused the naturalist to think that the men he was dealing with were not unacquainted with the secret of the flower of sleep.

A minute later, without them having had time to utter a cry, the three priests had fallen on the floor and were asleep, lying at the foot of the altar.

Bondonnat judged it prudent to deprive one of the bonzes of his ash-gray robe and don that costume, which ought to attract less attention. Then he crossed the entire length of the temple, passing in front of the monumental bronze door that, when it was opened during the day, gave access to the hemicycle where he had paused during the day on his way to visit Louis Grivard.

Finally, he went under an arch that led to a long corridor bordered to the right and left by cells; the sonorous snores that were escaping from them told him that the monks were at rest, and he did not think it appropriate to disturb their slumber.

At the end of the corridor there was a staircase, which Bondonnat went down, telling himself that if the Cossack really was a prisoner of the bonzes, they must have him locked in a dungeon.

The staircase had exactly sixty steps, and Bondonnat, in pitch darkness, the regretted not having brought some means of producing light with him. He was about to go back up to the temple to procure one of the lanterns attached to the vault when he perceived a faint gleam. He headed in that direction, following an interminable corridor, and soon found himself in the place from which the light was coming.

It was a vast crypt, which air only reached through occasional ventilation-shafts. It was illuminated by a large blue lantern; that was the gleam he had perceived from the steps of the staircase.

As he crossed the threshold of the crypt, Bondonnat saw a truly extraordinary spectacle.

At the back of the crypt stood a granite altar on which, seated in an armchair, there was a strange statue covered from head to toe in an infinite number of pearl necklaces. There was such a vast number of them that the torso was only visible in places.

Very intrigued, Bondonnat approached the altar were the porcelain armchair stood in which the idol was sitting. Suddenly, he emitted an exclamation of amazement. He had just seen the breasts of the statue rise and fall, as if by virtue of the respiration of a sleeping woman.

The idol was alive.

In a flash, Bondonnat remembered the artist's confidences.

"Lorenza!" he exclaimed. "The healer of pearls! It's her! It can only be her!"

Very excited by this discovery, he was preparing to wake the young woman up, to tell her that he had come to rescue her, when a bonze suddenly emerged from behind the altar.

Like Bondonnat, the newcomer had his head covered by a protective helmet. In spite of his surprise and emotion, the old scientist noticed that the helmet had small mica sheets fitted in the eyeholes, which permitted the wearer to see his surroundings clearly.

Against that unexpected aggressor, the flower of sleep would be ineffective; Bondonnat retreated in haste.

The bonze, Herculean in stature, rapidly caught up with the old man, snatched his bouquet out of his hand and threw it outside through one of the ventilation shafts. Then he knocked him down, put a knee on his breast, and tried to rip off his helmet.

Bondonnat understood that he was doomed. Breathless beneath his enemy's knee, half-stifled, he had a few seconds of atrocious anguish.

The bonze had succeeded in removing Bondonnat's helmet. He contemplated the old scientist's face for some time with a strange curiosity, as if he were astonished by his captive.

"Help!" shouted the naturalist, making a violent effort to free himself.

To make him shut up, the bonze set a huge brown hand, like an ape's paw, over his mouth in a brutal fashion, but he could not reduce Bondonnat to silence. The latter continued to call for help, shouting "Help! Murder!" and struggling in such a way that in order to master him, his adversary had to seize him by the throat.

He squeezed tentatively, and then more forcefully, and Bondonnat fell silent, gurgling, half-strangled.

It was at that moment that one of the crypt's lateral doors was broken down by the effort of a vigorous shove.

A man came in. Bondonnat was able to recognize Rapopoff.

"Help!" he croaked, desperately, making a supreme effort to free himself.

The Cossack was also dressed in a long ask-gray robe, which made him look ridiculous, and would have seemed comical in any other circumstances. He was brandishing a long wooden cylinder, whose precise usage was difficult to determine—but Rapopoff quickly found a means of utilizing it. He landed a mighty blow on the back of the bonze's neck, who fell upon his victim, knocked unconscious.

The Cossack was delighted with his exploit. He helped his master to get up and showed him the cylinder.

"Handy weapon, eh, Little Father?"

"What is it?" asked the naturalist, still winded and breathless.

"Simply a *kouroudou*…a prayer mill,[2] which I was condemned to turn in my prison cell. That instrument of piety has been very useful to me. I've already made use of it to knock out a couple of bonzes, including the one who brought me my food every day."

"How did you manage to arrive so opportunely?"

---

[2] The object is obviously a Tibetan prayer-wheel, sometimes known as a *khor*. The longer term used by the author is a version of the name of an island near New Guinea used by some French geographers; it had previously been used to refer to a prayer-wheel in *La Princesse des airs* by Le Rouge and Gustave Guitton, but I can find no evidence of anyone else having used it in that way.

"I wasn't far away. The dungeons are alongside the crypt, and in the silence of the night, I recognized your voice. I even made out the words "help" and "murder.""

"Let's go," said the scientist, already recovered from the shock he had experienced. "All's well! You can tell me your adventures later. The most urgent thing is to get out of here, taking this young woman..."

"That idol!" cried the Cossack, with a kind of terror.

"It's a living idol," said the old man. "We need to take her with us—or, rather, carry her, for she seems to be plunged in a sleep produced by some soporific drug. But first, I have to get my papers and my bank-notes back."

"I might be able to tell you where they are. They can only be in the superior's room. I've seen the whole monastery, and I know that in the cells of the ordinary monks there's nothing but a sleeping-mat and a pitcher of water..."

Bondonnat reflected momentarily. "All right!" he said. "Let's go see the superior—but make sure that you'll be able to find your way back, because you know that we'll have to come back for the young woman."

"Don't worry, Little Father; I know the monastery like the back of my hand, except for a part of the gardens I haven't been allowed to enter."

"I can guess why."

"Why?"

"I'll explain later. For the moment, let's hurry. We don't have a moment to lose."

They both went back upstairs. Beforehand, Bondonnat took care to put the helmet that he had taken off the unconscious bonze on the Cossack's head

The superior's room was only a few paces along the corridor bordered by cells, which Bondonnat had already traversed. They both went in.

Bondonnat was surprised to find it fitted out almost comfortably. There was even a clock with a brass frame and several items of European and Japanese furniture. The room was empty. The inhabitant had not left long before, however, for an oil-lamp was still alight on the table. It seemed a good bet that the superior was none other than the bonze who had tried to strangle the naturalist, and whom Rapopoff had so expeditiously knocked out with his kouroudou.

Bondonnat immediately started searching for his property. Fortunately, he did not have to search for long. When he opened the drawer in the desk he saw, at first glance, his banknotes, his papers and even the case containing his recording apparatus. He took possession of it all rapidly, and went back down to the crypt, still followed y the Cossack, who had not let go of his prayer-mill.

When they went into the subterranean temple, however, a terrible disappointment awaited Bondonnat. The living idol, the woman dressed in pearls, in whom the naturalist had recognized Lorenza, had disappeared. The altar was empty.

Bondonnat was in despair. "I would have one better," he wailed, "to leave the papers and banknotes and save that poor woman. But she can't be far away. It's absolutely necessary that we find her."

At that moment, the solemn and lugubrious clang of a great bronze gong resounded in the silence of the night.

"What does that mean?" demanded Bondonnat.

The Cossack was showing signs of frantic terror. "They don't make such a racket to summon the monks to prayer," he said. "I fear that they're aware of your presence. We'll be caught like rats in a trap, for I don't know how to get out."

"Just get me as far as the garden," Bondonnat said, "and don't worry about the rest."

They both ran upstairs again, four at a time, and then started running hectically through the corridors.

At the sound of the gong, whose booming clang continued to make itself heard, all the bonzes had woken up and were emerging fearfully from their cells. Lights appeared at the windows of the monastery. Everywhere, there were comings and goings, the sound of footsteps, exclamations and whispers.

"We have a lot to do to escape," declared Bondonnat as they emerged into the great temple, which it was necessary to traverse in order to reach the gardens.

He had hardly finished when a group of a dozen bonzes rushed the two fugitives. Rapopoff raised his terrible kouroudou and started whirling it around his head. The crack of breaking bone was heard; the Cossack had just fractured the skull of one of the monks. The others ran away, howling.

A few minutes later, Bondonnat and the Cossack arrived in the gardens, in the middle of which stood the great Buddha with the golden aureole. Without losing a moment, they headed for the secret passage. When they got half way, however, they were assailed by a hail of projectiles. Stones were being thrown at them, and arrows fired, and even a few gunshots burst forth—proof that the monks were equipped with a few modern weapons.

Bah! thought the naturalist. *When we arrive at a place I know well, they'll leave us in peace.*

In that, he was not mistaken. When the bonzes perceived that their enemies were heading toward the plantation of flowers of sleep, they stopped dead. Bondonnat was bold enough to uproot a few of the venomous plants before their eyes. That exploit accomplished, he hastened to regain the entrance to the subterranean passage, which he recognized without difficulty.

A quarter of an hour later, the Cossack and the naturalist were safe in the forest. Bondonnat carefully wrapped up the plants that he had just stolen in the bonze's robe. Only then did he remove his helmet. The Cossack followed suit.

The master and the servant breathed in the fresh morning air delightedly. The trees and plants of the forest were all covered by an abundant dew. The birds were waking up in their nests in thousands, and the sky was beginning to brighten in the east.

"I'm glad to have freed you," said the naturalist to Rapopoff, but I'll never forgive myself for not having been able to save my friend's wife, for I'm sure that it was her. I certainly can't abandon her. I know where she is; the bonzes will have to return her to us. As soon as I've had a few hours' rest, I'll go to Governor Noghi and speak to him in no uncertain terms.

On the way, the Cossack gave his master a brief account of his captivity.

One morning, Rapopoff had woken up in a monk's cell, without ever having been able to figure out how he had been transported there. There, he was only given a handful of rice and a little water every day, and he had been subjected to long and detailed interrogations.

Bondonnat was able to deduce that the Japanese governor was no stranger to Rapopoff's abduction, and that he had doubtless been mistaken, along with his master, for a Russian spy. That hypothesis explained the theft of the papers, and also the negligence with which the Japanese had searched for the guilty parties.

The result of Bondonnat's reflections was that it would hardly be prudent for him to prolong his sojourn on the island of Basan—but the old man was firmly determined not to abandon Lorenza to her jailers.

After that night of adventures, Bondonnat and the Cossack were exhausted by fatigue. It was with a veritable joy that they went back into the villa, firmly intending to sleep all morning.

Rapopoff immediately set about lighting a fire and making a pot of tea, while Bondonnat went into his bedroom and revived himself by washing in cold water.

He had scarcely concluded these hygienic measures when someone knocked loudly on the exterior door. He ran to the window and glimpsed in the dim light—the day was beginning to brighten—the gray robe of a bonze.

"Damn!" he muttered. "That complicates matters! The rogues are now coming all the ways to my home to harass me! But I'm determined not to let them intimidate me. I'll fight fire with fire."

He picked up his Browning and ran downstairs to open the door. He was extremely surprised to find himself in the presence of the painter Louis Grivard, whose supportive arm was around the waist of a woman with a horribly pale face, still clad in a bonze's robe, whom he immediately recognized as the living idol he had glimpsed in the crypt. A rapid glance allowed him to observe that she was still wearing the splendid armor of pearls that had been her only costume in the subterranean temple.

The artist was prey to a frantic excitement. "I've recovered my Lorenza!" he cried, enthusiastically, "but it's as if she were dead. One might think that her body was devoid of a soul. I've had to carry her almost all the way—and when she walks, she's like an automaton, or a phantom..."

"It's nothing," said the naturalist, having cast an eye over the young woman. "She's merely under the influence of some hallucinatory drug. I think I have precisely what I need to bring her round. The other day, Amalu gave me the formula of the beverage that brought me back to life."

Without losing a minute, the naturalist ran into his garden, and came back with the necessary plants, grated them, and, having expressed the juice, was soon able to present the healer of pearls with a glass filled with the beneficent beverage.

The effect was as immediate as it was efficacious. After a few minutes, Lorenza opened her eyes completely, and looked around with profound surprise. At the sight of her husband, a weak smile sketched itself on her features, hollowed out by fatigue.

"Where am I?" she murmured. "What's happened to me?"

She looked dazedly at the faces, unknown to her, of Bondonnat and the Cossack Rapopoff.

"Don't worry!" said Luis Grivard, swiftly. "You've been very ill, but you're cured now, my dear Lorenza, and you're with friends: Monsieur Bondonnat, a Frenchman, a great scientist, and this brave Cossack, who is devotion personified."

It was not without infinite precaution that the artist, aided by Bondonnat, concluded the process of telling the young woman what had happened to her.

"It seems to me that I've had a bad dream," she murmured. "I feel so weak that I'm scarcely capable of walking."

"We'll look after you," Bondonnat declared, paternally.

The scientist and the artist looked at one another.

"You know that the American steamer is lifting anchor at ten o'clock?" Grivard said.

"Then we still have time to take it!" the scientist exclaimed, joyfully. "I can't wait to get away from this accursed land. Hey, Rapopoff!"

"What is it, Little Father?"

"Hurry up and pack—parcel up our belongings anyhow. Then go along the shore until you can find a boat; hire it at whatever price is asked, without haggling, and tell the owners to bring it to the bottom of the garden."

"What if they ask where you're going?"

"Tell them that it's a simple excursion at sea. And above all, try not to be seen, as far as it's possible. You're not unaware that the bonzes must be annoyed with us."

"Bah!" retorted the artist, whom joy had transfigured and who had recovered all his natural joviality. "Those cowards won't be so quick to act. I believe that we have plenty of time to get aboard."

"But tell me," the naturalist demanded, abruptly, "how you managed to rescue Madame Lorenza."

The artist smiled.

"I had my idea yesterday when I asked you to lend me an iron bar. I'd noticed that the cave that served me as a habitation had been hollowed out by human hands, and I was convinced that it was merely the exit of a long subterranean corridor that had to end in the pagoda.

"Your confidences had led me to suppose that Lorenza must be a prisoner of the bonzes. I therefore conceived the plan of getting into their midst by means of the tunnel. You can guess now why I asked for the crowbar. As for the Browning, it was, of course, destined to shoot down the first rogue who tried to get in my way.

"It wasn't without hard work that I was able to clear myself a path through the rock-fall. As I'd anticipated, I found myself in a spacious subterranean corridor with walls ornamented by primitive sculptures. I took some branches of resinous wood to serve as torches, and advanced boldly into the darkness, disturbing thousands of bats as I went.

"Once I was some distance from the shore, fortunately, I only encountered a few insignificant rock-falls, and I arrived more rapidly than I could have supposed at the other end of my tunnel; there, however, my way was blocked by a solid granite wall. According to the calculations I'd made, I had to be directly under the monastery's foundations by that time.

"I was greatly embarrassed; I hadn't anticipated that obstacle. I tried to discover whether there was some secret door, so block that rotated on its axis—nothing. The wall rang solid under the blows of my iron bar."

"In your place," said Bondonnat, "I'd have tried to demolish it."

"That's what I did, but putting pressure on the cracks in the stone in order to make as little noise as possible. I was lucky enough to stumble upon a wall doubtless constructed in haste, which had only been designed to seal of the end of the tunnel leading down to the sea. The stones weren't very large and the mortar holding them together crumbled easily. I wonder what I would have done if it had been a matter of attacking the enormous blocks of granite constituting the foundations of the monastery.

"Soon, I sensed that the wall had become extremely thin, and I had to work very carefully to make sure that my iron bar didn't go through to the other side. Finally, the hole was large enough. With a single thrust of the bar I broke through the sheet of plaster that was all that was still barring my passage, and I leapt through the opening with a single bound.

"I found myself in a crypt lit by a large blue lantern. I looked around and thought I was about to go mad with joy. I saw Lorenza, naked and covered with pearls from head to toe, sitting on an altar like an idol.

"She didn't make the slightest movement.

All my blood froze in my veins. For an instant, I had the terrible thought that she might be dead and embalmed, changed forever into a mute idol.

"I leapt up on to the altar and discovered, to my indescribable relief, that my Lorenza, although very pale and very weak, was still alive. I seized her in my arms, and carried her to my hole, as a tiger might carry away its prey. I was sure that less than a minute had gone by between the moment I entered the temple and the moment I left again.

"With my torch in one hand, and holding Lorenza up with the other, while her head rested on my shoulder, I ran along the corridor, breathlessly. I stopped, though, and went back to fetch the iron bar, which I'd forgotten, and at a place where the roof was threatening to collapse, at the risk of being crushed, I provoked a rock-fall that would hold up anyone trying to pursue me for a long time.

"In any case, I thought that no one would notice my flight immediately, for the hole I'd made was directly behind the altar and the weak, smoky light shed by the blue lantern left all the corners of the large chamber in shadow."

"If you hadn't rescued Madame," said Bondonnat, "I would have saved her. It was less than a minute after you'd gone when I entered the crypt, which I'd already been in once."

In his turn, the naturalist told the story of his own adventure. "Now I think of it," he concluded, "what are you going to do with all those pearls? The picturesque costume that Madame Lorenza is wearing represents a fabulous sum of money."

"I'm keeping the pearls," Grivard declared, resolutely. "First of all, there are a large number among them that belong to me, or rather to my employer. As for the rest, I think it would give proof of a ridiculous delicacy to go and return them to the bonzes. What do you think?"

"I approve entirely."

"That reminds me," said Lorenza, in a voice as faint as a breath, "that it's still necessary to rid myself of all these necklaces, bracelets and girdles that are imprisoning me completely, and put on a costume more suitable than that bonze's robe, which Louis found behind the altar and wrapped around me in order to carry me away."

"Damn!" said Bondonnat. "I didn't think of that. But make a start by getting rid of your precious armor in my dressing-room. I'll find you some trunk in which to put it. As for a costume, I can only provide you with a Japanese dressing-gown."

"That will suffice," the young woman replied, swiftly. "If we add a belt, the dressing gown will be adequate to go from the shore to the steamer. We'll doubtless find what we lack on board."

Bondonnat looked at Louis Grivard for a few moments. "You aren't going to accompany me with those rags and that wild beard are you?" he said, abruptly. "You'd be all the more in error as I have everything you might desire here—jacket, trousers, short, even an excellent pair of scissors. I offer them to you with all my heart."

The artist accepted this proposal joyfully. Soon, he had taken on a more respectable appearance. He looked ten years younger. One would never have supposed that the elegant gentleman who had just appeared in Bondonnat's dining room was the same dirty, ragged and melancholy individual he had seen lying on the sand in the bay, eating wild fruits and raw mollusks.

Lorenza, too, was completely transformed. The silk dressing-gown with a pattern of foliage, retained by a light belt, molded itself to her slender figure; her beautiful black hair was coquettishly pinned up in the Japanese fashion, and her complexion had already lost its waxy pallor and resumed the colors of health.

"My God, how happy I am!" she exclaimed, throwing herself passionately into her husband's arms.

The two young spouses, holding one another tightly, whispered in one another's ears, kissing one another furtively like true lovers.

"What renders me most content, after the pleasure of recovering you," exclaimed Louis Grivard, "it that we'll be able to reimburse the advancements of our employer very handsomely!"

"You can send him a dispatch from the first port we reach that has a telegraphic station," said Bondonnat, who had never felt as happy.

This conversation was interrupted by the arrival of the Cossack, who announced that the requested boat was moored at the end of the garden.

They made the final preparations in haste. Bondonnat was careful not to forget the Japanese masks that had permitted him to traverse the pagoda's garden. Nor did he forget the plants that produced the flower of sleep, packing them personally into a special container.

The naturalist did not pay any heed to the villa's furniture, even though it was his property. He knew that the minutes were precious, and he would gladly have given all the banknotes that were in his wallet to be far away from the baleful island.

Although it pained him, he did not even want to take the time to say farewell to the amiable Hatouara and her father Amalu. He promised himself, however, that he would write to them and send them all the presents that he thought most capable of pleasing them, from among the products of western civilization.

Everyone cheerfully transported to the shore the scant baggage that they were taking away and took their places in the boat, which was manned by two robust Oceanian oarsmen with curly hair and smiling faces. Monsieur Bondonnat, guided by prudence, had instructed the Cossack not to hire any boatman of the Japanese or Tagal race.

The boat left the shore and headed—quite slowly, because of the coral reefs—toward the American steamer, whose hull was outlined clearly against the dazzling azure of the sky and the sea, and whose funnels were emitting torrents of black smoke.

"I'd like to be under the protection of the American flag already," said Bondonnat. "I won't be tranquil until we set foot on the deck of the ship."

"Bah!" said the artist. "You can see that no one's trying to stop us. The bonzes are too much in the wrong to try anything against us."

"Hmm!" said Bondonnat. "I have no great confidence in those fellows."

The scientist was interrupted by one of the native oarsmen who tugged his sleeve and pointed at something dark in the boat's wake. On looking more attentively, he realized that the dark patch was the head of a swimmer, for, after a few minutes, he recognized little Hatouara, who, cleaving through the water like a mermaid, was now only a few meters from the boat.

Bondonnat was profoundly touched.

"Poor girl!" he murmured. "She saw us leaving and didn't want us to quit the island without saying goodbye to us."

Hatouara arrived alongside the canoe. One of the oarsmen helped her to climb aboard. She was streaming wet and naked. She threw herself at Bondonnat's knees and kissed his hand. Her expression was profoundly melancholy and supplicant.

"Will you take little Hatouara for your slave?" she begged the botanist. "I no longer have anyone in the world."

"What about your father? Has something happened to him?"

"They've killed him—murdered him. I found him lying on the mat, his heart pierced by a dagger."

"Who are *they*?" asked Bondonnat, profoundly troubled and afflicted by the terrible news.

"The bonzes, the Japanese—how do I know? They haven't forgiven poor Amalu for being your friend and saving you from death. If you don't take me with you, I'll surely suffer the same fate. When I saw your boat leave the shore, I felt my heart squeezed, and threw myself into the sea to ask you if you wanted me."

"Well, yes, of course!" exclaimed Bondonnat, in one of the surges of generosity that were customary on his part. "You're a brave girl, and after all, it's me who is partly responsible for your father's death."

Hatouara's only reply was to kiss Bondonnat's hands affectionately, and bathe them with her tears.

He was doing his best to console the orphan when it occurred to him that Hatouara was leaving behind her small inheritance, and that, while taking her away, it might perhaps be a good idea to look after her interests. He asked the young woman if she had made any arrangements in that regard.

"Alas," sighed the poor girl, "I've already sacrificed all that I possessed. I knew that with my father dead, the greedy Noghi would not take long to get his hands on his possessions, so I decided not even to try to fight."

They had arrived in the vicinity of the steamer *Pacific*, and it was with genuine delight that, once the boatmen had been paid and dismissed, Bondonnat and his friends set foot on the ship.

The captain, a pure-blooded Yankee, did not ask the naturalist any questions. He contented himself with pocketing the banknotes that were offered to him and indicating the numbers of the cabins reserved for the five passengers.

The *Pacific* was primarily a merchant vessel, and was not equipped to carry a large number of passengers. Bondonnat observed regretfully that it was not fitted with wireless telegraphy equipment, without which he would be unable to notify his daughter of his arrival in San Francisco.

While everyone was unpacking, Bondonnat found an American newspaper in the passenger lounge. It was several days old; the captain of the Pacific had obtained it from one of his colleagues whose path he had crossed.

He unfolded it mechanically. Then his attention was caught by an article on the second page, and it was with profound astonishment that he read it.

AN IMPOSING CEREMONY

The city of San Francisco will soon be the theater of a very solemn occasion. The yacht Revenge, *which is due to bring back the mortal remains of the great French scientist Prosper Bondonnat, is impatiently awaited in the city.*

The handing over of the corpse to the French authorities will be the object of an official ceremony, at which the government of the Union will certainly be represented.

There is also talk of a delegation of American scientists, which, under the presidency of the celebrated Dr. Cornelius Kramm, the eminent physiologist popularly known as the sculptor of human flesh, will render a final tribute to the great scientist that Prosper Bondonnat was. The daughter and the ward of the deceased, whose dramatic adventures and heroic filial devotion are well known, will lead the funeral procession in person, accompanied by their fiancés and the family of the billionaire Fred Jorgell.

"What can this mean?" Bondonnat asked himself, pensively. "I'm not dead, damn it!"

He was interrupted by the strident clamor of the steamship's siren. The *Pacific* had raised anchor, the propeller was turning. The old scientist forgot other preoccupations momentarily in order to abandon himself to the pleasure of seeing the island of Basan gradually fading into the distance, and finally vanishing, like a wisp of azure mist, over the edge of the horizon.

14. THE BUST WITH EMERALD EYES

I. Resurrection!

All morning, the streets of San Francisco had been subject to an unaccustomed animation. Every hour, hundreds of trains disembarked thousands of travelers arriving from all over America.

In spite of the efforts of four regiments of mounted policemen, who carried out veritable charges from time to time, it was almost impossible to circulate through the multitude in which all the peoples of the world were rubbing shoulders: Americans, Chinamen, negroes, Oceanians and even Eskimos, still clad, in spite of the heat, in their sealskin blouses and thick furs.

At the windows of tall buildings, almost all reconstructed in steel after the last earthquake, numerous groups were crowded, and in places, speculators had set up stages on which places were being sold for twenty, fifty or a hundred dollars.

It was in the concourse and on the platforms of the Central Pacific Railroad Station that the animation was greatest of all. There, the policeman had a veritable battle on their hands; the human tide, incessantly swelling, was surging along all the adjacent streets , seeking to invade the broad avenue along which the cortege would pass whose anticipation had excite the curiosity of the inhabitants of "Frisco" to such an extraordinary degree.

In the midst of that crowd, three travelers installed in an automobile whose footplate as laden with numerous item of luggage, could not succeed, in spite of all the efforts of their driver, in fraying a passage.

In any other city than San Francisco, which serves as a meting-place for all the races of the world, the costume and appearance of the travelers would not have failed to attract the curiosity of idlers, but here, no one paid the slightest attention to them.

The first of the three individuals was a Cossack, easily recognizable by his slanting eyes, his prominent cheekbones and his flat nose; he was dressed in an old mariner's costume too small for his large build and a fur hat. The second was an old man with white hair and beard, and a physiognomy full of intelligence and benevolence. He was wearing an elegant suit of white twill and a Panama hat. The third was a young Oceanian girl, fifteen or sixteen years old at the most, bare-headed, with her hair put up in the Japanese style and held in place by long pins; she was dressed in a luxurious red silk kimono embroidered in gold.

"I believe," said he old man, who seemed to be observing the crowd with an ironic smile, that we'll never be able to get to the Palace Hotel. What do you think, my brave Rapopoff?"

"I think, Little Father," the Cossack stammered, to whom the surging multitude was giving a sensation akin to sea-sickness, or at least to vertigo, "that we'd be better off turning back."

"Impossible," the old man replied. "It's as difficult to go back as it is to go forward."

At that moment, ten howling voices became audible over the tumult of the crowd. It was a band of newsvendors for whom the doors of a printing shop had just been opened and who were running into the riot shouting: "Get the latest *Herald!* Portrait of the illustrious Bondonnat and details of his funeral!"

People were fighting to get hold of the sheets, for which some idlers were paying as much as a dollar. Five minutes had not gone by before the supply of papers was exhausted; more copies had to be thrown down to the vendors from the windows of the print shop.

The young Oceanian gazed at the spectacle with a surprise that was not exempt from a certain terror, watching and listening to it all with overexcited attention. Abruptly, she shivered, and turned to the old man.

"But it seems," she said, "that it's your name they're shouting!"

Monsieur Bondonnat made no reply. The slightly ironic smile that had cleared his features momentarily had disappeared. He was prey to a feverish impatience.

"It's important that we go forward," he said to the driver.

"Impossible," said the other, with a resigned gesture.

"There's a hundred dollars for you if you can get to the Palace Hotel, or even to a café from which I can telephone."

The man shrugged his shoulders. "If you promised me a thousand," he replied, "it would still be the same..."

He did not finish his sentence. An orchestra of five hundred musicians not far away had just launched into Chopin's *Funeral March*; the roar of the brass instruments and the lugubrious drum-rolls even drowned out the noise of the multitude.

At that moment, however, there was a formidable pressure in the crowd. The automobile, lifted up by a hundred vigorous hands, traveled thirty meters above the heads of the spectators. The three travelers were obliged to cling on to their seats.

Projected with an almost irresistible force, the vehicle was only halted in its surge by the regiment of policemen blocking the end of the street. Thanks to that brutal shove, however, it now found itself on the very edge of the avenue along which the funeral procession was beginning to move.

Bondonnat and his friends stood up on the seat in order to get a better view of the spectacle offered to them. A short distance away, they could see the Central Pacific Railroad Station, completely draped in black velvet ornamented with silver tears and transformed into a gigantic catafalque, lit by the green flames of bronze lamp-posts .The entire square in front of the station was nothing but an immense bouquet of flowers. Entire trainloads had been brought in, tributes from all the scientists in the world to the memory of the illustrious Prosper Bondonnat!

The avenue, from the station to the quays, was similarly draped in black velvet along its entire length. All the electric lights had been switched on, decked with large crepe veils of strange appearance. Finally, everywhere—at all the windows and all the branches of all the trees—thousands of American and French flags, similarly edged in black, were flapping in the wind.

In the center of the square, a stage protected by a tent of rich curtains was occupied by grave individuals dressed in black, diplomats and generals in bright uniforms.

Suddenly, cheers saluted the appearance of the procession, preceded by an imposing escort of mounted police accompanied by National Guardsmen, immediately followed by the five hundred musicians who were still playing Chopin's *Funeral March* and advancing slowly.

Monsieur Bondonnat experienced a strange seizure. His hands were trembling with emotion, and even if the tumult of the crowd would not have drowned out his voice, he would have been unable to speak, so tight was his throat. He rubbed his eyes to assure himself that he really was awake, and that he was not in the process of battling a nightmare. He could not help comparing himself to Charles V, who, according to tradition, had wanted to witness his own funeral ceremony at the monastery of Saint-Just, while lying in a coffin.

The procession, worthy of a king or a prince, continued to file before his eyes like a sparkling vision.

After the musicians came a dozen carriages laden with flowers; then came the hearse itself, ornamented at its four corners with torch-holders in which green flames were burning. It was surmounted by a dome of silver cloth supported by four ebony columns. The driver, who was guiding it with a solemn slowness, was dressed in a French uniform, pompously braided.

Behind it came several mourners' carriages with the blinds lowered.

At the thought that his daughter was in one of them, Bondonnat felt himself grow dizzy. He tried to launch himself forward, to cry out, but his movement and his cry were lost in the enormous rumor of the multitude and the thunder of the acclamations and the music.

The old man let himself fall back on his seat, pale and defeated, half-dead, gazing with dull eyes misted with tears at the majestic ceremony that continued to unfold according to its planned phases.

Protected by the policemen, whose task was becoming increasingly difficult, the representatives of the various scientific societies, American States and constitutional bodies took up their places on the various stages around the square that had been reserved for them.

One small group, in the middle of which three young women clad in long black veils were visible, went to take their places on a small stage more luxuriously decorated than the rest. And it was repeated in the crowd those people, honored by such a flattering distinction, were the relatives and friends of the deceased.

Bondonnat felt faint.

"My daughter!" he stammered. "My dear Frédérique! How can she be spared this dolor!"

Meanwhile, the funeral carriage stopped beside the stage where the scientists and diplomats were, and announcement was made in a clear voice: "Doctor Cornelius Kramm will speak on behalf of the members of the National Academy of New York."

Distraught, Bondonnat saw an individual with a singularly characteristic physiognomy rise to his feet. His clean-shaven face displayed regular features and his high forehead and enormous skull advertised a powerful intelligence, but his thin lips indicated a cold malevolence and behind his large gold-rimmed spectacles his lashless eyes were simultaneously staring and oblique, like those of certain birds of prey.

"Cornelius! The famous Dr. Cornelius!" repeated the crowd. "The sculptor of human flesh!"

The attentive silence of the multitude had become profound.

It was with a perfect ease that Dr. Cornelius Kramm began his speech.

"Gentlemen, the scientist to whom we have come here today to render just and public homage, was one of the noblest intelligences with which humanity has been honored. Thanks to him, human knowledge has accomplished immense progress, and if death had not struck him down in mysterious circumstances, he would doubtless have enriched our intellectual patrimony with further discoveries comparable to those that have contributed so much to his glory.

"Prosper Bondonnat died murdered by the sinister bandits of the Red Hand, on an island lost in the Pacific Ocean..."

Dr. Cornelius, prey to a sudden disturbance, stopped dead, and could not finish his sentence. His eyes, which were wandering distractedly over the audience, had just met those of Prosper Bondonnat himself.

The two gazes had interlocked, and Cornelius, in spite of all his audacity, had suddenly gone lividly pale. He could not remember a single word of what he had to say.

"Gentlemen," he stammered. "Excuse an emotion...very legitimate..."

Murmurs began to run through the crowd. Some were waxing ecstatic about the sensitivity of the good Dr. Cornelius; others found his attitude quite strange and incomprehensible.

The crowd murmured, but mutedly. There was a kind of dramatic atmosphere weighing upon all minds. It was one of those moments when one feels, without knowing why, that something extraordinary is happening. People were waiting for that extraordinary event.

It happened.

In the crowd, a few meters from the stage, a dog started barking furiously. It was a large black dog, of the barbet breed. Then it broke the chain that was held by a pale and puny young man, slightly hunchbacked, and, launching forth through the wreaths of flowers, it reached the automobile in which Monsieur Bondonnat was sitting in three bounds.

The dog licked his hands; it had leapt on to his knees, and the old man, moved to tears, exhausted by successive emotions, repeated in a feeble but satisfied voice: "Pistolet! But it's my dear old Pistolet!"

Numerous groups were commenting on the incident and wondering who the strange old man was when two policemen armed with whalebone nightsticks with lead balls ran up to capture the animal.

"This is no place for a dog!" said one of them, brutally. And he lifted his club to smash the barbet's skull.

"I beg you, gentlemen," stammered Monsieur Bondonnat. "Don't hurt my dog!"

The old man would probably not have got the better of the argument if the little hunchback, who was still holding the end of the broken chain had not suddenly intervened.

"Monsieur," be began, "the dog belongs to me..." But when he saw the face of the man who was holding the dog on his knees and protecting him as best he could, he uttered a cry of surprise and joy.

Launching himself into the automobile, he shouted: "Monsieur Bondonnat! It's him! Alive!"

He had seized his former master's hands, and was covering them with kisses and tears.

The two policemen stood there, stupefied, not knowing what to make of the scene. But the little hunchback's words had been heard by his nearest neighbors, who were almost all holding copies of the San Francisco *Herald*, containing the portrait of the scientist.

One glance sufficed for them to discover the resemblance between the portrait and the original, and a rumor immediately ran through the multitude, swelling and growing louder like the distant rumble of thunder.

Soon, the same cry was emerging from a hundred thousand throats: "Alive! Bondonnat is alive!"

"Yes!" cried the hunchback. "He's alive! Here he is! Come quickly, my dear master, to throw yourself into the arms of your children and your friends!"

"Long live Bondonnat!" someone shouted.

That was the signal for a general acclamation. People wanted to carry the old scientist in triumph. Fortunately, a squadron of policemen had arrived at a rapid gallop, and it was thanks to their protection that Bondonnat and Oscar, followed by the Cossack and the fearful and trembling Oceanian girl, were able to reach the foot of the principal stage.

On perceiving the old man, a young woman had risen to her feet, as pale as a corpse beneath her long mourning dress.

"Frédérique! My child!" stammered the old man.

"Father!" cried they young woman, holding out her arms. But the shock had been too brutal. Frédérique collapsed, inanimate, into the arms of the people around her.

"I've killed her!" cried the old man, in despair. Prey to a veritable madness, he tried to hurl himself upon the young woman's body.

At that moment, two policemen of athletic build took hold of him rudely and ragged him away.

"What are you doing?" cried the unfortunate scientist. "Let me go, I beg you."

"Come with us," the man replied, brutally. "I arrest you in the name of the law."

"What have I done?"

"You have the audacity to ask? You must be veritably bold to take the name of the great scientist and pass yourself off as him, at the very moment when all America is distraught at watching his funeral."

"But I swear to you that I really am Prosper Bondonnat!" replied the old man, losing his composure.

"He's a madman!" said the second policeman, who had not opened his mouth thus far. "In fact, he does resemble him slightly."

"I swear to you that I'm telling the truth," the old man repeated, obstinately.

"Come on, don't give us any trouble!" the first policeman said. "You can explain it to the chief."

While speaking, the two policemen, surrounded by twenty of their colleagues, dragged Bondonnat to the special police depot in the railway station.

He was left alone there in a kind of cell, whose only furniture was a stool and a camp bed.

The old man wondered sadly, on finding himself imprisoned again, whether the series of his misfortunes was about to recommence.

Outside, he heard furious cries and long acclamations: all the sounds of a popular tempest, a veritable mob.

In the midst of the confusion that had been produced when Frédérique collapsed, however, Oscar Tournesol had perceived that his master had been arrested and had immediately alerted Paganot and Ravenel, as well as Andrée de Maubreuil and Isidora, Frédérique's two best friends.

"Mesdemoiselles," he said, "Take care of your friend, I beg you. Monsieur Bondonnat has been arrested. We must go to his aid as quickly as possible. I fear that there might be some new move by the Red Hand behind this.

And having whispered a few words into their ears, Oscar led the engineer and the naturalist away with him.

Isidora and Andrée, who had been almost as emotional as Fréderique herself at the appearance of the specter of Monsieur Bondonnat, stiffened themselves against their emotion and, while waiting for the strange mystery to be cleared up, hastened to care for their friend.

They bathed her temples with cold water and made her breathe lavender salts, but the measures proved futile. Frédérique remained inert and icy.

"My God, she's dead!" cried Andrée. "Joy and surprise have killed her."

The two young women were panicking, losing their heads, in the midst of a crowd of people who offered their help to no effect.

Fortunately, Fred Jorgell arrived. He had succeeded, with great difficulty, in cleaving a way through the crowd to get to the stage. Isidora explained the situation to him briefly. His first concern was to appeal to the policemen, who knew who he was, and who, with the aid of their nightsticks, cleared a space around the stage. Then two of them carried Frédérique, who gave no sign of life, to the first aid post in the railway station. Dr. Cornelius followed behind them, in company with Fred Jorgell, to whom he had kindly offered his services. The latter had certainly not refused the illustrious practitioner's help.

Before following the billionaire, Cornelius had had time to say a few words in the ear of a correctly-dressed gentleman who had followed the entire scene with visible anxiety, and who was none other than the art dealer Fritz Kramm, the doctor's brother.

Throughout the city, however, the tumult was at its height; the crowd was exasperated by curiosity and also by expectation and disappointment.

"Come on!" cried some. "Is Bondonnat alive or dead? We need to know!"

"They're putting one over on us! The famous Frenchman is as alive as you or me. I've seen him!"

"No, I tell you. It's some crook who resembles him!"

"The proof that Bondonnat's alive is that the band's stopped playing, the speeches have stopped and Bondonnat's daughter was stuck dead on seeing her father!"

The capital fact that the music and the speeches had stopped had made a great impression on the crowd. Americans detest, more than anything else, anyone making a fool of them, and on this occasion, they were almost sure that they were the victim of some trickery. They began to manifest their ill humor by throwing stones, smashing the electric lights, and by overturning the stages from which the notable individuals had descended.

Chinamen, very numerous in the crowd, had been struck from the very start by the beauty of the black velvet fringed with silver, and began to tear off large pieces of it, which they slyly carried away. They were soon seconded in this work by bandits of all nations, who are abundant in San Francisco. As if by magic, the avenue that the funeral cortege had followed was stripped of all its finery.

The crowd, for whom that pillage had been, so to speak, merely an appetizer, now let loose. It howled like the sea whipped up by a hurricane. The policemen no longer knew which way to turn. It was a veritable mob that was growling; a few sailors were already beginning to break shop windows, and merchants were closing their blinds hastily.

In the midst of these scenes of disorder, the carriages bearing the wreaths were no more respected than anything else; the multitude tipped them over and took possession of some of the flowers, trampling the rest underfoot.

Forty mounted militiamen courageously defended the hearse in which Monsieur Bondonnat's remains—authentic or not—were contained. They had retrenched at the entrance to a little side-street, but they were undoubtedly about to be obliged to yield to the rabble, who were intent on taking possession of the silver torch-holders and rich draperies, when a luxurious automobile drew up behind the militiamen. It was escorted by twenty robust sailors, and the man leading them was the very same one to whom Dr. Cornelius had given mysterious instructions half an hour earlier, Fritz Kramm.

He told the chief of the militia that he had been given the mission of taking the great scientist's coffin to a place of safety; there was no reason not to believe what he said.

The coffin was therefore loaded into the automobile, which was soon lost in the tangle of small streets that extends between the port and the Central Pacific Railroad Station. The militiamen beat a retreat, and the crowd took advantage of it to demolish the superb funeral carriage entirely, the debris of which was shared out.

While this scene was taking place, Antoine Paganot, Andrée de Maubreuil's fiancé, and the naturalist Roger Ravenel, Frédérique's fiancé, had followed Oscar Tournesol to the police depot in the station. There, they demanded to see the man who claimed to be Monsieur Bondonnat. The dog Pistolet had followed them, and was continuing to bark energetically, as if exasperated by the error of which his master had been the victim.

The police officer began to prevaricate at first, but when Roger Ravenel, whom he knew to be a friend of the billionaire Fred Jorgell, had declared that he would post bail for any sum that was demanded, no matter how considerable, all objections were overcome and Monsieur Bondonnat as brought into the office, where the police captain and the three young men were already assembled.

Fortunately, the old scientist was carrying documents that established his identity, which had been in his wallet when he had been taken to the Island of Hanged Men. His resemblance to a photograph of Monsieur Bondonnat that Paganot was carrying in his pocket was also a serious argument. Finally, the barking and caresses of Pistolet did not permit any doubt to remain as to the real identity of the old man.

"But why," asked the police captain, in whom this incident inspired the greatest suspicion, "if you really are Bondonnat, didn't you inform your daughter of your arrival? You would have avoided the riot that is unfolding in the city at this very moment, for which you are responsible."

"That was absolutely impossible for me, Monsieur. It's only two hours since the steamer *Pacific*, on which I embarked at the island of Basan, dropped anchor in the harbor, and you know yourself that there was no way of traveling across town. I didn't know where my daughter was. I made great but vain efforts to reach the Palace Hotel, from which I hoped to telephone."

The captain reflected momentarily. "I'll clear all this up," he murmured.

"Monsieur Bondonnat will be set free, then?" asked Paganot.

"All right—but on condition that you answer for him. I'll let you know what sum I've fixed for his bail."

"Messieurs, I beg you," stammered the old man, completely exhausted by the succession of his emotions, "I implore you, tell me that my dear Frédérique is safe!"

"You'll soon know. The first aid post to which she must have been taken is in the station."

"I'll go get news of her!" cried Roger Ravenel, impetuously.

"I'll come too," added Bondonnat.

"No, my dear Master," said Paganot. "Stay here. It's more prudent not to expose Mademoiselle Frédérique to a second shock."

"You're right," the old man murmured, collapsing into a chair.

The engineer had not revealed the full extent of his thought, and, when he had retained Monsieur Bondonnat, it was partly because he was wondering, in anguish, whether the young woman might have died of the terrible shock she had suffered on seeing the specter of her father appear before her.

Fortunately, his fears were exaggerated. A few minutes later, the naturalist came back, his physiognomy radiant.

"Don't worry, my dear Master," he said. "Our dear Frédérique has finally recovered her senses—which is, I ought to say, thanks to the care of Dr. Cornelius, who called upon all his resources to bring her out of her faint."

From then on, it was no longer possible to restrain Monsieur Bondonnat. A moment later, the father and daughter threw themselves into one another's arms, weeping. As for Dr. Cornelius, he had modestly slipped away, doubtless to avoid thanks.

Paganot, Ravenel, Isidora, Andrée, Fred Jorgell and Oscar Tournesol were only slightly less emotional than Bondonnat and his daughter.

The police captain put an end to the tender scene by asking the billionaire and his friends to get into an automobile that he had summoned, and which would take them to the Palace Hotel under a strong escort. Everyone hastened to obey.

Half an hour later, all the friends met up again in one of the reception rooms of the luxurious caravanserai, which is reputed to be the largest in America.

There, Bondonnat's first concern was to telephone Police Headquarters, to offer a large reward to whomever could find the Cossack Rapopoff and the young Oceanian, who had been lost in the crowd while trying to follow him and about whom, in his emotion, he had completely forgotten momentarily.

Two policemen brought them back that evening.

Transported by joy and finding himself once again in the midst of his nearest and dearest, Bondonnat had forgotten all his fatigue. He gave a detailed account of his strange adventures.

"I shall adopt little Hadouara," declared Frédérique. "I want to provide the poor orphan with an appropriate education. But why, Father, didn't you bring the painter Grivard and the charming healer of pearls with you, to introduce us to them?"

"I begged them to accompany me, but Lorenza had experienced so much suffering during her captivity among the Buddhists that her health has been severely affected. She was obliged to remain aboard until she is well enough to take the first express train leaving for New York. They've both promised me, however, that we shall see one another again in France, and it's understood that, as soon as we've returned, Lorenza and her husband will come to spend a few weeks with us in our Breton villa.

"As for the Cossack, we'll make a first-rate laboratory assistant of him, if he succeeds in correcting his habit of emptying bottles of alcohol and making snacks with various chemical products."

After finishing the account of his adventures, Bondonnat was impatient to know how they had discovered where he was and how they had captured the Island of Hanged Men. It was Paganot who took charge of that narration, giving the most enthusiastic eulogies to the ingenuity and courage of Lord Astor Burydan. He explained how the eccentric had had the fortunate idea of taking all the clowns of the Gorilla Club into his service, how the swimmer Bob Horwett had destroyed the torpedoes, and finally, how the bandits, already terrified by the cinematographic visions projected from the deck of the *Ariel*, had been vanquished and annihilated in a pitched battle.

"But what has become of the bandits of the Red Hand?" asked Bondonnat. "There were a few among them who were brave men."

"The day after our victory, a navy cruiser, which Fred Jorgell had finally persuaded the American government to send to our aid, dropped anchor off the island and took all the bandits aboard. They're to stand trial in due course. As for the Eskimos, we left them alone."

"What about the Russians and the prophet Rominoff?" asked Bondonnat.

"The necessary measures were taken to return them to Europe."

"In sum," said the old man, "everything in the strange adventure has concluded better than we could have hoped. But there are three people missing from this reunion; firstly, the engineer Harry Dorgan, whose acquaintance I'd be delighted to make..."

"You'll see him here shortly," said Fred Jorgell. "He's in New York at present, where the expansion of the Lightning Steamship Company made his presence indispensable."

"But Lord Burydan and the Indian Kloum don't have the same excuse," said the old naturalist, laughing, "and it seems to me that their presence at my funeral was entirely requisite."

"As you know," said Ravenel, "Lord Burydan is the oddest man there is. He acts entirely as the whim takes him. As soon as we arrived in New York he left us, without saying where he was going, in the company of Kloum and a Frenchman named Agénor Marmousier, who is both his friend and secretary. Don't worry, though—Lord Burydan is one of those people who never remains out of sight for long."

Bondonnat and his friends went to bed very late that evening. They were all worn out by fatigue, but delighted that things had worked out so well.

The next day, Bondonnat's first concern was to go to Police Headquarters, firstly to deposit the bail he had promised, and secondly to find out what had happened to the embalmed cadaver to which the bandits of the Red Hand had succeeded in giving his own resemblance. He did not doubt that an attentive examination of that curious anatomical specimen would lead to singular discoveries.

Unfortunately, the chief of the San Francisco police told him that the coffin containing the corpse of the supposed Bondonnat had disappeared during the riot. The most scrupulous search had produced no result. It was assumed that after the riot, the coffin must have been thrown in the sea. It was necessary to renounce the possibility of discovering what had become of it.

Needless to say, the charges brought against Monsieur Bondonnat were dropped. The money he had deposited as bail was returned to him.

Soon, the newspapers announced that the venerable scientist, whose health was completely reestablished, had agreed to spend a few weeks in America in the estates of his friend Fred Jorgell before returning to France for good. The same newspapers announced the triple marriage of Harry Dorgan and Miss Isidora Jorgell, Roger Ravenel and Mademoiselle Frédérique Bondonnat, and Antoine Paganot and Mademoiselle Andrée de Maubreuil.

II. An Unexpected Visit

Three months after these events, a heavy automobile truck escorted by eight mounted men armed to the teeth was slowly following the beautiful road shaded by plane trees that runs along the southern shore of Lake Ontario.

In that locale, the landscape is one of the most beautiful to be found in North America. The immense expanse of the lake, of a very pale blue, is covered with hundreds of verdant little islets known as the Thousand Islands, which resemble as many bouquets floating on the calm surface of the limped waters. Delightful cottages are installed on many of these islets, constructed in brightly-colored bricks, which give the landscape the appearance, at a distance, of a magical kingdom. Luxurious launches made of maple-wood and mahogany, elegantly decorated and covered with multicolored tents, travel between the islands. Any suggestion of fatigue, labor and poverty is absent from the gracious décor.

That opinion was doubtless that of the riders who were escorting the trunk, for they were only advancing with leisurely nonchalance, pausing from time to time to admire the marvelous view in all its details. Meanwhile, they arrived at a place where the road was bordered by a monumental wall, above which the trees of a park almost entirely planted with gigantic thujas were visible. They went along that wall for about a mile, eventually arriving at a large wrought iron grille near to which was an elegant lodge that served as a guard-house.

A man with a long beard and spectacles, who seemed to be the leader of the little caravan, ran the bell intended to announce the arrival of visitors. Immediately, a robust individual with a rubicund face and vast shoulders emerged from the lodge and studied the newcomer suspiciously.

"What do you want?" he asked, curtly.

"Sir," the visitor replied, "I've been instructed to deliver into Mistress Isidora's own hands a gift addressed to her by her father-in-law, William Dorgan."

"I have very rigorous orders," the guard replied, suspiciously.

"I'm carrying a letter from William Dorgan."

"Possibly. In that case, I'll allow you to come in on your own and I'll take you to the senior steward, Mr. Bombridge. He'll decide whether or not your wagon can come through the gate."

"All right," said the stranger, without any impatience. "When he sees the letter, Mr. Bombridge will certainly let me in."

The stranger got down from his horse, came through a small lateral gate and followed the guard along a sandy pathway bordered with gigantic rhododendrons in cedar boxes. They soon arrived at a pitch pine chalet with elegant balustrades, shaded by magnificent maples. A young blonde woman who was standing on a first-floor balcony hastened to come out and meet the visitors.

"Good morning, Mr. Horwett," she said to the guard.

"Good morning, Miss Regina. "I've brought someone who wants to speak to your father."

"Come in, then. He's in his study.

The ex-clown Bombridge, now the senior steward of Harry Dorgan's estate, had lost none of his good humor. He was wearing a green velvet suit and a felt hat surmounted by a mallard plume, which gave him a very distinguished appearance. He invited his guests to take some refreshment, read William Dorgan's letter and then went out to telephone "the château." He soon came back, declaring that the truck could come in, but that the men of the escort had to remain outside the gate.

Matters having been thus arranged, he accompanied Bob Horwett and William Dorgan's representative in order personally to supervise the opening and closing of the main gate of the property—which, evidently, was well-guarded.

The truck, which Bob Horwett guided, went along an avenue of Virginia ash, at the end of which was a kind of drawbridge extended over an arm of Lake Ontario, which gave access to the heart of the park.

Harry Dorgan's magnificent house, an exact reproduction of the famous Château de Chambord, was contained, along with the vast garden that surrounded it, on one of the islands of Lake Ontario, and was only connected to the land by that drawbridge. The engineer had chosen the property not only because of its picturesque situation, but also with the objective of thwarting the assaults of malefactors—in particular, those of the Red Hand.

Once the drawbridge had been crossed, they entered another avenue, this one of sycamores, that led to the main courtyard.

While Bob Horwett drove the truck to the foot of the house's marble perron, Mr. Bombridge took William Dorgan's envoy to an arbor where Monsieur Bondonnat was sitting with three young women, all admirably beautiful, although in different ways.

"To whom do I have the honor of speaking?" the old scientist asked, courteously, coming to meet the visitor.

With a rapid gesture, the latter took off his spectacles and his false beard.

"Lord Burydan!" cried the three young women, with the same cry of surprise.

"He never changes!" muttered the ex-performer Horwett.

"I see, with pleasure," the old scientist said, cheerfully, "that your eccentric humor hasn't changed. But now, even though you're in familiar territory, permit me to make the introductions: Mrs. Harry Dorgan, Madame Paganot and, finally, Madame Frédérique Ravenel, née Bondonnat."

"I can see," said the eccentric, jovially, "that you haven't wasted any time in my absence. All my compliments, Mesdames. I hope that I shall have the pleasure of seeing your husbands?"

"No," Monsieur Bondonnat replied. "They're all in New York, and won't be back for two or three days. They've taken our friend Oscar with them."

"I don't know, Milord," said Frédérique, pulling a face, "whether we ought to speak to you. All three of us are very annoyed with you..."

"One doesn't desert friends like that!" Andrée put in.

"Not even to come to our wedding!" said Isidora, striving to assume a severe expression.

"Mesdames, I offer you my most humble apologies. It's not without reason that people call me eccentric. It's necessary, therefore, that my friends should be indulgent enough to close their eyes to my faults and accept me as I am."

"Should we forgive him?" asked Frédérique, turning to her two friends.

"Yes, indeed," said Andrée, "as long as he doesn't do it again."

"I can't hold it against him too much," added Isidora. "He's brought me a gift."

"And a magnificent gift!"

"But how is it," asked Bondonnat, "that William Dorgan has charged you with such a mission? Do you know him, then?"

Lord Burydan put a finger to his lips. "Yes," he said, smiling. "But shh—it's a secret."

The naturalist did not persist.

"Let's see the gift!" cried the three young women, simultaneously.

Bob Horwett ran to the truck and came back followed by four domestics, who were carrying, with great difficulty, a litter bearing a voluminous crate reinforced externally by sheet metal.

The domestics, their zeal stimulated by the young women, opened the case, not without difficulty. It contained a second crate, made of light white wood, which was similarly opened, and which seemed to be full of dense cotton wool.

"I wonder what it can be," said Frédérique.

"Some vase or precious trinket," Isadora replied. "I know that my brother-in-law Joe and my father-in-law are men of good taste."

"You're reconciled with Joe Dorgan, then?" asked Lord Burydan.

"Yes, it's better that way. My husband and I rarely see him, but they're no longer sworn enemies, as they once were."

Frédérique and Andrée had begun to remove huge handfuls of the dazzling white cotton wool that filled the case. Soon, something shiny appeared.

"Gold," said Andrée. "Some jewelry, no doubt."

"It's the bust of a woman! Of Isidora!" Frédérique exclaimed, having finished emptying the case with an impatient hand. "It's gilded bronze. It's magnificent."

"It's even more magnificent than you think," said the eccentric, teasingly. "Mistress Isidora's bust is made of solid gold. It's a true billionaire's gift."

"What folly!" murmured Isadora, who, in spite of her disclaimer, was blushing with pleasure.

Lord Burydan took the bust out of its container and placed in on the marble table in the center of the arbor. The art-work—by an illustrious French sculptor—was worthy of the precious material employed. The bust, slightly languid in its grace, was the equal of the most beautiful statues of the artists of the Renaissance. Jean Goujon and Germain Pilon would have thought it worthy of their chisel.

The eyes had been treated in the fashion of ancient Rome—which is to say that the irises, instead of remaining empty as those of modern statues generally are, has been represented by precious stones: two superb emeralds, exactly the same color as Isidora's eyes, blazed beneath the golden eyelids, giving the image an intense, almost disquieting vitality.

As Lord Burydan had said, it was a true billionaire's gift. Such a bust must have cost half a million.

The three young women remained mute with admiration for some time. The two Frenchwomen, far from being jealous, embraced and complimented their friend warmly.

"Where will you place this beautiful bust?" asked Frédérique.

"It seems to me," Isidora replied, after a moment's thought, "that its appropriate setting is the large Renaissance drawing-room."

"The one on the second floor, above the laboratory?"

"Exactly."

"Above all," said Lord Burydan, laughing, "put it in a room with a solid door. That bust would be magnificent prey for the gentlemen of the Red Hand."

The three young women laughed simultaneously, their laughter resounding in the silence of the arbors.

"Does the Red Hand still exist?" asked Isidora. "After the mass convictions that have recently been announced, and the hundreds of arrests made all over the Union, the famous association can surely be regarded as extinct."

"So much the better, then!" said the eccentric. "I'm not sorry to hear it. So people can finally sleep easy in the territory of free America?"

"At any rate," said Frédérique, "the Renaissance drawing room, where the bust will be placed, is fitted with solid armored shutters, and the door is lined with plates of sheet metal twenty millimeters thick—precautions taken, I think, because of the numerous precious objects the room already contains."

The young women wanted to go in and preside personally over the installation of the bust in the Renaissance drawing room. While they went to do that, Lord Burydan and Bondonnat walked with a leisurely stride along a watercourse covered with nymphea lilies and bordered with tulips in flower. Abruptly, the physiognomy of both men had become anxious, and they took twenty paces without saying a word.

"I've received your letters," said Bondonnat, finally, lowering his voice as if he were afraid of being overheard. "Have you discovered anything new?"

"I believe I'm on the right track, but I don't have any precise result as yet. I'm waiting. I don't want to take action until I'm certain."

"Be prudent."

"You don't need to make that recommendation to me. I didn't say anything in order not to frighten the ladies, but haven't you noticed, as I have, that all the members of the Red Hand who's been convicted recently are subaltern bandits? The highly intelligent men at the head of the association are not even under suspicion."

"I'm certain myself," the old scientist replied, "that the Lords of the Red Hand are not only intelligent men but veritable scientists. I'm still marveling at what I saw in the subterranean laboratory on the Island of Hanged Men. These people are as accomplished as Dr. Carrel.[3] I only know one man in America who has arrived at that level of expertise."

"And that is…?"

"Dr. Cornelius Kramm."

"That's curious," murmured Lord Burydan, seemingly preoccupied. "We've had the same idea. You know, I suppose—I only found out recently—that it's Cornelius' brother Fritz who is, in reality, the owner of the Island of Hanged Men? That seems very suspicious to me."

"Let's not go so fast. It appears that Fritz Kramm has established his innocence. It has been many years since he went to the Island of Hanged Men."

"That's possible, I suppose—but what seems less explicable to me that the investigation that should have been carried out into the existence of the subterranean museum whose location you've identified has produced no result."

"I did furnish the necessary indications," Bondonnat replied, "but it appears that the naval officer charged with the investigation found nothing at the location I had identified but a ravine ravaged by a dynamite explosion. The mysterious subterranean workings had been destroyed by an unknown hand."

"It must be admitted that the Lords of the Red Hand are very strong."

"To get back to Cornelius and Fritz Kramm, I know, from the story told by Lorenza, the healer of pearls, that they're capable of anything, having resorted to theft and blackmail."

---

[3] The French biologist Alexis Carrel (1873-1944), who emigrated to Canada in 1903 and worked in the U.S.A, after 1906, was renowned for his work in transplant surgery, for which he was awarded the Nobel prize in 1912; he was to go on to become even more famous for his work on tissue cultures, teaming up with Charles Lindbergh in the 1930s to improve the technology of transplant surgery.

"Undoubtedly," said Lord Burydan, "but there's no shortage of unscrupulous people who aren't Lords of the Red Hand. To bring such an accusation, it's necessary to have real proof."

The scientist reflected for a few moments. "There's another clue that might be of use to you," he said. "Recently, Dr. Cornelius—whose immense knowledge I admire sincerely—came to visit is us in the company of his brother Fritz. Joe Dorgan was there. At one time, all three of them were sitting next to one another. Well, do you know the strange impression I had? It was that I was in the presence of the three masked men whose commanded the Island of Hanged Men as masters and came on several occasions to dictate orders to me in my prison. I could have sworn that they had the same height, the same corpulence and the same voices. However, I know that it's necessary to be suspicious of such impressions."

"Yes," said Lord Burydan. "Obviously, all that doesn't constitute proof, any more than the barking of Pistolet, who seems to have a veritable hatred of the three individuals in question. I can't allow myself to be carried away by the desire to determine the truth, and I know full well that not all the people at whom Pistolet barks belong to the Red Hand."

"You can believe what you like, but my instinct tells me that those individuals are suspicious. Also, I'm sure that I've seen Joe Dorgan somewhere before...but let's leave that for the moment. Have you discovered anything?"

"Nothing worth mentioning, but I don't remain inactive for a single minute, and I'm admirably seconded, I must say, by my friend Agénor. That's why, a month ago, in disguise, I entered the service of William Dorgan, in order to be able to keep a closer watch on the actions and behavior of his son Joe. I confess that I haven't discovered anything so far. Joe Dorgan is very industrious and very ambitious. He's actively involved with his father's cotton and corn Trust. That might be evidence that he isn't affiliated to the Red Hand."

"He's intimately linked to Fritz and Cornelius."

"Undoubtedly, but there's nothing extraordinary in that. The two brothers own a great many shares in the Trust."

"You're right. And I don't know, after all, that I have any right to speak ill of Cornelius, who gave evidence of the greatest devotion to my daughter in San Francisco. He's the one who brought her round from an unconsciousness that might have proved fatal."

"It's all bizarre. At any rate, let's leave it there. I hope to have something new shortly. It's understood, of course, that this conversation must remain between the two of us. It would be too cruel to trouble the happiness of the three young households with such somber matters. They believe that they're rid of the Red Hand; let's allow them to maintain that belief until further notice."

"When shall I see you again?"

"I don't know. But you might receive a letter from me in a few days. If the recommendations I make to you have a special importance, I'll put an X underneath my signature. That sign will tell you that it's necessary to do exactly what I recommend in my letter, no matter how strange it seems."

"Understood."

"Now, not another word about the Red Hand. Let's go rejoin the ladies, who will certainly want to show us what they've done with the bust with the emerald eyes."

They both went to the Renaissance drawing room and admired William Dorgan's princely gift once again. It had been placed on an elegant pedestal, in a very favorable lighting. Isidora announced that on the day when her husband returned she would hide the bust behind a curtain in order to give him the pleasure of a surprise. In the presence of Lord Burydan she carried out a kind of rehearsal of the scene, and it was unanimously declared that Harry Dorgan was definitely the most fortunate of husbands.

It was, however, getting late. In spite of the efforts that were made to retain him, Lord Burydan bid his friends farewell, after having decked himself out once again in the false beard and spectacles that comprised his disguise.

III. The Bust with the Emerald Eyes

Andrée and Frédérique, sitting on a terrace of the house, were watching the sun disappear over the horizon of Lake Ontario, strewn with a hundred verdant islands. Majestically folded clouds were tinted with shades of deep violet, somber scarlet and orange. It was a magical spectacle.

"What a beautiful evening!" Andrée murmured, emotionally. "What calm! How soft the air is! It's a long time since I've been so happy."

Frédérique's only reply was a half-stifled sigh.

"You seem sad," said Andrée, taking hold of her friend's hands affectionately.

"No, I can assure you."

"Come on, Frédérique, you're hiding something from me. Do you think I haven't noticed that you've been pale and sad for several days?"

"Well, yes, it's true," the young woman murmured, reluctantly. "I'm not happy."

"But that's impossible!" Andrée replied. "What do you lack, then? You're rich surrounded by devoted friends, adored by your husband, and we'll soon be returning to France, where further happiness awaits you."

"My husband doesn't love me," murmured Frédérique, with a poignant anguish. "I'm sure of it."

"Really? But what gives you that idea? Roger shows every concern for you—you're all he talks about, all he thinks about."

"Oh," said Frédérique, having great difficulty holding back her tears. "Roger is certainly a model of courtesy in my regard. He deploys a solicitude that extends to the utmost details; he never gives me any pretext to address a single reproach to him—and yet..." Frédérique appeared to hesitate.

"Come on, Frédérique," said Andrée. "Don't stop half way. You know that you can have every confidence in me."

"I'll tell you everything. Roger doesn't love me as I'd like him to love me. He thinks more about his work than he does about me. But that wouldn't matter...I know that a scientist can't remain idle and that, if I want to be proud of him later, he has to work. That's not all. What if I told you, my dear Andrée, that for several nights, he's been getting up, leaving his room without making any noise, and only coming back after

84

an absence of two or three hours. I have a rival, I'm sure of it. Oh, if I believed that…!'"

"You astonish me—but you must be mistaken."

"I thought for a long time that I was making myself unhappy with baseless jealousy, but the facts are there. Why does he go out at night, as he does?"

"How can your husband have given himself to a rival in this house, which is sealed like a fortress and ten miles from the town?"

"When one is jealous one isn't stopped by reasoning like that. I suspect everyone!"

"Even Isidora? Even me?" asked Andrée, stung to the quick.

Frédérique threw herself into her friend's arms, weeping. "Forgive me, Andrée," she stammered, sobbing. "I don't mean you, of course, or Isidora…"

"Are you, by chance, jealous of the Oceanian girl that your father has brought back, then?"

"Oh, no! Of course not!" Frédérique exclaimed, her eyes flashing with pride. "I hope, in spite of everything, that my husband would prefer me to that bronzed skin."

"You can see that your suspicions are quite unreasonable. Roger undoubtedly only goes out to get a little fresh air in the lovely shade of the park."

Frédérique reflected. "For a moment," she said, "I thought of that Dorypha, that devilish dancer whom I detest with all my heart, even though she saved our lives—that hussy who had the impudence to kiss Roger against his will…"

"Think about it for a minute. You know full well that Dorypha, after having married her lover, the Belgian Gilkin, went to live a long way from here, in Arizona, where Fred Jorgell has entrusted her husband with the direction of a major enterprise."

"That's true. You're right. But how do I know that Roger isn't deceiving me with some chambermaid, or some girl who's smitten with him and comes to visit him secretly?"

"But you're crazy—absolutely crazy! Do you want me to talk to Roger?"

"Don't do any such thing! I'd die of embarrassment if he knew that I have such ideas."

The conversation was interrupted by the ringing of the dinner bell. Frédérique hurriedly went to her dressing-room, in order to efface the traces of her tears, and the two young women went down to the dining room.

As usual, the meal was very animated. Only Frédérique, in spite of all her efforts, took no part in the general gaiety. Nevertheless, in the tumult of conversation sand discussion, her melancholy went unobserved, except by her friend Andrée.

After the meal, the three young women went into the conservatory, which was adjacent to the dining room, in which they had the habit, every evening, while taking tea, of listening to the Scottish governess, Mrs. MacBarlott, read to them from the newspapers. In the meantime, Monsieur Bondonnat and his friends went for a walk along the shore of the lake, from which they could contemplate the admirable moonlight. It was not until later in the evening that Roger Ravenel came back to the room that he occupied, which was only separated from Frédérique's by a communicating door.

Roger knocked softly and, not receiving any response, went into his wife's bedroom. The darkness within was only tempered by the glow of an electric night-light suspended from the ceiling, which was hollowed out in the form of a dome.

He moved closer to the large four-poster bed and saw Frédérique, already in bed, motionless, with her eyes closed.

"She's asleep," he murmured. "I won't wake her."

And, advancing on tiptoe, he brushed the young woman's forehead with a kiss, and withdrew.

Frédérique was not asleep. As soon as she had heard the communicating door close again, he leapt out of bed, hastily slipped into a peignoir, threw a lace mantilla over her shoulders, and then, her feet bare in her slippers, moved to the communicating door and stuck her ear to the keyhole.

Roger was moving back and forth in his room. Frédérique heard him opening and closing drawers; then he went out.

"This time," the young woman murmured, quivering with anguish, "I'm going to know. I need to know!"

Silently, she went along the corridor into which the two bedroom doors opened. In the moonlight, she distinguished Roger's silhouette; he had already reached the top of the stairs and was starting to go down. She followed him, taking the utmost care not to be perceived.

Roger went out through a side door opening into the grounds on the side of the building opposite the main courtyard. Frédérique his behind the clusters of rare plants, and did not lose sight of him.

Perhaps, after all, she thought, *he simply wants, as Andrée said, to get a little fresh air under the trees. What joy, if I were sure that he isn't deceiving me!*

At that moment, however, she distinguished a feminine form in the distance, which seemed to be coming from the direction of the draw-bridge and heading toward the house. The unknown woman was advancing without hesitation, ducking behind tree-trunks and turning round frequently to make sure that she was not being followed.

Frédérique's heart was clutched by a mortal anguish. *My presentiments weren't mistaken*, she said to herself. *Roger is betraying me. He can't lie about it now. I've seen, with my own eyes, the odious rival who has stolen my husband's heart.*

Dazedly, she had moved forward into the moonlight; she only just had time to jump behind a clump of hortensias in order not to be seen by the unknown woman, who passed within a few feet of her hiding-place.

Frédérique could not see her face, which was hidden behind a thick lace headscarf. She felt a sharp pain in her heart. Her legs buckled beneath her; she thought she was about to faint—but hatred brought her upright again, and she continued on her way.

She looked for her rival. The latter had disappeared! Frédérique could only see Roger, who, having gone along the entire length of the façade, had arrived at the wing most distant from the room in which he lived, and was searching in his pocket for a key.

I'll follow him, she thought. The woman will join him, for sure. I'll catch them!

After waiting for a minute, Frédérique quietly opened the door that Roger had left unlocked and fooled him up the staircase that led to the first floor of the building.

Roger went some way along a corridor and stopped at the door of the laboratory that Fred Jorgell had placed at his disposition—for neither the naturalist nor Antoine Paganot had interrupted their work since arriving at the house. As he put the key in the lock Oscar Tournesol arrived at the far end of the corridor. He had come in on the opposite side of the building.

"I believe," he said, laughing, "That this is what's known as good timing."

"Yes," the naturalist replied, "it's perfect." While speaking, he opened the door. They both went into the first room in which the Cossack Rapopoff normally slept, having been promoted to the rank of laboratory assistant.

Oscar turned the light switch. Suddenly, he uttered a cry of fright on seeing the Cossack lying on his bed fully dressed, his head hanging down and his face contorted. Beside him there was an empty bottle.

"They've killed him!" exclaimed the hunchback, emotionally.

"No," said the engineer. "I think he's simply drunk."

"It's not ordinary drunkenness," said the adolescent, who had put his arm around Rapopoff's body, lifted him up and slipped a pillow under his shoulders.

The naturalist took a bottle of ammonia from a shelf and placed it near the Cossack's nostrils, but the revulsive, normally a sovereign remedy in cases of inebriation, had no effect.

"He must have been dosed with some narcotic," said Ravenel. "Fortunately, there's everything needed to render energetic treatment in the laboratory."

More anxious than he wanted to seem, Ravenel opened the door of the second room and, climbing on to a stool, reached out for the bottles arranged on a shelf.

Suddenly, a cry of amazement sprang from his lips. He had just perceived a faint ray of light under the door that gave access to the third room. Malefactors were undoubtedly there—the same ones, undoubtedly, who had dosed Rapopoff with a narcotic.

Roger remained hesitant for a few moments. *I don't see*, he thought, *what anyone could find to steal in that laboratory. There isn't a single object of value in there.*

Suddenly, an idea crossed his mind with lightning rapidity.

The bust with the emerald eyes! he thought. *It can only be that. The Renaissance drawing room is directly above the laboratory.*

Without reflecting on the risk he was running, he opened the door abruptly.

Three men were there their faces covered by masks. One of them was still mounted on the improvised scaffolding thanks to which they had just pierced the ceiling. He was holding the golden bust in his arms, gleaming in the light of the electrical ceiling-lamp, preparing to hand it to one of his accomplices.

Roger remained motionless momentarily, as if frozen by surprise. Before he had had time to make a decision, the three thieves had run to the door and slammed it behind them.

The hunchback had arrived; Roger swiftly brought him up to date with the situation. "Go fetch reinforcements," he said. "In the meantime, I'll stop them from getting away."

"But what if they attack you?"

"I'm not running any risk. I'll content myself with locking the outer door—the one that leads to the corridor. Before they've had time to break it down, you'll have returned with a few sturdy fellows..."

At that moment, the ray of light disappeared. At the same time, the door opened. With an irresistible surge, the three malefactors, knocking Ravenel and his companion down, ran through the two rooms and out into the corridor.

"It's not so bad," said the hunchback. "They haven't taken the bust. Our arrival surprised them, and their one thought was to get away."

"Yes, but we need to give chase without losing a minute. Fortunately, I have my revolver. Follow me!"

They both launched themselves into the corridor, arriving just in time to see the three bandits rushing headlong down the stairs. Roger and Oscar observed for a second time, with satisfaction, that the thieves were not carrying any kind of object.

Roger fired a revolver shot after them.

A loud scream—that of a frightened woman—responded to the noise of the gunshot.

Roger ran forward just in time to catch Frédérique in his arms as she fell, unconscious.

"Dead!" he cried. "She's dead! And it's me who has killed her!"

Mad with grief, he lifted up the young woman's body and ran with it to the laboratory, where he set her down in an armchair. "My darling Frédérique," he stammered. "But it's not possible. You aren't dead? Answer me! And you, Oscar, what are you doing there? Help me, then! Quickly—cold water, smelling salts!"

Prey to a veritable delirium, he covered the young woman's hands and face with kisses. After several seconds, she opened her eyes, and, darting stupefied glances at her husband and Oscar, she murmured, in a weak voice: "Oh! That woman...the bandits...!"

"Where are you wounded, my daring?" asked Roger, kneeling at Frédérique's feet.

"I'm not wounded—but I was so scared! The bullet whistled past my ear...."

"But what were you doing there?"

Frédérique blushed and bowed her head. Then, darting a rancorous gaze art her husband, she said: "I know everything! I followed you! I saw her, that wretched woman!"

"What woman?"

"The one with whom you're deceiving me! The one you go to meet every night! I couldn't see her face, but I'll be able to find her, and I'll take my revenge!"

Frédérique dissolved in tears.

"But that's crazy!" Roger exclaimed. "Frédérique, my love, I swear to you that I've never deceived you, that I've never had a rendezvous with any woman."

"Then why do you slip out of your room every night?"

Roger and Oscar looked at one another.

"I'm obliged to confess my secret," said the hunchback. "As you know, Madame, I'm going to marry Miss Regina Bombridge shortly. She has been kind enough to consent, in spite of the disgrace that afflicts me. I wanted to give her a surprise."

"What surprise?" asked Frédérique, suspiciously.

"A few years ago, science discovered a means of curing the infirmity from I suffer. Monsieur Ravenel has been generous enough to consent to apply the treatment that will rid me of my deformity..."

"And that's the reason," Frédérique asked, "why Roger leaves me every night?"

"Yes," the naturalist relied. "Poor Oscar asked me to keep it a secret. He wanted to give his fiancée the surprise of appearing before her one morning free of his hump and as upright as the common run of men."

Frédérique was half-convinced, but she was still hesitant. Her suspicious gaze went from Roger to Oscar, looking out for the blink of an eye that would allow her to deduce their complicity in a lie. But Oscar and Roger were being perfectly honest; they were telling the truth.

"What about that woman, then?" Frédérique demanded, insistently. "Why did I see her at the precise moment when you were in the park?"

Ravenel made a gesture of impatience. "What do you want me to say?" he demanded. "I don't know the woman. I know nothing more about her than you do. What explanation do you expect me to give you?"

"There must be one, though," said Oscar. "I'm sure, myself, that the woman was with the burglars. She was standing lookout while her accomplices were in the process of stealing the bust."

"The bust has been stolen?" Frédérique asked, the news making her forget her jealousy momentarily.

"No, it hasn't been stolen," the naturalist replied, "but we got here just in time..."

"So much the better!" exclaimed the young woman. "Isidora would have been heartbroken. You got it back, then? Where is it?"

"We got it back," murmured the naturalist. "Which is to say that we put the burglars to flight, and they left without taking anything with them."

"As long as they haven't extracted the emeralds!"

"I didn't think of that. Let's look for the bust. They must have left it in some corner."

Roger opened the door of the third room, which he inspected with a rapid glance. "I can't see the bust," he said, slightly astonished.

"Well, too bad!" said Frédérique, whose jealousy had revived. "You'll find the bust, since it's there. It's not the bust that interests me—it's that woman. Both of you ought to be in pursuit of the bandits. What are you wanting fir? They can't be far away, since the drawbridge is never lowered at this hour."

"All right," said the naturalist. "We'll set out in pursuit of the burglars—but before then, I want to get you safely back to your room."

"Certainly not. I'm going with you. I don't want the so-called female burglar to escape by means of some subterfuge. I want to know the truth, and I shall!"

Roger understood that there was nothing to be done against such obstinacy. "Well, come with us, then," he said. "But it's crazy. You'd be much better off in bed. You're risking getting hit by a bullet, as you nearly were just now."

"That's all the same to me. Let's go."

The three of them were about to leave the laboratory when they heard a kind of bizarre bellowing, which nailed them to the spot with astonishment.

"What's that?" demanded Frédérique, clutching her husband's arm with an instinctive gesture."

"Don't worry, Madame," replied the hunchback, who had just gone into the first room. It's simply our friend Rapopoff yawning.

Indeed, they saw the Cossack, alarmed by waking up in such numerous company, rolling his bewildered eyes and opening his jaws enormously wide. He ended up hiding under the bedclothes, doubtless ashamed of being caught in such an disreputable state.

"You, my lad," said Roger, who was deeply exasperated, "will have to reckon with me. We'll sort this out tomorrow morning. Everything that's happened is your fault. If you hadn't drunk the contents of that bottle...but enough..."

The Cossack made no reply. Huddled under his bedclothes, he let the storm pass.

"What a brute!" exclaimed the naturalist. Turning to Oscar, he said: "Quickly, run and wake up all the domestics. Tell the first one you meet to go and warn Harry Dorgan and Paganot. Since Frédérique demands it, we'll organize a search."

The hunchback departed at a run, while Roger carefully locked the external door of the laboratory.

Five minutes had not gone by when the entire domestic staff of the house was awake. Lights were moving back and forth in all the wings of the building.

Harry Dorgan, Antoine Paganot and even Monsieur Bondonnat, snatched from sleep, arrived in the summary costumes that they had hastily donned.

In a few words, Roger Ravenel told his friends what had happened, and the search was immediately organized. One party of domestics began to explore the shores of the lake, while another headed for the drawbridge. They were equipped with automobile headlights with which to search the thicker bushes, and a dozen dogs—including Pistolet, who had taken the lead—had been launched on the trail of the malefactors.

Frédérique and Roger followed the pack as closely as possible. Pistolet, who had taken the lead, soon retraced, baying in a plaintive fashion that attracted the young woman's attention.

"Pistolet's found something," she said. "We need to see what it is."

The dog led them into the heart of an inextricable thicket, in the middle of which a white object appeared, the nature of which Roger could not determine the nature at first.

Frédérique quickly guessed what it was.

"The woman!" she cried. "It's the woman! I recognize the color of her dress and headscarf. This time, I've got her! She won't escape me."

Abruptly pulling free of her husband's arms, she ran off at top speed. One might have thought that hatred was putting wings on her heels.

Having reached the bush she stood there, amazed and disappointed. She found herself in the presence of a young woman with a blooded face—and the woman was Regina Bombridge, the former bareback rider of the Gorilla Club, Oscar Tournesol's fiancée.

The young woman was not unconscious. She was uttering feeble groans. With the aid of Roger and Frédérique, who did not know what to think, she got to her feet and was able to go sit down on a rustic bench a short distance away, at the foot of a eucalyptus. Roger made her drink a mouthful of whisky, and bathed the wound on her head; fortunately, it was not serious.

Frédérique, having helped her husband, waited impatiently for the injured woman to be well enough to speak,

"I hope, Miss," she said, finally, in an almost menacing tone, "that you can explain how you come to be here, in the woods, at such an hour, when you ought to be peacefully asleep in your father's chalet."

Miss Bombridge bowed her head, utterly confused, but, after a long moment of hesitation, decided to speak. "Madame," she said, in a tone of noble sincerity that did not permit her words to be doubted, "I'm supposed to marry Oscar Tournesol in a few weeks, who, on his insistence, obtained permission to occupy a room in my father's house until we're married."

"I know that," said Frédérique, in a tone quivering with impatience. "Get to the point, Miss."

"I perceived that for some time, Oscar was going out every night. I tried to find out where he was going; he answered me evasively. What can I say? I thought that he was deceiving me." With real chagrin, the young woman added: "Unfortunately, Madame, I still believe it. I have the proof."

"What do you mean?"

"This evening, I had the unfortunate idea of spying on him, and I can assure you that I've been well punished. I had arrived, while following Oscar, at the door of the stairway to the laboratory, when I perceived a woman carefully veiled by a mantilla, who was moving in the same direction. This time, I could no longer doubt. I received such a blow to my heart that I didn't have the courage to go any further. I retraced my steps, with death in my soul. I was getting ready to go back to my father when three masked men abruptly appeared in front of me. Before I had time to flee, I was struck on the head and fell down. The men continued on their way, doubtless thinking that they had killed me."

Frédérique was pensive. "What did the woman you saw look like?" she asked.

"I don't recall, exactly," Regina replied, searching her memories. "She was about your height, with her head enveloped in a mantilla like yours."

"It was me."

"You, Madame?"

"Yes, my child. I too, I confess, was anxious about my husband's nocturnal absences..."

"There's no need to go into all that," said Roger, impatiently.

Frédérique threw her arms around her husband's neck and hugged him recklessly, then whispered in his ear: "Let me confess everything. It will be my punishment." Aloud, she went on: "Yes, Miss, I had the same suspicions as you, and I too thought, on seeing you, that I was sure of my facts—but I can now tell you the whole truth. If my husband and Oscar have been meeting every night for several days, it's because they were preparing a surprise for you."

"A surprise? For me?"

"Yes, Miss—but permit me not to say any more."

"In any case," ad Roger, insistently, "it's time to go back in. It's necessary that I put a better dressing on your wound. Believe me, Oscar has had no intention of deceiving you, and in a few days' time you'll know his secret."

While this scene was unfolding in a solitary corner of the grounds, the two parties carrying out the search had met up. The burglars' tracks had been followed to the edge of the lake, to a place where the ground was trodden and the reeds broken. It was there that the burglars must have got back into the boat thanks to which they had been able to get into the property. The following day, moreover, a billhook was found, with which they had cut the rope in order to get away more rapidly.

Miss Bombridge went back to her father's house, under the safe-guard of her fiancé. Frédérique went furtively back to her bedroom, still ashamed of her unjust suspicions.

The domestics received permission to go to bed, and Monsieur Bondonnat, who, being too lightly dressed, had caught a chill while walking through the dewy grass, declared that he would do the same.

Harry Dorgan remained alone in the company of Ravenel and Paganot.

"Since we're awake," the last-named proposed, "let's go to the laboratory to see what damage has been done, and whether, as I fear, the burglars have got away with the emeralds."

"Let's go," said Harry Dorgan. "I don't feel the slightest desire to go to sleep."

They went back up to the laboratory, going through the first two rooms without waking the Cossack, who had fallen profoundly asleep again.

The third room had been completely turned upside-down by the burglars, who must certainly have been professional burglars possessed of an extraordinary skill. They had begun by closing the thick shutters of the window overlooking the main courtyard, from which the light might have been seen. Then, with two tables and some chairs, they had constructed a genuine scaffold immediately under the location of the bust. The improved drill-bits and saws that they had used to pierce the ceiling were found.

"The people who did this," observed Harry Dorgan, "were very well-informed. They weren't unaware that the door and windows of the Renaissance room are armored and virtually impenetrable."

"I can't see the bust, though," said Paganot, who had been hunting high and low since entering the room.

"I'm quite certain," Roger said, "that they didn't take it away."

"We'll find it," said Harry Dorgan.

"Let's search!"

"Let's search."

All three of them explored every corner of the room. They even went up, with the aid of the hole in the ceiling, into the Renaissance room. The bust remained undiscoverable.

"We'll continue searching tomorrow," said Harry Dorgan, slightly nervously, "but I think it would be the most elementary prudence to put two strong men on sentry duty at the laboratory door."

"I think so too," Roger agreed. "We can scarcely count on the Cossack."

The three of them withdrew.

As they had agreed, they met again early the next day, in order to continue their investigation.

Following the advice of his friends, Harry Dorgan had given orders that no one was to tell Isidora about the theft. They all thought it best only to inform her once they had found the bust. They knew how fond the young woman was of it, and judged it unnecessary to worry and upset her before being certain of the situation.

They did not take long to be convinced. The most scrupulous investigations produced no result. The bust with the emerald eyes had disappeared as if it had gone up in smoke.

Rapopoff, when interrogated, could provide no information. The Cossack had found a bottle labeled *Whisky* beside his bed and thought it was a gift from one of his masters. Conscientiously, he had drunk half of it. The analysis of the liquid that remained showed that a powerful narcotic had been added to the whisky. If the Cossack had emptied the bottle entirely, he would certainly be dead, in spite of his robust constitution. The bandits had overshot their aim. The dose of the narcotic had been too strong. Rapopoff had gone to sleep after the initial draughts, which had saved him from emptying the bottle completely.

The entire day was spent in futile searches. Toward evening, it was necessary to bite the bullet and go to tell Isidora the sad news, by which he was sincerely upset.

"However," Roger Ravenel never ceased repeating, his words supported by Oscar, "I'm sure—perfectly certain—that the bust didn't leave the house, or even the laboratory.

IV. The Lava Tub

The theft of the bust with the emerald eyes had upset Isidora greatly. She wondered whether this latest crime might be due, once again, to the bandits of the Red Hand. At any rate, she was exasperated.

Perhaps for the first time in her life, she had an argument with her father.

"What!" she said to him. "You're a billionaire, you've made your own fortune, and even with the immense wealth that the whole world envies, the intelligence and energy that everyone cites as exemplary, you can't guarantee your personal security and that of your daughter?"

"I confess," the billionaire replied, "that I haven't paid enough attention to it. My friends, Rockefeller, Pierpont Morgan, Mackey and others, are surrounded by hundreds of detectives and visible guards..."

"Well it's necessary to do as they do!" the young woman replied, a trifle nervously.

"All right. I'll give orders to that effect. But I thought that the precautions I'd taken were sufficient, and also that the Red Hand was no longer to be feared."

"Whether it's the bandits of that terrible association or others, it's indispensable that we're better guarded and better defended."

"Don't get angry, my dear child. I'll order half a dozen motor launches today, which will patrol the waters around the island all night. That way, I hope you'll be able to sleep peacefully."

"I'm not only worried about myself but about you and our friends. I'd be eternally remorseful if anything happened to Frédérique, Andrée or their husbands through our fault. But that's not all. It's now necessary to tell William Dorgan what's happened. He won't be pleased, I'm sure, to see the negligence with which we've looked after the royal gift he sent me."

"Don't worry about that. I've already had a long letter to William Dorgan taken to the Post Office in which I've told him all the circumstances of the theft. He's too intelligent to hold us responsible for an event of which we're the primary victims. Since there's a mysterious aspect to the theft of the bust, which hasn't yet been clarified, William Dorgan will be the first to make urgent efforts to that end."

This conversation took place in the evening on the day after the theft.

Three days later, a laconic telegram announced the arrival of the billionaire.

Contrary to what Isidora had said, William Dorgan did not manifest any annoyance.

"I'll give you another bust, my dear child," he said, "if it turns out that this one is conclusively lost—which isn't proven."

"Obviously," said Isidora, "if we could find a few skillful and experienced detectives..."

"There's no lack of them," William Dorgan interjected. "And damn it, an ingot of that weight, and two gems that are known to every jeweler in America, can't disappear as easily as that."

"In any case," said Fred Jorgell, who had just shaken his rival financier's hand cordially and sat down beside him in a rocking-chair, "We've already taken effective measures. I've sent off a hundred telegrams. The police in all the large cities of the Union have been alerted. I'll do everything necessary to recover Isidora's portrait. My self-respect is at stake; it's necessary that the thieves are caught, no matter how much it costs."

"Well, good luck," said William Dorgan, in a perfectly detached tone. But we'll talk at our leisure about the incident tomorrow. Personally I don't attach enormous importance to it. I've come here primarily for the pleasure of seeing you all. Your friends from France have definitely won me over, and I have a veritable admiration for Monsieur Bondonnat's genius. He's had such extraordinary adventures!"

"Here he is, in person," said the old scientist, appearing at the door of the room. "But not so many compliments on my count, I beg you. I'd never have believed that Americans were such flatterers."

Bondonnat and William Dorgan shook hands effusively, and struck up a conversation with the most frank cordiality.

Paganot, Ravanel, Frédérique and Andrée, who had been informed of the billionaire's presence, arrived in succession.

William Dorgan even wanted to meet the Oceanian girl Hatouara, the Cossack Rapopoff and, most of all, Oscar Tournesol, about whom the engineer Harry had told him a great deal.

The billionaire was happy in the midst of that family meeting, from which the only one missing was Harry Dorgan, retained in New York by the interests of the Lightning Steamship Company.

"Do you know what I intend to do?" said the billionaire, suddenly. "It's isn't because of the theft of the bust that I've come. My friend Fred Jorgell's letter only brought forward the date of the trip. I'm going to take you all to a delightful property that I've just bought in Florida, where the climate is delightful."

"Why not spend a few days with us here?" asked Fred Jorgell. "That would be much simpler."

"Don't worry, I'll come back. First, I want to have the pleasure of having you as my guests."

The invitation was accepted in principle by everyone, and the conversation became general.

The two billionaires disagreed about business matters, but in an entirely amicable and courteous fashion.

"I won the first round," said William Dorgan. "I beat you with regard to the corn and cotton Trust, but I dare say that you'll have your revenge."

"It's certain," said Fred Jorgell, with a malicious smile, "that if the Lightning Steamship Company continues to succeed as it has done so far, we'll do battle again."

"Of course! When you've monopolized all transport by water, we'll only be able to move our corn and cotton at the tariffs you fix."

"You'll still have the railways."

"You know very well that railway companies demand too high a price when it's a matter of cumbersome materials like cotton and corn."

"Don't worry—we can always come to an arrangement. There won't be any recurrence between us of the conflict of interests that drove us apart for such a long time."

"I'm glad to find you so well disposed, and we're ready to pay you a profitable rate. You're not unaware, moreover, that in the financial duel that nearly caused us to fall out permanently, I was primarily guided by my son Joe—but he's become much more reasonable. He's reconciled with his brother, and has ended up understanding, with him, that good relationships and family affections are worth more than a few million dollars."

"However," Fred Jorgell put in, "you now have associates who might not be so accommodating. I mean Dr. Cornelius Kramm and his brother, the art dealer."

"I can assure you that they too are charming people. They only do what I tell them to do. In any case, their share isn't very considerable, and the sums that advanced or procured for the Trust have already been partly reimbursed."

The conversation had reached that point when Oscar, who had left the room for a few moments, came back in and went to whisper a few words in Bondonnat's ear. The old scientist nodded affirmatively to the adolescent, and they both slipped out, unnoticed, on to a large balcony ornamented with marble bases and shrubs, which was like a verdant annex to the room.

"You've received a letter from Lord Burydan?" asked the old man.

"Yes, my dear Master. Here it is."

Bondonnat read the letter; as he did so, he face expressed a certain surprise.

"That's curious," he said. "I wouldn't have thought of that. If Lord Burydan isn't mistaken, American thieves are much cleverer than ours."

"I don't understand what Lord Burydan means when he talks about chemical methods."

"I'll explain. Let's go to the laboratory first."

They headed toward the wing of the house that had been the theater of the theft a few days before.

On the way, the hunchback asked Bondonnat why the eccentric had not written directly and had made use of an intermediary.

"I understand that perfectly," the old man replied. "Lord Burydan, rendered very suspicious by recent events, probably feared that my correspondence might be intercepted. He assumed that yours would be less closely monitored."

"Lord Burydan asks us whether anyone has recently come to deliver chemical produces and take away unnecessary glassware. He seems to attach considerable importance to the matter."

"We'll soon find out."

They arrived at the laboratory. They were welcomed by Rapopoff, who, as usual, gave them a military salute."

"Good day," Bondonnat said to him. "Can you tell me what day the last delivery of chemical products came?"

"Yesterday, Little Father," the Cossack replied. "The two men who came were very pleasant and very generous. They gave me a twenty-cent piece for helping them to carry two carboys downstairs."

"Were the carboys full or empty?" asked the naturalist swiftly.

"Full, Little Father, and quite heavy."

"That's it!" murmured Bondonnat in Oscar's ear. "I'm beginning to think that Lord Burydan isn't mistake. But let's see... What were they full of, Rapopoff?"

"I don't know."

Bondonnat and Oscar went into the third room, and at the first glance the scientist perceived a large lava trough that was standing in a corner, and which served to wash glassware, volcanic lava being immune to corrosion by acids. It was quite empty.

"Was it you who emptied that tub?" Bondonnat asked the Cossack.

"No, Little Father."

Bondonnat did not say anything more. He leaned over the edge of the trough, where a little liquid still remained. He took out a few drops with a spatula and then took some bottles of reagents from one cupboard and a touchstone from another. He performed a number of operations that Oscar and the Cossack watched with interest.

"Lord Burydan was definitely right," he said eventually. "I can now reconstitute the extremely skillful means by which the theft was committed. Lord Burydan mentions a chemical means in his letter. Personally, I couldn't see how such a voluminous mass could be taken away. It was simply dissolved."

Oscar opened his eyes wide.

"Yes," said Monsieur Burydan. "That's what happened. As I've just confirmed with the aid of reagents, the lava trough was filled with *aqua regia*, and you're not unaware that *aqua regia*, formed of a mixture of nitric and hydrochloric acids in equal proportions, is the only liquid that has the property of being able to dissolve gold. The burglars, or bandits, simply placed the bust in the tub, and when they were sure that it had dissolved, they filled the empty carboys with *aqua regia*, and had the aplomb to get the worthy Rapopoff to help them carry it away."

"What about the emeralds?" asked Oscar.

"They found them intact at the bottom of the tub. Doubtless they took care not to forget them."

"That's amazing."

"Oh, their precautions were well taken. They foresaw everything. Thus, the *aqua regia* had been tinted with a substance whose nature I haven't yet been able to determine, so that the liquid became sufficiently opaque for no one to perceive the bust."

"That's nevertheless making fools of us all!" exclaimed Oscar. "To think that we searched the laboratory from top to bottom, without thinking of looking in this trough!"

"Oh, they're evidently intelligent people. But one question: who is our supplier of chemical products?"

"Mr. Gresham."

"Get him on the telephone. We need to straighten this out straight away."

Oscar hastened to obey, and a few moments later he obtained the telephonic connection.

"Gresham and Co. in New York?" asked Bondonnat.

"Yes, sir. Who's speaking."

"It's on behalf of Mr. Harry Dorgan."

"Good."

"Can you tell me, Monsieur, when you made your last delivery to out laboratory on Lake Ontario?"

"It was at least a fortnight ago, sir."

"You didn't send anyone yesterday, then, to pick up empty glassware?"

"No one."

"Thank you, Monsieur."

Bondonnat replaced the receiver. "You see, my dear Oscar," he said, "that there's no more doubt possible. Miss Isidora has lost the bust with the emerald eyes forever."

"We must tell William Dorgan and Fred Jorgell immediately."

"No," the scientist replied, after a moment's reflection. "I'm not sure that's the right thing to do. Until further orders, we ought to keep this secret between the two of us. I'll simply write a note to Lord Burydan, who ought to be fully informed."

"I believe you're right, my dear Master; but that doesn't affect the fact that the Red Hand—assuming that it's them—have affiliates skilled in chemistry. It's obvious that they must have true scientists among them."

V. The Scaffolding Bridge

Americans never lose sight of the axiom that "Time is money." They do not recoil from any audacity when it comes to a matter of eking at that precious capital. Thus, for instance, here, people wait for a railways system to be completed before risking themselves in it, and for the bridges, tunnels and other works of art to be fully installed and offering a proven solidity. In America, on the other hand, they start by placing the rails haphazardly in order to out trains in circulation on the provisional track, leaving all the necessary supplementary work to be done at a later date, in a more serious fashion.

Do they encounter a watercourse? They put up a wooden bridge until the company's receipts are sufficient to put up a steel or stone one. American carpenters have no rivals in the art of constructing such bridges, with the aid of wooden scaffolding, which sometimes reach sixty meters in height and are installed with a great simplicity of means and an amazing audacity.

Is there a deep valley to traverse? They begin by laying a bed of hard stones. Then they put up the firs support, in which they rest the second, a third or a fourth—as many as it takes to reach the level of the track. On the last support, two beams are set, and on those beams two rails.

These audacious constructions are not maintained by St. Andrew's crosses or by iron T-bars; they are only held together by dowels and a few crossbeams that maintain the separation of the beams at intervals.

It was on a scaffolding framework of that sort that the New York railway was once supported a few kilometers from Rochester station. The bridge, thirty meters high, straddles a broad and deep valley, at the bottom of which lies a marshy stream that flows into Lake Ontario a few leagues further on. Today, the bridge in question has been replaced by a monumental bridge of granite and iron.

The landscape offers a savage and desolate aspect. As far as the eye can see, the edges of the stream are covered with rushes, reeds and dwarf willows, which serve as a refuge for aquatic birds.

It was about ten o'clock in the evening, and a thick fog occupied the entirety of the valley's depths, when three men wrapped in thick hooded cloaks ventured through this muddy and damp terrain, into which they sank continually.

"I know longer know where we are," said one of them. "There's no means of getting one's bearings here. One can't see four steps ahead of oneself."

"My dear Cornelius," another said, "I believe that I'd do well to switch on my electric lantern."

"That's not very prudent. You know, Baruch, that the light of the lantern might be visible from the height of the bridge."

"That's impossible in this fog." Turning to the third individual, who had not yet opened his mouth, he said: "What do you think, Fritz?"

"I agree with you. We're not taking any great risk in fog like this."

Baruch flicked the switch of a pocket torch; thanks to its aid, the three Lords of the Red Hand were able to follow the path snaking along the bottom of the valley without overmuch difficulty.

After a quarter of an hour of slow and difficult walking, they reached a wretched hut built of will branches and covered in reeds, similar to those used by hunters of snipe and wild duck. A man could scarcely stand up inside it. It had no other issue than the door, which faced the railway bridge, the base of which faced the railway bridge, presently drowned in the mist, although the upper part was outlined with a fantastic clarity against the pale moonlit sky.

Each of the three Lords sat down on bundle of reeds, which was the only available seat.

Baruch displaced one of the bundles and pulled out a square box from underneath it, to which was attached a metallic wire protected by a green cotton sheath. The box contained an electric telegraph-key for sending Morse code, the mechanism of which was carefully checked by Baruch and Cornelius.

"It's in good condition," said Fritz. "I fear that the humidity might have put it out of order."

"No," said Baruch, "this cabin is a little more elevated than the level of the surrounding soil. But what time is it?"

Cornelius checked his chronometer. "Ten past ten at Rochester station. We still have twenty-five minutes to wait. Don't forget my instructions, will you? As soon as the lights of the train draw level with the signal at the entrance to the bridge you throw the switch."

"It will be a fine collapse!" sniggered Fritz. "There's ten kilos of panclastite under each of the main beams. Would like one of us to stay to keep you company?"

"No. Your presence in the immediate vicinity of the Rochester station at the moment when the detonation occurs is indispensable—so it'll soon be time for you to leave me. What I have to do isn't very difficult.

"As I've explained," said Cornelius, "you're not running any risk. Because panclastite always acts in a vertical direction, the beams will break from the bottom upwards. Anyway, you're far enough away from the bridge here to have nothing to fear."

"I know. I won't be staying for long here. As soon as the explosion occurs I'll only take the time to thrown my devices into the river mud and go back to my auto. I've very keen that my presence in New York should be observed in the morning."

"I believe," said Cornelius, "that our preparations have been made in the wisest fashion. We have another role to play, which is no less difficult."

"Everything will go to plan," said Fritz. We need a catastrophe of this sort. It will clear up the situation completely."

"You must understand," said Cornelius, "that enterprises such as the theft of the bust with the emerald eyes only offer us a precarious resource. It's necessary to get our hands on a veritably considerable capital, at a stroke."

"I received the last information from my agents less than an hour ago," said Fritz. "All our enemies will be on the train: William Dorgan, Isidora and your real father, my dear Baruch, Fred Jorgell."

"Oh, he's the one I detest the most," the bandit replied. His physiognomy had taken on an expression of savage ferocity."

"There's also the entire French party," said Cornelius, with a mocking smile, "beginning with my savant colleague Prosper Bondonnat, and that malicious little hunchback who has caused us so much trouble."

Baruch's face darkened. "I would have dearly liked to save Andrée, though," he added.

"What childishness!" Fritz exclaimed. "At the point we've reached, we can't stop at quibbles. It's necessary that they all die. It's the only means of getting out of the situation. Andrée has to die with the others. She has to."

"Well, then she'll die," murmured Baruch, with a sigh.

Cornelius took out his chronometer again. "Hmm!" he said. "We only have a quarter of an hour left; that's just enough time to get there. Until we meet again, my dear Baruch, and good luck! Tomorrow morning you'll get a coded telegram, which will tell you everything."

"Goodbye, Doctor, Fritz!"

The three bandits exchanged a cordial handshake and parted.

Baruch remained alone, lying on a bed of reeds. He switched off his electric torch and waited.

From time to time, a gust of wind caused the beams of the immense supportive structure to creak. It seemed to the murderer, who was shivering involuntarily, that plaintive voices were mingling with the sighing of the wind in the reeds. At the entrance to the bridge, whose scaffolding emerged from the ocean of fog, the huge red signal looked like a bloody eye open in the black night.

At the very moment when Fritz and Cornelius took their leave of Baruch, two luxurious automobiles deposited outside the station on the New-York-Rochester railway an active and joyful band. The guests at the property on Lake Ontario had come together, with the exception of Harry, who had been retained in New York for some time by the heavy workload imposed upon him by the administration of the Lightning Steamship Company.

After long hesitation, it had been agreed that everyone would spend a month in the property that William Dorgan had just bought in Florida. The billionaire, pleased that his invitation had finally been accepted, went in person to buy the Pullman car tickets in which the entire party was to travel.

"The express leaves at ten thirty-five," he said, cheerfully. "We'll be in New York by ten past twelve."

They were just about to go on to the platform, while a squad of domestics under the direction of Bob Horwett was busy registering the luggage when a cyclist dismounted in front of the station and headed for the group formed by the family and friends of the two billionaires.

Bondonnat was very surprised to see that the cyclist, who was covered in sweat and dust, was the Indian Kloum. He immediately came up to the old scientist.

"What is it, my dear Kloum?" Bondonnat said. "You're completely out of breath."

"Dispatch from Lord Burydan," the Indian announced, laconically.

"For me?"

"Yes, for you."

Kloum handed Bondonnat a letter, which the latter opened feverishly and read.

My dear Master

Don't take the express that leaves Rochester at ten thirty-five, and make sure that all our friends put off their journey until tomorrow. Insist on retaining them; otherwise, they will be in terrible danger. I have my reasons for not being more explicit.

Lord Burydan.

The eccentric's signature was accompanied by the X that signified, as had been agreed, that the instruction contained in the letter must be carried out to the letter.

The old scientist could find no better way than to take Fred Jorgell, Paganot and Ravenel to one side. They yielded to his reasoning and took responsibility for persuading Isidora, Andrée and Frédérique of the necessity of putting back their departure by another day. As for Oscar Tournesol, he knew Lord Burydan too well not to know that the latter must have had important reasons for writing such a letter.

It only remained, therefore, to alert William Dorgan—but the latter did not want to listen, even when Bondonnat, after some hesitation, showed him Lord Burydan's letter. He was even somewhat annoyed that his daughter-in-law, who had promised him formally to accompany him, along with her friends, was changing her mind so abruptly.

"Everyone is free to do as he wishes," he declared, dryly, "but I've decided that I'll take this train, and I'll take it. Neither Lord Burydan nor anyone else will change my opinion. I truly wonder what danger I can be in, comfortably installed in a luxury compartment. With reasoning like that, one would never get into a carriage. I have several important meetings in New York tomorrow morning, and I won't cancel them for such a trivial reason."

"It's not a trivial reason," Isidora replied, holy. "Who knows whether the bandits of the Red Hand might have decided to attack the train?"

"No—the Red Hand has never been as terrible as that. All of its members are locked up, anyway. You're forging chimerical fears..."

All arguments, and even pleading, collided with the unbreakable obstinacy of the old man. When the train appeared in the station he climbed aboard and leaned out of his carriage window to give his friends one last handshake—but he seemed genuinely annoyed by the defection of his guests.

"I hope you won't hold it against us," said Isidora.

"Not at all," replied the billionaire, who had recovered his good humor. "I understand the reasons for your action, although they appear insufficient to me."

"You're wrong, Father-in-law, and I'll spend all night worrying about you. At least promise to send me a telegram as soon as you arrive, to reassure me."

"I promise. But now I think about it, when shall we see one another again? I hope that your departure, in spite of Lord Burydan's mysterious warning, isn't conclusively adjourned? Oh, if you knew how delightful that corner of Florida is, with its great palm trees and odorous creepers. When you've seen it, you won't want to leave again."

"We have no desire to refuse your invitation," the young woman replied, swiftly. "The proof is that at noon tomorrow, without fail, we'll be in New York, from which we'll all depart for Florida together."

"Unless, of course," the billionaire replied, mischievously, "you receive another mysterious warning from the mysterious lord."

"That's unlikely."

"Who knows?" murmured Bondonnat, who had been prey to multiple anxieties once he had read the letter bought by Kloum.

At that moment, the enormous locomotive of the express emitted a shrill whistle, its funnel launched forth a torrent of smoke mixed with wisps of steam, the axles grated, and the train moved off. Isidora, who had climbed up on to the carriage's footplate, only just had time to jump down.

The massive train had moved off slowly, effortfully climbing the stiff slope at the extremity of which was the red signal placed at the entrance to the wooden bridge.

Fred Jorgell's guests climbed into the automobiles that had brought them, sadly heading back to the house. They were all deeply upset, especially Isidora and her two friends. Fred Jorgell tried in vain to reassure them.

"I really don't know," he said, what kind of peril William Dorgan can be in. His train will deposit him at New York Station, where he'll find his chauffeur waiting to drive him directly to his home. Even if he were to be attacked by the Red Hand—if that happens, it'll be solely due to his own stubbornness—he's been warned. He's armed. Anyway, I repeat, I don't see how and when he can be attacked. When he arrives, many districts of the city will still be very busy."

"Doubtless you're right," said Andrée de Maubreuil. "And yet, if Lord Burydan has warned us, we can trust that he must have a serious motive."

"I wish it were tomorrow morning," said Isidora.

No one attempted to continue the conversation, and the journey continued in profound silence.

Fred Jorgell and his friends had only just left Rochester station when an automobile covered with a layer of dust that was evidence of a long journey pulled up facing the station entrance. Two men got out. They were Lord Astor Burydan and his friend Agénor. They both seemed prey to a marked overexcitement.

Lord Burydan went through the halls in a few strides, raced on to the platform and, perceiving the station-master, ran toward him.

"Sir," he said in a voice full of anguish, "has the New York train gone?"

The functionary believed, as often occurs, that he was confronted by a traveler who had just missed his train. "You're unlucky," he said. "It's only a few minutes since the train pulled out. Look—you can still see it in the distance. It's about to go through the signal at the head of the..."

There was no time to finish his sentence. A jet of livid flame shot into the sky, illuminating, for the duration of a lightning-flash, the town, the countryside and the double steel ribbon if the railways track. Then a formidable detonation rang out.

The red signal had disappeared, as if blown out by an invisible breath, and where the bridge and train had been, there was no longer anything but a vast white cloud rising and spiraling into the sky, where there was a resplendent full moon.

The station-master had gone white.

"Someone's blown up the bridge!" he cried, despairingly. Thinking of all the responsibilities that might weigh upon him, he added: "But it's not my fault!"

"No one can accuse you of anything—but it's necessary immediately to go to the aid of all those unfortunates who are dying at the bottom of the ravine." Lord Burydan grabbed the station-master's arm as he moved back and forth along the platform, half-crazed. "One more thing.

Tell me, I beg you, whether Fred Jorgell—whom you doubtless know—got on the train with his friends."

"No," the station-master replied, mechanically. "They bought their tickets, but at the last moment, they stayed here. Only one of them departed."

"Which one?"

"A billionaire from New York…in truth, I can't recall his name."

"Might it have been William Dorgan?"

"Yes, that's it."

Lord Burydan heard no more. He got back into his automobile with Agénor and sped in the direction of the bridge as fast as the engine could contrive.

In the meantime, help was being organized at Rochester station. The famous Doctor Cornelius and his brother Fritz, who happened to be passing through the town, were the first to put themselves at the disposal of the authorities and to be transported to the site of the catastrophe.

15. THE LADY OF THE SCABIOUS FLOWERS

I. After the Bridge Disaster

Unknown malefactors had just blown up the bridge over a profound valley a few miles along the track from Rochester station. The New York express had been hurled into the abyss. The carriages had been smashed, the majority of the passengers killed or atrociously mutilated.

Lord Burydan, who happened to be at Rochester station with his friend Agénor Marmousier, had hastened to climb into his automobile and race to the scene of the disaster. The spectacle he saw was horrific. Carriages had caught fire in the depths of the valley and the injured, burned alive in the wreckage, or scalded by the boiling water escaping from the disemboweled locomotive, were uttering lamentable screams. A few carriages remained caught on the rocks, suspended twenty or thirty meters in the air. The scene of desolation was lit by the moon, then full, and by the reddish flames of burning materials, which permitted the sides of the gulf to be seen.

Brave as he was, Lord Burydan was moved to pity and horror. He forgot momentarily the reasons that had brought him to that valley of death. The poet Agénor was scarcely less fearful; he thought he was seeing a nightmarish vision of the apocalypse looming up before his eyes.

"Fortunately," murmured Lord Burydan, "I was able to prevent our friends from taking the train. Only William Dorgan is among the passengers. We have to try to find him."

The automobile was left behind a clump of willows half way down the road that led to the bottom of the valley, and the two friends advanced through the rushes and reeds to the heap of debris, from which a concert of heart-rending screams was rising. They had only taken a few strides in that valley of horror when Agénor uttered an exclamation. He had just perceived the inert body of William Dorgan beneath a tangle of wheels and cross-ties, which, forming a kind of vault over him, had been able to protect him, up to a point. The billionaire had a deep wound on his temple.

"I strongly doubt that he's alive after such a fall," said Lord Burydan, shaking his head.

"His heart is beating, though," said Agénor, who had gone to the wounded man. "What should we do?"

"First, help me carry him to the car. Then you can take him..."

"To Rochester?"

"No. I have reasons for not wanting him to be seen in Rochester. Go to Syracuse, which is only an hour away, and deposit him in my little house in the suburbs...being careful to avoid being seen, as much as possible. Kloum will come to help you soon."

"I'll do exactly as you say. You can be sure that William Dorgan will be cared for admirably."

The two of them picked up the body of the billionaire, which they had a great deal of difficulty removing from beneath the debris, and carried it to the automobile. When they arrived there, Lord Burydan took all the papers out of the injured man's pockets. A strange plan had just taken form in his mind. He took possession of a check-book, a wallet containing identity papers, two railway tickets and several letters and telegrams. He also took a diamond ring that William Dorgan wore on his right hand, and a tie-pin ornamented with a large pearl.

Agénor watched him do it with surprise.

"What do you intend to do?" he asked.

"It would take too long to explain. Only know that I might perhaps find a means of annihilating the Red Hand. Adieu, my dear Agénor. Take good care of our patient."

The automobile moved off and disappeared into the night. Lord Burydan hurriedly went back down to the field of carnage. He examined several atrociously-disfigured cadavers successively, until he found one whose head was no longer anything but a bloody pulp, and who had the same height and almost the same build as William Dorgan. The unknown cadaver was also dressed with a rare elegance.

"I don't think I could find a better one," murmured the eccentric, emotionally.

Without hesitation, he placed the diamond ring on the finger of the unknown man, ornamented him with the pearl tie-pin, and slipped he check-book into an inside pocket, not without carefully removing all the papers that the dead man—a certain Mr. Murray, the director of a Brooklyn steel-works—had on him.

Lord Burydan had scarcely finished making this substitution, which would have seemed suspicious to anyone who did not know him, when his attention was attracted by feeble groans that were coming from a Pullman car that was lying upside-down. He immediately went to it.

He bloodied his hands on the broken glass of the compartment, and was half-stifled by acrid smoke, but he succeeded in pulling an extremely beautiful woman out of the wreckage. He was struck by the fact that she was wearing a large bouquet of scabious flowers on her bosom[4] and that she was dressed in mourning.

Scarcely had he succeeded in getting her out than she fainted in his arms, after having darted a dazed glance of gratitude at him.

Lord Burydan carried the young woman to a place about fifty yards away, and set her down gently on a mound covered in thick grass. Then he went down to the stream that ran through the bottom of the valley, and dipped his handkerchief into it in order to moisten the injured woman's forehead and temples.

Then he perceived a troop of men armed with torches and electric lamps who were coming down the path into the valley in haste. At a glance, he recognized Fritz and Cornelius Kramm among them—which gave him pause for thought.

The station-master from Rochester, who was also among the rescue party, had seen him; they exchanged a few words, and Lord Burydan confided the young woman he had just snatched from the jaws of death to his particular care. Then he joined the rescue party, among whom were a dozen robust railways workers armed with pick-axes and crowbars with which to clear the debris.

The work was organized with the silent rapidity that is perhaps found only in America. The dead were laid out side by side on the bank of the stream, the wounded temporarily installed on mattresses that two Railway Company tenders had brought from the town. Thanks to first-aid kits, the wounded began to receive the most urgent care. Their number was, in any case, not very considerable. In that catastrophe, the memory of which still lingers in America, almost all the passengers had been killed. Out of a hundred and ten, only a dozen, more or less mutilated, had survived.

Among these survivors, a little girl about four years old was found lying in the baggage-net; she had survived the fall without a scratch. She

---

[4] Presumably *Scabiosa atropurpurea*, otherwise known as Mourning Bride or Mournful Widow.

smiled, looking around in astonishment, as if she had only just woken up. She was taken away, in order that she would not see the body of her mother, cleanly decapitated by one of the wheels of the locomotive.

Further away, a gentleman with a white beard, caught in a tangle of axles and wheels, was calling desperately for help. When they tried to free him, they perceived that his two thighs and been cut through just below the abdomen. He died almost immediately.

A young woman who had gone mad was holding her husband's head in the flap of her skirt.

Lord Burydan had never seen such a harrowing spectacle.

The rescuers' task was, moreover, full of difficulties. It was necessary to summon a fire engine urgently from Rochester to put out the blaze that had taken hold in the wreckage of the carriages and threatened to consume everything. The search for the dead and wounded continued in the midst of wooden beams that were still smoking and steel bars that had not cooled down.

Lord Burydan performed prodigies of heroism. Twice he was nearly crushed while trying to lift up a carriage, and he burned his hands grievously extracting one old lady who was buried under the seats. The latter had no injuries; she had simply been almost asphyxiated and slowly roasted.

Cornelius and Fritz also pretended to deploy great zeal, but their veritable preoccupation was not at all philanthropic. Both of them, convinced that Fred Jorgell, his family and their French friends had been on the train, were waiting with ferocious impatience for the bodies of their enemies to be recovered.

Lord Burydan, whom neither of them had recognized, watched them from the corner of his eye, attentively observing their actions and gestures.

The two bandits seemed put out. However, when the disfigured corpse of Mr. Murray was brought to the temporary field hospital, and Cornelius recognized William Dorgan's diamond ring on his finger, he could not suppress a smile of satisfaction. He searched the cadaver, and found the check-book that Lord Burydan had placed in an inside pocket.

"Here's one of them," he said to Fritz, who had come running in response to his brother's signal. "We're bound to find the others somewhere nearby."

The two bandits judged it necessary to put on an ostentatious display of the grief that they would be assumed to feel at the death of their friend and associate.

"Dear William Dorgan!" exclaimed Fritz, appealing to the stationmaster and other people present. "To think that we were dining cheerfully together only a week ago. Why did hazard have to give me the dolorous mission of being the first person to recognize my friend's body?"

"You'll make certain, won't you," said Cornelius, in a tone adapted to the occasion, "that our friend's body is put to one side, until we can inform his two sons."

"It's still lucky that it was only him," murmured the honest stationmaster, as he came closer. "Did you know that the entire family nearly got on?"

"What are you saying?" demanded Fritz, his eyes suddenly harsh and his features contracted.

"I was saying that it's lucky that Mr. Fred Jorgell—whom I know by sight—and all his friends didn't accompany Mr. Dorgan, as they had intended to do. They changed their minds at the last moment and didn't board the train."

"That is, indeed, very fortunate," Cornelius replied, in a constrained tone. He had great difficulty concealing his vexation and ill humor.

"It's definitely rotten luck!" exclaimed Fritz, angrily, once the witnesses to the scene had moved away. "We thought we were getting rid of the entire band at a stroke."

"Too bad! We'll have to start again."

"What a pity—it all went so well!"

"I'd taken the most scrupulous precautions. I've even brought a special flask, from which it would have been sufficient for me to let a single drop fall on to each dressing to provoke the instant death of any survivors."

"Let's not despair, though," said Fritz, after due reflection. "We have one result. The death of William Dorgan will put our friend Baruch in possession of vast sums. One of our objectives will thus be obtained."

While the two Lords of the Red Hand held that cynical discussion in the midst of the dead and dying, Lord Burydan continued to expend his strength and energy unsparingly, risking his life a hundred times in order to extract bodies from beneath the framework of the smashed carriages, which were mere cadavers more often than not.

When the sun rose on that scene of desolation, Lord Burydan was exhausted by fatigue, and the cuts and burns he had sustained were causing him considerable suffering. He thought about retiring, all the more so because his presence had become totally unnecessary. Those passengers who were still alive had been taken to a place of safety, and the number of rescuers was increasing by the minute; they were arriving from all directions.

One fact will give an idea of American activity. They were still busy clearing the floor of the bloody valley when a squad of a hundred carpenters, summon by telegram and brought by a special train, set about reconstructing the scaffolding of the bridge.

Lord Burydan was about to leave, taking advantage of one of the numerous taxis that had arrived from Rochester, when he suddenly remembered the beautiful young woman who had been the first person he had rescued, with the pale complexion, the mourning-dress and the scabious flowers on her bosom.

Forgetting his fatigue, he went precipitately to the temporary field hospital that Cornelius was just leaving, after having made certain that William Dorgan was the only enemy of the Red Hand who had perished in the catastrophe.

Not perceiving the young woman among the wounded immediately, Lord Burydan went in search of the station-master, to whom he had confided her. He did not find him. In the disorder, no one could give him any information.

Mechanically driven, perhaps by a presentiment, he went to the place where the cadavers had been deposited. Scarcely had he cast a glance over the disfigured remains than he recognized, with an indescribable dolor, those of the beautiful young woman in mourning. On her ribs, doubtless to make it easier for her relatives or friends to identify her, someone had replaced the bouquet of somber violet flowers.

"The only woman that I might have loved!" he stammered, dolorously.

He brushed the icy forehead of the dead woman with his lips, and fled, despair in his heart.

II. "Celerity!... Discretion!..."

For Lord Burydan, the weeks that followed were full of trouble, agitation and neurasthenia. To begin with, William Dorgan, whom Agénor had taken to the cottage that the eccentric owned on the outskirts of Syracuse, had not been able, in spite of all the care lavished upon him, to make a complete recovery from the shock he had suffered. He had become entirely aphasic, no longer able to articulate more than a few unintelligible stammers.

Lord Burydan almost repented of the substitution he had effected. He suffered from belated scruples, wondering whether he had really had the right to do what he had done.

With his usual frankness, he thought that the simplest course of action was to acquaint William Dorgan fully with his plans.

The billionaire, who, apart from being unable to speak, had completely recovered his intellectual faculties, listened gravely to the eccentric aristocrat's confidences. For a few minutes, he remained deeply plunged in reflection. Finally, he seized the notepad of which he made use to communicate with those around him, and with a firm hand he wrote;

You have my confidence, and I approve entirely of what you've done. So far as everyone else is concerned, I'm dead, and I'll stay dead until further notice.

In spite of the lengthy explanation he had given the billionaire of his plans, Lord Burydan was slightly surprised by the facility with which he gave his assert.

"Don't you want to inform your son Harry?" he asked him again.

The aphasic shook his head negatively.

"And your son Joe?"

William Dorgan repeated the negative gesture, in a more emphatic fashion.

That was because the billionaire, during the long meditative hours of his convalescence, had had time to reflect upon a host of petty events to which, until then, he had paid no attention, and, without knowing them in their entirety, had divined enough of Lord Burydan's plans to take account of the fact that it was ninety per cent certain that the eccentric was right. He could not forget that Lord Burydan had saved his life. Finally, there had been two or three confidential conversations between the two of them in the course of which Lord Burydan had succeeded in winning the billionaire over to his way of thinking.

For the latter, it was extremely important to have won the assent of William Dorgan, to whom he had made his real identity known.

Nevertheless, by a curious contradiction, Lord Burydan, prey to a black melancholy, went for rather a long time without giving any thought to the Red Hand. In spite of all his efforts, the young lord could not forget the tragic physiognomy of that beautiful stranger—"the lady of the scabious flowers," as he thought of her—whom he had only glimpsed and held momentarily in his arms, only to lose her almost immediately. He tried in vain to free himself from that haunting. In spite of all the resources of his imagination, the poet Agénor was unable to distract him from it.

Various circumstances reanimated that chagrin. One day, Lord Burydan, who had gone into a café for refreshments, found a copy of the *New York Illustrated News* on the table at which he sat down. Having riffled through it, distractedly to begin with, his attention was caught by a double page spread in which there were portraits of all the victims of the Rochester catastrophe. At the first glance he recognized the lady of the scabious flowers, whose picture offered a striking resemblance.

"Is that image going to pursue me everywhere?" he stammered, and closed the magazine again.

He was about to leave when his attention was invincibly attracted by a striking advertisement on the back cover of the same periodical:

SPIRITUALIST INSTITUTE
For the Relief of Inconsolable Ladies and Gentlemen
DIRECTOR: EZECHIAS PALMER, MENTALIST PSYCHOLOGIST
Member of Several Academies

All of you who have lost a dear one, who are mourning a mother, a spouse, a fiancée, or an adored son, do not abandon hope! Come, in all confidence, to find the honorable Ezechias Palmer. He will console your grief. He will cause to appear before your eyes the familiar and blessed features of the dear departed, miraculously delivered from the inexorable chains of death. This is no deceptive promise. Let the incredulous come; they will see and be convinced.

Lord Burydan reread the strange advertisement twice more; then, shrugging his shoulders, he murmured: "He must be some charlatan!"

However, he took the issue of the *New York Illustrated News* away with him, because he wanted to cut out the picture of the lady of the scabious flowers, in order to keep it.

Three days later, a business matter having taken him to New York, hazard took him to Fifteenth Avenue. Without having sought to do so, he found himself in front of a large bronze door, above which was inscribed in golden letters *Spiritualist Institute*. The plaque was fixed in the middle of a very high wall.

In Lord Burydan, curiosity was more powerful than any other sentiment. He rang the bell, and found himself in a courtyard planted with venerable yew trees and cypresses, from which a domestic clad in a violet smock that made his resemble an archbishop escorted him to a reception room of severe aspect, singularly original in style.

The massive items of furniture were made in ebony encrusted with little mother-of-pearl stars. The dark blue draperies were fringed with silver. A large incense-burner hung down from the dome-shaped vault. The vault itself formed an azure sky strewn with smiling angels. On the fireplace, a marble group represented Death, in the form of a hideous skeleton, in the chest of whom a genie was planting his knee, while taking away his scythe. Tall stained-glass windows spread a mysterious light over that décor.

"A funny drawing-room!" murmured Lord Burydan, looking around.

119

Five minutes later, one of the two blue velvet door-curtains parted, to give passage to a correctly-dressed gentlemen who bowed ceremoniously to his visitor.

"To whom do I have the honor of speaking?" asked Lord Burydan.

"I'm Ezechias Palmer." Without giving Lord Burydan time to introduce himself, he added; "You've doubtless lost someone dear to you."

Lord Burydan had entered the bizarre establishment under the impulse of curiosity, but now that he found himself face to face with its director, he no longer knew what to do in order to mount an honorable retreat. Fundamentally, he was convinced that he was dealing with a charlatan.

"That's true, sir," he relied, a trifle embarrassed, "but I'd like to ask you for some information. I won't hide the fact that I'm a skeptic, and I'm wondering how you can possibly realize the seductive promises in your prospectus."

Mr. Palmer gazed at his interlocutor in an imposing fashion, and it was only after having looked him up and down that he replied, with a sort of disdainful pity: "Sir, the means that we employ are partly natural and partly occult. But what does it matter, if we attain the goal that we have proposed. None of those who address themselves to me, I can assure you, ever experience disillusionment."

Lord Burydan felt drawn, in spite of himself, to set Mr. Palmer a challenge. He took the photograph of the lady with the scabious flowers from his pocket.

"Can you," he asked, "enable me to see the person whose portrait this is?"

"Of course," replied Mr. Palmer, with aplomb.

"Will you employ supernatural means or the others?" the eccentric could not help enquiring.

"That will depend…in any case, it's indispensable that I know, in the minutest detail, the circumstances in which you saw this person for the last time."

Very discontented, deep down, to have ventured into this den of mystery, Lord Burydan gave a brief account of the catastrophe of the wooden bridge, and asked Mr. Palmer when he ought to come back.

"I'll write to you," the latter replied, "but to do that it's necessary for me to know your address."

"I don't want to tell you my name. Write to me at *poste restante*, Syracuse, under the initials A.B."

"As you please," replied the director, with the same coolness. "But you should know that, in those circumstances, the policy of the establishment is to ask for a deposit."

"Your demand is perfectly legitimate. Here's five hundred dollars."

"That's sufficient for a down payment. If you're satisfied, you'll have to pay us a similar sum. If not, you'll be reimbursed in full."

Mr. Palmer escorted his visitor to the door of the Spiritualist Institute, and, before parting from him, said: "I've been occupied with the science of the soul for a long time, you know, and no one can suspect how impassioning that study is. I began with the study of mental illnesses, and was the director of Greenaway Lunatic Asylum for a time; it's only by degrees that I've arrived at a knowledge of the Occult..."

The word *Greenaway* was a flash of enlightenment for Lord Burydan, He understood that he was in the company of the former jockey who had been his jailer for a time, in the madhouse from which he had escaped with Oscar Tournesol's aid, and he congratulated himself sincerely for not having made his true identity known to that singular businessman.

Lord Burydan went back to Syracuse that same evening. Several days went by without him hearing any mention of Mr. Palmer. He was beginning to think that the five hundred dollars he had shelled out could be regarded as lost when he received a curt note asking him to come to the Spiritualist Institute at ten p.m. precisely the next day, and to "be prepared for any emotion."

The eccentric began to feel increasing annoyed with himself for having got mixed up in that business. However, curiosity drove him to see how Mr. Palmer kept his promises. The next morning, therefore, he took the train to New York.

He spent part of the day making visits. As the time fixed by the thaumaturge drew nearer, he could not prevent himself experiencing a muted impatience. For him, time was marching with desperate slowness.

At ten o'clock precisely, he rang the doorbell of the Spiritualist Institute.

The same violet-clad manservant opened the door to him. Without a word, he led him through a side door into an avenue bordered with dark fir-trees and holly bushes with scarlet berries, at the far end of which was another door with a double batten, surmounted by a cross.

Lord Burydan shivered. Was he about to be taken into a cemetery, then? He was indignant in advance at the macabre comedy, but he had come too far to turn back. It was necessary to go on to the end.

His guide opened the door to the funereal enclosure, making him understand by signs that he could not accompany him any further, and eventually left him alone.

In the moonlight, scarcely veiled by thin cloud, the eccentric was able to examine the place in which he found himself.

It really was a cemetery, but an exceedingly luxurious cemetery. The pathways, well-graveled, were bordered with bronze sphinxes, and in the thickets of funereal verdure, tall columns surmounted urns, while Gothic chapels and statues were silhouetted in their marmoreal whiteness. The penetrating perfumes of flowers rose from the bushes, mingled with a vague odor of incense and aloes.

Continuing on his way, Lord Burydan went past the edge of a pond on which black swans were sleeping. He passed close to an immense jasmine covered in flowers, and heard a few notes of the song of a nightingale chirping in the branches of a laurel.

He was grateful to those who had contrived this stage-set for having spared him banal phantasmagorias: the hooting of owls, skeletons rubbed with phosphorus or specters wrapped in bed-sheets noisily dragging rusty chains.

This Palmer definitely has more taste than I would have thought, said Lord Burydan to himself. *Now I'm wondering how this is going to end.*

He went into a path bordered by myrtles and rose-bushes, which emitted a delightful odor. Glow-worms were crawling in the grass, and fireflies fluttering from flower to flower like little souls in torment. Gradually, he forgot where he was and continued walking, plunged in a profound reverie.

Suddenly, he shivered. He thought he had heard something like a stifled groan nearby.

He raised his eyes. He found that he was a short distance away from a chapel with a pointed roof, from which he was only separated by a clump of somber bushes of broad-leaved acanthus. At the very moment when he looked at it, the chapel was illuminated by a blue-tinted glow. The iron door swung soundlessly on its hinges. A woman dressed in mourning advanced slowly along the path. She was holding a large bouquet of scabious flowers.

Breathless with emotion, in spite of his determined incredulity, the eccentric aristocrat remained motionless, his heart palpitating. He contemplated the apparition with wide eyes. She passed within a few yards of him, without appearing to see him, and making no more noise than a veritable phantom.

He had not been able to make out her features until then, but at a given moment she reached an empty space that was brightly illuminated by the moonlight, and slowly turned her head.

Lord Burydan uttered a terrible cry. What he saw could not be an actress. It really was the lady with the scabious flowers that he had pulled out of the smoking wreckage. They really were her features, so pure and gracious in design. And yet, he had seen her lying among the dead; he had brushed her already-icy forehead with his lips.

He remained where he was, nailed to the spot by what was perhaps the most violent emotion he had ever experienced in his passionately active life.

At the resounding cry of supreme anguish that he had uttered, the apparition had turned her pale face toward the nocturnal visitor. Their eyes met.

"Him!" she exclaimed. "It's him!" And she ran forward, as if to throw herself into his arms.

Lord Burydan ran to the far end of the pathway that went around the clump of bushes, in order to meet her. In the course of that movement, he lost sight of her momentarily behind the thick foliage.

When he arrived at the place where she had been an instant before, she was no longer there. She had disappeared.

She seemed to have dissolved, like a light vapor, into the azure-tinted mist that enveloped all that décor of prodigies and enchantments.

He wandered through the pathways of the luxurious cemetery, in vain. He searched the thickets and spinneys in all directions, in vain. The lady of the scabious flowers, who had perhaps been no more than a phantom, had vanished like a phantom.

The only trace that Lord Burydan found of her was one of the somber scabious flowers that had dropped from her bouquet. He picked it up piously.

Utterly distraught, he found himself, without knowing how, in front of the gate of the strange cemetery, and allowed himself to be led away by the silent servant in the violet smock, like a child, into the street.

III. The Lady of the Scabious Flowers

Staggering like a drunkard and prey to alternations of fever and depression, Lord Burydan had great difficulty getting back to the hotel where he was staying. There he was obliged to go to bed, laid low by the commencement of a neurasthenia provoked by the violence of the emotions he had experienced.

Agénor, immediately summoned from Syracuse, installed himself at his bedside and cared for him with his habitual devotion. At the end of a week, Lord Burydan, although still very weak, was able to get up and resume his occupations.

His first concern was to return to the Spiritualist Institute. Mr. Palmer's first words were to ask his client whether he was satisfied.

"Very satisfied," relied the young lord, agitatedly. "I've scarcely recovered from the shock I experienced."

"In that case, you know what we agreed. That's five hundred dollars you owe me."

"Here they are. And you'll earn many more if you can allow me to see, once again, the person I'm mourning…"

"To my great regret, what you're asking of me is impossible. The prodigy operated once in your favor cannot be repeated."

"Let's talk seriously!" exclaimed the eccentric, shrugging his shoulders. "You mustn't try to take me for a ride. I'm certain that the apparition I saw is a clever actress who possesses a strong physical resemblance to the person whose loss I deplore."

"You might be mistaken," Mr. Palmer replied, gravely. "You've seen the person you desired to see. Don't try to get to the bottom of things."

"Let's speak clearly. I'll offer you ten thousand dollars if you enable me to see the lady with the scabious flowers again. Whether she's a specter or an actress is of no importance to me."

The former director of the Lunatic Asylum, who, in spite of his connections with the infernal spirits, had not yet succeeded in curing his passion for racecourses, where he consumed the greater part of his profits, seemed strongly tempted by his rich client's offer.

"Damn!" he murmured. "The fact is, as I told you just now, that I can't produce the prodigy twice. I'll try, though. I'll send you a note a few days from now."

"Try to do it as soon as possible!"

Lord Burydan withdrew, seething with impatience at the thought that Mr. Palmer was playing hard to get simply in order to make him pay more dearly. Nevertheless, several days went by without him hearing anything further from the director of the Spiritualist Institute.

Meanwhile, William Dorgan's death certificate had been drawn up and his succession opened, in accordance with all the legal formalities. Harry Dorgan then found out that all the contracts signed with regard to the corn and cotton Trust that his father had directed, half of which should have reverted to him, had been redrafted in such a way that he was almost excluded from it. Cornelius, Fritz and Joe had made use of front men and created fictitious identities, and, in brief, had arranged matters in such a fashion as only to leave the engineer a number of derisory elements.

Furthermore, numerous lawsuits had been launched, and the business affairs had been so confused that it seemed evident that the Trust, of which Joe had himself appointed temporary director, could not be liquidated for many months.

In his retreat, William Dorgan, who would have been quite well had it not been for the mutism by which he was afflicted, followed all the ups and down of the legal battle in which the two brothers were engaged, with a passionate interest, keeping up to date with the proceedings.

It was in the context of these lawsuits that Harry Dorgan asked Lord Burydan to go on his behalf to see Cornelius Kramm, to ask for duplicates of various documents that had not been disclosed in court.

The eccentric accepted this mission, not merely to render a service to his friend, but because he was also desirous of seeing Dr. Cornelius on his own terrain—which is to say, in the laboratory in which he conducted his audacious experiments in human grafting.

Although he was not unaware of the part that Lord Burydan had played in the siege of the Island of Hanged Men, the doctor welcomed him with the greatest cordiality. He explained the lawsuit that had divided the two brothers so skillfully that Lord Burydan began to wonder whether it might not be Harry who was in the wrong.

During the conversation with his visitor, Cornelius took him on a tour of the majority of the rooms in the magnificent house in which he lived. The only place to which he did not take him was, in fact, the laboratory in which he carried out his most interesting experiments, to which he never admitted anyone.

Lord Burydan and the doctor were walking together amicably in the beautiful gardens surrounding the hotel when an old Italian named Leonello, who had been in the service of the sculptor of human flesh for many years, came to tell the latter that someone was asking to see him.

"Wait here for me for a moment," said Cornelius, "I only have a few words to say to the lady who wants to see me. I'll come back right away."

Lord Burydan agreed, and continued walking along the pathways on his own, reflecting on the strange, enigmatic man, almost a genius, in whose home he found himself.

A few minutes went by. Lord Burydan had reached the part of the gardens that was situated directly behind the house when he perceived, on the sill of a first-floor window, a large bouquet of scabious flowers set in a vase full of water, as if to preserve them for as long as possible.

"This is a veritable obsession," the young man murmured. "Those flowers pursue me everywhere."

He was still gazing at the bouquet when a feminine silhouette appeared in the depths of the room, and then approached the window.

With an indescribable amazement, Lord Burydan recognized the disquieting lady of the scabious flowers, the victim of the collapsed bridge, the apparition of Mr. Palmer's cemetery.

This time, he thought he must be losing his mind. He wondered whether he was not the victim of a hallucination. He gazed suspiciously at the apparition, convinced that she was about to vanish, or dissolve into a puff of smoke.

Nothing happened. The weather that day was perfectly clear, and it was scarcely two o'clock in the afternoon. Lord Burydan was able to convince himself that, although she was very pale, the woman he was looking at really was a creature of flesh and blood, not a vain phantom.

Had the victim of the catastrophe been brought back to life? Was he confronting her twin? He did not want to try to settle the question.

In her turn, the young woman had seen him, and she seemed just as frightened—and, most of all, just as surprised—as he was. Nevertheless, her physiognomy gradually cleared. As if she had come to an abrupt decision, she leaned over the widow-sill.

Lord Burydan drew nearer. He was about to obtain the key to the mystery. Unfortunately, almost at the same moment, he saw Dr. Cornelius in the distance, coming to rejoin him.

The young man only just had time to put his finger to his lips to make the lady of the scabious flowers understand that the moment was unfavorable for an explanation. She understood so well, having seen Cornelius in the distance, that she hastened to close the window.

Lord Burydan remained at the house for a further hour. He was only listening with a distracted ear to the captious reasoning of the sculptor of human flesh. When he took his leave of the latter, he had only one thought in his head: to make contact with the mysterious woman, at any cost.

He went back to his hotel, absorbed by that unique thought, swearing to himself that he would not leave New York without having the solution to the enigma.

By a rather curious coincidence—which in reality, was perfectly natural—he found on his return a letter from Mr. Palmer announcing that, to his great regret, he could not enable him to witness the supernatural apparition for a second time.

This Palmer, he thought, *is certainly in communication with Cornelius. He undoubtedly hopes to extort a large sum from me by making me believe in imaginary difficulties. He's grossly mistaken. Now that I know where my unknown woman is, I no longer need him.*

Lord Burydan was malicious enough to send Mr. Palmer an ironic reply, in which he told him not to disturb the spirits that he had at his service needlessly, in view of the fact that he had reckoned with the matter by himself and was now entirely consoled.

Lord Burydan had already made a plan.

After dinner, he went out in the company of the faithful Indian Kloum, with whom he had had a long conversation.

That evening, the lady of the scabious flowers was reading, next to her open window, pausing from time to time to gaze at the beautiful trees in the garden. Her pale face, illuminated by a moonbeam, veritably seemed to belong to a supernatural being.

Suddenly, something passed over her head with a faint sound reminiscent of a flutter of wings. There was then the dry sound of an impact against the partition wall.

She turned round, more surprised than frightened. A short arrow had just plunged into the woodwork, where it was deeply embedded.

The young woman's first impulse was to close the window. On looking at the arrow more closely, however, she perceived that it was ballasted by a small paper scroll attached with a violet ribbon.

She took possession of it, but, before unrolling it, she went back to the window, and hr anxious gaze scanned the moonlit gardens with a rapid glance.

Facing her, at the top of a high wall crowned with ivy, she made out the face of the young man she had glimpsed that afternoon. Beside him, another individual, with a red-tinted complexion, sitting astride the wall, was still holding the bow of which he had just made use.

Certain that their message had reached its destination, the two strangers disappeared. The young woman closed the window and, with a slightly tremulous hand, she opened the scroll and read the few lines written in violet ink, in a noble masculine hand.

Madame,

Whether you are, as I thought for some time, and still think at times, an immaterial being, or whether you are merely, as seems more probable, a victim of the sculptor of human flesh, I am entirely devoted to you. My life, my heart and my fortune belong to you.

If you are, as I have every reason to dread, detained here against your will, tomorrow, at the same time as today, the side door to the grounds will be opened to you, and I shall be at your orders to take you wherever you wish. I have already been able to ascertain that you are permitted, every evening, to stroll in the grounds between nine and ten o'clock, under the surveillance of the old rogue who is in the doctor's service. Don't worry about him, for I have taken the measures necessary to make sure that he cannot oppose your escape.

Believe, Madame, that it is under the impulsion of a profoundly pure and disinterested sentiment that the signatory of this letter is permitting himself to intervene in your existence and ask you for permission to be your very humble servant and friend.

Lord Astor Burydan.

After having read the note twice more, the young woman, not without a profound emotion, had the prudence to burn it, in order that it should not fall into the hands of her jailers. Then she went to bed. Once her lamp was extinct she tried to go to sleep, but her preoccupations kept her awake, and dawn was about to break when sleep finally came to claim to her.

The next day seemed to her to be interminably long. Every time she heard the sound of footsteps in the grounds, she ran to the window to see whether she might not find herself once again in the presence of the young lord, so handsome and so brave, who appeared to have such a noble affection for her. She waited impatiently for the moment when she was permitted to take in the evening air in the gardens.

At nine o'clock precisely, as he did every evening, old Leonello, Dr. Cornelius' trusted servant and laboratory assistant, came to find the young woman. He escorted her silently into the grounds, and, as he always did, silently started walking by her side beneath the large trees.

The captive was profoundly emotional. Her heart was beating rapidly. Her throat taut with anxiety, she listened for the slightest sound, waiting for the propitious moment when the side entrance would open abruptly to give passage to her rescuer. The silence was only disturbed by the melancholy sound of the wind moaning in the foliage, and, far away, the distant rumors of the sea and the city.

In her state of nervous excitement, she could not help speaking to Leonello. She felt a compulsive need to talk, walk and fidget.

"When will I be able to get out of here?" she murmured.

"I am unable to give you any information in that regard," the Italian replied, with glacial irony.

"But after all," she said, "you don't have any right to keep me here."

"Be sure that those who have arrogated that right have done so in your own interests. You're in the home of a knowledgeable physician. He perceived that you were in need of care, that you were ill, and he won't let you leave until you're completely cured."

At that moment, ten o'clock chimed in the bell-tower of a nearby church.

The young woman was no longer alive; she was trembling with anguish. "Well, I shall escape!" she said, abruptly, to Leonello.

The Italian laughed briefly; his voice rang false. "Ha ha! One doesn't get out of here as easily as that. And sometimes..."

He did not finish his sentence.

"And sometimes?" demanded the young woman, insistently

"Well, Madame, since you insist, I'll tell you...sometimes, one never get out!"

They both fell back into silence. The prisoner was scarcely breathing. She felt an oppressive atmosphere of terror and nightmare weighing upon her. She thought she was about to faint.

Suddenly, it seemed that she heard an imperceptible sound in a nearby bush. She uttered a profound sight, and began to hope again.

For a few seconds, Leonello watched her from the corner of his eye, prey to vague suspicions.

"It's time to go back in," he declared. "We've been walking for an hour. You'll catch cold."

"But...I'd like to walk for a few minutes more..." she stammered.

"No," he said, brutally. "That's enough. We're going back!"

He reached out to grab the young woman by the arm.

Before his hand could touch her black mourning-dress, an Indian—the same one who had launched the arrow the day before—leapt out from behind a bush and seized Leonello by the throat.

The attack had been so sudden and unexpected that the Italian did not have time to utter a cry. In the blink of an eye, the Indian knocked him down, tied him up and gagged him.

Almost at the same moment, the side-door to the grounds opened noiselessly, and Lord Burydan entered in his turn. Bowing respectfully to the captive, he simply said: "Come, Madame. Thank you for having believed in me."

So emotional that she did not have the strength to say a single word, she accepted the arm that Lord Burydan was offering to her, and they both went out. Kloum, who was the last to leave, locked the door again with the duplicate key that he had.

A few minutes later, an automobile carried all three of them away, and did not stop until it reached the door of the Preston Hotel, where Lord Burydan was staying. As was well-known, the hotel in question had had a moment of celebrity while the city of New York was being terrorized by the exploits of the Knights of Chloroform.

On the terrace, which was decorated with orange-trees and laurels in pots, Lord Burydan had ordered a light snack in advance, to be served at half past ten; old wines sparkled in crystal bottles in the light of electric bulbs, discreetly veiled by silk lampshades, and the dishes that the stewards hastened to bring on silver trays exhaled an appetizing aroma.

At a gesture from Lord Burydan the hotel servants withdrew. Only Kloum remained, who was more a friend than a servant, and in whose presence they could talk without constraint.

"I believe, Madame," the young lord murmured, in a voice vibrant with contained passion, that we're admirably situated here. With a broad gesture, he indicated the distant sea, where the lights of ships were moving back and forth, the giant bronze Statue of Liberty overlooking the harbor, and the enormous panorama of the city, punctuated by dense shadows and harsh lights.

The young woman cast an ecstatic glance over the grandiose view that extended before her eyes, and silently held out her hand to Lord Burydan in an adorable gesture of gratitude.

"I hope that you'll accept a few refreshments," he said.

"I confess that it will be a pleasure. I was so emotional this evening that I could only take a few spoonfuls of broth, and, to tell the truth, since the terrible catastrophe at the wooden bridge, I haven't had a single day of tranquility. I've undergone terrible ordeals...but you need to know the whole truth."

"I haven't dared ask you for confidences. However, I'll admit to you frankly that my curiosity has been keenly excited. We became acquainted in such an extraordinary fashion!"

"I have absolutely nothing to hide from you. I've experienced terrible misfortunes, it's true, but I have no reproach to address to myself."

Lord Burydan looked at the young woman, as if in ecstasy. The very sound of her voice was the most delightful music to him.

"Speak," he murmured. "I don't even know your name."

"My name is Ellenor, and I'm the daughter of Lord Beresward, who, having abandoned England ten years ago, came to seek his fortune in the New World. He died four years ago, only leaving my mother modest resources. It was only by dint of privations that Lady Beresward succeeded in completing my education and that of my sister Clara. As you can see, my misfortunes up to that point were utterly banal."

"Believe, Miss Ellenor, that I'm listening to you with the most earnest attention. Nothing concerning you is indifferent to me."

"In New York, my sister and I had found modest employment as bookkeepers in the offices of the billionaire William Dorgan, when my mother, who still lived in the town of Rochester, suddenly died. Our grief was immense. Our mother was the only relative and friend that we had. She had devoted her entire life to us, and we had never had the slightest secret from her."

"You had, no doubt, gone to Rochester to take part in your mother's funeral and to occupy yourselves with the liquidation of her succession?"

"That's right. As soon as the terrible news reached us, Clara and I left in haste, after having asked for a few days' leave. It was while coming back from that journey that we were victims of the catastrophe."

The young woman's voice trembled, and she could not hold back her tears. Lord Burydan began to glimpse a few glimmers of light in what had appeared until then to be completely inexplicable. After giving Miss Ellenor time to collect herself, he said: "Forgive me for reminding you of your grief, but Miss Clara presumably perished in the accident?"

"Alas, that is only too true, and until today I bitterly regretted not having shared my sister's fate..."

"Why until today?"

Ellenor lowered her head and blushed, ashamed of the confession that had just escaped her. Lord Burydan understood, with a quiver of joy, that the orphan's heart already belonged to him.

Now, he understood perfectly the error of which he had been the victim. It was indeed Ellenor that he had pulled out of the wreckage, but it was Clara that he had seen lying among the dead. The resemblance between the two sisters, their identical mourning dress and the bouquets of scabious flowers had completed the illusion.

Ellenor had been more frightened than hurt. She had not even lost consciousness entirely, since the features of the man who had saved her had remained profoundly engraved in her memory. She recounted that when the physicians—among whom was Cornelius—had not found any serious injury, she had been taken back to Rochester early that night, and put up in a hotel at the railway company's expense. She had stayed there for several days in order to arrange her sister's funeral.

Another reason retained her there after the funeral ceremony. Her sister Clara had been carrying in a wallet the few banknotes that henceforth constituted the sisters future. In spite of all research, that wallet had not been found. The inquest permitted it to be established that many of the dead and injured had been robbed, by criminals who had joined the rescuers and had raced to the theater of the disaster from every direction, like vultures that have scented the odor of a battlefield from afar.

"Misfortunes never come singly," she continued. "On arriving back in New York I found that I had lost my job. William Dorgan had perished in the catastrophe himself, and the personnel in his offices had been reduced to what was strictly necessary; they had profited from the fact that I had extended my absence without permission to sack me brutally.

"I was devoid of resources. I went to the officers of the railway company to ask for compensation. They replied, cynically, that if I thought I had a right to any, I only had to bring a lawsuit, the company not being in the habit of paying compensation of that sort unless they were constrained by a legal judgment.

"I went out with tears in my eyes. I only had a few coins left. I saw the moment approaching when I would no longer have any option, in order to find shelter, but to appeal to some charitable institution.

"I stiffened myself, however, against weakness and discouragement. In a bar, into which I had gone to drink a glass of milk and eat a slice of bread, I consulted the offers of employment that covered the whole of pages seven and eight of a daily paper. Alas, I couldn't find anything suitable. I spent the afternoon going from door to door offering my services. All the positions were filled.

"I went back to my hotel exhausted by fatigue. The manager, fortunately, consented to extend me credit for the cost of my room for that night, but he told me that if I hadn't paid by noon the next day, I would be pitilessly thrown out. At the same time, he handed me a letter that had arrived for me.

"I was very surprised, on reading it, to learn that the honorable Ezechias Palmer was asking me to go to his office and offering me an advantageous position."

"That was, no doubt," said Lord Burydan, "A few days after the visit in the course of which I had shown him a photograph of Miss Clara."

He briefly recounted the circumstances in which he had been led to address himself to the director of the Spiritualist Institute.

"I understand everything now," the young woman murmured. "But I'll continue my story. Mr. Palmer welcomed me kindly. He immediately took charge of me. The only work he demanded from me was to read aloud from a few manuscripts, which was not tiring. I thought I was saved.

"Here, I must confess to you that, either by virtue of my education or my temperament, I'm very superstitious. My mother's death and that of my sister had further accentuated my tendency to mysticism."

"That tendency has its good side."

"Undoubtedly, but not when it's exploited by a brazen charlatan of Ezechias Palmer's stripe. He had me witness all kinds of fantastic scenes, and was artful enough to persuade me that he had the ability to put me in the presence of my sister, poor Clara. I was naïve enough to believe him."

"What an infamous rogue! I'll take a veritable pleasure in going to give him a good hiding and demolishing his sorcerer's paraphernalia. I have an old score to settle with him as well. I haven't forgotten that he nearly let me die of starvation at the Lunatic Asylum."

"One evening," Ellenor went on, "he instructed me to take a bouquet of scabious flowers—which possessed, he assured me, powerful evocative virtues. He took me into the garden of the establishment, which he arranges to resemble, especially by night, a luxurious cemetery.

"He took me to a cellar, in which he left me, instructing me not to be astonished by anything I might see and slowly to follow the pathway that starts leads away the chapel. 'You'll suddenly be surrounded by a soft blue light,' he told me. 'That will be the moment to emerge from your retreat and advance to meet your sister, who will appear at the far end of the path. Above all, don't say a word, even if you see something extraordinary! Speaking would expose you to grave danger and prevent the apparition from occurring.' He left me alone in the darkness, very intimidated, waiting for the apparition. A few minutes went by, and soon, as he had said, I was surrounded by a soft blue light."

"Due, no doubt, to electric lighting."

"Probably. Faithful to the orders I'd received, I opened the bronze door of the monument, whose worn hinges didn't make the slightest sound, and I advanced along the pathway, summoning up all the strength of my soul to render myself favorable to supernatural powers. I'd only take a few steps when I heard a slight noise on a lateral pathway. Mechanically, I turned to look in that direction..."

"It was then that I uttered the exclamation you heard!"

"An exclamation to which I replied with my own cry of surprise, for I had just recognized, in the nocturnal walker in the cemetery, the generous man who had snatched me from the jaws of death. But as, in order to join you, I passed behind a clump of bushes that hid me from your view momentarily, two men—one of whom was Palmer—threw themselves upon me and shoved me into a subterranean passage ending in a sort of dungeon.

"There, Palmer heaped me with reproaches and insults, forgetting in his fury where to find all the affected kindness with which he had succeeded in persuading me. 'Stupid girl!' he shouted, squeezing me brutally with his fists, 'we have an imbecile in our hands who would have taken you for a spirit and would have given you as many banknotes as you wished, and you've spoiled it all with your incompetence!' With a harshness that revolted me, he added: 'Do you think I have the means to feed you for doing nothing? From now on, you have to do as I say, or else...'

"Weeping, I stammered: 'But you promised to enable me to see my sister!

'To believe such nonsense,' he said 'you must be as naïve as the gentleman who's in the process of running all over the garden imagining that he's going to see apparitions!

"By this time, I was utterly disillusioned with regard to the wretch. After that, I only had one objective: to get out of that den in which the most sacred thing in the world—the memory of the dead that were dear to us—was being exploited."

"Oh, if only I'd known your lamentable story sooner!" murmured Lord Burydan. "But don't worry. Mr. Palmer will lose nothing by waiting. I intend to regale him with a little boxing match that he'll remember for a long time."

"He's more of a swindler than a wicked man. Seeing that I was good for nothing, he was doubtless about to let me go when he received a visit from Dr. Cornelius. What was agreed between them? I don't know—but the doctor, who had already had occasion to see me on the day of the catastrophe and with whose immense reputation I was familiar, took me to one side and offered me an employment with which he assured me that I would be fully satisfied.

"I accepted. I would have accepted anything rather than remain in that so-called Spiritualist Institute, where I was witness to the most brazen frauds every day. I was somewhat reassured, in addition, by my new master's scientific renown."

"Naturally," Lord Burydan put in, seething with impatience and anger, "Cornelius treated you no better than Palmer?"

"I'd be lying if I said that I've suffered any injury or brutality—but I was a prisoner. I was forbidden to go out, and every day, Leonello forced me to take several spoonfuls of a medicine, on the doctor's orders, which he said would restore my health..."

"Did this medicament really do you good?"

"On the contrary. Every time I've taken it, I've been subject to dizzy spells, and I've been getting paler every day..."

"My God! The sculptor of human flesh was testing some diabolical mixture of his invention on you. But be patient—I'll get to the bottom of all that. If some of my suspicions are confirmed, Cornelius will have terrible accounts to settle!"

This conversation was interrupted by the arrival of a servant who brought a bouquet of spacious flowers. Ellenor took them, and thanked Lord Burydan with a tender glance.

"I noticed," he said, "that you liked those flowers. Isn't it thanks to them that I was able to discover your retreat and rescue you? When I didn't know your name, I called you 'the lady of the scabious flowers.'"

"It's true that I'm fond of these violet flowers, to which are attached—I don't know why—the idea of mourning. There are white ones, pink ones and lilac ones; I like them all equally...."

The two young people chatted long into the night. Lord Burydan spoke in his turn and held Ellenor under a spell with the story of his prodigious adventures. Then the conversation took a more intimate turn, and when they separated, they had exchanged the sweetest and most solemn promises.

The hacienda of San Bernardino was situated in the state of Arizona on the Mexican frontier. It was built in the middle of a verdant valley watered by a multitude of little streams coming down from the nearby mountains, and its red brick roofs stood out cheerfully against the foliage of the sycamores and laurels that shaded it.

That farm, lost in the heart of nature, far from railways and cities, was a veritable oasis, a delightful retreat. Trout pullulated in its streams; innumerable flocks grazed the prairie grass that covered the neighboring hillsides; the orchards were overflowing with fruits of every kind: pears, apples, grapes, pineapples, figs and oranges; and in the gardens, the vegetables of the Old World grew alongside those of tropical countries.

Game was abundant in the forests. There were quail, long-eared hares, "cottontails," "jackasses," wood pigeon, grouse and even duck, wild geese and antelope. It is true that one also encountered wildcats, rattlesnakes and the occasional puma, or Californian lion, of which only a few specimens remain; but rattlesnakes do not inspire as much terror in Arizona as might be believed; if, by chance, a hunter is bitten, he contents himself by way of treatment of drinking as much whisky as he can. If the whisky fails to kill him, he is certain to overcome the snake venom.

The hacienda of San Bernardino, situated in the middle of that miniature terrestrial paradise, belonged to the New York billionaire Fred Jorgell, who had installed there as caretakers a Belgian former mariner named Pierre Gilkin and his wife Dorypha. A short while before, the married couple had had occasion to render the billionaire's family important services and he had rewarded them by confiding this outpost to them, which constituted for them the most delightful of sinecures.

At any rate, Pierre Gilkin, who was very active and very serious, gave every satisfaction to the owner, and the revenues of the hacienda had almost doubled since it had been confided to his management. Lively, cheerful and sparkling, like the true Spaniard she was, Señora Dorypha supported her husband admirably.

It was said that prior to her marriage, Dorypha had led a scarcely exemplary existence, and sometimes, on feast days, while the Indians and vaqueros employed by the enterprise got drunk on whisky and pulque, she danced habaneras to the sounds of the Mexican guitar, which

Pierre Gilkin had learned to play, that were so voluptuous and intoxicating that people came from several leagues around to admire her. In the opinion of the old men, an honest woman ought not to possess such talents, and it was deduced therefrom that the señora had performed as a dancer in some theater before becoming a *haciendera*.

It was also remarked that no woman knew better than she did how to drape a silk mantilla over her shoulders, or decorate her blonde hair with a ribbon or a simple flower. There the rumors stopped. Señora Dorypha's conduct was exemplary and, in a country where passions are ardent and mores a trifle relaxed, she was considered to be a model wife. No one, even among the most malevolent, had the slightest coquetry for which to reproach her.

Dorypha and her husband were perfectly happy, and they could not have asked for anything better than to continue that peaceful and hardworking existence. Nothing was calmer than the life they led at the hacienda of San Bernardino. Weeks went by without any other incident than the capture of a wildcat or the sacking of an Indian convicted of theft or drunkenness.

One morning, Gilkin received a long letter from Fred Jorgell, who almost never wrote to him. The billionaire announced the imminent arrival at the hacienda of a young woman, whom he recommended to the hacienda, asking that she be welcomed there as one of his closest relatives.

A week later, Gilkin went to the settlement at Cucomongo in his cart, hitched to four mules, and came back with an admirably beautiful young woman with black hair and dark eyes. Her name was Ellenor.

It was at the personal request of Lord Burydan that the lady of the scabious flowers had quit the Northern States in order to go to the part of the United States that was still wild, some areas of which had not yet been put to the plough. The eccentric had decided to pursue to the end the battle in which he was engaged with the Lords of the Red Hand, whom he had sworn to discover, unmask and deliver to justice. In such an enterprise, it was necessary that he not be hindered by the presence of someone he cherished.

It had not taken him long to realize that a smile from Ellenor was sufficient to reckon with his grimmest resolutions. He knew that he was dealing with redoubtable enemies, who would not take long to discover the young woman he loved and take vengeance on her for the checks that Lord Burydan had inflicted on them. He trembled at the mere thought that Ellenor might become the victim of the sinister bandits of the Red Hand.

After long discussions with his fiancée, both of them were convinced that she ought to go to wait in some retreat unknown to anyone, while Lord Burydan completed his plans. In any case, in order to achieve that, he only asked for a few months, or a few weeks. In a short time, in fact, he had discovered a host of indications that would lead him infallibly to success.

He therefore took action to find the young woman a safe haven, unknown to anyone. After having reflected for some time, he thought that he could find nothing better than the verdant solitude in Arizona, placed, so to speak, on the margin of the civilized world. He had, moreover, been able to appreciate Pierre Gilkin's devotion. Finally, he was familiar with the picturesque region on the Mexican frontier, which contains admirable locations and enjoys an exceptional climate, from having visited it during his sojourn in San Francisco.

Although it would cost her dearly to be separated from her fiancé, Ellenor therefore consented, without overmuch difficulty, to go spend some time at the hacienda of San Bernardino.

Fred Jorgell, to who Lord Burydan had confided his plan, gave it his entire approval and assured him that the young woman would not find a more pleasant and more tranquil residence anywhere in America.

Señora Dorypha gave the most cordial and enthusiastic welcome to Fred Jorgell's protégée. She installed her on the first floor of the farmhouse, in a bright and cheerful room from which one could see the gardens arranged in flowery and verdant terraces all the way to the foothills of the Sierra, the blue-tinted summits of which limited the horizon.

Dorypha quickly became fond of Ellenor. She went to some trouble to provide her with distractions and render her life agreeable. Sometimes she took her fishing in the little torrents that came down from the Sierra; sometimes she took her for long horseback rides. Emerging from the valley, they traversed deserted plains strewn with cacti, wild palms and "bunch-grass," to visit one of the local Mexican landowners, where Dorypha, as a Spaniard, was always very courteously welcomed.

That existence of healthy exercise, in the midst of the pure air of the mountains, son had a good influence on Ellenor's health. The pallor that had worried Lord Burydan was colored by the lively incarnadine of health. Her beauty, in its full bloom, took on a character of robust vigor that did not take away any of its charm.

Under Dorypha's direction, Ellenor became an intrepid Amazon. She sometimes rode for tens of miles in a single day mounted on one of the half-wild mustangs that are the only horses found in the region.

Two months went by like that. Outside of her excursions and a few hours devoted to reading, the young woman had no other serious occupation than replying to the long letters overflowing with impetuous passion and delicate tenderness that Lord Burydan wrote twice a week. By means of that intimate correspondence, in spite of the distance that separated them, the two fiancés learned to know one another a little better every day, united by a narrow communion of ideas and sentiment, and their love for one another only increased.

In the early days, Lord Burydan had manifested his anxiety on the subject of the adventurers of all kinds who roam Arizona, either prospecting for mines or exploring valleys propitious for agriculture or breeding livestock. Ellenor soon reassured him by explaining that the inhabitants of the hacienda of San Bernardino had nothing to fear from the vagabonds of the frontier.

To begin with, the hacienda was outside the routes generally followed by the "desperados," and the Indians who comprised the majority of the enterprise's personnel were numerous and well-armed. In addition, Pierre Gilkin, in conformity with the customs of the region, offered those who came to knock on his door a generous hospitality. He knew that it was extremely rare for a hacienda that showed itself to be humane and welcoming to be the objective of bandit attacks. He was liked by everyone in the region.

Several times, when he was taking livestock to Cucomongo, the Belgian was intercepted by desperados; quickly recognized by them, instead of stealing his animals or his cash, they contented themselves with drinking a cup of "aguardiente" from his gourd and going along the road peacefully with him, following the same mountain path for several miles. They knew full well, in any case, that Pierre Gilkin was not one of those cowards who hand over their wallet at the first threat, and that he would have fought to the death rather than allow himself to be robbed.

One morning, Pierre Gilkin and Dorypha, both mounted on horses, had gone to inspect the livestock in the mountain pastures. Ellenor refused to go with them. She had just received a parcel of magazines from New York, and preferred reading to an excursion.

Installed in an arbor shaded by the odorous flowers of Virginia jasmine and large red honeysuckle, she let herself drift into a reverie. At the

140

far side of the vast courtyard, Indian servants were busy milking superb cows of the Norman breed, which Fred Jorgell had brought from France at great expense; further away, others were busty threshing ears of corn, and the rhythmic sound of the flails dominated all the other sounds of the valley.

The young woman had just read, with interest, an account of a party given by a billionaire at which, to complete the extravagance, after the meal and before the commencement of the dancing, the lawns of the garden had been watered with the aid of silver watering cans filled with champagne of the highest quality.

Ellenor raised her eyes distractedly, and perceived, at the exterior fence of the courtyard, a vagabond of the most lamentable appearance.

His long, tangled gray beard was covered with dust, and his features were hidden beneath a sombrero so faded by the rain and the sun that its color had become almost indefinable. His clothes were in rags, and through the gaps, the skin was visible, tanned by the weather. His feet were bare within his enormous boots; he was limping lamentably, leaning in order to walk on an enormous gnarly staff. Finally, he had a gray canvas sack slung over his shoulder, which, to judge by its weight, must have been filled with stones.

The vagabond was in the process of negotiating with one of the vaqueros when Ellenor, impelled by her kind heart, hastened to intervene.

"Eduardo," she said to the servant, "let the poor man in, so that he can sit down on the stone bench facing the door."

"It's just, Señora," the servant replied, "that the master had forbidden us to allow anyone into the hacienda during his absence."

"Bah!" said the young woman. "He doesn't look very dangerous. Anyway, I'll take the responsibility."

The vagabond had listened to this dialogue in silence. Leaning on the fence, he seemed exhausted by fatigue. "Thank you, Señora," he stammered, when he saw that Ellenor had won the argument.

He came in, limping, and sat down on the stone bench. On the young woman's instructions, Eduardo brought him a piece of bread, a bit of dried meat and a pitcher full of wine—which, in Arizona, is very abundant and very strong.

Without saying a word, the man threw himself on these provisions like a hungry wolf, and had soon consumed them all.

Ellenor contemplated him with a curiosity mingled with profound pity.

"Here," she said, putting a dollar in his hand. That's to help you on your way. Are you going far?"

"I'm going to Cucomongo. I've come from the other side of the Sierra, where I've been doing a little prospecting. Unfortunately, I've skinned my heel on the rocks, and I've had a great deal of difficulty getting this far."

"Have you had good results?"

"I'm not discontented." He took a few stones from his bag in which little particles of metal gleamed. "Look, these are the mineral specimens I've collected. There's copper, silver and even a little gold."

"Who knows?" said Ellenor, laughing. "Perhaps you'll be a billionaire one day. For that, it would be sufficient to lay your hand on a productive seam."

"Who knows?" he repeated, in a singular tone that made the young woman shiver. Involuntarily, she looked at him, but is features were hidden by the broad-brimmed hat and she could not see the expression in his eyes.

There were a few moments of silence.

"Do you want anything else?" the young woman asked.

"Yes, Señora. To be frank, it's been a full week since I've had a drop of whisky or smoked a pipe..."

Ellenor brought a bottle, a glass and a packet of Virginia tobacco herself, which she handed to the vagabond, who dissolved in thanks.

"If you'd like to wait for the master of the hacienda," she said, "he'll be back soon, in half an hour or so."

That proposition did not seem to be to the man's taste. Doubtless he had some private reason for not wanting to find himself in the presence of Pierre Gilkin and his wife.

"Thank you, Señora," he said, but I'll get back on the road. I don't walk very quickly, and I won't get to Cucomongo until dusk. Thank you very much for your generosity; I won't forget it."

He put his bag of stones back on his back, raised his hat politely and left.

Eduardo followed him with this gaze until he had disappeared at a bend in the road. Then he came back into the courtyard shaking his head.

"That's singular," he murmured "That's a man who didn't make a good impression on me. I don't like people who are afraid to look you in the face. That fellow looks more like a tramp than an honest prospector..."

So long as he was within sight of the hacienda, the vagabond continued to hobble when he walked. As soon as he was on the road bordered with cacti and acacias that led to the highway to Cucomongo, however, he stood up to his full height and started walking with long strides, like a man who does not feel the slightest fatigue. A little further on, he emptied the so-called mineral specimens with which his bag was stuffed into a pond, stuffed his clay pipe with the tobacco that Ellenor had given him and started whistling as he walked.

It was scarcely half an hour after he had left the hacienda that he made out the silhouettes of two riders in the distance, who were coming toward him. That encounter was doubtless not to his taste, for he immediately went into a field of corn, the tall stems of which completely hid him from view, and he watched the riders pas by from his hiding-place. They were a man and a woman, both dressed in the Mexican fashion, with vast sombreros, ample sarapes and boots equipped with immense spurs.

"My God!" murmured the vagabond, when they had disappeared. "I believe I did well not to remain in their path. But all's well! Now I'm certain; I know what I wanted to know."

The man resumed his route. This time, he did not walk as rapidly, and mumbled unintelligible words from time to time, as if absorbed by his preoccupations. It was thus that he reached a miserable taverna, whose walls were made of clay mingled with mashed straw and the roof of worm-eaten planks. He went in to refresh himself. An old Mexican with a hooked nose and a swarthy complexion brought him, in response to his request, a glass of *aguardiente* and an *alcarazas* full of fresh water,

He had just taken a mouthful of the beverage distractedly when another client came into the taverna. He was a robust fellow with faded blond hair and a beard. His hair was cut very short and his beard, irregular and ill-shaped, must have been a fortnight's growth.

The new arrival was even dirtier and more ragged than the man with the bag, and a large revolver made a bulge in the pocket of his jacket. He looked around as a hungry tiger might on entering a sheepfold. The old Mexican could not help trembling before the ferocious expression of his gaze.

"What can I get you, Señor?"

The stranger did not reply. He had just perceived the so-called prospector, and his physiognomy now expressed sharp surprise, mingled with a certain constraint.

"You here, Mr. Slug?" he exclaimed.

"As you can see, Mr. Edward Edmond," the other replied, with a snigger. "You've renounced the service of billionaires, then? Sit down. Will you take a little something with me? I'm delighted to have run into you. Where have you come from like this?"

"I've just got out of prison," Edward Edmond replied, piteously. "I have no money or domicile. I'm reduced to despair!"

"You should never despair," Slug replied, with a philosophical gaiety. "Here, have a drink. That'll set you right."

He poured a large draught of *aguardiente* into the glass that the Mexican, slightly reassured, had just brought.

Edward Edmond drank it in a single gulp. "What about you, Slug?" he suddenly asked. "You don't appear to be much better off than me."

"That depends. There are days when I'm rich, and others when I'm poor. I make arrangements to get by."

"You're satisfied, then?"

"I don't have too much to complain about."

"But you're still traveling on behalf of the Reed Hand?" Edward Edmond asked, after a certain hesitation.

"Still."

"The association hasn't been exterminated, then?"

"It's never been as solid."

Edward Edmond laughed bitterly. "That's easy to say," he said, "but the Island of Hanged Men has been occupied, hundreds of affiliates thrown in prison, lynched, hanged or electrocuted. Every day, the police take more severe measures. And the famous Lords, who were said to be as powerful as gods, are no longer giving any sign of life."

"You're not very well informed. Mr. Edmond."

"Well enough to know that I'm not mistaken." His eyes shining with hatred, gradually becoming more animated as he spoke, he added: "I'm content, anyway, with what's happened to the Red Hand…it's that, and you, Slug, who caused me ruination!"

"What?" said the bandit, starting in surprise.

"Yes. But for you, I'd still be with Fred Jorgell, where I was well-paid, well-nourished and had already saved up almost enough to go back to Ireland and live on my income. Curse the Red Hand, and all those who are part of it!"

Instead of being annoyed by that violent outburst, Slug smiled indulgently. "You're a child, my dear Edmond," he said. "Say rather—and it's the exact truth—that if you hadn't been stupid enough to become infatuated with Dorypha, you'd still be with your billionaire. What did the Red Hand do, in sum? What did I do myself? I prevented you from committing suicide; I advanced you considerable sums, in return for a few small services. Don't blame the Red Hand, only blame your own stupidity and your vices."

Edward Edmond bowed his head and remained silent. He understood perfectly well that Slug was right.

"Yes," he stammered, after a pause, "I acted like an imbecile. It was Dorypha, that creature of perdition, who caused my ruination. The slut! I detest her! It would give me infinite pleasure to crush her head with a paving-stone. Yes, that woman, not content with taking my money and betraying me in every manner, also tried to murder me."

"Yes, indeed," said Slug, negligently. "I'd forgotten about that. Last time we saw one another, aboard the yacht *Revenge*, of which I had the honor of being captain, you'd just received a nasty thrust from a knife. How were you able to get out of that?"

"After the taking of the Island of Hanged Men I was arrested like all the others and taken to Chicago aboard a naval vessel. Because of my wound, I was unable to appear in court, so I was given a hospital room for a prison, where I was under the guard of two detectives. I was tried and sentenced a long time after the others, and was lucky that neither Dorypha nor my former master was called as a witness. An advocate, to whom it was necessary to give all the money I had left, took advantage of that situation. They weren't able to establish the exact extent of my guilt and ended up releasing me after a few months of imprisonment. I was thrown out on to the street, having only just recovered, without a cent. Since then, I've been wandering miserably."

"That's not very pleasant," said Slug, politely.

"Say that it's lamentable. But what about you? I thought you were dead or in prison."

"I wasn't even arrested," said Slug, with a certain vanity. "When I saw that things were beginning to go bad I made myself scarce. Anyway, I'll tell you about all that another time. For the moment, let's talk about Dorypha..."

"If I knew where to find her..." muttered the Irishman, shaking his fist.

"Oh, she's a clever woman. She was able, as they say, to pull her irons out of the fire. She's married, and has been placed by Fred Jorgell at the head of a very prosperous agricultural enterprise."

"She's married?"

"You really don't know anything, do you? She married Gilkin, that big Belgian who incited my sailors to revolt. They're a very happy couple..."

Edward Edmond ground his teeth in rage. "Even so," he cried, thumping the table furiously, "if I have to go on foot from one end of America to the other, I swear that I'll find her!"

"If you're a good boy," said Slug, greatly amused by the conversation, "I'll tell you where she is. I can even tell you, right now, that she isn't far away. So close that it was at Dorypha's house that I ate my morning meal."

"What are you telling me?"

"The exact truth."

"I beg you, Mr. Slug, tell me where she is."

"You're in too much off a hurry, my lad. Before that, we need to have a serious talk. You are, from what I can see, at your wits' end."

Edward Edmond cast an eloquent glance at the rags he was wearing.

"Well," said Slug, "perhaps I have a means of coming to your aid. Jut now you were slandering the Lord of the Red Hand. You were wrong to do that, and I'll prove to you that the Red Hand never abandons its friends, any more than it leaves its enemies in peace. You only have to say the word for me to come to your aid, in the name of the Lords."

"Well, so be it!" murmured the Irishman, with a somber expression. "Anyway, isn't it the only resource I have left? Speak—I'm ready to do anything."

"I'm glad to see you so well-disposed. You'll see very quickly that it's entirely to your advantage to listen to me."

"Will I be as well paid as before?" asked the Irishman, his eyes sparkling with a flame of cupidity.

"Why not? That will depend, of course, in the services you render. Know that, in spite of the recent checks it has suffered, the Red Hand is far from having exhausted its resources."

Slug had taken a solid wallet from beneath his rags, which he opened, displaying a wad of banknotes to the Irishman's astonished eyes. "As you see," he said, "the Lords are far from being ruined."

"What do I have to do?" asked the Irishman, meekly. "I'm all yours, body and soul."

"First of all, we're going to go to Cucumongo. There, I'll buy you some decent clothes. We'll dine together, nothing but the best. Then I'll give you an advance, and you'll spend a good night in a comfortable bed. You look as if you need it. It's not until tomorrow, or even the next day, that I'll need you."

"To do what?"

"You're very curious! Bah! I might as well tell you what it's about today as later. It's a matter of paying a visit to Dorypha."

"A visit?" murmured Edward Edmond, stupefied.

"Oh, let's understand one another: it will be a visit of a very particular kind. It will take place during the night, and we'll be accompanied by a few well-armed comrades."

"I understand. You want to kill Dorypha. Well, I'm in!"

"It's not her that it's about. All the same, you can satisfy your rancor at the same time. I don't have any objection to that. At the moment, there's a young woman at Pierre Gilkin's hacienda whom the Lords have given me orders to abduct. It seems that she's the fiancée of one of the association's most redoubtable enemies. She'll be a precious hostage in our hands. Are you a good horseman?"

"I can ride like a cowboy. Why ask?"

"Because we'll all be on horseback, and it's in that fashion that we'll abduct the girl. Ten miles from the hacienda, an automobile will be waiting for us with a few reliable men."

"Why not have the car come closer?"

"It's obvious that you don't know Arizona very well. In this region, almost everywhere, there are only scarcely-marked trails; horses and carts with massive wheels are the only means of locomotion employed."

"I've never been here before. Anyway, I'll do anything you want me to, provided that I'm allowed to kill the slut who caused my downfall."

"Agreed," said Slug. "Now, let's get going. We need to get to Cucomongo before nightfall. We can make small talk on the way."

Slug had thrown the dollar the Ellenor had given him on to the table. He took the change that the Mexican offered him and left, followed by the Irishman, whose face was radiant with joy.

V. The Mockingbird

That day, the heat had been overwhelming. Ellenor, whose room let out on to a balcony and a veranda shaded by Virginia jasmine and honeysuckle, left the large windows overlooking the gardens wide open.

The atmosphere was remarkably mild; a fresh and embalmed breeze was making the foliage of the nearby forest murmur. In the great silence of the slumbering countryside, the slightest sounds were discernible: the gurgle of the little torrents coming down the mountain; he distant lowing of the large herds of cattle in the pasture, and, dominating all the rest, the shrill notes of the nightingale's song, the crystalline whistling of giant toads and the ululation of nocturnal predators.

Clad only in a light peignoir, and her feet bare except for dainty Mexican mules, the young woman was leaning on the balustrade. For some time she contemplated the country, drowned in a magical silvery mist, and the sky, strewn with a dust of diamante stars. The profound calm of the beautiful night entered into her. It seemed to her that mysterious voices were talking to her in an unknown language in order to appease her sadness; she had only to close her eyes to see the smiling face of her fiancé appear.

Her breast swelled with a sigh. "I'm too happy!" she murmured. "I fear that something bad is going to happen."

She had pronounced those words almost in a whisper, but above her head a bizarre voice repeated the intonation of her phrase, without giving any meaning to the words.

Ellenor smiled and looked up at a wicker cage suspended from one of the hooks on the veranda.

"Shut up, Coco," she said. "It's time to go to sleep."

A chirping, coming from the cage, replied to that injunction. The mockingbird had understood.

The creature in question—one of the curiosities of natural history— is very common in Arizona, where it lives in the cactus-covered plains. It is easily tamed and, the bird having an instinct for imitation, often begins to reproduce everything that it hears in its vicinity, from the croaking of frogs to the human voice, the sound of a coffee-grinder or the crackling of a fire in the hearth.

The Americans of the South value mockingbirds highly and often pay as much as forty of fifty dollars for them when their education leaves nothing to be desired. There are not many houses in which a few of them are not kept in cages.

The one that Ellenor possessed had been given to her by Dorypha; he was entirely tame. Most of the time, he was left at liberty in the farm, and in the evening he never failed to return punctually to his cage. One of the young woman's favorite distractions was listening to Coco's imitations or playing with him. She fed him herself, every day, on finely-minced raw meat, for he mockingbird, approximately the same size as our blackbird, is essentially insectivorous and carnivorous.

Ellenor savored the charm of the beautiful night for a long time before finally retiring to her bedroom, but she left her window open, as she almost invariably did.

It was already some time since the inhabitants of the hacienda had gone to sleep when ten men who had been patiently waiting, hiding in a little wood some distance away, leapt over the fences surrounding the courtyard and disappeared one by one into the buildings where the vaqueros and the Indians were sleeping—building situated on the far side of the open space from the lodgings occupied by Pierre Gilkin, Dorypha and Ellenor.

The bandits, led by Slug and Edward Edmond, spent a long half hour in those buildings, adjacent to the stables. Then they crept out and headed into the garden overlooked by Ellenor's window and that of the spouses' room.

"You've understood what we need to do?" whispered Slug to his accomplices, grouped around him behind a hedge of orange-trees. "The girl's room is the third counting from the right. The first one is Dorypha's and her husband's; it's situated directly above the entrance door. Wait for me at that door, ready to bar the way to anyone who tries to get out. Keep your eyes open for trouble! Above all, don't kill anyone without telling me."

"What about you?" asked the Irishman.

"I spotted a ladder under the balcony. I'll make use of it to get into the girl's room without making a noise. If I'm lucky enough to find her asleep I'll tie her up and gag her before she has time to make a sound."

The bandits went to the post assigned to them, while Slug, following the plan he had mapped out, arrived under the veranda, found the ladder and set it up, leaning it on the edge of the balcony exactly opposite Ellenor's window.

When he was half way up the ladder Slug made certain that his revolver was in his side-pocket, and cocked it, making a slight click.

To the bandit's profound surprise, however, another sound exactly similar to that one replied to it. Someone lying in ambush on the balcony had doubtless cocked a revolver and was taking aim at the assailant. That, at least, is what Slug thought.

Without giving his supposed adversary time to make use of his weapon, the bandit fired first, aiming at hazard, a little above his head, and precipitately beat a retreat.

To his great surprise, no one responded to that attack.

Slug had no idea that the noise that had caused his alarm had been produced by the mockingbird, which, having heard the hammer of his revolver click, had hastened to offer further proof of its talents.

Ellenor, woken with a start by the detonation, which had resounded almost in her ear, leapt out of bed and, half-dressed, chilled by fear, opened the door that let out into the corridor, in order to seek refuge in the bedroom of the two spouses—but she recoiled precipitately on perceiving, in the moonlight, a group of hideous faces blocking the corridor a little further on than the door of Dorypha's room, which they were trying to break down with thrusts of their shoulders.

They were the bandits commanded by Edward Edmond, who, on hearing the gunshot, had hastened to invade the house and climb the stairs to the first floor.

Mad with terror, Ellenor went back into her room, closing and bolting the door. Then, hearing shouts and further gunshots, she ran toward the balcony and the veranda, scarcely knowing what she was doing.

Fortunately, Slug had left his ladder there. Without thinking, the young woman made use of the ladder to descend into the garden, and started running through the dark pathways in the direction of the building occupied by the servants, in order to raise the alarm.

Dorypha and her husband had also been woken up by Slug's revolver-shot, but the two spouses were brave, and at first, they were not extraordinarily excited. They had often had to deal with bandits in the past.

Pierre Gilkin hastily put his trousers on, seized the Browning placed beside his bed and went out, determined to shoot the first person he saw. In the meantime, Dorypha hastened to light an oil lamp set beside the bed.

Pierre Gilkin started down the stairs as the bandits were coming up. He only just had time to take refuge in his room and lock the door.

"We're under attack by the Red Hand!" he cried, fearfully.

"Well, too bad!" said Dorypha. "We'll defend ourselves, if that's so. You're very strong, Pierre, and those rogues aren't as brave as people think. Anyway, are you quite sure that it's the Red Hand?"

"I'm certain. There are no bandits in these parts, as you know very well."

"Kiss me, Pierre. We'll defend ourselves and die together if we must."

The two spouses threw themselves into one another's arms in a passionate embrace. Their lips met in a burning kiss that might perhaps be their last.

"What about Miss Ellenor?" Dorypha cried, despairingly.

"We can't worry about her right now—we've got enough to think about ourselves."

At that moment, the bolt fell to the ground, torn away. The door opened. Two or three hideous faces appeared.

Pierre Gilkin fired into the crowd, almost at point-blank range, twice in rapid succession. Two men fell. Cries of fury rose up.

"Surrender, swine, or we'll flay you alive!"

"We'll set fire to your hovel!"

"Bastards!" riposted Pierre Gilkin, exasperated. "You haven't got me yet." And he fired a third time, wounding another bandit.

While those words were exchanged at hazard, bullets whistled through the room. Pierre Gilkin had already been nicked in the ear and the shoulder.

Suddenly, a loud and harsh voice momentarily drowned out the crackle of gunfire and the shouts of the combatants. "Long live the Red Hand! Death to the traitors!"

Dorypha had recognized that voice, and had gone pale. "The Irishman!" she stammered. "We're doomed! Oh, how I regret not having killed him!"

With all the composure of hatred concentrated by long rancor, Edward Edmond took careful aim at Pierre Gilkin and fired.

The shot struck home. The master of the hacienda was thrown backwards, dropping his Browning. Edward Edmond's bullet had broken his arm.

"Give me your Browning!" Dorypha shouted, in panic.

But the Irishman had already rushed into the room and was taking aim at Pierre Gilkin, who was wounded, disarmed and incapable of defending himself.

Dorypha launched herself to his rescue. A frightful struggle began. But Dorypha, half-naked, was not in any shape to defend her husband against the Irishman, who was endowed with an uncommon vigor. With his right hand he squeezed the dancer's throat as if in an iron vice, and laid her down on the bed, while with the left he fired at Pierre Gilkin—who, hit full in the chest, collapsed, bathed in his own blood.

"I've killed him, that rascally Belgian!" he sniggered. And now it's your turn, you accursed bitch! You're going to die! Your time has come!"

He was getting ready to blow the gypsy's brains out when his arm was seized by an iron grip. He turned round, furiously, and found himself face to face with Slug.

"You mustn't kill the woman," he said, curtly.

"I thought..."

"I've changed my mind. Content yourself with tying her up securely."

Edward Edmond lowered his head, utterly crestfallen—but he had not the slightest inclination to resist Slug's command.

"Everyone else, help me to search the house," the latter continued. "The other woman's got away. We need to find her, at all costs!"

Dorypha, who was writhing on the bed although the cords were cutting into her wrists and ankles, was uttering loud screams, and the bandits could not help experiencing a certain emotion.

Perceiving that, Slug said: "Gag the slut, so that she stops ripping our ears. She'll soon find out what the cost is of betraying the Lords of the Red Hand."

The order was immediately carried out. Then the tramps spread out through the house, even searching the bushes in the garden and exploring every corner—but in vain. Ellenor had disappeared, and it was impossible for the bandits to work out which way she had gone.

The young woman had reached the buildings occupied by the vaqueros and the Indians without incident, but when she opened the door her feet collided with a body lying in the middle of a large pool of blood. Before going into the masters' house, the bandits had murdered the servants.

Shivering with terror and on the point of fainting, the young woman remained in the same place or some time, and it was from there that she watched the bloody drama of which Dorypha's room was the theater. Convinced that the gypsy and her husband had both been murdered, Ellenor had but one thought: to get away, as far as possible from that scene of carnage.

She made her way to the entrance to the corral where the mustangs were, and, leaping on to the back of the first, without the aid of saddle and stirrups, she launched forth at hazard across country, clinging to the animal's mane and exciting it with her voice and gestures.

The mustang, which was not accustomed to being ridden in that fashion, raced as if it had had the bit between its teeth through the meadows and the plantations of vines and orange-trees. It was probably that hectic race that saved the young woman. The animal did not come to a halt until it was in the middle of a field of corn, the stiff and resistant stems of which prevented it from going any further.

It was from there that Ellenor saw the troop of bandits pass by, during the night, like an infernal cavalcade, having taken possession of the hacienda's best horses.

One of the blackguards was carrying the inert body of Dorypha, brutally thrown across his saddle; her white peignoir stood out clearly in the darkness.

The fugitive contemplated that spectacle with eyes widened by horror. Soon, the silhouettes of the horsemen faded away into the night and disappeared in a northerly direction.

Worn out by fatigue and shock, the young woman wondered briefly whether it might be best to return to the hacienda, a few of whose inhabitants might perhaps have escaped death. She was about to head in that direction when tongues of red flame rose into the air, while agonized whinnying and bellowing burst forth. Horror! Infamy! The tramps had set fire to the hacienda, after taking care to lock the doors of the stables.

Having escaped for a second time, she rapidly turned around, more dead than alive. She resumed her hectic course at hazard.

Half an hour later, vaqueros who had seen the light of the blaze from afar had had hastened to Pierre Gilkin's said found her, almost unconscious, and took her to Cucomongo, to a hotel, where she was cared for solicitously, and where she remained for three days, suspended between life and death.

When she had recovered from the frightful shock, she was told that Dorypha had disappeared, but that Pierre Gilkin, mortally wounded, had not yet succumbed to his wounds and was being treated at the local hospital. The vaqueros had found him and carried him out just as the flames were about to reach the bedroom where the murderers had left him lying in the pool of blood shed by his wounds.

Exhausted by so many terrible emotions, Ellenor thought that there was nothing she could do but return to New York. That same day she sent a long letter to Lord Burydan.

Four days later, she got down from a train at the Central Pacific Railroad Station in New York.

Lord Burydan was the first person she saw on the platform. He was holding a large bouquet of scabious flowers. Ellenor smiled palely on recognizing the flowers that had become even dearer to her. The fiancés climbed into an automobile without delay, which bore them away rapidly to the Preston Hotel.

In memory of their first conversation, Lord Burydan had ordered a table set on the terrace overlooking the city.

During their meal, they had a long and tender conversation. Ellenor recounted, without omitting anything, all the events of the drama in which she had played such a terrible role.

Her fiancé listened very pensively, without interrupting to make a single observation. "My dear Ellenor," he said, finally, "since I received your letter, I've thought a great deal. I think, this time, that I've found you an absolutely inviolable retreat."

"I'll go anywhere you tell me to go," the young woman replied, with an obedient smile. "I know that everything you advise me to do is in the interests of our love."

"In Canada," he went on, "I own immense properties, and I have friends who are entirely devoted to me. It's to them that I want to entrust you. The Red Hand will certainly not go looking for you in the forests on the shore of Lake Winnipeg. I hope that the decision doesn't cause you any chagrin?"

"My only chagrin is in being so far away from you."

"You know very well that it's necessary. Be patient—this separation won't last much longer. In a little while, I'll attain the goal that I've set for myself."

"When shall I leave?"

"As soon as you've had some rest. I'll warn you, as well, that you'll have a traveling companion, a venerable old man who is one of my best friends."

"I'll be slightly anxious about traveling with a stranger."

"Oh, don't worry. He won't be any trouble. After a terrible trauma, the man has been completely deprived of the power of speech. It's impossible for him to say a single word."

"What is his name?"

"Mr. Clark."

Three days later, Ellenor, whom Lord Burydan accompanied to the station, took her place in a Canadian Railway Pullman car, in the company off the billionaire William Dorgan, who had been introduced to her under the name of Clark, and who was rendered quite unrecognizable by large dark glasses.

16. THE FEVERISH TOWER

I. In Florida

On that torrid morning at the end of summer, only two travelers got off the train that had just stopped at the station in Tampa, at the southern tip of Florida. Each of them was wearing a khaki suit and a cork hat, and each was followed by a black servant carrying his bags. Each of them cast the same weary and distracted glance at the white buildings of the town of Tampa, above which the wind was blowing swirls of dust, and which stood out starkly against a dazzling blue sky.

Each of them took a few steps toward the station exit, and, when they found themselves abruptly face to face with one another, they each uttered similar exclamations of surprise.

"You here, Lord Burydan?"

"You're here yourself, my dear Oscar. But looking at you, it seems to me that something about you has changed?"

"You're not mistaken," the young man replied, cheerfully. "The last time I saw you, I was still slightly hunchbacked; now I'm completely free of that deformity, thanks to the treatment applied to me by the illustrious Monsieur Bondonnat, my master and friend, and his son-in-law, Monsieur Ravenel."

"All my compliments!" said Lord Burydan, shaking the ex-hunchback's hand warmly. "That why no one has see you for such a long time?"

"Yes. I've had to remain absolutely immobile for several weeks, with my spine held in traction. Now it's all over…but would it be indiscreet to ask you where you're going?"

"A carriage belonging to our friends ought to be waiting for me outside the station."

"Just like me! I'm also expecting to find a carriage…in fact, perhaps it's the same one?"

"It's not impossible. At any rate, there's a vehicle here—but there's only one."

They both approached a kind of charabanc harnessed to two frisky mules, protected against the ardors of the sun by an awning of waxed canvas. A black man was asleep on the driver's seat, in the shade of a huge parasol. Oscar shook him to wake him up, and asked him whether he was in the service of the honorable Mr. Bombridge.

"Yes," the black man replied, yawning. "I've come to pick up two passengers."

"Well, here they are," said Lord Burydan. Turning to Oscar, he added: "I wasn't mistaken, you see. It's written that we're to take the same vehicle."

The two friends installed themselves on the cushions. The black man cracked his whip joyfully, and the mules set off at a rapid trot, with a tinkle of bells, shaking the brightly-colored woolen pompoms with which their harness was decorated, by way of fly-whisks.

They raced through the dusty and deserted town. At that hour, everyone had already begun the siesta. They soon found themselves on a highway bordered to either side by clumps of palm trees, tulip trees and eucalyptus. Further on, a fertile valley extended, covered with fields of fully ripe tobacco, the bronze-colored leaves of which exhaled an acrid perfume in the hot sunlight.

Eventually, after a two-hour journey, which the dust and the mosquitoes rendered less than agreeable, they climbed a hill crowned by a forest of oaks, cypresses and pines. There a delightful coolness reigned.

The travelers mopped their sweat-bathed faces and began to breathe more easily. They were able to resume the conversation they had begun at the station when the charabanc, slowing its pace, turned into a sandy driveway, above which arborescent myrtles with a delightful perfume formed a vault of verdure impenetrable to the sun's rays.

"I haven't asked you the purpose of your journey?" Oscar remarked.

"It's a rather serious matter that brings me here. You know that, until recently, the Lightning Steamship Company directed by Fred Jorgell and his son-in-law Harry Dorgan, had obtained a great success relative to the public and its shareholders, well merited by virtue of the speed and comfort of its steamers?"

"I'm aware of hat. The first dividends to be distributed were quite high."

"Unfortunately—it's a secret that I think I can reveal to you—the Company is undergoing a crisis. In less than a month, two of its largest ships have been lost, with all hands and cargo."

"Oh! I didn't know that…that's very unfortunate."

"Well, I believe, personally, that the two disasters, occurring in the same region, off the coast of Florida, were no accidents. I'm convinced that they're attributable to malevolence rather than chance."

"Do you have proof?"

"I only have suspicions. Admit, nevertheless, that it's at least singular that the catastrophes occurred in the same place, at the precise moment when Harry Dorgan, the company's co-director, is entering into overt conflict with his brother Joe, who has taken over the direction of the cotton and corn Trust since the death of William Dorgan."

"I don't see what interest…"

"You will. The Lightning Steamship Company having taken control of water transport, has considerably raised the freight charges on cotton and corn. Joe Dorgan and his two associates, Fritz and Cornelius Kramm, would, I think, willingly pay out a few million dollars to drive Lightning Steamships into bankruptcy."

"I don't yet see what the connection is between the two shipwrecks and your journey?"

"I've simply come to make discreet enquiries, in the theater of the catastrophe, in order to try to identity its true cause, and I naturally thought of asking for hospitality from our friend Bombridge, who is now a millionaire."

"I'd rather he hadn't become one," said Oscar, with a sigh. "I curse the fatal idea he had of buying a ticket in the Confederate States lottery, in which he won a million dollars."

"Why is that?" asked Lord Burydan, surprised.

"Because," Oscar murmured, effortfully, "I was engaged to Miss Regina Bombridge."

"Aren't you any longer, then?"

"No, I understood that my situation is no longer comparable to Regina's and I thought in all honesty that I ought to release her from her promise."

"Oh! What did Bombridge and his daughter think of that?"

"Regina was desolate. She begged me not to change our plans, but Bombridge père put so little insistence in trying to retain me that I understood that he wouldn't be displeased to have a son-in-law richer than me."

"That astonishes me," said Lord Burydan, pensively.

"I must say," Oscar said, "that there hasn't been a definitive break. I received a letter from Regina a few days ago, which asked me to come and spend a few days in her father's house."

"A singular course of action!"

"In reality, several suitors have announced their candidacy for Miss Regina's hand. Père Bombridge, who is aware of his daughter's affection for me, is very indecisive. It is, apparently, this week that the matter is to be settled. Bombridge, as a former clown, is something of a humorist. He's assembling the competitors for his daughter's hand at his table for a few days, in order to make comparisons."

"I wish you the best of luck with all my heart," said Lord Burydan. "If I can influence Bombridge's decision in any way, you can take it for granted that I shan't fail to do so."

At that moment the charabanc passed through a portico, the columns of which were bizarrely surmounted by two huge golden snails. Those ornaments piqued Oscar's curiosity.

"Is Bombridge going to be ennobled, and has he chosen snails to decorate his coat of arms?"

"You haven't heard, then?" relied Lord Burydan. "After quitting the job of general steward that he held on Fred Jorgell's estate near Lake Ontario, Bombridge has gone into business in a big way. He's organized intensive edible snail-farming on a large scale. His establishment is, it's said, very curious to visit. After all, the Escargot Trust might become as brilliant as any other.

The carriage had stopped in front of a charming dwelling in the Creole fashion, build in the midst of an immense garden in which parasol pines, large laurels and cypresses offered protection against the ardors of the sun.

The habitation was small, but very comfortable. A "varangue," or covered gallery, extended over its entire length, sustained by bamboo columns around which wound the stems of climbing vanilla, Angola peas and Florida jasmine.

Among the trees, Oscar noticed magnolias and flame-trees with bright flowers, which were shedding their petals over lawns in the English style, embalming the atmosphere. "One can see," he murmured, delightedly breathing in those heady scents, "that we're truly in the land of flowers in Florida!"

Oscar was abruptly wrenched from this contemplation of vegetal magnificence by the arrival of Regina Bombridge herself. Having perceived the new arrivals from afar, she had hastened to welcome them.

"If you knew," she said to the young man, "how glad I am to see you! I was afraid you might not come." She added, uttering a slight exclamation of surprise, almost of fright: "But what's happened to you?" She too had just perceived that Oscar Tournesol had been relieved of his hump.

There were endless explanations, bursts of laughter and, finally, congratulations.

"How glad I am!" cried the young woman, clapping her hands. "You weren't mistaken in thinking that you'd give me a pleasant surprise! That's another one of my father's prejudices against you completely annihilated."

"Are the other contenders for your hand numerous?" asked Lord Burydan, smiling at the two lovers' tender protestations.

"There are only two. One is the conjurer Matalobos, a former member of the Gorilla Club. I haven't met the other one as yet, but I believe he's occupied with the Occult Sciences."

"What's his name?" Oscar asked.

"James Rollan."

"Never heard of him," said Lord Burydan.

"In any case," Regina went on, decisively. "I'm digging my heels in. I've promised myself that I'll marry Oscar, and I'll marry him, whatever my father might say."

At that moment Mr. Bombridge himself appeared on the threshold of his abode. He came to meet his guests, shook Lord Burydan's hand cordially, and then Oscar's, perhaps a trifle coldly. All in all, however, his welcome was hospitable.

A black man conducted Lord Burydan and his friend to their rooms, which were equipped with bathrooms where they were able to refresh themselves and wash off the dust of the journey.

When they came back downstairs, they were thoroughly rested and ready to do honor to the meal prepared for them, the fine odors of which were already rising from the kitchens located in the basement.

The dining room was fitted out with the luxury particular to the creoles of Florida and Carolina. Enormous blocks of ice in marble vases maintained a delightful coolness there; the silverware and crystal sparkled, and, and behind each guest stood a black servant, exclusively occupied with the individual to whom he was attached.

Lord Burydan was about to sit down at the table when Mr. Bombridge handed him an envelope bearing the postmark of Winnipeg in Canada. "I nearly forgot this letter, which arrived this morning," he said.

"Thank you. It's the very letter that I've been waiting for, impatiently."

Lord Burydan immediately broke the seal of violet wax and absorbed himself in his reading.

"I observe," said Oscar, in a low voice, "that it's not bad news. Your face has suddenly become radiant."

"Indeed," Lord Burydan replied. "It's Miss Ellenor who's writing to me. As you now, she's in Canada at present. The excellent Mr. Pasquier has taken charge of her for a while, along with another of my friends, an old man who has been completely deprived of the power of speech following the trauma he experienced in the Rochester railway disaster."

Oscar would have liked to know more about the old man who had been struck dumb, but he dared not question Lord Burydan. He was not unaware that the eccentric's discretion was proof against anything when it came to certain matters, and that he would only allow himself to be questioned when he was ready.

They both fell silent. Each of them was going back, in their thoughts, to the time they had spent in the verdant forests extending around the Blue House, where the mad murderer Baruch, after having escaped from the Lunatic Asylum, had found a refuge.

Oscar asked Lord Burydan how the madman was faring.

The question seemed to displease the eccentric. "The invalid's condition is quite satisfactory," he replied, evasively. "His physical health is excellent, but I fear that he might never recover his reason."

Oscar did not persist.

Matabolos had just come into the dining room. The conjurer, since he had aspired to Regina's hand, had begun dressing with the elegance of a true gentleman. Diamond buttons sparkled in his cuffs and the front of his frilly shirt. His physiognomy, which had once reflected malice and gaiety, had taken on an expression of stiff solemnity. He was wearing a monocle, and his fingers were charged with rings. He bowed to Oscar and Lord Burydan.

A general conversation was engaged, in which the Gorilla Club cruiser formed the principal subject-matter, everyone evoking some episode of the taking of the Island of Hanged Men.

The meal continued joyfully.

They had reached dessert. Composed of magnificent fruits of a kind that only ripen under the ardent skies of Florida, when a black man brought in a telegram addressed to Lord Burydan. The latter scanned it, and his face immediately took on an expression of extreme discontent.

"Gentlemen," he said. "Fred Jorgell has just informed me that another of the Lightning Steamship Company's ships has just perished, with all hands and cargo."

"Where?" asked Mr. Bombridge.

"In the same location again, off the Florida coast. People can say what they like; it's something other than mere coincidence."

"Is it far from here?"

"According to the information that Mr. Jorgell has sent, it's on the reefs of Oyster Bay that the three steamers traveling from New Orleans to New York have been successively wrecked."

"There was, in fact, a terrible tempest the day before yesterday," said Regina. "I know that several ships ran aground on the coast."

"Oyster Bay," Bombridge put in. "But that's only a few miles from here."

"I'd like you to take me there," said Lord Burydan.

"If you insist...." said Bombridge, hesitantly.

"The proposition doesn't seem to please you?"

"I'll tell you frankly that the region neighboring Oyster Bay is one of the mot sinister in the world. It's nothing but an immense swamp populated by alligators and snakes. Furthermore, it's the favorite abode of yellow fever, which is propagated by millions of mosquitoes born in the stagnant waters."

"That is, indeed, not very inviting."

"That whole part of the coast is deserted. Once, before the Spaniards sold Florida to the United States, there was a black village in Oyster Bay, but it's now almost a century since the entire population died of the fever or took flight. The coast is bordered by reefs, and sharks swarm there. It's such a dangerous place that even though pearl oysters are abundant there, only a few poor blacks go there in their boats, when the season is most favorable, to fish for them. I don't know of any shore that's more inhospitable."

162

"It's necessary, however," said Lord Burydan, "that I go to see all that at close range."

"The government would do well to install a lighthouse in such a location," said Oscar.

"There already is one," said Bombridge, "at the mouth of the river that connects the sea to Lake Okeechobee, but as you can see, it's not much good for anything."

The conversation was suspended there. Everyone left the table to go take coffee, which was served on the varangue, and savor the excellent cigars that Mr. Bombridge harvested from his own property.

II. The Escargot Trust

Mr. Bombridge's guests lingered for a long time, idly extended in rocking chairs, abandoning themselves to the charm of the enervating climate.

As the master of the house explained, no white man could devote himself to any work whatsoever in such heat.

When the sun had gone down somewhat, Mr. Bombridge suggested to his guests that they go and visit his snail farm.

"It's an immense and curious enterprise," he said, "which has no parallel in America, and you won't be sorry to have seen it. Anyway, it isn't far away...about a mile from here."

They took their places in a carriage harnessed to four mules, which took no more than ten minutes to travel the length of the long eucalyptus avenue that led to the enterprise.

The snail farm comprised a vast enclosure surrounded by a brick wall, the summit of which was fitted with sheet metal inclined inwards in such a way as to make escape impossible for Mr. Bombridge's livestock.

Once they were inside the enclosure, everyone continued on foot, and went into in the park, properly speaking. It consisted of a series of enclosures in the form of parallelograms, separated by brick walls of slightly lesser height than the enclosing wall, but similarly provided with metal sheets intended to prevent any initiative to independence on the part of vagabond mollusks.

"As you can see," explained Mr. Bombridge, with the self-satisfaction of a proprietor, "the park in installed on a sandy hill. Snails love furnished ground, where they can easily dig holes and lay eggs. These little plank bridges permit free circulation in all directions within each enclosure and the collection of the animals when they've reached the regulation size that permits them to be sold."

"That's very interesting," said Lord Burydan. "Hold on! What are those metallic masts terminated with large balls?"

"Each of them is a gigantic vaporizer designed to produce a fine drizzle on dry days. You're not unaware that when the weather is too dry snails retreat into their shells, growing thin, and there growth is interrupted, sometimes remaining static for several months."

Oscar enquired in his turn about the purpose of a vast brick hangar with a glazed roof, which was visible at one of the extremities of the enterprise.

"That's the shipping hall," Mr. Bombridge explained. "Five hundred negroes are employed there night and day packing up the mollusks in glass-sided crates, which each contain a thousand of them, and which are sent from America to every country in the world. The trademark of the Bombridge farm is already celebrated, and its products fetch high prices in Australia, at the Cape and in the markets of Old Europe.

"It's indispensable that the snails should be sealed in order to be transportable, especially over long distances. That cave-like structure whose entrance you can see over there is a subterranean hall with walls made of exceedingly dry rock. That's where the escargots seal themselves of their own accord while awaiting packing and transportation to market."

Mr. Bombridge and his friends had been following the paved path established between the enclosures for nearly an hour, and they had not yet covered a tenth of the enterprise.

"We can easily form an idea of the rest," Lord Burydan declared. "We mustn't abuse your kindness."

"You haven't seen everything yet..." said Mr. Bombridge, with a proud smile.

He was interrupted by a shrill whistle. A minuscule locomotive, driven by a negro with curly hair, ran rapidly through the enclosures, towing fifteen wagons laden with verdant foliage.

"That's a forage train arriving," Mr. Bombridge went on. "Four miles from here I own several hundred hectares of marshland, which I've sanitized somewhat with eucalyptus plantations. The terrain remains damp enough to produce rapidly-growing vegetation with an abundance that would astonish you, including watercress, giant radishes and Florida cabbages, which are harvested every day by my black workers.

"A week before being put on sale, my boarders are nourished exclusively on vine leaves. For that, I grow Japanese vines, the vegetation of which is exuberant, especially in this latitude. That gives my produce an exquisite taste, much sought-after by gourmets."

During this explanation, the Decauville railway locomotive had stopped on a little iron bridge that spanned the largest of the enclosures.

"Look!" exclaimed Bombridge. "No one can have any idea of the voracity of escargots."

A robust black man caused one of the small wagons to tip. A heap of tender verdure fell into the enclosure; immediately, there was a general stir among the snails. They hastened forward in their hundred, thousands and myriads, and the astonished spectators distinctly perceived the sound of mastication, which resembled that which might have been made by thirty rats.

After a few minutes, nothing remained of the wagon-load but a few stems and fibrous ribs deemed too tough. The black man then started pouring out the contents of the second wagon.

"That's admirable!" declared Matalobos. "That mass of forage was spirited away almost as rapidly as if I had had a hand in it."

"Truly," said Oscar, "I don't regret having seen that. But I can perceive veritable phenomena: snails as large as two fists, and others of a soft pink or bright yellow color, as beautiful as the prettiest marine seashells."

"It's necessary to tell you," Mr. Bombridge explained further, "that, like every serious livestock-breeder, I take a keen interest in the amelioration of the race. The snails that have attracted your admiration I've imported at great expense, some from the Greek islands, others from Madagascar. It's those countries that produce the largest individuals of the species, but they're a trifle tough. I haven't despaired of succeeding, with the aid of a series of selections, in obtaining a variety as tasty and also a tender as the Burgundy escargot, which will be as large as a medium-sized tortoise."

""What astonishes me," said Lord Burydan, "is that in such a short time you've acquired the knowledge necessary to direct, as you do, such a vast and ingeniously designed establishment."

That compliment went straight to Mr. Bombridge's heart. "It's true," he said, lowering his eyes modestly, that few people could teach me anything about escargots. However, I owe a great deal to reading the works of a French scientist, Raphaël de Noter, who has written a definitive textbook on the subject.[5] It's to him that I address myself every time I find myself in difficulties."

---

[5] Raphaël de Noter (1857-1936) was a celebrated French botanist, horticulturalist and agronomist. His *L'Héliciculture: élevage et industrie de l'escargot: manuel pratique de la plus rémunératrice des industries agricoles moderne* [Heliciculture: The Breeding and Commercial Production of Edible Snails: A Practical Manual of the Most Profitable of Modern Agricultural Industries]

Regina, who was standing a little behind Oscar and slightly to one side, whispered in his ear: "What my father isn't saying is that he's discovered a certain intelligence in the escargot, and that he's presently engaged in domesticating some of the best-endowed of his inmates."

"Perhaps he intends to put them on stage in the music-halls," said the young man, laughing.

"I don't know about that, but even though he's become very rich, it's impossible for him to forget that he was once a member of the Gorilla Club."

"Gentlemen," Mr. Bombridge suddenly interjected, his expression having darkened, "I've shown you everything interesting that there is. I believed that it would be as well not to stay here any longer; one of those terrible storms is brewing—one of the tornados that are the scourge of the region." With his finger he pointed at the sky, which had suddenly become a livid white, while large coppery red clouds were massing in the west.

"Do you know what I propose?" he added. "We'll all climb aboard the Decauville. It will take us back to the house faster than the mules would, and it will permit us to cast an eye over the crops as we pass by." He turned to the white-haired negro who had been guiding the group thus far. "Jupiter," he said, "Give the order to hitch up the excursion wagon to the locomotive. We'll go back to the house via the track."

This order was immediately carried out. Five minutes had not one by when Mr. Bombridge's guests, and Jupiter himself, took their places inside a long wagonette, very comfortably furnished, which could easily carry a dozen people.

The miniature locomotive emitted a shrill whistle-blast; the train moved off, traversed a series of enclosures over a long iron viaduct, in which millions of snails were swarming, and which seemed to go on forever. Finally, it went through a kind of postern and, increasing its speed, sped over flat terrain. The landscape was no longer enlivened by forests or gardens. It was a bare, bleak plain, where only a few clumps of bamboo, stunted willows or eucalyptus trees twisted by the wind grew at intervals.

Old Jupiter, at a sign from his master, had taken an ice-bucket, bottle of sherry, lemon and other refreshments out of a little cupboard set at one end of the wagons, which he deposited on a narrow side-table.

(1911) presumably inspired this chapter. Le Rouge, an enthusiastic gourmet, was doubtless inspired to see the book as a significant pointer to the future.

"The heat is overwhelming," declared the host, "and it wouldn't be a luxury to refresh ourselves a little."

No one replied. Sweat was running down ever face. There was not a breath of wind in the air, and the croaking of bullfrogs, which pullulated in the region, was audible in the distance

While chilled beverages were avidly absorbed, the train had moved into a verdant plain punctuated by low hedges of mimosas and dwarf eucalyptus. They were the crops that Mr. Bombridge had mentioned. Black men armed with long scythes were cutting the forage necessary to the snails. They bowed respectfully to the train as it passed by, removing their vast hats of woven rattan.

The train had further increased its speed. The cultures, which covered several hundred hectares, were surpassed. Again they found themselves in the midst of a bare and desolate landscape. Without waiting for his master's order, Jupiter had abruptly closed the windows and was spraying the floor with strong-smelling antiseptics. Now the train was traveling with the rapidity of an express.

"Why all these precautions?" asked Lord Burydan, slightly surprised.

"It's because the vapors exhaled by these marshes are deadly. Those who venture into the marshes without precaution, especially at dusk, are sure to die of a malignant fever in a matter of hours. Only the negroes, especially when they've already recovered from one bout of yellow fever, can resist the mephitic atmosphere." He pointed with his finger at the swamps strewn with large pools of water, beyond which they could perceive the sea, barring the horizon like a lividly colored ribbon.

"Do you see those yellow fumes," Mr. Bombridge continued, "and that gray mist, almost at ground level, which seems to be agitated by a perpetual movement? That mist is constituted by millions of mosquitoes. The fumes are the deleterious exhalations rising from decay. There are places here where even the blacks can't survive, and where a white man would be incapable of remaining even for a matter of minutes without perishing."

"Aren't you exaggerating a little?" asked Oscar. "It seems to me that over there, on the sea shore, I can see something resembling a village, in the middle of which stands a bell-tower. If the region is as unhealthy as that, no one would ever have had the idea of building a church there!"

"It is indeed a church—but didn't I tell you a little while ago that it's been abandoned for nearly a century, and that all the inhabitants of the village died or fled? The negroes dare not go near that bell-tower, even in broad daylight, and they call it 'the feverish tower.' Extraordinary things happen there, according to them."

Everyone looked curiously at the ruined church, the square tower of which, brown in color as if baked by the sun, stood out against the pale sky in a lugubrious and seemingly menacing fashion.

"A strange land!" murmured Lord Burydan. "It's necessary, however, that I see that feverish tower at close range."

At these words the old black man made a gesture of terror. His complexion took on a grayish tinge—which is, for negroes, a manner of going pale—and his large bulging eyes rolled as if they were about to emerge from their orbits. He pronounced a few words in a jargon that was part-Spanish and part-English, of which Lord Burydan only seized a few words.

"What does the black man mean?" he asked Miss Bombridge.

The young woman smiled. "The brave Jupiter," she said, "is frightened by the mere idea that you might go to the feverish tower. He says that there's not a black man for ten leagues around who would serve as your guide."

"Evidently, it's not a very healthy place. By taking certain precautions, however..."

"It's not just for their health that the blacks tremble. They're afraid of the evil spirits that haunt the tower. You'll find some who claim to have seen the demon of yellow fever in person."

"I'd be curious to know what it looks like."

"I can give you an exact description. According to Jupiter, it resembles an enormous spider; its head is as big as a bull's, and is fused with the body. Furthermore, it has the expression of a hideous human face, or, rather, death's-head, with large liquid and phosphorescent eyes, like those of an octopus. Two holes take the place of the nose, and it has a mouth split all the way to the ears, garnished with sharp little teeth. That horrible head is blood red and bristling with spikes like the carapace of a marsh-crab. It has six legs on either side, of a beautiful bright green color, which end in suckers. The most extraordinary thing of all is that its irises are bright blue, and child-like in their softness."

"That's an exceedingly fantastic monster!" said Oscar, in his turn. "Since you're so well-informed, do you know what its habits are?"

"By day, it lurks in the depths of the fetid mud of the swamp. By night it roams, and if it encounters a sleeping negro, it pumps out all his blood with its suckers. The next day, the negro is found dead of yellow fever. It's also said that it sometimes lives in the damp crypts of the church. When there's an epidemic of yellow fever in the region, it announces itself by ringing the bell that has remained in place in the tower."

"And has anyone ever heard that bell?" asked Oscar impressed by the story in spite of himself.

"Jupiter claims to have heard it twice. The first time, ten thousand people died, the second time, fifteen thousand. The blacks also say that the Spanish Jesuits tried to exorcise the strange demon, but that it was the demon who came out on top in the struggle. They all died of the fever." The young woman concluded: "It's certain that, for my part, I wouldn't like to hear the bell of the feverish tower ring."

There was a moment of silence. During the young woman's story, clouds the color of soot and sulfur had gradually invaded the whole extent of the sky. A mist with a fetid odor had completely submerged the marshes. The feverish tower was no longer visible.

The atmosphere had become stifling. One might have thought it the ardent breath escaping from the mouth of an oven. In spite of the care with which Jupiter continually sprinkled the floor of the wagon, all the passengers were panting, their throats dry and their hearts gripped by the kind of physical anguish that even takes hold of animals at the approach of storms in tropical countries.

"Fortunately," exclaimed Bombridge, with a sigh of relief, "in another five minutes we'll find ourselves in a beautiful forest of pines where the air is pure, aromatic and salubrious. In a quarter of an hour we'll be at the house, where we can brave the fever and the tempest."

As if in response to that reassuring affirmation, there was a dull rumble of thunder, and sheaves of blinding green lightning-flashes were scattered over the four corners of the sky like a gigantic firework display. The sun launched one last macabre white beam between two clouds and then disappeared completely; the rain had begun to fall, not in large drops but in bucketfuls, and in jets the thickness of a wrist; it was no longer a downpour but a deluge.

The roar of the mountains of water that were running down the slopes in torrents was mingled with the weakening rumbles of the thunder and the whistling of the wind whipping the tall reeds and the trees of the forest.

Then, as can happen in such abrupt hurricanes, there was a calm, and for a few minutes, there was almost silence.

It was then that, with a fear they could not dissimulate, Lord Burydan and his friends distinctly heard the distant tolling of a bell.

Jupiter's teeth chattered; his hear was standing on end. "The bell of the feverish tower!" he stammered, trembling in his every limb.

"Yes, it really is," murmured Bombridge, in an ill-assured voice. "There's no other bell for twenty leagues around."

"You're sure that you're not mistaken?" said Lord Burydan.

"No," replied the former clown, in an abrupt tone.

Again silence reigned in the wagon, which was not speeding through pitch darkness beneath the dense foliage of the pine forest. As happens, in the tropics, night had succeeded day in a matter of minutes. They were now in the most profound darkness.

The voyage ended sadly, and it was with a genuine sentiment of joy that they set foot on the ground and they all perceived the façade of the house, brightly illuminated, where the black servants were already busy with the preparations for dinner.

The meal was considerably less cheerful than the earlier one.

Mr. Bombridge would have blushed at the idea sharing the ridiculous superstitions of old Jupiter; nevertheless, he could not help thinking that, for three weeks, cases of yellow fever had been unusually frequent among his blacks, and he thought that he could still hear the sound of the fatal bell ringing in his ears.

After the meal, however, there was a recrudescence of good humor and enthusiasm among the guests. The tempest had died down as rapidly as it had been unleashed; the atmosphere, purified by the rain, was delightfully fresh; the flowers and the foliage were exhaling their embalming odor and the powerful scent was rising from the ground that is always disengaged after a storm.

The tautened nerves had also rediscovered their calm, and no one was any longer experiencing that bizarre tightness of the heart, that physical anguish from which they had suffered so much.

Mr. Bombridge proposed that they go to take in the fresh air on the terrace that overlooked the house. Everyone accepted enthusiastically, and they were able to admire the magnificent landscape, lit by the rays of the moon.

On the horizon, they could see the red gleam of the lighthouse situated at the mouth of the river in the depths of Oyster Bay, which resembled a star about to fall into the sea.

Lord Burydan contemplated that distant light for a long time. He did not share his reflections with anyone, and all of Mr. Bombridge's guests soon retired to their rooms to savor a little well-deserved repose.

III. The Red Star

One moonlit night, about three weeks before Lord Burydan's arrival in Florida, a coastal sloop had dropped anchor in Oyster Bay. A launch had set off from that sloop, propelled by four vigorous black oarsmen. In the greatest mystery, it had disembarked three individuals and several large crates, directly opposite the feverish tower. Then the launch had returned to the ship; the sloop had raised anchor and had set out to sea again, without having been seen from any of the rare boats of the inhospitable coast.

In that location, the coast was bordered by large mangroves, the roots of which, plunging into the mud, were laden with clusters of oysters. Those roots, twisted and tangled, formed profound caverns, which served as shelters for huge land-cabs, snakes of every sort and a host of dangerous animals.

That rampart of mangroves had not been crossed without difficulty by the three travelers, still encumbered by their luggage. At every step they slipped on the roots and sank into the mud, or tore their hands on mollusk-shells.

Their arrival disturbed a whole society of swarming creatures.

"Brr!" said one of the three individuals. "I think I put my hand on a toad."

"You must have been mistaken," his companion replied. "I think it was more likely on a snake; there aren't any toads this close to the sea."

"A jolly place, this Florida, about which you've told me so many marvelous things! I'm wondering what we're going to do here?"

"That's not your concern," the other replied, harshly. "You're here to obey the Lords of the Red Hand, and me, their representative—so hurry up. In a few minutes we'll be out of these accursed mangroves and we'll set foot on firm ground."

Edward Edmond did not reply, and continued to advance, still muttering complaints.

As for the third person, a woman, her companions were careful to push in front of them, as if they were afraid that she might try to run away, and every time she stopped, Slug put the barrel of his revolver to her head.

"Keep moving, Dorypha," he told her, "or I'll kill you like the gypsy bitch you are."

Dorypha did not reply, but her rage and humiliation were at their peak, and she proffered the most terrible oaths mentally.

Finally, the three of them reached more solid ground. It was the square, once paved with large flat stone slabs, that extended in front of the church, and which was ordered to the left and the right by dilapidated houses, the former dwellings of Spanish colonists.

Having taken a small electric torch from his pocket, Slug got his bearings amid the debris.

"What are we doing?" asked Edward Edmond, who seemed to be in a very bad mood.

"First I'm going to put Dorypha in a safe place. Then we're going back for the crates that I was obliged to leave at the foot of the mangroves. Afterwards, you can rest for as long as you wish. Don't complain! We'll have almost nothing to do during our sojourn here; it's a real holiday!"

"Some holiday! A country were there's nothing but venomous beasts, where people die like flies of the *vomito negro*.[6] I can't wait to get out of here!"

"Coward! You know full well that we've nothing to fear from the fever—me because I've had it, and you because one of the Red Hand's doctors vaccinated you with a special serum before we set out."

"You can say that as often as you like, but I'm not reassured."

Dorypha had not missed a word of this conversation. Slug noticed that she was listening, and immediately had a fit of rage. "Have you finished spying on us?" he said. "Walk in front of me, so I can take you to the niche intended for you."

The gypsy obeyed, trembling with fury, and went into the church.

The vast nave, constructed in the Spanish style of the eighteenth century, was cracked in numerous places. The vault, damp and whitened by saltpeter, still bore traces of gilding in places.

The beam of the torch picked out a moldy picture in one corner, which represented a Black Madonna, proof that colored people had been the most numerous worshipers in the church. Long sprigs of moss, mingled with bright red poisonous mushrooms, covered the pavement of the sanctuary.

---

[6] The Spanish term for yellow fever.

Slug, who consulted a greasy notebook from time to time, steered to the left of the nave and opened a small door, the hinges of which grated lamentably in the silence. The door gave access to a spiral staircase that occupied the interior of a tower adjacent to the main building.

Slug went on ahead, then Dorypha, and finally Edward Edmond. The anguished gypsy wondered whether she might not have been brought into that sinister place in order to be hurled from the top of the bell-tower. As she went up she looked back, to dart a glance at Edward Edmond so melancholy and supplicant that the Irishman, in spite of all his hatred, felt moved to the utmost depths of his soul.

The gypsy had gown thinner by virtue of the privations and the ill-treatment to which hr jailers had subjected her, but she had lost none of her beauty. Her appearance had merely taken on a grimmer aspect. The corners of her mouth, as if tightened by suffering, gave her face a poignant expression to which one could not remain indifferent. Her eyes were burning with a somber fire in the depths of their orbits, hollowed out by grief and tears.

After having gone up thirty-five steps, Slug stopped on a landing that gave access to a square room occupying the entire first floor of the tower. On the upper floor, it was the bell itself that could be glimpsed through the interstices of the woodwork.

"We've arrived," said Slug, consulting his notebook again. Then, without hesitation, he went to the wall facing the entrance, in the middle of which there was a large rusty nail. He leaned forcibly on the nail. Immediately, a door opened, revealing the interior of a square chamber about eight feet wide. The external surface of the door had been so skillfully covered with slender bricks and cement that if one did not know the secret, it was impossible to distinguish it from the rest of the wall.

Externally, the cell was fitted into a bulbous protrusion fitted into one of the corners of the bell-tower. Hiding-places of that kind can be found in many old Spanish churches, and it was thus that on many occasions, in the early times of the conquest, missionaries were able to escape—miraculously, so to speak—from the pursuits of rebellious Indians.

Slug shoved the gypsy brutally into the cell and closed the door again.

"Now," he said to Edward Edmond, "let's go back down. You can see that your former mistress will be admirably well accommodated."

"How did you discover that hidey-hole?" asked the bewildered Irishman.

"I didn't discover it. It was indicated to me. Almost all of this region belongs to the Red Hand. It's not long since the crypt was entirely filled with stolen goods. There's no place in the world where there's less chance of being disturbed. The local people have a mortal fear of fevers. The Lords of the Red Hand have been careful to spread certain terrifying legends among the negroes, which makes sure that none of them dare come near this place, even in broad daylight."

At that moment they were on the landing, on to which a small square window opened.

"Anyway," said Edward Edmond, "it's a terribly unhealthy place." And with his hand he indicated the lugubrious extent of the marshes, which, in the nocturnal darkness, were radiant with a faint blue light, due to the phosphorescence of putrescence, while in other places, hundreds of fire follets were dancing round pools. "If I were alone here," he concluded, "I think I'd be terrified."

Slug, who was a strong-minded man, merely laughed at those terrors. "Imbecile," he said. "Don't you know that those wandering flames are merely a kind of lighting-gas, or something similar. There really isn't anything much to be afraid of."

While arguing thus, the two bandits had gone back down into the church. Then they went back to the place where they had left their crates.

It was not without difficulty that they succeeded in bringing them through the cluster of mangroves. Edward Edmond wondered whether they might yet be obliged to haul the heavy packages up to the summit of the tower.

Slug reassured him. "There's a very spacious crypt under the church," he explained, "the entrance to which isn't easy to detect. That's where we'll deposit our baggage."

He showed the Irishman one of the flagstones in the choir, in the center of which a ring was fitted. Afterwards, they went behind the altar to find an iron lever, of which they made use to lift the slab. It uncovered the entrance to a flight of stairs that ended in a subterranean room lined to the right and left by tombs.

"You can see that the place leaves nothing to be desired," said Slug. "One could leave merchandise here for ten years without anyone daring touch it."

"I'm wondering why we're taking all these precautions," said the Irishman. "If no one dares come near this place, it's not worth the trouble of putting ourselves out."

"You can't see further than the end of your nose. It's possible that the police might come to search the tower before long, and it's prudent to anticipate anything."

The Irishman would have liked to ask more questions, but he understood that Slug was not disposed to enlighten him with regard to his plans, so he resigned himself to staying silent.

Edmond and Slug were beginning to feel weary. They took a tin of corned beef and a bottle of alcohol out of one of the crates. After eating with a hearty appetite they went to sleep on the first floor, contenting themselves that first night with their overcoats as mattresses and pillows.

No one would have suspected that the tower, supposedly haunted by demons and ghosts, now had residents of flesh and blood.

In the days that followed, their life was organized. Slug and Edmond collected armfuls of rushes to make mattresses, and unpacked some of the provisions contained in the crates. The latter contained everything indispensable to life, including tobacco, whisky, weapons, ammunition and medical supplies.

Dorypha's two guardians spent all day smoking, sleeping or fishing along the shore, which was teeming with fish. They remained perfectly healthy, doubtless due to the febrifugal medicines that they were careful to take every day, in accordance with the instructions they had been given.

The Irishman would have that life of idleness quite comfortable had he not sensed a mysterious danger hanging over them. Slug sometimes spent all night at the summit of the tower, scanning the horizon anxiously; at other times he slept tranquilly on his mattress of rushes. The Irishman was unable to figure out the reasoning behind his actions. Slug remained impenetrable. Edmond had not yet been able to extract any information from him regarding the fate in store for the gypsy.

In fact, as time went by, Slug seemed to redouble his precautions. Every morning, he demanded that the rushes should be spread over the whole surface of the floor, in such a way that if anyone came they would not suspect that anyone was sleeping there. Doubtless for the same reason, he forbade the Irishman to leave any object whatsoever in the tower that might reveal the presence of a human being. It was in the crypt that they took all their meals, and there that they took shelter during the hottest periods of the day.

The Irishman was intrigued to the highest degree, for every day he discovered further facts capable of stimulating his curiosity. One morning, Slug opened a crate that had remained intact until then and took out several large and carefully-wrapped bottles filled with a colorless liquid. He took one of them and went out into the swamp. From a distance, Edmond saw him occupied in distributing its contents in the stagnant water; then he came back to get another, and repeated the procedure until all the bottles were empty.

On another occasion, Slug decided to open the largest of the crates, but closed it again almost immediately. The Irishman only had time to glimpse metal, glass and wires: the dismantled components of some machine whose purpose he could not determine.

Finally, there were days on which Slug went away without wanting to be accompanied, and only came back at nightfall, sometimes even the following morning.

The Irishman ventured a thousand conjectures, but did not arrive at any conclusion.

In the meantime, Dorypha was leading a thoroughly miserable existence. The redoubt into which she had been thrown only received daylight through a narrow rectangular opening. It was cluttered by miscellaneous objects that one might find in the loft of any church: broken wooden candlesticks, caved-in chairs, even an armless statue of St. Rose of Lima,[7] to which a barbaric coloring lent an appearance of life in the dim light. The gypsy was almost afraid of it.

She remained lying on a bed of rushes for entire days, prey to sadness and despair. She scarcely touched the food that Slug brought her once a day. The poor dancer was waiting to die; she would have like to die, but she had attained that phase of physical and mental depression when one no longer even has the courage to commit suicide.

Eaten away by ennui, she began mechanically to create puerile distractions for herself, as children and old people do. She spent hours weaving the dry rushes that composed her bed, and fabricated in that fashion a crown for the statue of St. Rose.

---

[7] The ascetic daughter of a Spanish colonist, who became a lay associate of the Dominican order, St. Rose of Lima (1586-1617) was the first person born in the Americas to be canonized.

178

One day, she had the joy of discovering, in one corner, an old pewter crucifix that had been lying under the dust for more than a century. She cleaned and polished it, and attached it to the wall.

Dorypha's principal consolation was, however, "her star."

The narrow window that illuminated the cell was placed so high and orientated in such a fashion that even by hoisting herself up the gypsy could only perceive an expanse of sea and a distant fraction of the coast, but every evening, in the same direction, a red gleam lit up, brighter than a star, which subsisted all night long.

Dorypha had never been able to work out exactly what that light was; but she contemplated it tirelessly, and attached a superstitious importance to its presence. On the days when the fog hid her star the gypsy was even sadder and more despairing than usual, and every evening she waited impatiently for the dear little light to spring forth in the crepuscular mists.

"There it is! It's alight!" she exclaimed. "I'm not entirely abandoned yet."

Her eyes ardently fixed on the distant star, she plunged into reveries in which all the scenes of her old life passed through her imagination like the fleeting silhouettes of a dream.

In that monotonous reclusive existence, there were some days that were more terrible for her to bear. That was when there were storms. Then Dorypha could not sleep; the atmosphere in her narrow cell became suffocating. She soon emptied the pitcher of water that Slug brought at irregular intervals, and was ravaged by thirst.

Once, when one of those formidable tropical storms had been unleashed, battering the also of the old tower with its blasts of rain and launching furious waves over the rampart of mangroves, the gypsy was lying on her miserable bed, prey to an immense depression. She was hoping that the night might be more peaceful, and that she might finally get a little sleep. Her nerves, further exasperated by privation and illness, were tautened to breaking point. She shivered at the slightest sound, breathing in with an unhealthy voluptuousness the perfume the poisonous flowers of the great marsh, brought to her by the wind.

Night was about to fall and the storm had lost none of its violence.

"My red star!" Dorypha suddenly cried. "I must see it light up!"

Nervously, she leapt to her feet and hoisted herself up until her eyes were level with the loophole.

Almost immediately, the light sprang forth in the darkness, a little weaker than usual, but still visible through the confusion of the downpour, beneath the sky of black clouds, ripped occasionally by flashes of lightning.

"One might think that it was waiting for me!" the gypsy murmured, her eyes moistening with tears.

She was torn from her contemplation by the sound of unaccustomed comings and goings. Someone was going up and down the stairs precipitately. Then there was a kind of metallic clang in the upper floor of the tower. Finally, the blows of a hammer resounded.

"What can they be doing?" the gypsy wondered, anxiously.

Suddenly, she raised her hand to her eyes with an almost dolorous cry of amazement.

From the summit of the tower a sheet of red light emerged, harsh and blinding. A few rays of that light penetrating through the loophole had been sufficient to force the gypsy to close her eyes, where she was now experiencing a painful burning sensation.

"I don't understand that at all!" she stammered. "I think they'll end up driving me mad. They would have done better to kill me at a single stroke, at the same time as my husband."

Gradually, Dorypha opened her eyes; they slowly became accustomed to the light.

Renouncing any attempt to understand, she contented herself with contemplating the red star.

Suddenly, she uttered a cry. The red star had disappeared.

Dorypha waited for long hours. Her avid gaze scrutinized the profundities of the night and the thicker darkness outside the inexplicable circle of light surrounding the tower, but in vain.

After a time, the fulgurant aureole was extinguished as suddenly as it had lit up. Dorypha found herself once again in the profound darkness of her prison. She hoisted herself up to the loophole. Less than five minutes had gone by when, to her profound surprise, the red star scintillated again, this time not winking out again until daybreak.

It was incomprehensible.

The next day, the gypsy waited with feverish curiosity for sunset to come.

On that night and the subsequent ones, the red star did not suffer any sudden eclipse. On the other hand, the mysterious light in the tower that had shone for two hours was not reilluminated.

Was there a correlation between the two facts? Dorypha did not even try to work out what it might be. She might perhaps have forgotten the inexplicable event, coming to regard it as a hallucination, had not the same thing happened a week later in identical circumstances. As on the first occasion, the gypsy heard a great stir on the stairway of the tower. The bell-tower lit up, and the red star disappeared; its disappearance lasted more than three hours.

The same thing happened again a few days later, for the third time.

Dorypha came to think that it was doubtless once a week that the bizarre event occurred. Now that she expected it, however, almost on a particular day, it was no longer a source of distraction for the gypsy.

Her existence resumed its monotonous course, without being troubled by any incident for some time.

On the same day that Mr. Bombridge took his friends to visit his enterprise, Edward Edmond and Slug were smoking their pipes philosophically, sitting on the capital of a fallen column. They were both silent, Slug as a matter of habit, the Irishman as a matter of necessity—for his companion had only responded thus far with monosyllables to all the attempts he had made to strike up a conversation.

For a few minutes, Slug had been attentively observing the livid sky and the sea whitening beyond the reefs.

"I'm going for a walk," he said.

"Do you want me to go with you?"

"No need."

"When will you be back?"

"I don't know."

"All right. See you later, then. Have a good time."

The Irishman started whistling between his teeth to hide his irritation, while Slug headed nonchalantly toward the mangroves on the strand.

Edmond followed him with his gaze for some time. When he finally saw him disappear, he gave free rein to his ill humor. "I've had enough of this life!" he exclaimed. "I'm dying of boredom. I have to obey, like a valet, whatever command that old rogue gives me, without even knowing what he's doing! Why have I been stupid enough to enslave myself to the Red Hand again? I have dollars in my pocket, it's true, but I'm more miserable than I was when I was a simple tramp wandering the roads."

He looked around as if searching for inspiration. Suddenly, his faced brightened. He rubbed his hands, like a man who has made an interesting discovery.

He slipped a half-full bottle of whisky into his pocket and headed for the church.

Having arrived in the nave he went straight to the stairway in the tower and climbed as far as the first floor landing. There he stopped and, leaning out of one of the loopholes, looked n the direction of the shore. In the distance, he could see Slug, so far away that he now looked no bigger than a pygmy.

Reassured by the certainty that his tyrant had really gone, Edward Edmond deliberately went to the secret door, pressed the nail the commanded the lock, and found himself in the presence of Dorypha, sadly lying on the rushes that served as her bed.

He could not help being moved by the lamentable state of the gypsy, whose face was emaciated and whose blonde hair fell in disorder over her shoulders.

They looked at one another for some time in silence. Edmond did not know how to begin the conversation, and Dorypha was too proud to speak first.

Finally, the Irishman plucked up his courage. "Hello, Dorypha," he said. "I've come to bring you a drop of whisky, taking advantage of the fact that Slug isn't here."

"You don't think I'm dying quickly enough?" she said, bitterly.

"Are you afraid that my whisky might be poisoned? Here, look!" He took a copious swig straight from the bottle.

The gypsy's eyes suddenly sparkled. She had just had an idea. Her bleak and dejected physiognomy suddenly became almost smiling.

"Well, give!" she said. "I'm too unhappy to have the right to be proud."

She drank in her turn. It seemed to her that the burning liquor gave her a superhuman energy. "It's better than Slug's pitcher of water," she said, with a faint smile. It's him I hate most of all. You..."

"Me, I'm obliged to obey the Red Hand. Anyway, I have the right to hate you. Didn't you try to kill me?"

"Let's not dwell on the past," said the gypsy, with a simplicity that did not lack nobility. "All that's far behind us. Let's be good comrades, as we once were. Don't you think that they way I'm being treated is vile?"

The Irishman had abruptly forgotten all his rancor. He felt over-whelmed once again by that voice, with its tender inflections.

"I'll do what I can to be useful to you," he stammered.

"You say that! But I'm sure that I've only been brought to this accursed tower to be murdered with impunity. The first day we arrived here I heard you say that everyone dies here of yellow fever."

"That's true," said Edward Edmond, lowering his head.

"Except," said the gypsy, with a burst or ironic laughter, "that what Slug doesn't know is that I've had yellow fever too, when I was in Havana."

The conversation continued for a while in that tone. The bottle of whisky had been empty for some time, and Dorypha had deliberately encouraged the Irishman to drink the greater part of it. Neither of them was paying any attention to the storm that was gradually rising in the sky.

It was the gypsy who noticed it first. "I'm stifling in this cell!" she said. "If you were kind, you'd let me out for a while to stretch my legs."

"Impossible! If Slug found out, he'd blow my brains out without the slightest scruple—and then again, if I did what you ask, you'd try to escape."

"No, I promise you. Just let me go up to the bell-tower to get a little air."

After a long negotiation, the Irishman ended up giving his consent. They both went up to the circular gallery above the belfry.

Edward Edmond had the idea of taking out his collapsible telescope, and was amusing himself studying various parts of the swamp when he suddenly uttered an exclamation of surprise and fear.

"What's the matter?" asked the gypsy.

"I can see Slug down there. He'll be here within the hour."

"So what?"

"I need to put you back in your prison. Besides, there's a storm brewing. It's already raining."

"Well, all right," she said, meekly. "I'll go back down, but at least promise to come and see me again."

"Agreed."

They went back down to the floor below. As they went past the bell, Dorypha asked to look at it more closely. The Irishman agreed, and was the first to venture on to the latticework frame encasing it. Dorypha followed him. Half way through the perilous traversal, the gypsy suddenly uttered a brief burst of laughter and, tripping him up, caused the Irishman to lose his balance. He disappeared through one of the yawning gaps and fell bruised and shaken, on to the litter of rushes that—fortunately for him—covered the floor of the chamber below.

"Slut!" he cried.

He tried to get up, but could not do it, and thought that he had broken his back.

Without paying him any further heed, the gypsy had seized the bell-rope, and she started ringing the bell with a desperate energy.

Night had fallen abruptly; the tempest was raging over the land. Dorypha continued ringing. The deep note of the bronze bell mingled with the rumbling of the thunder.

Someone might come, she thought. *I know the region is inhabited.*

She continued to ring until she had exhausted her strength; then another idea suddenly occurred to her. In spite of what the Irishman had said about the impossibility of crossing the marsh, she thought she might be able to do it. It was dark; she would find a hiding-place where Slug and Edward Edmond would not be able to find her.

She ran full tilt down the stairs, but just as she was about to cross the threshold of the church she found herself face to face with Slug.

"Aha!" the bandit sniggered. "It seems that we want to escape. Fortunately, I'm here!" While speaking, he leapt upon the gypsy and seized her by the throat before she had time to raise her arms defensively.

In the blink of an eye he knocked her down and tied her hands and feet securely. Only then did he wonder what had become of the Irishman.

He had no difficulty finding him, moaning pitifully in the chamber on the first floor.

"Was it you who rang the bell?" he demanded, in a terrible voice.

"No, I swear!"

"Then it was you who opened the door to the gypsy?"

"That's true—but I've been cruelly punished." And he recounted what had happened.

"That's all right," said Slug. "I'll let you off this once—but don't do it again! Anyway, I'll make sure that witch doesn't cause us any further inconvenience of that sort. Do you know that her idea of ringing the bell might have put us in danger? Fortunately, the weather's so bad that no one will have heard it, I hope."

Slug helped the Irishman to get up. He felt him, making sure that nothing was broken, and finally rubbed his back with whisky. Then he went back down and returned to the gypsy, still tied up. He carried her away on his back and deposited hr, without saying a word, in her former prison.

"Now I'm going out again," he said to the Irishman. This time, I hope, you won't take it into your head to open Dorypha's cage.

Without waiting for the Irishman's reply, he left, and did not come back for two hours. He was bent over by the weight of a voluminous sack.

"What's that?" asked the Irishman.

"Something to reinforce the gypsy's prison. I don't think that imitation stone door is secure enough. I'm going to put up a real one...but you'll see that tomorrow. I'm too tired today. I'm going to sleep.

The Irishman had not fully understood what Slug intended. So, a quarter of an hour later, during their meal, he asked him if he was going to take any food to the gypsy.

"No," the bandit replied, coldly. "It's not worth the trouble. She has no need of it."

"What do you mean?"

"Haven't you understood my plan? The sack I brought is full of cement. I'm simply going to wall Dorypha up in her hole. That way, she won't trouble us again."

"But what will the Lords of the Red Hand say?" stammered the Irishman, his blood congealed by fright.

"What they'll say is purely my concern. It's none of your business."

The conversation ended here. The Irishman could not imagine that Slug would actually carry out his horrible plan.

In that, he was mistaken. Slug never went back on a firm decision, on principle. The next morning, he set about transporting large stone blocks, which could be found in abundance in the ruins, up to the first floor of the tower. Then he took the door off its hinges, and, before the eyes of the gypsy and the Irishman, who were almost as frightened as one another, he started laying down the foundations of a wall.

In order that the new masonry he was building should be indistinguishable from the old in its color, he took the precaution of mixing soot with the cement that he was using.

The work made rapid progress. By noon, it only remained to place the final row of stones.

IV. The Pewter Crucifix

It was in the role of jockey that Ezechias Palmer, the son of an honorable clergyman of the state of New Jersey, had made his start in life, leaving incomplete the theological studies that he had undertaken under the parental aegis.

A sudden gain in weight forced him to renounce the hippodrome, and he was lucky enough to obtain a position as director of a Lunatic Asylum, only retaining from his original métier a remarkable aptitude for losing his money at racecourses.

Mr. Palmer rapidly wearied of the society of madmen—who, in any case, did him a series of bad turns—and he quit the Lunatic Asylum to establish, thanks to the capital of benevolent shareholders, a Spiritualist Institute, in which people afflicted in their affections by death could see their dear departed appear at will, and even converse with them.

Mr. Palmer's clients declared themselves to be quite satisfied. The materializations left nothing to be desired; money was flowing into the coffers of the ingenious spiritualist when the New York Police chanced to discover that the souls evoked were represented by young ladies whose attractions had nothing immaterial about them and whose morals were deplorable, especially for pure spirits. The Spiritualist Institute was closed, by order of the authorities.

Mr. Palmer then fell on hard times. He had spent his last dollar and was wondering, while wandering the streets of New York in a melancholy fashion, what the most rapid, most economical and least painful means of suicide was. He ended up concluding that a plunge into the Hudson would meet all three conditions in a satisfactory manner.

The result of this meditation was that he took to a gun-dealer the superb Browning with which he had initially planned to blow his brains out, and came away with four dollars, which put him momentarily in a good mood.

That was definitely his lucky day. As he was coming out of the gun-merchant's shop he perceived a group of women, young and old, stationed around a shoemaker's shop in the open air. He went over, impelled by curiosity, and his attention was immediately caught by the strange remark: "That young woman is wearing away her heel, she's so dark, soft and faithful."

In that simple sentence there was an entire revelation. Benevolent hazard had pushed Mr. Palmer into the vicinity of the boutique of a podomancer

Podomancy, as everyone knows, is the art of diving a person's character, and even their future, by means of the way in which they wear their shoes.[8] After an hour, Mr. Palmer knew that, if brunettes wear away their heels and are faithful, blondes were away their toes and are flighty, that noblemen and cunning people wear away the arches of their feet, prodigals and the stupid the uppers—and a host of other notions of similar force.

Dazed with joy, Mr. Palmer ran all the way to a newspaper office and, with the little money he now possessed, inserted an advertisement conceived as follows:

Would you like to know
YOUR QUALITIES, YOUR FAULTS AND YOUR FUTURE?
Pay no heed to charlatans and tricksters!
Be practical!
Appeal to the exact sciences and consult
The famous JAMES ROLLAN
The greatest podomancer in the whole of America.
It is sufficient to send him a pair of shoes that have been worn, but not worn out,
to know the secret of your destiny by return of post.
Tell me how you walk
And I will tell you who you are!
N.B. No reply will be made to people
who send shoes in poor condition.

Mr. Palmer had had an idea of genius. The day after he had inserted this advertisement, he received an avalanche of shoes of every kind, the majority of which were those of women.

Without losing any time, he drafted four notices, which, reproduced in large quantity, ought to suit all the possible and imaginable cases.

---

[8] Strictly speaking, podomancy, once popular in China, is the pedal equivalent of palmistry, involving the consultation of the lines on the sole of the foot, but the Western habit of wearing shoes obviously confuses the relevant indications and the artistry of their interpretation.

They were conceived in a style so vague that everyone was bound to find something true therein.

A week later, he was obliged to hire three employees to sort out his vast correspondence, and he possessed a vast hangar entirely filled with shoes. Others would have sold that merchandise wholesale for next to nothing, but Mr. Palmer had too much business acumen to commit such a blunder. He increased his staff by three master cobblers and, before the end of the first month, had inaugurated, in New York itself, two superb stores in which excellent shoes were released to the public at bargain prices.

The name of James Rollan was already almost celebrated. The famous podomancer's portrait was on the eighth page of the newspapers, framed by stunning testimonials. His offices occupied a vast building and he was able to set up branches in Chicago, New Orleans and San Francisco.

His success grew with hurricane rapidity. Mr. Palmer founded an Academy of Pedicure, and launched an unparalleled corn-plaster. Finally, he set the seal on his renown by publishing, under his pseudonym of James Rollan, a brochure on *The Esthetic Rationale of the Foot*, which was a great success.

All that his happiness lacked was to find, among the richest and most beautiful heiresses of the Union, a companion worthy of him. He was in no hurry, though, for he only wanted to make his choice in the perfect knowledge of the circumstances. He even rejected several very advantageous matches in succession.

It was then that, in the course of a business trip to the southern States, that hazard put him in the presence of Mr. and Miss Bombridge, who were traveling in the same railway carriage as him. He was charmed by Regina's beauty and grace, and after a quarter of an hour, he swore to himself that he would never have any wife but her. It was a thunderbolt!

Without deciding as rapidly, Mr. Bombridge was not hostile in principle to the idea of giving his daughter to the obliging and polite gentleman in question, who talked about nothing but millions of dollars, and cited stupefying turnover figures.

It was thus that Mr. James Rollan, like Matalobos and Oscar Tournesol, was invited to come to Florida for a brief period, at the end of which Mr. Bombridge would make his final decision known.

James Rollan was such a busy man that, in spite of his good intentions, he was only able to arrive two days after his competitors. He was made no less welcome in consequence, and was ceremoniously introduced to his rivals, Oscar and the prestidigitator, and also to Lord Burydan.

It seemed to the eccentric that the newcomer's face was not unknown to him, but he could not recall exactly where he could have seen it before. For his part, Palmer recognized at first glance the man who had come to the Spiritualist Institute to ask him to make the lady with of scabious flowers appear, but he thought that his former client would not recognize him under the name of James Rollan, given certain changes that he had made to his physiognomy and his costume. Instead of being clean-shaven, as before, he wore a thin moustache and blond side-whiskers, which made him look like some elegant Austro-Hungarian diplomat.

James Rollan was given a perfect welcome by Mr. Bombridge and his friends. His presence was a fortunate diversion from the bad weather that had not ceased to rage since the arrival of Oscar and Lord Burydan, which prevented more interesting excursions in the neighborhood. On the day of the podomancer's arrival there as a frightful storm, and the little society had no other recourse than to organize a game of bridge in the large drawing room of the villa while the rain drummed the closed windows noisily and the wind wailed in the trees of the forest.

The evening concluded in a rather sullen fashion, and everyone retired early to their bedrooms.

Lord Burydan could not sleep. Once he was alone he tried to read, but he soon perceived that he had scanned two or three pages without having taken in a single word. His mind was elsewhere. Then again, although the window was still open by a crack, it was unbearably hot.

The young man took advantage of a calm interval to go up to the terrace go smoke a cigar. The wind, steeped in rain, refreshed his burning brow and soothed his nerves. He started walking back and forth slowly, gazing distractedly at the landscape.

Suddenly, he stopped.

The red gleam of the little lighthouse at the entrance to Oyster Bay had disappeared. Much more surprising was that another gleam, of the same color but more intense, had lit up some ten miles away, to the north.

Lord Burydan calculated that it was in approximately that direction that the feverish tower stood. Evidently, something extraordinary was happening. Lord Burydan went back downstairs to find a waterproof coat—for the rain had begun to fall violently again—and returned courageously to his observation post.

He had imagined at first that, for some unknown reason, the lighthouse had moved. After an examination, he realized that he was mistaken. After an hour's sentry duty on the terrace, Lord Burydan saw the new light go out. Almost immediately, the lighthouse lit up again.

The eccentric understood that nothing else would happen that night, so he returned to his room, very preoccupied.

The following morning, the weather was superb. Oscar Tournesol got up early and went to knock on Lord Burydan's door in order to invite him to go for a matinal stroll. The eccentric had already gone out. Oscar was told that he had left the house an hour earlier, in the company of the old negro Jupiter, whom he had taken as a guide.

They waited for him in vain all morning. He only came back at midday, just as Mr. Bombridge's guests were about to go to lunch. He seemed tired and discontented. He asked for permission to go and change his clothes, for he was covered in mud from head to toe.

When he came back down, he was bombarded with questions.

"I hope you're going to tell us about your walk?" said the conjurer.

"You should have taken us with you," added James Rollan.

When Lord Burydan made no reply, Regina, pretending to be annoyed, said: "Perhaps Lord Burydan doesn't want to tell us where he's been. It would be indiscreet to insist."

"I don't have any reason to hide it from you," said the eccentric. "I had a whim to go and visit the feverish tower."

"You've been there? What imprudence!" cried the guests, with one voice.

"Don't worry—I took my precautions. I've obtained from my knowledgeable friend Prosper Bondonnat a febrifuge of his invention, thanks to which one can remain in the most unhealthy places, at least for a few hours. I confess that the precautions were far from unnecessary. Nor did I forget to cover my face with a mosquito net and take a small medical kit with me."

"Are the marshes as terrible as that?" asked Oscar.

"More terrible than is believed! In addition to the clouds of mosquitoes and venomous insects that form dense swarms over the stagnant waters, the swamp is the refuge of the most hideous reptiles I've ever seen. As well as the inoffensive bullfrogs, one sees toads of prodigious dimensions, and the famous coffin snake, bright pale green in color, which hunts its victims like a dog. Some of the pools are full of poisonous oysters and hideous scarlet crabs, which do battle around sleeping alligators that can easily be mistaken for fallen tree-trunks.

"In the places where a few trees grow and the ground is firmer, one encounters giant ants, so numerous and voracious that they're capable of reducing the cadaver of a man to a perfectly clean skeleton in less than an hour."

"You dared to go through all that?" asked Regina, suppressing a shiver of disgust.

"I obtain no great merit from that, since I had the brave Jupiter for a guide, who knows the swampland very well and took me via relatively safe paths. In sum, I only skirted those horrors at a distance.

"The most singular thing of all is that in those putrid waters and venomous muds, admirably-perfumed and headily-scented flowers bloom. In the midst of that pandemonium of reptiles, sky-blue and crimson blossoms open, with glistening metallic foliage. In some places, the black water is covered by a carpet of flowers in which one can see the flat heads of serpents looming up.

"I had to go through a clump of huge mimosas that exhaled an intoxicating perfume, and which moved their branches away from me with a slight hiss, for they're shrubs endowed with almost as much sensitivity and nervousness as human beings.

"Elsewhere, in the midst of jalap vines with blue corollas, huge grey and pink wading birds were feeding on snakes and lizards, and took off with a loud clatter of wings as we approached. There were also immense sulfur-yellow butterflies, spiders as big as my fist, and caterpillars the size of small snakes.

"It was through that entire swarm of more-or-less suspect insects that I had to walk for nearly three hours before reaching the feverish tower. When I arrived at a certain distance, Jupiter refused to accompany me any further, and he stopped, after showing me that route that I still had to follow."

"So you've seen the sinister tower?" asked Mr. Bombridge. "All my compliments. I wouldn't have had the courage."

"Let's not exaggerate. The feverish tower and the ruins that surround it are built on a plateau that overlooks the nearby marshes, and the air there must be much less unhealthy, all the more so because of the proximity of the sea..

"I climbed up to the top of the tower. It's a ruin, and a ruin abandoned for a long time. I saw the bell that frightened us so much the other day. It must be very old, because it's covered in Latin mottoes and armories. As for the sounds we heard, it's not impossible that in a strong wind, the bell might be agitated. There's nothing marvelous in that."

"With your manner of explaining things," said Regina, "you're taking the poetry out of the legend of the feverish tower for me."

"No," murmured Lord Burydan. "I even experienced a real disappointment, for I thought I was on the track of an interesting discovery. However, I've omitted one rather bizarre fact. As I was coming down the stairway of the tower, I thought I could make out muffled groans. I went back up, but I could no longer hear anything. I looked everywhere, and couldn't see anything. There's no place where anyone could hide. I concluded that I was the victim of a hallucination, or that the apparent grounds were only one of those vibrations caused by the echoes that one often heard in the immediate vicinity of bells."

The narrator was suddenly interrupted. A black man came in, saying that a man was asking to speak to Lord Burydan.

"Who is he?" asked the eccentric, hurriedly getting up from the table.

"He looks like a tramp," the black man replied, astonished by the nobleman's urgency.

At the door, Lord Burydan was surprised to find himself in the presence of Pierre Gilkin, Dorypha's husband, who, after having been left for dead by the bandits of the Red Hand in the hacienda of San Bernardino, had been obliged to spend months in the hospital at Cucomongo in Arizona.

"You, here!" exclaimed the astonished aristocrat.

"Yes," Gilkin murmured. His clothes were covered in mud; his pale and distraught visage and slightly curbed stance indicated great fatigue. "As soon as I was capable of standing up, I set out in search of Dorypha. I've traveled all the roads of America, dressed as a vagabond, trying to make the acquaintance of all the bandits I encountered."

"What have you discovered?"

Gilkin, whose hands were trembling with emotion, handed Lord Burydan an ancient pewter crucifix that he had taken out from inside his jacket.

"See for yourself!" he said, excitedly. "That's what I found just now at the foot of the feverish tower!"

Lord Burydan took the crucifix and examined it. A few words had been engraved by an awkward hand, and the inscription, to judge by the brightness with which the letters stood out from the duller metal, seemed very recent. Not without difficulty, he deciphered the message:

Am walled up alive in the tower. Help. Dorypha.

Beneath the signature, by way of an afterthought was added: *First floor.*

Lord Burydan remembered the groans that he had heard and was chilled by horror. "You haven't tried to discover where she is?" he asked Gilkin.

"I didn't find anything," murmured the gypsy's husband, dejectedly. "Then too, I'm not entirely cured. I have a fever. It was only with great effort that I dragged myself this far, where I knew I'd find you, as a letter from Fred Jorgell had informed me."

"We mustn't lose a minute! We must go in number to the feverish tower. Dorypha will be saved!"

"As long as there's still time," murmured Pierre Gilkin, bleakly.

Lord Burydan was about to go and inform Oscar Tournesol when a servant handed him a telegram. The young man opened it rapidly, read it sat a glance and then stuffed it in his pocket, crumpling it nervously.

"What's the matter?" asked Oscar, who had come in search of his friend.

"Another of the Lightning Steamship Company's steamships sank last night."

"That's really bad luck."

"It wasn't bad buck; it was a crime. But I'm determined to know the truth, and today! I'm going to the feverish tower."

"In that case, I'll go with you."

"Right! But tell old Jupiter that we need him; he's the only one capable of guiding us through the swamp."

Mr. Bombridge was brought up to date briefly. A few minutes later, Lord Burydan, Oscar and Pierre Gilkin set out for the feverish tower, escorted by four robust black men armed with rifles and revolvers.

In spite of his extreme weakness, Pierre Gilkin had insisted on accompanying his friends.

Mr. Palmer and the conjurer apologized for not taking part in the expedition, offering the excuse that they had to stay behind to keep Regina company. The truth was that they had no desire to traverse the accused marshes.

V. The Feverish Tower

When Slug had sealed the massive stone filling in the last gap in the wall constructed instead of the door to her cell, Dorypha abandoned herself to despair for some time. This time, she was doomed, devoid of resources. No one would come to her rescue; there was nothing left but to die.

She bitterly regretted having had the idea of ringing the bell instead of fleeing as far away as possible.

If I'd taken advantage of Slug's absence, she thought, quivering with rage and writhing in the bonds that were cutting into her ankles and wrists, *I'd have been able to reach the sea shore and I'd be free, instead if which, nothing remains for me to do now but die of starvation.*

Fortunately, the gypsy possessed one of those temperaments formed for struggle, which react vigorously against circumstances after being subject to a few moments of temporary depression. Less than a quarter of an hour after the last stone had been placed in the wall of her covert, Dorypha had already made a start on trying to free herself from the cords binding her wrists.

There was no possibility of untying them; the knots had been too skillfully and tightly made; Dorypha had only one means of getting out of them, and that was to cut through them by wearing them away, little by little, against the stone.

The gypsy chose the roughest granite she could find along the walls of her cell and set to work. The task was exceedingly difficult, however; while fraying the cord she also scored the skin of her hand and wrist. When she was finally able to break the cord, after an hour's work, she was covered in blood—but her hands were free and that was a great step forward.

Encouraged by that first success, she waited for her numb and swollen hands—or she had been tied up since the day before—to recover their movement and elasticity; then, without overmuch difficulty, she undid the cords binding her ankles.

Then she looked around to see whether, among the various objects to be found in the cell, any of them might be of use to her.

First of all, she discovered an old brass candlestick that she carefully put to one side, with the idea of using it as a weapon or a lever. It was then that she noticed that it had a sharp spike, on which candles had been fixed. It was an instrument entirely appropriate for scraping mortar and unsealing the stones.

Without waiting for the complete exhaustion of her strength, diminished by long fasting, the gypsy, the gypsy immediately set to work.

She thought that there was no point in attacking the wall that Slug had built, made of heavy blocks united by cement; she thought that she might triumph more easily over the old mortar, already friable, and the less voluminous stones of which the old wall was constructed.

The point of attack that she chose was at floor level. The recluse told herself that the hole she proposed to make would remain unnoticed for some time because of the thick litter of rushes covering the flagstones of the chamber.

She worked patiently for the rest of the day. Alas, when the sun set, she perceived that she had achieved very little. The hole she had made in the wall appeared to her to be ridiculously tiny—and yet, she was exhausted by fatigue.

Night forced her to interrupt her work. She lay down, with the firm intention of resting well in order to continue as soon as it was daylight.

All through the next day she worked with the same courage, although hunger was tormenting her entrails. She found some relief in chewing the stems of the rushes that served as her bed: a measure that was palliative but anodyne, for, that evening, she had completely exhausted her strength.

Her efforts had not been futile, however; the stone she had been attacking was now almost completely loose; it would only required simple pressure to remove it from the mortar, which was no longer adhering to it.

That night, the captive heard the movements on the stairway to the bell-tower that ordinary preceded its illumination. As on the other occasions, through the loophole, she saw the red star on the horizon go out while a bright light shone down from the top of the tower.

The interior of the cell was brightly lit. One ray of light, penetrating obliquely through the loophole, fell directly upon the pewter Christ that the gypsy had cleaned and hung on the wall in the early days of her captivity.

"Who knows?" she murmured, struck by an inspiration. "Perhaps I have there, in my hands, a providential means of making my situation known outside.

She took the crucifix off the wall and, making use of the sharp spike of the candlestick as a stylet, albeit with considerable difficulty, she engraved a few words on the back of the cross. Then, hoisting herself up as high as she could, she threw it out of the window.

It was that crucifix that Pierre Gilkin was to bring to Lord Burydan the following day.

That effort had exhausted the captive's strength. A fever caused by deprivation of nourishment as also devouring her, and, in spite of her lassitude, did not permit her to sleep. The poor gypsy spent a horrible night. Hunger was clawing at her; her ears were ringing; she seemed to see fireflies dancing before her eyes.

At daybreak, she got up and tried to go back to work—in vain! She was so weak that after a few minutes she felt faint and lost consciousness. A profound sleep followed that loss of consciousness without transition.

Like all those suffering from hunger, the gypsy dreamed that she was taking part in magnificent feasts. It was the inarticulate words she pronounced during her dreams that Lord Burydan heard during his visit to the tower.

She slept for several hours. There were such resources in her robust constitution that the short period of rest sufficed to return a fraction of her energy.

When she woke up, she heard the sound of voices in the room adjacent to her prison. She stuck her ear to the wall, and thought she understood that it was Slug, who, before leaving on one of his mysterious expeditions, was giving his instructions to Edward Edmond.

She was not mistaken. Footsteps resonated on the stairway of the tower. Slug had gone, and Dorypha soon heard the Irishman uncork a bottle, open a tin and begin to eat. Through the wall, she could even make out the clicking of his jaws.

The gypsy's hunger was increased by those sounds, which seemed to add insult to her distress. She swore that she would have her share of the Irishman's meal.

With infinite precaution, she pulled away the stone that she had had so much trouble freeing from its cement.

Suddenly, Edward Edmond, who had heard nothing, entirely absorbed in his occupation, saw a long thin brown arm emerge from the rushes, take hold of the bottle of whisky and the tin of corned beef, and then disappear.

That larceny was accomplished so swiftly that the Irishman, with his mouth full, did not have time even to think about preventing it. The surprise that he experienced extended into fear,

"Is that you, Dorypha?" he stammered, trembling all over.

A burst of mocking laughter replied to him from the other side of the wall.

He had not yet recovered from his stupefaction when the brown hand reached through the hole again and stole the rest of his provisions—which is to say, a packet of sea biscuits and a slice of ham.

Dorypha had thrown herself avidly upon the unexpected victuals. She constrained herself, nevertheless, only to eat very sparingly and a little at a time. She had heard it said that nourishment should only be taken with extreme moderation after a long fast. She drank a mouthful of whisky. Oh, how willingly she would have sacrificed all she possessed for a pitcher of fresh water!

The gypsy felt life and hope reborn within her. With the little food she had, she felt capable of making a hole big enough to crawl through. Then, in order to escape, she would take advantage of a moment when her torturers were absent or asleep. She did not want to pause over the thought that the Irishman would denounce her to Slug and that the latter might perhaps kill her with a revolver shot fired through some hole in the wall.

Edward Edmond was far from having any such intention.

He parted the rushes, uncovering the gaping opening, and, lying flat on his belly, he called: "Dorypha!"

"Let me eat in peace," the walled-up women replied.

"You're not dead, then?"

"I don't die as easily as that!"

"What did you use to pierce the wall?"

"That's not your concern."

"Oh!" murmured the Irishman, with a sigh of regret. "If only you weren't so perfidious and false, if you hadn't acted to treacherously! But you can't be trusted!"

Dorypha was profoundly astonished. After having thrown the Irishman from the height of the belfry, she had not expected such affability.

"What are you getting at?" she asked.

"Listen!" he went on, with slight hesitation. "I've had enough of the Red Hand. If you hadn't tried to kill me as you did, I'd have helped you to escape. Now, I know you too well. This evening, I'm going to show Slug the hole you've made, and he'll be quick to block it up with good cement. It's not the lunch you've stolen from me that will get you out of here."

The gypsy reflected. *Evidently*, she thought, *he has a plan, and I don't think it'll be difficult to lead him by the nose.*

"Listen!" she said to him in her most seductive and tender voice. "I recognize that I've treated you very badly, but you must understand that I had some excuse. If you care to do as I tell you, a brilliant future will open up before you. Let me escape, follow me in my flight, and I swear to you that your old job, with Fred Jorgell, will be returned to you, or, better still, the billionaire will give us enough money to go and live in Europe, far from the Red Hand. You know that he can't refuse me anything, since it's me who saved all his friends..."

"Oh, that Slug!" murmured the Irishman between his teeth. "I detest him! He orders me about as if I were his slave."

"If you tell certain people I know what you know about the Red Hand, your fortune will be made," the gypsy insinuated, perfidiously.

"That requires reflection!"

The conversation continued for an hour in that tone. Dorypha, to whom the imminence of the peril lent a veritable eloquence, put to work all protestations and all promises. Forewarned as he was, Edward Edmond could not believe that she was not speaking in good faith.

"Let me escape!" she repeated, in an imploring voice. What's to stop you restoring the wall to the same state once I'm out? Slug won't notice anything. I'll find some place to hide in the ruined village until we can run away."

That final argument completed the Irishman's persuasion.

"Well, all right!" he muttered. "Too bad! I'll risk everything to gain everything. But this time, at least, don't betray me! You know that you can do anything you want with me."

He went down to the crypt to fetch the iron lever. In a few minutes, he had increased the size of the opening sufficiently for Dorypha to crawl through it and out of her cell.

"Oh, what joy to be free!" she exclaimed, stretching hr limbs.

"Yes," said Edward Edmond, anxiously. "But go down quickly and hide in the ruins of the village. I have to hurry up and repair the wall before Slug gets back."

Dorypha hastened to obey. For the moment, she was acting in good faith.

Scarcely had she gone down four steps of the stairway, however, than she perceived through a loophole, a hundred yards away, a troop of men with rifles on their shoulders heading toward the feverish tower. Among them, she seemed to recognize Lord Burydan, and—which brought her emotion to a peak—Pierre Gilkin himself.

She felt a shock to her heart so violent that she almost fainted. That only lasted a moment. With an irresistible surge, she leapt down the remaining steps in order to run as quickly as possible toward her friends.

She had counted without the Irishman. He too had recognized, at a glance, Lord Burydan, Oscar and Pierre Gilkin. He perceived, furiously, that it was for the benefit of others that he had risked so much. He overtook the gypsy and forced her back up the steps.

"You shan't go with them!" he cried, foaming with rage. "You'll stay with me or I'll kill you!"

Recklessly, Dorypha ran up to the topmost platform of the tower. She knew that her friends would be able to see her there, and she set about uttering loud cries and waving her arms to attract their attention.

Edward Edmond, overcome by exasperation and fury, ran after the gypsy, with his revolver in his hand, and fired at her, at almost point blank range.

Ducking rapidly, Dorypha avoided the bullet, and, remembering her old métier, deftly kicked the weapon out of the Irishman's hand.

The later fell upon her, his hands open, in order to strangle her.

An atrocious struggle began.

Pierre Gilkin, who was marching at the head of the little troop, saw that scene from a distance. Realizing the peril that Dorypha was in, he started running as fast as he could in order to go to her rescue, without waiting for his friends.

Edward Edmond had seized Dorypha by the throat, but she bit him so cruelly that that he had to let go and jump backwards. In that abrupt movement he forgot completely where he was; his heels collided with the stone balustrade; he lost his equilibrium, and fell head first into empty space.

All that had happened so rapidly that the gypsy wondered at first how she had been able to hurl the robust Irishman from the top of the tower.

Then, she felt a kind of vertigo. After the desperate effort she had just made, and the battle she had fought, her weakness abruptly returned, worse than before. She felt that she no longer had the strength of a little child. It was slowly and painfully that she began to go down the stairway.

She was about to reach the first floor when a terrible apparition barred her way.

Slug, his pipe between his teeth, was advancing toward her, his expression mocking, with a Browning in his hand.

"Aha!" he said. "It seems that when the cat's away, the mice dance! Truly, that Irishman's an imbecile. I can't go away for an hour without him doing something stupid."

Dorypha had gone as pale as a bedsheet. All her blood flowed back to her heart.

Then, at the moment when Slug extended his hand toward her, a shot rang out.

The bandit fell to the floor, his shoulder shattered..

Behind him, still holding his smoking gun in his hand, Dorypha saw Pierre Gilkin with his arm extended.

She leapt over the bloody body of the old tramp and plastered herself passionately against the spouse that she had believed to be dead, and whom she had rediscovered so miraculously.

They both considered one another delightedly, so emotional that they could not speak at first.

"Hw pale you are, my poor Dorypha!" said Pierre Gilkin, finally. "It's true then, what was on the tin crucifix—that the wretches had walled you up alive?"

"Yes…come and see!"

Dorypha dew her husband into the first room. She showed him the gaping opening through which she had been able to escape.

"Oh, it's like that, is it?" cried Pierre Gilkin, trembling with hatred and anger. "Well, you'll see!"

"What are you going to do?"

"Something that will amuse you. Come with me, and you'll see."

The Belgian went back to the place where he had left Slug. He tied up the injured man's hands and feet with the bandit's own red belt. Then, with Dorypha's help, he took the old tramp, who was cursing them with all his might, into the first room.

"I understand!" cried Dorypha, clapping her hands. "I wouldn't have thought of that!"

"Good. I was about to forget something. It's necessary to gag him, for Lord Burydan and his friends are close behind me, and won't take long to get here—and I don't want them to free the bandit, even to put him in prison."

"You're right. Hurry up."

In spite of his somersaults, Slug was shoved head first through the hole in the wall. The stones were put back in place as well as could be contrived, and Dorypha hid the traces of the work by heaping up a large quantity of rushes there. She and her husband promised one another to return the following day and complete the work of vengeance. Wounded as he was, Slug would not be able to escape before then.

Pierre Gilkin and Dorypha had scarcely finished with their prisoner than Lord Burydan and his friends came into the ruins in their turn.

Dorypha was warmly congratulated on her escape. Then the eccentric asked her some questions. Thanks to the gypsy, it did not take him long to clear up the mystery that had intrigued him so much.

"It's not surprising," the young woman said, "that you didn't find anything when you came. There's a crypt under the church, and that's where the bandits hid their food, their baggage and all their equipment."

"It's absolutely necessary that I visit that crypt," Lord Burydan declared. "If I'm not mistaken in my suppositions, the discovery I've just made will permit me to save thousands of lives."

Two of the black men were summoned and, with the aid of the iron lever, had no difficulty raising the stone that covered the entrance to the stairway leading to the crypt. There were all kinds of objects there.

Lord Burydan immediately spotted a large crate on which he noticed the address of a supplier of scientific and optical apparatus. The crate contained a huge acetylene lamp and colored glass lenses: in brief, everything that Slug had used to change the belfry of the feverish tower into a lighthouse'

"I now know," said Lord Burydan gravely, "how the successive disasters to the Lightning Steamship Company's ships were provoked. The keepers of the lighthouse at the entrance to the bay are certainly affiliates of the Red Hand. Now I have the proof of it! So, on stormy nights, when they were aware of the presence of a steamer in the vicinity, they put out their light and Slug lit his. The captains, misled by the change, steered on to the reefs, thinking that they were heading for the river estuary, where they would have found a haven from the tempest. They perished miserably."

"It only remains to know," said Oscar, "who the people are who have an interest in ruining the Lightning Steamship Company."

Lord Burydan did not reply to that observation. He had just perceived some large bottles, which, according to their labels, must have contained microbial cultures. That was a flash of enlightenment for him. He suddenly understood what was responsible for the recrudescence of contagious maladies that had been raging for weeks.

The apparatus and the bottles were carefully placed in the crates and the blacks were charged with transporting them to Mr. Bombridge's house.

That same evening, Lord Burydan wrote Fred Jorgell a long letter of explanation.

The next day, the Tampa police picked up the keepers of the Oyster Bay lighthouse.

Pierre Gilkin and Dorypha kept the secret of their vengeance jealously. No one ever found out what had become of Slug.

17. THE MADMAN OF THE BLUE HOUSE

I. The Choice of a Son-in-Law

Mr. Bombridge, famous throughout America for the near-genius with which he had organized the intensive production of edible snails, had brought together a few friends in the superb property he owned in Florida, a few miles from the town of Tampa.

Among his guests were Lord Burydan, famous for his eccentric adventures; the prestidigitator Matalobos; the honorable James Rollan, the owner of a shoe-retailing business; and a young Frenchman, Oscar Tournesol, who was attached to the laboratory of the illustrious naturalist Prosper Bondonnat. The three last-named individuals had announced their candidature some time before for the hand and the millions of Regina Bombridge, but thus far, it had been impossible to say which of the three had the greatest change of success.

Miss Regina, it was said, was very fond of Oscar Tournesol. On the other hand, Matalobos was an old friend of Mr. Bombridge, who held him in high esteem. As for James Rollan, his millions, the distinction of his manners and his perfect elegance made him a redoubtable competitor for his two rivals.

After long hesitation, Mr. Bombridge had finally declared that at the end of the great feast given in honor of the suitors, he would announce the name of the fortunate mortal called to become his son-in-law.

That singular conduct had attracted a few courteous observations on the part of James Rollan.

"You've doubtless made your choice?" the distinguished gentleman had enquired.

"That might well be the case," Mr. Bombridge had replied.

"Then why not make it known immediately? There's a certain cruelty in putting our patience to the proof any longer."

"Let me be; I have my own ideas on that subject."

James Rollan had not been able to get any more out of Mr. Bombridge. In spite of all his solicitations, that latter had remained locked in an impenetrable discretion.

The meal was worthy of the hospitable reputation of the master's house. On the printed menu, truffled green turtle liver was juxtaposed with Mexican crayfish, Florida pheasant and one of the delightful iguana lizards common in Central America, which was served with a Carib sauce. Let us also cite, among the gastronomic curiosities, tender and savory okra, and palm cabbage. Mr. Bombridge's cook had been careful not to forget a dish of escargots, expertly grilled and served with a sauce of which Madeira, of the celebrated Barnum brand, formed the principal element.

The guests took their places around the table ornamented with magnificent flowers. Regina, whose beauty was brought out by a brightly colored dress of Indian lawn, was seated in the place of honor between her father and Lord Burydan. She seemed to be in a very good mood and quite cheerful, but deep down she was troubled, and from time to time she darted covert glances in Oscar's direction that were anxious, almost consternated.

Mr. Bombridge's guests had just savored the oyster soup—which is, so to speak, the foundation of Yankee cuisine, and which no serious meal is without—when Lord Burydan took a letter out of his pocket that he had just received, and gave it to Oscar to read.

After scanning it, the latter smiled at Regina, and also stared at James Rollan with a fixity that seemed to the honorable gentleman to be in rather poor taste. That rapid incident passed almost unperceived, however, and the most cordial gaiety soon reigned among the guests.

First, they drank a toast to Miss Regina, then to her father, and then, by turns, to the health of everyone present. The black servants had difficulty uncorking the bottles of extra-dry fast enough, and replacing them with others. The enthusiasm had arrived at its peak. Now, everyone was toasting on his own account, without worrying about his neighbors.

"To the father of the escargot industry!" cried the prestidigitator, in a slightly hoarse voice.

"To his charming daughter!" said Oscar Tournesol, for at least the fourth time.

"To His Majesty the King of England!"

"To the illustrious Prosper Bondonnat!"

"To France!"

"To America!"

That joyous racket was suddenly interrupted by the arrival of a black servant, old Jupiter, who seemed terrified. "Master!" he cried. "Come quickly!"

"You're annoying me," replied Mr. Bombridge. "I've forbidden you, once and for all, to disturb me when I'm with my friends."

"To the door, Jupiter!" cried the assembly, with one voice. "Leave serious business until tomorrow!"

The black man seemed unintimidated by this poor welcome. "Master," he repeated insistently, "Come quickly. It's very serious. You're wanted on the telephone."

"Well, let them call back. I'm not to be disturbed!"

"Master," replied old Jupiter, stubbornly, "it's the director of your South Carolina branch."

"What does he want?"

"A terrible catastrophe has occurred. I can't explain..."

"All right," said Mr. Bombridge, getting up with an irritate expression. "It'll have to be me that gives in!" Turning to his guests, he said: "Gentlemen, I beg you to excuse me; I'll be back in a minute. But don't worry—I'm sure it's nothing serious."

Mr. Bombridge went out, and the guests looked at one another silently. Their gaiety had vanished as if by magic. The word "catastrophe," pronounced by Jupiter, rendered the most dazed anxious, and everyone waited impatiently for the master of the house to return—but the latter's absence was prolonged far beyond what would have been necessary for a simple telephonic communication.

Very anxious, Regina was about to go in search of her father when the latter reappeared. His expression was distraught; his head was bowed like that of a man overwhelmed.

"What's the matter, my dear friend?" asked the conjurer, in a tone full of solicitude. "I hope that you haven't suffered any misfortune."

"Gentlemen," said Mr. Bombridge, with impressive simplicity, "Jupiter wasn't exaggerating when he pronounced the word *catastrophe* just now. I'm completely ruined."

That declaration produced a profound impression among the guests, and it was In the midst of the most religious attention that Mr. Bombridge continued.

"You're not unaware that I possess an establishment in South Carolina as large as the one in Florida. That's where I bought together three million subjects destined for export, which I was causing to fast until they sealed themselves naturally. I've already, explained to you, haven't I, that in order to be transported over long distances, my mollusks need to be sealed?"

"Well?" said Regina, impatiently.

"As usual, the animals had been shut in three greenhouses specially constructed for that purpose, each of which can contain a million of them. Last night, a cyclone ravaged the entire region of South Carolina. The glass in my greenhouses was entirely destroyed; a diluvian rain immediately following the passage of the cyclone restored all the vivacity to the escargots and, alas, all their appetite."

"I deduce," said Lord Burydan, "that they must have escaped and committed a certain amount of damage in the vicinity."

"A certain amount of damage!" cried Mr. Bombridge, tearing his hair. "You don't know, my lord, what hungry escargots are capable of, especially when there are three million of them! You have, however, seen with what rapidity, even when they're not famished, they can make an entire trainload of forage disappear.

"By virtue of one of those misfortunes that only happen to me, the neighboring property belongs to the celebrated horticulturalist Brigmann, who specializes in the production of orchids and early vegetables. The fugitives fell upon his cultures and consumed the plants, herbs and flowers right down to the roots. The disaster was consummated in a matter of hours, at a cost of millions of dollars. When I've compensated Mr. Brigmann, as I'm obliged to do, I'll hardly have enough left to live on."

A deathly silence greeted this fatal news. The guests looked at one another, consternation painted on their faces.

"Gentlemen," Mr. Bombridge continued, "it's obviously a misfortune, a great misfortune...but it mustn't prevent us from dining. It was very impolite on my part to importune you with the tale of my misfortunes..."

Everyone protested. Everyone attempted to console Mr. Bombridge, telling him that the disaster might not be as great as announced. Beneath those words, however, embarrassment and vexation was detectable, and it was in the midst of the most painful constraint that the meal continued that had begun so cheerfully.

In spite of the exquisite and precious wines, no one was any longer hungry or thirsty.

Regina maintained an imperturbable silence. Nevertheless, she was visibly making considerable efforts not to weep, and everyone wondered with a sincere pity what the young woman must be feeling. Was she not the first victim of the catastrophe, and the most cruelly afflicted? Everyone understood how false the situation was for Regina and her suitors, and everyone was expecting the inevitable denouement.

It was Mr. Bombridge himself who took responsibility for bringing it about.

"Gentlemen," he said, turning to the suitors, "it's understood, is it not, that all three of you are released from your promises? Miss Regina is now merely the heiress of a former clown, a ruined man who can no longer give her the most modest dowry..."

Matalobos raised his yes hypocritically to the heavens. "Alas," he said, "how unfortunate it is that I am not myself favored with a fortune. It would have been a joy for me to share everything I have with my old friend Bombridge...but alas, I'm poor, very poor...

"It's very painful for me to renounce Miss Regina's hand...it is, however, my duty to do so, since I not have the fortune that would permit me to create for her an existence worthy of her, or to assure her of the necessary comfort..."

"Mr. Bombridge's ruination dies not alter my intentions in the slightest," Oscar declared. "I loved Miss Regina before she was rich, I still love her just as much, and if such a sentiment were not egotistical on my part, I would even applaud an event that puts us on an equal footing with regard to fortune."

Regina thanked Oscar with her gaze and a smile. Mr. Bombridge declared in a sulky tone that, now he no longer had a dowry to give his daughter, he no longer wanted her to marry.

There was only James Rollan who had not yet said anything, and the distinguished gentleman was visibly very embarrassed. In spite of Regina's beauty, he was not at all disposed to take a wife who would not bring a single dollar to the conjugal association. On the other hand, he thought that Matalobos had revealed the foundations of his thinking a trifle too crudely; he, James Rollan, determined to act as a veritable man of the world.

"It seems to me," he said with a smile, "that this is hardly the time to talk about marriage. Let us leave Mr. and Miss Bombridge to recover from this rude shock, and accustom themselves to a change of fortune that might, after all, not be irrevocable." He added Jesuitically, putting his hand on his heart: "As regards myself, nothing could change my sentiments in Miss Regina's regard; they have never changed, and never will."

On hearing that ambiguous declaration, Oscar and Lord Burydan exchanged a rapid glance.

"I fear," said the eccentric, suddenly, "that Mr.—let's say Mr. James Rollan, since that's the pseudonym he has presented—will shortly have preoccupations sufficiently serious to be obliged to postpone any marriage plans indefinitely."

James Rollan had suddenly gone very pale, and then very red. He darted an instinctive glance in the direction of the window.

"Permit me to ask, my lord," he said, in an ill-assured voice, "why you have employed the word 'pseudonym' in my regard?"

"Because," the eccentric replied, tranquilly, "where I met you previously, you were known simply as Ezechias Palmer, and you were the director of an establishment in which the afflicted were able to see the soul of people dear to them appear."

Palmer leapt from his chair as if he had been suddenly bitten by a snake.

"When I met you," Oscar said in his turn, "you were the director of a sanitarium, and if I remember correctly, you nourished your inmates rather poorly."

Mr. Palmer, who was endowed with a redoubtable aplomb, had already had time to collect himself.

"I cannot contradict Lord Burydan," he said, with an ironic politeness. "My true name is indeed Ezechias Palmer. But since when, in free America, has it been a crime to adopt a pseudonym for business purposes? I have directed a madhouse, and a Spiritualist Institute. Where is the harm in that? Not everyone is capable of doing as much." He added, with a Mephistophelean smile addressed to Lord Burydan and Oscar: "It's certainly easier for anyone to have himself locked up as a madman than to run a lunatic asylum. In sum, at the present moment, thanks to my intelligence and energy, I'm at the head of a superb business, and I can cite the highest references as to my honorability."

Lord Burydan marveled at the man's aplomb. "Mr. Palmer," he replied. "It's certainly not to Police Headquarters that it's necessary to go to obtain sound information on your account. And I have good reason to believe that the 'superb business' that you direct is going bankrupt in a future that appears to me to be very imminent."

"Milord," replied Mr. Palmer, with perfect self-composure, "I scorn insinuations of that sort."

"They're not insinuations, alas," said the eccentric, taking from his pocket the letter he had read at the commencement of the meal. "I know from a reliable source that hundreds of your clients have formed a syndicate to sue you for fraud..."

"Lies! Slanders!" protested Mr. Palmer.

"I very much fear," said Mr. Bombridge, in his turn, taking a copy of the New York *Herald* from his pocket, "that milord is right." And he pointed out an article in the paper, circled in red ink. "My word yes," he added. "That's extraordinary. It says here that a certain Palmer, alias James Rollan, former jockey, former director of a sanitarium and former spiritualist, is being actively sought by the police. Several detectives have been launched in his pursuit, and his arrest is merely a matter of hours."

Palmer was a tragic sight. "It's all lies!" he stammered, weakly.

"Listen to me carefully, Mr. Palmer," Bombridge went on. "I've received you under my roof. I have no intention of playing the role of informer and handing you over to the police. In your own interest, however, I think that the best advice I can give you is not to extend your stay here too long."

Perceiving that there was no immediate threat to his liberty, Palmer had regained all his self-control and aplomb. "That's excellent advice you're giving me, Mr. Bombridge," he replied. "I'll leave for Tampa right away, where I'll take the express to New York. My presence there is necessary to defeat the machinations of my competitors. As for the newspapers that have defamed me by affirming that a complaint has been made against me, I shall launch a lawsuit and demand a hundred thousand dollars in damages and compensation. *Au revoir*, gentlemen. *Au revoir*, Miss Regina. I'm sure that you haven't believe a word of all these infamies that have been alleged against me. You will soon have news of me. Oh, certainly, it costs me dearly to leave you at a moment when you're undergoing such a cruel ordeal!"

Mr. Bombridge, who had risen from the table at the same time as Palmer, left the dining room, but came back almost immediately.

"Have no fear regarding Regina's fate," he said. "I'm happy to tell you, as Jupiter has just informed me, that the telephone message announcing my ruination was the work of a practical joker. Goodbye, Mr.

Palmer. I'll have the buggy harnessed. Jupiter will take you to Tampa station."

This time Palmer understood clearly that he was being mocked. Incapable of conserving his mask of politeness any longer, he left, slamming the doors, after having darted a furious glance at Lord Burydan and Oscar.

Matabolos was scarcely less put out. He too was exasperated by having fallen head first into the trap that the mischievous Bombridge had set for him.

As for Regina she was having great difficulty suppressing her desire to laugh.

That attitude put the lid on Matabolos' fury. He rose to his feet in his turn, stammering that he was expected in New York on urgent business, and that he too would take advantage of the buggy to go to Tampa station.

"Good riddance!" said Bombridge, when the conjurer had turned on his heel. "I don't like schemers."

Regina had thrown her arms around him affectionately. "Tell me, Father," she murmured, with a smile, "Are you going to continue to drive away my lovers like this?"

"Don't complain, since I'm leaving you the best of all." And he added, in a grave tone: "Oscar, you have my permission to kiss your fiancée."

The two young people fell into one another's arms.

"It's curious," murmured Lord Burydan, "but I foresaw this denouement. I even took the precaution of bringing one of those baubles that it's customary to offer young women in such cases. Delving into his pocket with an affected negligence, he drew out a small jewelry-box, which he handed to Regina.

She opened it impatiently, but closed it again almost immediately, dazzled. The box contained an engagement ring ornamented with a large diamond.

Lord Burydan was thanked warmly; then Mr. Bombridge filled the glasses again and declared: "Now that we're rid of the spoilsports, we can drink a toast to the health of the two lovers. Well, Milord, what do you think of my stratagem? If I hadn't made those two fellows believe that I was ruined, poor Regina might perhaps be going to marry one of them."

"No!" cried the young woman, swiftly. "I had promised Oscar to be his wife, and I would have kept my word!"

The party did not break up until late in the evening.

It had been agreed that the marriage of Regina and Oscar would take place as soon as possible.

II. An Abduction

The day after that memorable engagement dinner, Mr. Bombridge got up early, as was his custom, to take a stroll under the large trees before the ardent sun had caused the dew to evaporate entirely, in the brief and charming interval that follows sunrise in the tropics. He was astonished to find that Lord Burydan was ahead of him. The eccentric was in the process of talking to the boy who came from Tampa every morning on horseback to bring the mail.

"Well, Milord, is there any news?" asked Mr. Bombridge, after having asked after his guest's health.

"To my great regret, I shall be obliged to leave you," Lord Burydan replied.

"Not today, I hope?"

"Today, in fact. I've just learned that my yacht *Ariel* arrived in Tampa yesterday, where it is anchored in the bay. It will return to sea as soon as I'm aboard."

"That's very annoying," murmured Bombridge, seemingly put out. "I'd hoped that you'd be present at Regina's marriage to your friend Oscar."

"That was certainly my intention, and perhaps I shall be able to be there." Changing his tone abruptly, he went on: "By the way, would you like to take advantage of my yacht for an excursion at sea? I was planning a charming excursion for you just now."

"Of which the itinerary…?"

"Consisted of going along the coast as far as Oyster Bay, or even, if you have the time, going around the Florida peninsula as far as Port St. Lucie, from which you can return to Florida by rail."

"I won't say no," said Mr. Bombridge, slightly hesitantly. "I don't know that part of the coast very well."

"The supervision of your establishment," Lord Burydan went on, "doesn't require your presence so imperiously that you can't absent yourself for two or three days?"

"It's not that. The organization of my snail farms is such that I could go away for two or three months. All the managers and overseers I'm selected are trustworthy men."

"In that case, it's agreed!" exclaimed the eccentric, joyfully. "I'll tell Oscar and Regina. I'm sure they'll be delighted with the little voyage."

The necessary preparations were rapidly made, and two hours later, a buggy deposited the four tourists on the quays of the port of Tampa, where they perceived the gracious silhouette of the *Ariel* anchored just outside the harbor, and whose funnels were already releasing torrents of black smoke.

Oscar and Regina furtively squeezed one another's hands. At the sight of the yacht they had both experienced the same charming emotion; they recalled the long crossing that they had made together from Vancouver to the Island of Hanged Men, and could not forget that it was in the course of that journey that they had made the mutual confession of their love for the first time. It was with a genuine pleasure that they climbed aboard the *Ariel*.

They had scarcely set foot on the deck of the yacht, closely followed by Mr. Bombridge and Lord Burydan, than a middle-aged gentleman came to met them. He was accompanied by an old Indian who emitted a cry of joy at the sight of Oscar.

"Hello, my dear old Kloum!" said the young man. "Bonjour, Monsieur Agénor." Not without pride, he added: "May I introduce my fiancée, Miss Regina!"

While the blushing young woman received the compliments of the poet Agénor Marmousier and the Indian, Lord Burydan conversed with the captain.

"Do we have enough coal?" he asked.

"The bunkers are full, Milord."

"And provisions?"

"I've embarked all the best fresh food we could find in Tampa; with the provisions we have aboard we could almost go around the world."

"That's good, Captain. I don't see any reason why we shouldn't leave, then?"

"The boilers are lit; we're about to raise anchor. We'll be under way in a quarter of an hour."

After giving orders that were carried out with an entirely military rapidity and precision, Lord Burydan only occupied himself with his guests. A large drill tent had been set up in the aft section of the yacht. Everyone took their places in light and comfortable bamboo chairs, and prepared to admire the beautiful landscapes that were about to succeed one another uninterruptedly until the end of the excursion.

The anchors had already been raised; the engineer stimulated his fires, and the town of Tampa, with its white houses set against a bright blue sky, its palm trees and somnolent little port, began to decrease on the horizon.

The coast, deeply indented, spread out in all its wild majesty, with its reefs and its bays bordered by old mangroves, whose roots extended to bathe in the sea. At rare intervals on the deserted shore they perceived a hut covered in palm leaves or the boat of a negro pearl-fisherman.

"Poor black men," murmured Regina. "I feel sorry for them." She pointed with a fearful gesture at three sharks that were frolicking in the wake of the yacht, patiently following it in the hope that they would be thrown something on which to feed.

"The blacks aren't as fearful of sharks as you think," said Lord Burydan. "They're accustomed to that fishing from infancy, and they're all armed with sharp cutlasses, with the aid of which they're well able to defend themselves."

"What are those ruins?" Agénor suddenly interjected. "How desolate the landscape seems!"

The *Ariel* was, at that moment, passing a region of more sinister appearance; the shore was strewn with an assortment of broken rocks that rendered it unapproachable. Behind the ribbon of reefs was a marshy coast in the midst of which stood a bell-tower surrounded by ruined houses.

"That's the feverish tower," said Lord Burydan gravely to his friend Agénor, drawing him slightly to one side. "This is the very coast on which several of the Lightning Steamship Company's ships perished."

"I know from your last letter that you connected that investigation brilliantly and rapidly. You're still certain that it was the Red Hand who caused the shipwrecks?"

"Absolutely. You'll understand how it happened. You see that little white lighthouse about ten miles to the south? It's situated at the entrance to Oyster Bay, which serves as a haven for ships during storms. The keepers of the lighthouse, presently under lock and key, were affiliated to the Red Hand. When one of Fred Jorgell's steamers left New Orleans, its departure was signaled to the wreckers. In this season, storms are frequent and terrible. What would happen? The steamer's captain, thinking to take refuge in Oyster Bay, steered straight for the light identified on his chart. But the light was no longer in the same place; the lighthouse-keepers had extinguished their beam, and another was shining from the top of the feverish tower we can see from here. The steamer was infallibly drawn to break up on the rocks."

"Those are very serious facts," said Agénor, pensively. "Only three people could have an interest in sinking Fred Jorgell's steamers."

"I'll wager that you've had the same idea as me."

"I don't know, but the ruination of the Lightning Steamship Company can only interest its financial rivals—which is to say, Joe Dorgan and Cornelius and Fritz Kramm."

"That's what I told myself. And do you know that it was the same bandits that pillaged the hacienda of San Bernardino and almost killed Pierre Gilkin who were drawing the steamers on to the rocks?"

"That's extraordinary!"

"One of them," said Lord Burydan, "was none other than the Slug who played the role of captain of the *Revenge* so well, and who somehow slipped through our fingers on the Island of Hanged Men."

"Did you catch him?"

"No, he escaped again, but he must have met the same fate as his accomplice Edward Edmond, whose skeleton was found, picked clean by the red ants and reptiles of the swamp.

Lord Burydan then recounted, in detail, how Dorypha had been saved, and told him that the gypsy and her husband, both seriously ill as a result of privations and injuries, were presently being cared for in an isolated pavilion in the grounds of Mr. Bombridge's house.

In his turn, Agénor brought Lord Burydan up to date with Fred Jorgell's plans. The latter was proposing to buy the immense marsh surrounding the feverish tower and to dig canals that would transform the stagnant pools into running water and to sanitize the accursed region with eucalyptus plantations, poplars and fields of a species of potato of Brazilian origin, *Solanum commersonii*, which grows admirably in damp soil.[9] Before then, the mosquitoes would be destroyed by means of petrolage and the reptiles exterminated with the aid of predatory snakes

---

[9] Le Rouge probably derived this information from Ernest Roze's *Histoire de la pomme de terre* (1898), which includes a detailed description of the species in question (the South American potato vine), praising its resistance to disease and its productive employment in breeding programs for the genetic amelioration of commercial potato crops.

inoffensive to humans, such as the mussurana,[10] which can rid an entire region of the venomous animals it contains in a short time.

This project, which Fred Jorgell would put into execution as soon as he was free of some more immediate concerns, would be completed by the construction of a lighthouse for which the feverish tower would furnish the materials, and by the destruction of the reefs with the aid of dynamite.

While Lord Burydan and Agénor were engaged in this conversation the Ariel was drawing away at full steam from the dangerous region, and the feverish tower soon disappeared in the distance.

The landscape had changed completely. Forests of tall palm trees, mahogany and cedars undulated as far as the eye could see; the beaches were covered in fine glittering sand, and pretty fishing villages were reflected indolently in the blue water.

They ate lunch on deck. Regina, her appetite excited by the lively sea air, did honor to the on-board cuisine, which lost nothing by comparison with that served to her at the paternal villa.

In the afternoon they rounded Cape Sable and skirted the little islands with which the Florida channel is strewn.

In the evening, they all returned to their cabins. As he wished Lord Burydan goodnight, Mr. Bombridge asked Lord Burydan when they would reach Port St. Lucie.

"Tomorrow, no doubt," the eccentric replied. They separated after exchanging a cordial handshake.

The next morning, Mr. Bombridge came up on deck early. He was surprised to see that the Florida coast had completely disappeared. In every direction there was nothing but the sky and the sea, immense and blue.

The "Escargot King"—as the newspapers were beginning to call him—was utterly amazed. He rubbed his eyes to make sure that he was really awake, and wondered anxiously where, once again, he might be the victim of some subtle machination of the bandits of the Red Hand.

---

[10] Some South American farmers kept the ophiophagic snakes known as mussuranas as pets, in order to keep their habitations clear of deadlier snakes like the pit viper, but it was not until the 1930s that the Brazilian government attempted a large-scale release of mussuranas in a major field-experiment in ecological engineering (it was not a great success) so Le Rouge was somewhat ahead of his time in setting out this plan.

He noticed with a certain anxiety that the *Ariel*, fitted with the new engines invented by Harry Dorgan, was traveling with the rapidity of an express train. No one, moreover, was on deck.

Increasingly anxious, he headed toward the bow, and, spotting a cabin boy, asked him if he could see the captain. The boy replied that the captain was always available, and took Mr. Bombridge to the officer's cabin.

With the most exquisite politeness, the latter gave his interlocutor to understand that he could not furnish any information with regard to the progress of the vessel, milord having commanded the greatest discretion in that regard.

"But I'm Lord Burydan's friend," Bombridge replied, choked by astonishment.

"Perhaps, then," said the captain, "he will have the pleasure of informing you himself. And look—there he is!" He pointed at Lord Burydan, who, clad in an elegant striped flannel suit and a vat Panama hat, was walking nonchalantly toward the stern.

Bombridge hastened to catch up with him.

The eccentric could not help smiling on seeing his passenger's discomfited expression. "Ah, my dear Bombridge!" he said. "You look as if you're going to a funeral."

"Well," the Escargot King replied, piteously, "You must admit there's good reason. I embarked yesterday for a brief excursion, and now I find myself in mid-Atlantic."

"It's true," replied Lord Burydan, coolly, "that we're presently on the edge of the Sargasso Sea."

"I was just wondering whether I might be the victim of some plot by the Red Hand."

"No," said Lord Burydan, laughing. "The only guilty party is me. I couldn't resist the pleasure of playing a trick on you, in my own fashion. Didn't you tell me, yesterday, that you could absent yourself for months without your interests suffering as a result?"

"Yes," the ex-clown retorted, discontentedly, "but it's still necessary for me to keep in touch with me people, to issue orders."

"Don't worry. The *Ariel* is equipped with wireless telegraphy apparatus. Everything has been anticipated, you se."

"But in the end, milord," Bombridge demanded, ready to become angry, "where are you taking me?"

"To Canada," the eccentric replied, with perfect composure.

The Escargot King was so astounded that at first, he could not say a word. Eventually, he murmured: "This is a practical joke, isn't it?"

"Nothing is more serious, I assure you."

"But what will my daughter and future son-in-law say? And to begin with, what am I going to do in Canada?"

"Don't worry. First of all, Regina and Oscar are in on the conspiracy..."

"That's very naughty of them."

"And you'll be the first to thank them for having brought you. Didn't you say that you wanted me to be present at Regina's marriage?"

"Yes, but..."

"Not only will I be present at that marriage, but you shall be present at mine. Know, my dear Bombridge, that I'm inviting you to my wedding, which will take place at the same time as that of Oscar and your daughter."

"I can see," said Bombridge who had rapidly come to a decision, "that there really is no need to be sorry. I ought to be grateful enough to you not to take umbrage at the joke..."

"Which was fundamentally well-intentioned. Besides which, they don't call me an eccentric for nothing."

Regina and Oscar who had been waiting for the conclusion of the explanation before appearing n deck, showed themselves then, laughing uproariously, and congratulated Lord Burydan on such a well-planned and well-executed abduction.

At that moment, a sailor brought the eccentric a marconigram that had just been received by the on-board apparatus.

"Well!" said the young aristocrat, after reading it. "That's new. Do you know who's just been found walled up in the rubble of the feverish tower? Slug himself—the famous Slug. An old black man whose hobby is searching for treasure perceived that a wall had been recently repaired. He excavated a hole, and discovered the bandit, still alive but in a parlous state."

"What has been done with him?"

"He's been taken to your house, but if he recovers, I'll give orders for him to be brought to Canada under escort. It's through him, I'm sure, that we can discover the ultimate chiefs of the Red Hand."

"Hmm. Will he be willing to talk?"

"It doesn't matter. I'll employ whatever means are necessary to achieve my goal. Until later—I want to attend to this matter myself; I attach great importance to that rogue's capture."

And Lord Burydan went precipitately to the cabin that accommodated the wireless telegraphy equipment, with the operation of which he was thoroughly familiar.

III. The Amnesiac of the Blue House

The Canadian spring manifests a vigor and a force that is not found in any other country in the world; the thick layer of snow and ice with which the country has been covered for many weeks melts in a matter of days. Suddenly reawakened, generous nature seems then to employ all her creative and fecund power in hastening to cover the ground anew, with a verdant décor. Then, as if by magic, the white, blue and pink violets bloom, along with orchids, sunflowers, tiger lilies and a thousand other flowers.

The majestic avenue of maples, black ash-trees and birches leading to Lord Astor Burydan's manor house near Winnipeg was beginning to take on an attractive appearance. Birds were fluttering joyously in the thickets covered with buds and new shoots. In the distance, a cheerful sun was rising over the blue roofs and gilded weathervanes of the house.

The morning was radiant, and Lord Burydan, who had only been married for a few weeks, prey to a pleasant reverie, was contemplating the young spring horizons when a heavy automobile, painted gray, whose construction was not at all suggestive of luxury, advanced slowly along the lordly avenue.

The driver was a man of colossal stature. Beneath his leather jacket enormous biceps could be seen swelling, and his shoulders, imposing in their breadth, immediately suggested the idea that the Hercules could easily have lifted the weight vehicle that he was steering.

At the sight of the vehicle the eccentric made an abrupt gesture, and was unable to suppress a shiver. His smiling face had suddenly become grave.

After traversing the main courtyard, where nothing remained of the sordid vestiges that Matthew Fless had left behind, the car stopped in front of the perron, now ornamented with two bronze nymphs and beautiful marble vases.

"Good day, my brave Goliath," said Lord Burydan, taking the giant's hand; the latter gratified him with a handshake capable of bending an iron bar. "The journey was uneventful?"

"Yes, Milord. Nothing remarkable occurred. Following your orders, some time before crossing the frontier, the prisoner was made to inhale the contents of the flask, which took effect immediately. We told the customs officers that we were escorting a man who was dangerously ill, and they didn't raise the slightest objection."

"Good. I thought it better to do things in that way."

"Where should we take our man?"

"I'll show you myself. But don't stay in front of the perron; I'd be desolate if Lady Burydan and her friends perceived that hideous villain's face."

Goliath climbed back into his seat, turned the car around skillfully, and took it into a smaller courtyard situated behind one of the wings of the manor. Then Goliath opened the rear door, which was exceptionally solid and locked with a key.

Two men got down from inside the vehicle. One was only a little less robust than Goliath; the other had his arm in a sling, and was pale and weak. The former was the swimmer Bob Horwett. He was still in the service of Harry Dorgan. The latter, at Lord Burydan's request, had entrusted him with the delicate mission of transporting Slug from Mr. Bombridge's villa to the manor that the eccentric owned on the shore of Lord Winnipeg.

The bandit maintained a grim silence, and although he seemed considerably debilitated, he raised his head proudly from time to time and darted a challenging glance at his enemies.

"I've made all the necessary arrangements," Lord Burydan explained, "to lodge this scoundrel in such a way that it will be impossible for him to escape. The windows of the first floor room that he'll occupy are fitted with iron bars as thick as a man's wrist; the oak door is armored and it opens into a room where one of you, either Goliath or Bob Horwett, will be permanently stationed."

"We'll work in three-hour shifts," said Bob Horwett.

"Arrange the matter as you please. The essential thing is that Slug is never without surveillance. If you need reinforcements..."

"No need," said Goliath. "The two of us are perfect adequate to the task. If the wretch makes any attempt to escape, I'll flatten him like a medlar." And the giant lifted his formidable fists, with which he made a game of smashing a coconut with a single blow or killing an ox with a well-judged punch to the head.

"I confide him to you," said Lord Burydan, handing Bob Horwett the keys to the first floor room. After consulting his watch, he added: "I'll leave you to it. If you need anything, don't hesitate to ask."

"In truth," said Goliath, "I could do with a bite to eat." He displayed a row of teeth that would have been a credit to a young shark.

"I believe," said Lord Burydan, "that it wouldn't be prudent to let you go for long without something to eat. But don't worry—you were expected, and your table is set upstairs. You'll see that you'll be quite content with Canadian cuisine."

Hastily quitting Slug and his guardians, Lord Burydan went through the entire length of the house and arrived at the perron, where Mr. Bombridge, his son-in-law Oscar, Agénor and he famous naturalist Prosper Bondonnat were already assembled.

"The ladies are holding us back!" exclaimed Bombridge, impatiently.

"Don't worry, Father!" cried a joyful voice.

Regina appeared on the threshold. She was closely followed by Lady Ellenor Burydan—the lady of the scabious flowers—and her friends Madame Andrée Paganot and Madame Fréderique Ravenel. Scintillating with beauty, radiant with health and happiness, the four young women were wearing simple but exquisite spring dresses. Monsieur Bondonnat contemplated them momentarily with affection.

"Mesdames," said Lord Burydan, I can announce the arrival at the manor of a distinguished guest---one of our old acquaintances."

"Who's that?" asked Frédérique, curiously.

"Captain Slug in person. The honorable gentleman has come to spend a short holiday with us, in order to recover from the consequences of a wound received in the service of the Red Hand."

"You're joking, milord," murmured Frédérique fearfully. "I wouldn't sleep peacefully if I knew that that execrable bandit was living under the same roof."

"Don't worry, beautiful lady. He's in a solidly-barred cell, and I've given him as guards the champion swimmer Bob Horwett and the giant Goliath, who can break chains and bend an iron bar between his index-finger and thumb as if it were a stick of marshmallow"

"Why are you still concerning yourself with those wretches, my dear Astor?" asked Lady Burydan, tenderly. "Aren't we happy?"

"Yes, my darling, you're right; we're very happy. But we'll only continue to be on condition that we triumph over the enemies who have done so much harm, to you, to me and to our friends. I've sworn to exterminate the Red Hand, and I shall!"

While these words were being exchanged, a superb mail-coach, harnessed to four Irish horses that the stable-hands were having difficulty restraining, came to a halt in front of the perron. Everyone installed themselves on the vehicle's banquettes. Lord Burydan took the reins. The rig set off like a train, while Oscar, putting the horn to his lips, woke up the sleeping echoes with joyful fanfares.

Regina was sitting next to Lady Ellenor, for a profound sympathy had developed between the great lady and the former circus rider. It was not without considerable sorrow that the lady of the scabious flowers was seeing Regina and her husband leave the manor house.

The mail-coach was going through a wood of wild cherries in full bloom and birches whose sap exhaled an aromatic scent.

"Look, Regina," said Ellenor. "You're leaving at a good time. The Canadian countryside is never more pleasant to behold."

"Believe me, milady, I'll never forget the happy days I've spent with you," Regina replied, "but we can't extend our holiday any further. My father can't neglect the enterprise he directs any longer. And as you know Lord Burydan has given my husband and Mr. Agénor important missions to fulfill in New York."

"But you'll come back?"

"Certainly. For your part, it's necessary not to forget that we're expecting you in Florida this winter. When your Canadian forests are covered with a thick layer of snow and ice, you'll be glad to find yourself in the shade of palm trees and orange trees, among the flowery arbors of our garden."

"I promise you once again that I shall come to see you."

"And so will we," said Andrée and Frédérique, with one voice, having followed the conversation distractedly.

While the four young women made plans for future holidays and excursions, the mail coach, devouring the distance, came into the city of Winnipeg, which it passed through like a gust of wind, and stopped in front of the railway station.

Everyone got down, and while the domestics registered the baggage, Regina said goodbye to her three friends. In the meantime, Lord Burydan and Monsieur Bondonnat gave Agénor and Oscar their final instructions.

"Above all," said Monsieur Bondonnat, "I beg you to send me the detailed reports that Police Headquarters must have regarding the manner in which the arrest of the murderer Baruch was carried out."

"Another document that will be indispensable to us," Lord Burydan interjected, "is as full a list as possible of the cures and official transformations effected by Dr. Cornelius."

"I'll do my best," Oscar replied, "to send you the relevant information."

"In any case," Agénor put in, "you doubtless know that Fred Jorgell has put numerous expert detectives on campaign, who will certainly discover new facts..."

The conversation was still going on when the train pulled into the station with a thunderous din. Mr. Bombridge, Regina, Oscar and Agénor bade their friends a final farewell and took their places in the luxury compartment that had been reserved for them.

The train was about to move off when Lord Burydan shouted to Mr. Bombridge, who was waving to him through one of the windows: "I forgot to ask you not to fail to send me news of Dorypha and her husband!"

Bombridge nodded his head in assent as the train pulled away.

Lady Ellenor and her two friends had a few purchases to make in Winnipeg; it was agreed that the domestics would take the mail-coach as far as the outskirts of the city, Lord Burydan and Monsieur Bondonnat having visits of their own to make.

While the three young women went around the shops, the eccentric and the old scientist headed for the residence of Mr. Pasquier, a lawyer of great integrity and a friend of Lord Burydan's, to whom a considerable part of his business affairs was entrusted. It was Mr. Pasquier who had helped Lord Burydan, after his internment in the Lunatic Asylum, to obtain the recognition of his rights and to expel the baronet Matthew Fless from his relative's estates, of which he had entered unduly into possession.

The Canadian lawyer gave his rich client the most cordial welcome, and introduced his visitors into the simple but comfortable study where he generally spent every morning.

"Well?" asked Lord Burydan, once the conventional polite remarks had been exchanged. "How is your boarder?"

Mr. Pasquier shook his head. "Mr. Clark's health is excellent," he murmured, "except in one respect; he's still aphasic, and I don't believe that he'll ever recover the power of speech."

"Who knows?" murmured Bondonnat, who had suddenly become pensive. "I've seen the most extraordinary cures. Science knows very little about these nervous maladies. Personally, I believe that we may still hope."

"Would you like to see the patient?" asked Pasquier.

"Yes," said Lord Burydan. "I'm sure that my visit will give him pleasure. In any case, I need to reach an agreement with him on certain matters."

"I think it might be better if I don't go with you," said Bondonnat.

"Indeed…"

"No need to show me the way," said the eccentric to Pasquier, who had risen to his feet. "I know the house."

Lord Burydan left the study, went through a beautiful garden in the French style, with pathways bordered by box-trees, and knocked on the door of an isolated lodge constructed some way behind the main building.

At his friend's request, Pasquier had agreed to surrender that part of the house to Mr. Clark—or, rather, to the billionaire William Dorgan.

A domestic specially assigned to the invalid's service introduced Lord Burydan into a luxurious reception room, where William Dorgan was already present.

Since the terrible catastrophe at the Rochester bridge, in which he had almost perished, the old man had changed considerably. His hair was now completely white, and his physiognomy, furrowed by wrinkles, was imprinted by the melancholy that one encounters in almost all of those who are deprived of speech.

William Dorgan had got to his feet hurriedly on seeing Lord Burydan, for whom he had a thoroughly paternal affection. The old man picked up his notepad and hastily scrawled: *Will my reclusion end soon? Are we nearing the conclusion?*

"Be patient a little longer," the eccentric replied. "You know that in the game I'm playing against the Red Hand, an imprudent move might have the gravest consequences. Indeed, I've come to see you before I make certain decisions…"

Have I not told you a hundred times, the billionaire wrote, *that I approve I advance of everything you do?*

"There are, however, matters about which I need to consult you."

A discussion began, and it was only after half an hour that Lord Burydan emerged from William Dorgan's residence. He seemed quite satisfied.

He rejoined Bondonnat in the lawyer's study, and the two of them, after exchanging a few polite words with Pasquier, took their leave of him and went to the location where the mail coach was waiting for them.

The three young women were already at the rendezvous and the domestics had just finished relieving them the various parcels they had acquired *en route*. They climbed back into the vehicle and set off at a rapid trot toward the manor.

Half way back, Lady Ellenor and her friends declared that they wanted to get out and go back to the house on foot. In the beautiful sunlight, through the countryside full of flowers, accompanied up by the songs of thousands of birds, it would be a charming stroll.

Lord Burydan gladly acceded to his wife's request. "Agreed," he said. "We'll dine together in an hour and a half. I'll make use of the time to go to the Blue House with Monsieur Bondonnat."

"With Monsieur Bondonnat?" repeated Frédérique, slightly surprised. The young woman knew that her father had always refused previously to go to the Blue House, presently inhabited by Noel Fless, who had been looking after the murderer Baruch since his escape from the Lunatic Asylum. Until today, the old man had experienced an insurmountable horror at the thought of being in the presence of the murderer of his friend, Monsieur de Maubreuil.

"Yes," said Lord Burydan. "Monsieur Bondonnat is accompanying me."

"It's necessary," said the old man, in a grave tone.

The three young women had dispersed into the undergrowth. For some time it was possible to see their bright dresses shining like huge flowers through the thickets that were not yet clad in foliage, and the crystalline notes of their joyful laughter could be heard in the limpid atmosphere.

Lord Burydan and Bondonnat were left alone on the platform of the mail coach; the domestics, who had taken the seats inside the vehicle could not hear them, so their conversation immediately took on a confidential complexion.

"William Dorgan is now aware," said Bondonnat, "that you've told me that he's still alive?"

"Yes, and he doesn't seem displeased, but he's very keen that you should be the only person who knows the secret."

"But shouldn't we inform Harry Dorgan and Isidora?"

"The father has strictly forbidden that. 'It's not yet time,' he said."

"Perhaps he's right, all things considered," murmured the old scientist.

There was a moment's silence. Nothing could be heard but the rumble of the torrent that was flowing to the left of the road, the sound of which was growing louder by the minute.

"That's the Roaring Stream you mentioned to me?" asked the old man.

"Yes; it's the watercourse that separates my land from Pasquier's. You'll soon see the pretty stone bridge I had constructed in place of the worm-eaten footbridge whose beams that old rogue Matthew Fless—justly nicknamed Baron Skinflint—had sawn through in order to drown me in the torrent. That way, he would have remained in sole possession of my house and estates."

"What's become of the old miser?"

"He's returned to his own estate, which is almost as big as mine. He has nothing about which to complain, believe me. I'm told that he's furious about my marriage."

"I can understand that."

"Let's not talk too loudly about Baron Skinflint." Pointing through the trees at the elegant mass of a chalet with balconies, and large overhanging roofs, sky-blue in color, Lord Burydan added: "That's the Blue House. That's where my cousin Noel Fless, Barn Skinflint's son, lives."

At that moment the mail coach was rolling along a side-road carpeted with grass, which zigzagged through the forest. Lord Burydan let the horses go at their own pace. Like Monsieur Bondonnat, when they went through the gateway of the Blue House, he experienced a profound emotion.

"I confess," said the scientist, "that I'll need all my courage to tolerate the presence of that wretch."

"Stay firm until the end. I've made you party to the strange conclusion at which, by virtue of a chain of reasoning and deduction, I've eventually arrived. It might well be that I'm right—and to arrive at that certainty, your judgment is absolutely necessary to me."

"Well, so be it," said Bondonnat, firmly. "We're here. I'm ready."

The domestics took the horses' reins. The aristocrat and his friend got down and were greeted, from the threshold of the house, by a robust and smiling young woman, who hastened to put down the child that she was in the process of breast-feeding, in order to greet the visitors.

Ophelia was blonde, with a delicately pink complexion and limpid blue eyes, which expressed tenderness and generosity. She found the means to be distinguished while offering a typically Canadian robust splendor of form.

"How are you, my dear cousin?" exclaimed Lord Burydan, depositing a kiss on Ophelia's rosy cheek.

"Very well, cousin. But to what do we owe the pleasure of your visit? You've been neglecting us, along with Mistress Ellenor and her friends. It's at least a week since we've seen you."

"We've been so busy! But we haven't forgotten you. Is Noel here?"

"Alas, no," replied Mrs. Fless. "He left early this morning to visit a lumberjack camp, and won't be back until this evening."

"Too bad! But his presence isn't absolutely necessary."

"What is it about?"

"This is my friend, Monsieur Bondonnat, a scientist whom I've brought expressly to examine our invalid."

"I doubt that anyone can cure him. The poor innocent is in the garden at present, where he takes great pleasure in weeding, and pruning the hedges. I'll fetch him."

In the meantime, Bondonnat had gone back to the mail-coach and had taken a long box out of the trunk of the vehicle. He rejoined Lord Burydan just as the escapee from the Lunatic Asylum was introduced, rather fearfully, to presence of the visitors. He was clad in a coarse overall. His physiognomy was delicate and distinguished, but his eyes retained a vague and bewildered expression.

Bondonnat examined him attentively for some time, and an exclamation suddenly escaped his lips. "This isn't Baruch! I don't recognize him! It's impossible that this is Monsieur de Marbreuil's murderer!"

"Watch," said Lord Burydan, in the old scientist's ear. He handed the young man a notebook and a pencil. "Write your name," he said to him.

Without hesitation, the young man wrote, quite legibly, the words *Joe Dorgan*.

"What do you think of that?" said Lord Burydan.

"It's frightful!" murmured the old man. "I daren't believe, as yet, that you're right. It's so implausible as to be almost crazy. Would you like me to examine the invalid with the aid of X-rays? Perhaps that way we'll be able to ascertain the truth."

"Oh, one moment more, if you please. This is a letter written by Joe Dorgan before he was captured by the tramps. Compare the two signatures."

"They're absolutely identical! You must be right!"

"Wait! I haven't finished. I'll order the poor fellow to write the name of Baruch Jorgell, the supposedly his own."

The amnesiac obeyed meekly, but it required a great deal of time and effort for him to write the two words, and the letters making it up were exactly similar to those of Joe Dorgan's signature.

"You understand," said the eccentric, "that there is no residue in the memory or the hand of that signature, which I'm now certain is not his."

"And you conclude?" asked Bondonnat, prey to a violent emotion.

"That the man standing before us isn't Baruch Jorgell. It can only be Joe Dorgan."

Bondonnat did not reply. He was reflecting. "In that case," said, abruptly, "the Joe Dorgan we know must be..."

"Baruch Jorgell, the murderer, miraculously transformed by Cornelius' diabolical science."

"It's almost impossible," murmured Bondonnat, hesitant and stupefied. "If Cornelius has been capable of realizing such a *tour de force*, he almost deserves to be pardoned."

"That's going a little too far. Before anything else, let's see what results you get from the examination by means of X-rays."

Bondonnat opened the box containing his apparatus and went into the dining room, accompanied by Lord Burydan, the amnesiac and Ophelia, whose curiosity had been keenly excited by the whole scene.

There were a few moments of silence while Bondonnat methodically set up the screen, the tubes and other accessories.

Scarcely had the apparatus been aimed than confused lines became gradually clearer on the white surface of the screen.

"Look!" said Bondonnat. "It's just as I thought. The patient has been treated by Dr. Garsuni's method. Look, one can clearly make out, under the epidermis, the masses of paraffinated Vaseline, with the aid of which the subject has, so to speak, been given a new face. You can also see, in some parts of the skeleton, the cushions and deformations that have resulted from the surgical operations. Now I can affirm, without the slightest hesitation, that we're in the presence of a fake Baruch, of a man whose face has been manipulated and retouched by a great surgeon, who has given him a physiognomy quite different from the one he possessed before. It remains to determine who the virtuoso is who is capable of obtaining such a marvelous result...”

“Do they not call Cornelius Kramm the sculptor of human flesh?” Lord Burydan replied, simply.

“My conviction is now complete. Cornelius is guilty, and Baruch—the real Baruch—is his accomplice.”

“What are your intentions, my dear Master?” asked Lord Burydan.

“It seems to me that the first thing o do is to return to this poor fellow the physiognomy that has been stolen from him.”

“Is that possible?”

“It’s not so very difficult, since I know the means that have been employed. From today onwards, the invalid will be subjected to energetic treatment. I’ll come to see him twice a day, and I’m sure that before long, he’ll have recovered the face that nature originally gave him.

“But can you also return his memory and his reason?”

“No, I don’t believe so. The operation that has been carried out on his brain has produced lesions such that the damage is irreparable...” The venerable scientist, prey to a slight impatience, broke off and exclaimed: “Damn it! Let’s not go too quickly. I’ll undertake to restore the man’s true physiognomy—that’s already something, it seems to me. After that...we’ll see.”

Holding her baby in her arms, Ophelia had followed the phases of that scene with an amazement mingled with respectful terror. The application of X-rays, which she was witnessing for the first time, appeared to her to be something marvelous and diabolical. Obedient to an irrational impulse, she had moved as far away from the strange apparatus that permitted the sight of what was happening inside the body.

Bondonnat read in her expression the impression that she was feeling, and could not help smiling. “Don’t think, Mistress,” he said, “that I’m a minion of the Devil. My boots, I beg you to believe, don’t contain cloven feet. I don’t employ any other magic than the knowledge—very incomplete, alas—of the laws of nature.”

Reassured by Monsieur Bondonnat’s words and the expression of serene bonhomie imprinted on his features, she said: “Will our innocent be cured, then?”

“We’ll do everything we can to achieve that. Here, let me have some paper and ink—I’ll write you a prescription that you’ll need to fill as soon as possible.”

The old man covered an entire sheet of paper with handwriting that was as neat and clear as if it were printed.

"But Noel's away," Ophelia objected, "and won't be back until this evening. I can't send him to Winnipeg until tomorrow."

Lord Burydan intervened. "Give me the prescription," he said. "I'll send a domestic to the city and have it filled out. He'll come back at top speed, and will be back in two hours.

Bondonnat had fallen silent again. He was attentively studying the young man with the rosy cheeks and vague expression, who had to be Joe Dorgan. He could not find in those features, whose expression as very gentle, any of the physiognomy, energetic to the point of cruelty, that was Baruch Jorgell's.

"I understand what has happened," he said to Lord Burydan. "The resemblance must have remained perfect while Cornelius had his subject in his hands, while he could hold back the effects of nature that were tending to destroy his work. For many months, the invalid has been out of the claws of the sculptor of human flesh. Nature has been able to resume, on the sly, as it were, her slow work of reconstruction. It's not yet Joe Dorgan that we have before our eyes, but it's already no longer Baruch Jorgell."

"It's up to you to complete nature's work," said Lord Burydan.

"I'll do everything possible to that end!" said the illustrious scientist, modestly.

The amnesiac seemed to have understood the meaning of that statement. A gleam of intelligence appeared in his extinct gaze. He stood up, came over to Monsieur Bondonnat and took him by the hand. "Won't you, sir," he stammered, in a dull voice, "do everything possible?"

"Why not, my friend?" said the old man, deeply moved.

"To heal me! Here! Here!"

And the amnesiac put his hand to his head with an urgent gesture, and then fled into the garden of the Blue House, uttering a savage howl.

IV. The Dramas of Fire

Along the border of the estates of Astor Burydan and Mr. Pasquier, for an extent of more than five miles, ran woods and fields belonging to the baronet Matthew Fless. In the middle of that estate, one of the largest in the vicinity of Winnipeg, stood a farmhouse solidly constructed of stone blocks, which had the appearance of a gentleman's dwelling.

It was there that the old miser had retreated when Lord Burydan's unwelcome return had forced him to abandon the latter's manor house.

Since the fatal day when he had been obliged no leave that princely residence, the old man's wrath had not cooled. He caused his creditors to expiate, by means of a thousand harassments, the bitter disillusionment that he had experienced.

Rising before dawn, he rode from farm to farm mounted on a wheezy mare that could have given Rosinante points in regard to thinness, which one might have thought a refugee from the knacker's yard.

The baronet had conserved the appearance familiar to us. As in the past, he resembled the picture of the Wandering Jew in our old *Images d'Épinal*. His beard was, however, a little longer, his face a little more wrinkled, and his vestments a little dirtier. His hair, which hung down over his shoulders, was, as before, protected by a hare-skin bonnet which bore some resemblance to a helmet, a beret and an Episcopal miter.

He had not ceased to wear his green dressing-gown, warmly lined with rabbit-skin and ingenious patched up with fragments of cloth in all the colors of the rainbow. His fingers were still as thin and crooked; his fingernails were as long as those of certain mandarins. His health, however remained excellent. His little dark eyes still sparkled, as keen as those of a blackbird behind his bushy eyebrows; and his appetite, maintained by the austere diet imposed on him by his avarice, seemed to increase instead of diminishing with age.

That morning, the baronet had got up even earlier than usual. His first concern, on leaping out of the settee with broken springs that served as his bed, was to concoct a refreshing soup with wild sorrel, which he had picked in a nearby clearing, and crusts of dry bread, kept from the previous day, which even a not-overly-fussy dog would have refused with scorn.

The miser swallowed this laxative soup to the last spoonful with delectation.

"Excellent!" he murmured, between his teeth. "In spring, the blood needs to be refreshed…and now I'm well-fed, let's hit the road! I'll go have lunch with my farmer Flambard, who only lives eight miles away…a mere stroll…and on the way, I'll see whether the barley and oats are thriving."

The baronet put on his hare-skin bonnet, picked up his holly-wood staff and set our briskly. His hamstrings were as sturdy and muscular as those of an old stag, so he marched with a rapidity that a professional runner would have envied.

He paused from time to time, making sure of the good progress of his numerous cereal crops, tore up the occasional weed, and set off again more forcefully.

Without suffering the slightest symptom fatigue, he covered the distance that separated his dwelling from Flambard's farm. He arrived just in time to sit down at table. A vast cauldron of cabbage soup was fuming, hanging from the pot-hook, exhaling a vapor that tickled the miser's nostrils agreeably.

The farmer, although discontented by the visit, could not avoid inviting the baronet to sit down at the communal table. The new guest astonished the farm-hands by his appetite, for, although Baron Skinflint was very sober at home, he was avid and even gluttonous when he ate out. Jokers claimed that, like a boa constrictor, he could eat enough for a fortnight.

Having devoured like an ogre and drunk like a Templar, the baronet collected the hundred dollars that was due to him from his tenant, and, well restored, set out for the farm of another of his debtors, who lived ten miles away.

He arrived there at nightfall, collected fifty dollars, and ate dinner.

Not a bad day, he thought, as he lengthened his stride in order got go back home. *I haven't spent too much today. Everything would be well but for these diabolical sabots, which seem to be visibly wearing away. I'll have to put some big nails in them one of these days. I've already picked up a dozen that will do the job perfectly.*

It was ten o'clock in the evening when the miser went through his kitchen door. He scarcely felt any fatigue, and in spite of the wear on his sabots, he was, in sum, delighted with his day.

He stuck a match cautiously and made use of it to light the extremity, sharpened in advance, of one of the resinous pine branches that one finds in peat-bogs. That luminary gave off an acrid and nauseating smoke but it had, in the eyes of Baron Skinflint, the inappreciable advantage of rendering unnecessary the employment of candles, oil and other expensive means of lighting.

By the light of his torch, the miser carefully reread his account-book. Then he went to lock his money in a special room, carefully sealed with locks and bolts. Finally, wearied by such a busy day, he threw himself down on his bed, after taking care to remove his sabots and his hare-skin bonnet.

He went to sleep almost immediately.

He had only closed his eyes for five minutes when someone knocked rudely on his door.

The baronet, as a man accustomed to alerts of that sort, leapt rapidly out of bed, armed himself with the large revolver he kept under his pillow and advanced bare-footed toward the door, on which someone was continuing to knock, ever more insistently.

"Who's there?" he growled. "Go away. This is no time to be waking honest folk." He punctuated his speech by cocking his weapon.

"It's me, Father," replied a strong, clear voice. "Your elder son. Quickly, open up. The wind's icy."

The miser has recognized the voice of his son, attached to the English embassy in New York, of whom he had not had any news for a week. By virtue of a residue of suspicion, he did not hasten to open the door. "Is it really you?" he said. "Say something else, so I can be sure of not being deceived."

"Father, I beg you, hurry up!" cried the visitor, impatiently. "The wind is pricking my ears like a thousand needles."

"Don't be so impatient! I believe it really is you. I'll open the door."

Slowly, the baronet drew the bolts and turned the key in the lock. To begin with, though, he only opened the door by a crack, while a solid chain maintained it ajar. Then, raising his resin torch with one hand and holding his revolver in the other, he made sure with a circumspect eye that it really was his elder son who was hammering on his door at this undue hour.

Finally, the chain fell. The door opened wide, and the baronet's elder son was able to come into the kitchen.

Tall and robust, he was wrapped up to the ears in a black fox-fur coat and coifed in an elegant traveling-cap. There was a complete dissimilarity of appearance and bearing between the son and the father; the former was as elegant as the later was dirty and neglected, but both their gazes shone with the same gleam of cupidity, and Fless the diplomat, setting aside the matter of age, resembled Fless the miser feature for feature.

"What are you doing here?" the baronet demanded of his son with surprise. "I wasn't expecting you. Are you on leave, then?"

"There's no longer any question of leave for me, Father," said the young man, agitatedly. "I've been sacked."

"Sacked!" cried the old man, shocked.

"Yes! And it's thanks to my cousin, Lord Burydan. He's used the highly-placed connections he has in England against me. I've been accused of gambling, of having mistresses and of being part of an association of bandits known as the Red Hand."

The miser was dazed by stupor and chagrin. He cherished his elder son in his own fashion. As much as he detested Noel Fless, Ophelia's husband, the inhabitant of the Blue House, he loved the diplomat. The latter had always been able to make his father believe that he was as "economical" as he was, and he had been artful enough to have his bother Noel entirely disinherited, to his own advantage.

"Is there any truth in these accusations?" the baronet asked, anxiously.

"Not a word. They're atrocious calumnies. Lord Burydan—who has just got married expressly to disinherit us—has never forgiven me for my part in his internment in the Lunatic Asylum, in the same way that he'll be eternally resentful of you, my dear father, for having entered a little too quickly into the possession of his estates when everyone thought that he was dead."

"Oh, the fine estates!" murmured the miser, with a sigh of regret. "The beautiful forests! The lovely wheat-fields! The excellent pasturage! To think that I've been robbed of all that! I received such a blow that I'll never recover from it."

The diplomat looked around the miserable fire-less kitchen, in which the provisions amounted in total to a hunk of black bread that looked as hard as a stone and must have been at least a week old, with a grimace of disgust. Fortunately, he had taken the precaution of dining in Winnipeg. "Lord Burydan is a bad relative," he said, after a momentary pause. "It's to him that I owe the loss of my employment and the accusation that weighs upon me."

"An accusation?" exclaimed he old man. "What do you mean?"

"Didn't I just tell you," the young man replied impatiently, "that it's been claimed that I belong to the Red Hand? It's better that you know the whole truth. A arrest-warrant has been issued against me, and I had to flee in haste..."

The old man sat down on a stool, prey to a veritable chagrin.

"But at least you're not guilty?" he murmured, anxiously.

"Lord Burydan is responsible for all of it!"

"You're not at risk of being arrested here?"

"They'd have to extradite me for that..."

His head in his hands, the old man remained plunged in sinister reflections for a few minutes. "Do you're reduced to expedients," he said, bitterly, "and you've come to ask me for money! Truly, I have no luck at all!"

"No," said the young man, in a somber voice. "I don't want anything. I haven't come to deprive you of the savings you've taken such trouble to amass..."

"I don't have a sou saved," the miser replied, automatically.

"Understood. But you'd be very glad, I'm sure, to recover possession of the manor house and the lands surrounding it?"

"What would I need to do for that?"

"Simply give me a free hand to act. I've vowed a mortal hatred against Lord Burydan. One of us has to die."

"But he's married!" murmured the miser, frightened by his son's bloody plans.

"His wife will suffer the same fate as him."

A tragic silence hung fir several minutes over the glacial kitchen. Neither Matthew Fless nor his son dared say aloud what they were thinking.

"Lord Burydan's a rogue," the miser murmured, finally. "If I were sure of killing him without running any risk, I wouldn't hesitate for a moment."

The diplomat sighed loudly. "That's it, Father," he said. "No weakness. No futile scruples. Be energetic! I'm glad to see that you share my way of seeing." As if he wanted to bring matters to a head and prevent the miser hesitating any longer, he added: "The wind is very violent tonight. It's blowing from the west…and Lord Burydan's lands are situated due east of yours."

The old man had understood. "You want to set a fire?" he said, trembling in every limb.

"Did I say that? Well, I won't go back on my word. A forest fire, in this season, would do incalculable damage. The manor house is situated in the middle of resinous woods."

"But what about my forests?" replied the old man, swiftly.

"Haven't I told you that the wind's blowing from the west?"

"That's true. Even so, even if the wood and the manor house burn, that won't get rid of the eccentric for us."

The diplomat shrugged his shoulders. "You haven't understood?" he murmured. "The fire is only the pretext. Under cover of the disorder caused by such a disaster, all kinds of things might happen." And the wretch made a significant gesture, putting his hand to the butt of his revolver. "Besides which," he continued, "the city of Winnipeg is too far away for help to arrive in time."

"But won't the Blue House, where your brother Noel and his wife Ophelia live, inevitably be caught up in the blaze?"

"Well, too bad! I detest Noel. The best I can wish on his behalf is that he doesn't find himself in front of me during the few hours that go by between now and sunrise!"

The baronet dared not reply. He was afraid of the son that he had raised in accordance with his own principles, and whom he had taught, since early childhood, to put wealth ahead of everything else. The old man understood that it was too late to prevent the wretch from carrying out his plan, and, by virtue of a rapid reflection, he began to tremble for himself and his treasure.

"Let's make haste, then," the son said. "Time is precious! Are you coming with me?"

"I…I don't know…" stammered the baronet.

"I can see that you don't like it. All right! I don't need anyone else to act. Oh, one last recommendation. If I don't come back, don't worry. If I succeed, I'll make arrangements to disappear for a while, so that no suspicion will fall upon me. I've got a little boat in Lake Winnipeg, with which I can go wherever I want. In any case, don't admit, whatever happens, that you've seen me this evening."

"All right, all right!" murmured the miser, anxiously. "Good luck."

Mathew Fless's son had already disappeared into the night.

Baron Skinflint remained motionless for some time on the threshold, overwhelmed. Then, suddenly making a desperate resolution, he picked up his revolver and disappeared in his turn into the forest.

The night was cold and foggy, and a furious westerly wind as making the elastic trunks of the fir trees moan in a melancholy fashion, seemingly murmuring confused and terrible words in the miser's ears.

The baronet shivered, and, pulling his hare-skin bonnet down over his ears, he headed toward the part of the forest that confined Lord Burydan's estates.

He had hardly taken a hundred steps when he saw a little gleam spring up between the trees some distance away, which slowly grew larger.

The crepitation of a fire that was beginning to take hold reached his ears. The light, meanwhile, became fuliginous. In spite of the furious wind that was stimulating it, the fire was brooding, devouring bushes and twigs until it encountered a clump of resinous trees that would provide it with fuel.

Retained by a terrible curiosity, the baronet continued to move along the sunken fence that separated his property from Lord Burydan's.

One after another, he saw two more fires ignited. A moment would come when the three conflagrations would become one, when the forest would blaze like an immense torch, encircling the eccentric's manor house with a sea of fire.

An hour went by.

The fire grew with an imposing slowness.

It was like a bloody aurora gradually rising between the trunks of the fir-trees, the white boles of the birches and the maples.

Lord Burydan's forest was now covered with a dome of black smoke, from which millions of sparks were springing. The miser was no longer cold. The intense radiation of the blaze penetrated through his rags and he recoiled, frightened by the glow that was climbing higher, more terrible with every passing minute.

Suddenly, loud screams erupted in the silence, followed by the sound of a bell and the blasts of an automobile horn.

Through the moving curtain of flames, the miser perceived shadows moving back and forth with panicked gestures. Ax-blows resounded, punctuated with brief orders.

As is done in such cases, Lord Burydan was trying to limit the scourge by felling trees; at the head of his servants he was fighting the invading fire himself. He was valiantly seconded by his friends. Goliath was felling ask-trees with three blow of his ax. Bob Horwett and Kloum were directing the manor's servants to the most threatened locations.

Then a squad of woodcutters arrived, under the guidance of Noel Fless.

Hidden behind the trunk of an oak, the miser watched the poignant spectacle, and he too, in his hiding place, was impassioned by that battle against the most destructive of the elements.

"They're capable of stopping the fire in its tracks." he muttered, furiously. "Already one whole area's been preserved. Fortunately, we have the wind in our favor!"

Half an hour went by. The number of workers was increasing from one minute to the next. The miser's fury no longer knew any bounds when the two automobiles and the mail-coach, sent in all haste to neighboring villages, disembarked a new troop of woodcutters.

All those efforts would have come to nothing had not Lord Burydan had an idea of genius.

"We'll never stop the scourge alone," he shouted. "There aren't enough of us. Everyone leave the felling and head for the Roaring Stream!"

He was immediately understood.

"The lord's right," cried voices in the crowd of laborers.

"We need a barrage."

"Only water is capable of fighting fire."

"The torrent will defeat the fire!"

Stones, tree-trunks and bags of band were hurled into the bed of the torrent. In less than a quarter of an hour, a solid barrage had been erected. Tumbling impetuously down the slope, the waters were precipitated toward the fire, which was reflected in them as if in a mirror. Then there was a long, loud hiss; the battle between the elements commenced.

The entire forest was invaded by an acrid fog of smoke and water vapor. There were great trees whose feet were entirely bathed, but which continued to burn like torches, projecting their branches in all directions in incandescent brands. Some thickets formed little islands of fire, which the action of the water gradually shrank from one minute to the next, and which ended up collapsing with a strident din, leaving vast clouds of white vapor behind.

Fortunately, the fire had not reached the higher ground, with the result that the Roaring Stream, whose waters never ceased to pour, eventually reckoned with it.

From his hiding place, Baronet Fless had followed the phases of the drama while grinding his teeth. Overwhelmed by rage, he saw that his son had committed a futile crime. But it was written that the old rogue would drain the cup of horror to the dregs that night.

In the midst of the laborers who had been fighting the fire from the start, the Indian Kloum had, at one moment, perceived a man who lying face down and taking the greatest precautions, was heaping twigs on a fire set in a hollow in an old fire-tree.

Taciturn by nature, Kloum did not mention his discovery to anyone else, but, drawing apart from his companions, he had set off in pursuit of the incendiary, and, with the special skills of the people of his race, had followed him at a distance without being perceived.

At the moment when the wretch, believing his work to be complete, was preparing to flee along a path leading to the lake, the Indian appeared in front of him and, before he had time to take any action, leapt at his throat and knocked him down. Then, putting his knee on the chest of the man thus felled, he considered him attentively by the ruddy light of the blaze.

"Ha!" he said. "The son of Baron Skinflint! That doesn't surprise me."

"Let me go!" croaked the half-strangled incendiary.

"No," said Kloum, cocking his revolver

"Mercy! I have a wallet full of banknotes in my pocket. It's yours if you let me go."

"No."

"At least," the miser's son murmured, hoarsely, "don't kill me now. Take me to your master. Lord Burydan is my cousin, my brother's friend—he'll show me mercy. You don't have the right to kill me."

"Well, I'll take it," said Kloum, impassively.

And, putting the barrel of his weapon to his enemy's temple, he blew his brains out.

The body was agitated by a long tremor, and then became immobile. Baron Skinflint's heir was dead.

At the sound of the gunshot, a man had emerged suddenly from behind the oak where he had been hiding until then. It was the miser. He ran to the bloody corpse, which he had recognized at a glance, while Kloum vanished, like a shadow, into the thick smoke.

The miser saw his son with a hole in his skull, his face hideously distorted by a supreme grimace of hatred and terror.

He did not say a word. He lifted that dead head, which the reflection of the flames surrounded with a bloody aureole, brushed the still-moist forehead with his lips, and fainted.

When he came to, he found himself surrounded by bright light; clumps of blazing larch were emitting a dazzling white light. Every branch, swollen with moist sap, burst like a firework. It was the sound of those detonations that had roused the old man from his torpor.

Strangely enough, he could no longer see his son's body beside him. Someone had taken advantage of his faint to take it away.

The author of that disappearance was none other than Kloum. Not being certain how Lord Burydan would react to the execution of the incendiary, the Indian had thought it prudent to carry the body to a place where the flames were more ardent.

The baronet looked around for a few moments, in bewilderment. Suddenly, he uttered a cry of terror and amazement. He was surrounded by a circle of flames that was gradually shrinking.

"Fire!" he cried, desperately. "Fire! And it's my own wood that's burning! How did that happen?"

Bounding through the flames, he fled, howling. He went straight ahead, not knowing what he was doing.

What had happened was that while Lord Burydan, his friends and his servants had been busy fighting the scourge, the wind had shifted from the west to the north-east, and it had eventually been perceived that it was toward the forest belonging to the miser that a rain of sparks, hot embers and flaming branches was pouring.

Entirely given over to his preoccupations, the baronet had not noticed that the fire, creeping insidiously along at ground level, had made a long detour and had gradually encircled him

His beard grilled and his hare-skin bonnet roasted, he found himself, without knowing how, back in his own house.

He ran out again almost immediately to cry out, to call for help— but his voice was drowned out by the tumult of the fire.

Almost extinct on the neighboring property, the fire seemed, so to speak, to be taking its revenge by devouring the woods belonging to the miser.

The woodcutters had not noticed for some time that Baron Skinflint's woods were also on fire. When they did realize it, they refused forcefully to go continue their work of preservation on the baronet's land

"That old egotist can burn alive in his lair!" said one of them. "I'm not the one who'll lift a finger to save him."

"He's never helped anyone," said another. "It's only just that no one comes to his aid."

"Let him die," said a third. "Good riddance."

By virtue of a misfortune that was considered later to be a providential punishment, the water of the Roaring Stream found the limit of its natural flow along the ditch of the sunken fence that surrounded the miser's woods, with the result that the fire was given free rein in that area. The fire therefore devoured several hectares without meeting any obstacles, and stopped of its own accord at the uncovered space surrounding the farmhouse.

Lord Burydan was too generous by nature to allow the flames to devour his enemy's property. He made the laborers ashamed of their egotism and, followed by Goliath, Bob Horwett, Kloum, Noel Fless and Ophelia, he went into the miser's wood. But the eccentric arrived too late. He and his friends were able to observe one thing, which was that the disaster had, in the end, only damaged Baron Skinflint's forest. He therefore contented himself with circumscribing the fire with a number of ditches, which brooded dully, propagated by tree-branches. A light rain that began to fall completed the extinction of the burned stumps. They withdrew, completely reassured.

Noel Fless and Ophelia, who were the last to remain behind, were about to leave too when they distinguished, in the midst of a heap of ashes, a completely charred skeleton. Ophelia almost fainted, convinced that they were the miser's remains.

"Great God!" she cried. "My father-in-law has fallen victim to the fire—and it's our fault; we weren't quick enough in coming to his aid."

Noel had gone very pale. "It would be an eternal remorse for me if that were so," he murmured, "but I doubt that those blackened bones are my father's. He's never worn shoes as fine as those." And he pointed at the dead man's elegant shoes, which had chanced to escape the fire.

"That's true!" exclaimed the young woman, whose face cleared. "I've only ever seen him shod in crude sabots."

"It doesn't matter—I don't want to remain in doubt. Let's look for my father. It's rather surprising, you must admit, that no one saw him while we were fighting the disaster."

The two young people were only a short distance away from the miser's house. They found the door wide open and went in.

The furniture and utensils were in a state of disorder; evidently, Baron Skinflint's dwelling had been the scene of some drama.

Anxiously, Ophelia and her husband went through all the rooms on the ground floor and the first floor. They even explored the barns, the stables and the garage, without any result.

"There's only the grain-loft where we haven't looked," said Ophelia, suddenly.

"Let's go up there," murmured Noel, striving to hide the anxiety that he felt.

Ophelia climbed the staircase that led to the grain-loft. By the livid gray light of the dawn, they saw a frightful spectacle.

Baron Skinflint, reduced to despair, had hanged himself from one of the beams supporting the roof.

Having remained economical to the last, he had taken care to put his hare-skin bonnet, his green dressing-gown and sabots to one side before deciding to put the fatal slipknot over his head. At his feet, the stool on which he had stood in order to carry out his funereal project could still be seen.

Fortunately, Ophelia was a woman of action, to whom life in the open air and tiring excursions through the woods had communicated an almost virile strength and energy. Her first movement was to cut the rope that encircled the old man's neck, without even waiting for her husband to help her.

When Noel Fless reached the stair-head in his turn, the young woman had already laid the baronet down on a bundle of straw, and, observing that the body was still warm and supple, had started to lavish all the cares usual in such cases upon him.

"Is he dead?" exclaimed Noel, terrified.

"No," said Ophelia, "but he's not much better."

"Poor father!" murmured the young man, profoundly troubled.

"It's not a matter of wasting our time in useless lamentations! Help me! Perhaps he can still be saved."

Both of them, fortunately, being up to date with the latest progress in science, they carried out artificial respiration, and rhythmic tractions of the tongue.

After quarter of an hour, the miser opened his eyes, and then closed them again after uttering a profound sigh.

"He's saved!" cried Ophelia, joyfully.

V. A Double Cure

Monsieur Bondonnat was walking slowly along one of the pathways of the garden behind the manor house. Plunged in his reflections, he did not even give any thought as he usually did, to classifying in his mind the numerous specimens of Canadian flora that were blooming in the flower-beds, mingled with plants originally from Old Europe.

The naturalist seemed preoccupied. From time to time, he took a notebook from his pocket, whose pages were covered in figures and for-mulae, and consulted it with an expression of discontentment.

"Obviously," he said, forgetting himself sufficiently to speak aloud, "I've only achieved half a result as yet."

"Well," said a joyful voice a few yards away from him, "it's neces-sary to try obtain the whole of it, that famous result!"

Lord Burydan emerged from behind a clump of sorb-trees, where he had hidden in order to give his old friend a surprise.

"I perceive, milord," said Bondonnat, smiling, "that you've been spying on me—but that's my fault. I have no need to say what I'm think-ing out loud."

"I'll wager that I can guess what the famous result is to which you made allusion."

"That's not very difficult. You know that I'm only thinking about one thing at present—of curing the so-called madman of the Blue House completely, who certainly isn't insane, but hasn't recovered his intelli-gence or his memory."

"You've seen him?"

"Yes, I've just come from the Blue House, where I also had the op-portunity to see your dear cousin, Baronet Fless."

"What did the old rogue say? His son was really exceedingly gener-ous not to leave him where he was."

"Don't say that. The baronet is entirely converted. He's recognized his wrongdoing, and begged pardon from his son and daughter-in-law for all the miseries he's inflicted on them. He's changed so much that he talks about nothing but spending money. It's almost a prodigy."

"Get away!" said the eccentric, amazed.

"It's exactly as I have the honor of telling you. The baronet has new clothes. He's sacrificed his hare-skin bonnet and green dressing-gown, which now serve as a scarecrow. He's cut off his bushy beard; he looks ten years younger. A pedicurist from the city has filed his diabolical claws; a few baths in soda ash have got rid of the inveterate dirt that fitted him like a carapace. He's now as neat as a newly-minted coin.

"So much the better!" said the eccentric, very amused by that metamorphosis. "I must give myself the satisfaction of going to admire him in his new aspect. Then we'll arrange an interview with his former servant Slug. That will be pleasant! For the moment, though, let's set Baron Skinflint aside and get back to our invalid."

"As I told you, there's been no change in his condition. He's almost entirely recovered his physical identity, and there's no doubt that he's the true Joe Dorgan, but his intelligence and memory leave much to be desired."

"Perhaps it's me," said Lord Burydan, taking a letter out of his pocket, "that will give you the means of making is cure complete. Oscar has written to me..."

"What does he say?"

"He's sent me some very interesting information. Read it. Thanks to certain medical journals and Cornelius' own pamphlets, he's been able to reconstitute the methods employed by the sculptor of human flesh to bring about some of his most marvelous cures."

Bondonnat took the letter that Lord Burydan was holding out to him and read it attentively.

"Here," he said, pointing to one of the paragraphs in the missive, "are some details that are particularly valuable. It's the formula for the operations employed by Cornelius to cure a rich old lady who had gone mad with grief following the death of her son. To succeed in that, he was content to abolish her memory of things past for a period of time—only a few months."

"So what?"

"You don't understand? Cornelius must surely have used the same means in the case that occupies us, and as the treatment has been published several years ago, n a medical journal, I only have to follow Cornelius' own procedure to cure our invalid."

"Oscar is decidedly a precious fellow."

"Without losing a moment, I'll make up the potion indicated in our friend's letter. If he's not mistaken, the result of the medication will be very rapid."

"When will it take full effect, then?"

"With the substance employed here, if my assumptions are correct, a few hours should suffice to expel from the body the stupefying substances that have paralyzed the brain, and render the invalid's memory complete clarity."

"That would be excellent," murmured the eccentric. "We'll finally be able to see..."

Bondonnat returned to the laboratory that had been installed for him n the manor house. An hour later he emerged again, holding a flask of the powerful medicament indicated by Cornelius. The latter had doubtless never thought that he would be beaten by his own weapons and that Bondonnat would make use of an article in a medical journal in which the sculptor of human flesh had recorded one of his marvelous cures.

The old scientist wanted to go to the Blue House himself to give his instructions to Noel Fless and his wife regarding the manner in which they should administer the potion to their patient.

Bondonnat scarcely slept that night. He was anxious to know whether his treatment would succeed, and could not help thinking that, if the means he had employed were to fail, he could not envisage any other that might be efficacious. He was up at dawn, and headed for the Blue House along the paths through the forest, that part of which had fortunately been spared by the fire.

It was Ophelia who opened the door to him, her eyes still puffy with sleep.

"What an early riser you are, my dear Master!" said the young woman, smiling.

"Yes, yes," the old man replied, impatiently. "How is our invalid?"

"I don't know. He must still be asleep. No one has one into his room."

"I'll go myself. Don't disturb your husband. I'm in a hurry to make certain."

Bondonnat climbed the stairs to the first floor precipitately. Having reached the patient's room he stopped, turned the key quietly in the lock, opened the door without making a noise, and went in on tiptoe.

The room was in near-darkness. Ample curtains had been drawn over the window. Bondonnat drew them back cautiously.

A few rays of spring sunshine then ventured into the room, furnished in bright colors, revealing the old man's patient, still asleep. A vague smile was wandering over his lips, as if he were under the influence of a pleasant dream.

Gently, Bondonnat woke the young man, who initially looked around in amazement. Then, taking him by the hand he said: "How are you this morning, my dear Joe?"

"Quite well, Monsieur—but it seems to me that since yesterday, there's been a great change in me..." He fell silent abruptly, and drifted away into a profound reverie.

Bondonnat studied him anxiously.

"That's strange!" murmured the invalid in a faint voice. "It seems as if a blindfold has been removed from my eyes...that a darkness enveloping my memory has dissipated."

"May you be telling the truth!" murmured the aged scientist, emotionally.

Joe put his hands to his head with a kind of fatigue. "It seems to me," he said, "that I've been traveling in unknown regions during the night. I seem to be waking up from a dream." Suddenly, however, he uttered a piercing cry, and stood up, under the impression of a frightening thought. "The bandits!" he exclaimed. "Everyone around me was killed! What will my father say? I must have been in great danger...must have been delirious...for a long time..."

He had hidden his head in his hands and had started to weep copiously. After a while, he looked at Bondonnat, as if he had never seen him before—but, reassured by the old scientist's benevolent physiognomy, he smiled at him.

"You seem very interested in me, sir. You must have helped me recovery my memory. But who are you?"

"I'm a physician who has been caring for you for some time," Bondonnat hastened to say, "and who is very glad to see that you're on the way to a full recovery."

"Where's my father?"

"Your father is well. You'll see him soon. For the moment, let's not talk about him. You need to tell me, in detail, what you feel, and what you can remember."

"Let's see," said the invalid, with a sort of hesitation. "My name is Joe Dorgan, isn't it? The son of the billionaire, the brother of Harry the engineer.

"Yes, my friend. How far back, in your estimation, does the loss of memory you've suffered extend?"

"I don't know exactly," Joe replied, effortfully. "I've lost any notion of time, as it were. But what I can remember, exactly, is a bloody drama...after which I don't remember any more..."

"Tell me about it, briefly."

"My father had sent me to the South to collect a large sum of money. I had an escort of a dozen men. We were attacked by tramps in a gully near the Black Canyon. All my men were killed. I was taken prisoner. When they took me away, one of the bandits put something cold over my face, with a strong odor."

"A chloroform mask?"

"Yes, that's it. And it's from that moment on that there's a shadowy gap in my memory, like a dark lacuna. It's like an interminable night full of one of those nightmares that leave hardly any trace when you wake up...there was a place where I was maltreated, from which I escaped...my memories become only a little more precise from the time I arrived in this forest...in this house..."

"All is well! Bondonnat interjected, joyfully. "You're saved. It's up to me, now, to explain everything that seems to you to be incredible. You've been the victim of a frightful machination. A scientist of genius, who is also a great criminal, has modified your personality, and in the meantime, you've worn—like a mask, so to speak—someone else's appearance. But you shall know everything."

Bondonnat spent hours recounting to Joe Dorgan the bloody odyssey of the Red Hand and the audacious crimes perpetrated by Baruch and the Kramm brothers.

In the course of that conversation, Bondonnat observed, with an indescribable satisfaction, that Joe had not only recovered his memory, but all of his intelligence. No trace of the metamorphosis brought about by Cornelius remained. Save for a few scars and a few imperceptible deviations of certain organs, he was his old self again.

It was with a sentiment of infinite bliss that Joe breathed, through the open window, the embalmed air of the garden; he seemed to have been born for a second time. Everything delighted him; he was glad to be alive.

Finally, he experienced an immense gratitude to all those who had saved him, sheltered him and cured him. He shook Monsieur Bondonnat's hand, weeping. He wanted to go and embrace Noel Fless and Ophelia, and kiss their child. He even embraced Baron Skinflint, who was unused to such effusions.

"Al this is very good," said Bondonnat, addressing both Noel and Joe, "but you know what I've said to you. I'm going to Winnipeg. Make sure everything's ready for my return."

Half an hour later, the old man had rejoined Lord Burydan, who leapt into an automobile and had himself taken to Mr. Pasquier's house.

The lawyer introduced him almost immediately to the lodge inhabited by William Dorgan, still hidden under the pseudonym of Clark.

"You need to come with me immediately," said the eccentric to the aged billionaire.

Where to? wrote the mute on his notepad.

"You'll see. Hurry up."

What's it about? wrote William Dorgan again, seemingly disinclined to put himself out.

"It's a surprise!" cried Lord Burydan, impatiently. "But you *must* come."

The billionaire ended up giving in to his friend's persistence and took his place at his side in the automobile, which set off in fourth gear, only to stop again in front of the door of the Blue House.

A numerous society was already gathered in the dining room. William Dorgan saw Andrée, Frédérique, Ellenor, Bondonnat, Kloum and Bob Horwett. There were several other people that the billionaire had never seen before, who were none other than Baronet Matthew Fless, his son and daughter-in-law.

On the express instruction of Bondonnat, no one appeared to recognize William Dorgan, who sat down on the chair that the scientist offered him.

William Dorgan was prey to a strange emotion. He understood that this as a solemn moment.

The witnesses of the scene were no less emotional. It was only that morning that they had learned that William Dorgan had not been killed in the Rochester Bridge catastrophe, so everyone understood that momentous events were in the making.

"My friends," said Lord Burydan, in the midst of a profound silence. "I've asked you to come here to associate you with an act of justice and reparation. I have great news to reveal to you. First of all, our friend William Dorgan is alive, very much alive. To escape the murderers who were threatening him, however, it was necessary to let them believe that he was dead, in order to bring out the truth."

With a rapid gesture, the eccentric had removed the dark glasses the old man was wearing.

Every hand was immediately extended toward the resuscitated man, who, not knowing the exact purpose of the scene, was profoundly troubled.

"I haven't finished," Lord Burydan went on, gesturing to everyone to sit down. "William Dorgan had a son whom he loved dearly. That son was kidnapped by bandits, and then returned after a few months of captivity…or, at least, it was thought that he had returned, for it was an impostor who had taken on the features, the physiognomy and physical appearance of the veritable Joe Dorgan.

"A criminal of genius, a scientist devoid of conscience, Cornelius Kramm, the sculptor of human flesh, had realized the prodigy of giving Baruch Jorgell the features of Joe Dorgan and Joe those of Baruch.

"While the victim, atrociously mutilated, languished in a madhouse, the murderer, hidden behind the mask of living flesh that the infernal Cornelius had placed over his features, sowed death and ruination around him. It was Cornelius and Baruch who blew up the Rochester Bridge; they were the owners of the Island of Hanged Men; they are, in fact, the Lords of the Red Hand."

A silence of consternation hung over the audience for a few moments. Everyone was alarmed by these revelations. It was in the midst of the most profound meditation that Lord Burydan continued.

"Fortunately, the bandits have met opposition. Thanks to the science and courage of our friends, we're on the point of triumphing in the struggle. First of all, we've found the real Joe. We have given him back his true physiognomy…"

Lord Burydan did not finish his sentence. With an impetuous gesture, he whipped away the curtain behind which Joe had been hiding throughout the scene.

The young man threw himself into his father's arms.

"My son!" cried the billionaire, to the amazement of everyone present.

The violence of the mental commotion experienced by the billionaire had been such that he had been abruptly cured of his mutism.

"My hope has been realized!" exclaimed Bondonnat, excitedly. "I knew that only a violent emotion was capable of undoing the harm caused by another violent emotion. I attempted this audacious experiment, and am happy to see that it has succeeded completely! Mr. Dorgan, you're cured—completely cured!"

That *coup de théâtre* had been so gripping and so poignant that all those who had just taken part in it remained dazed by amazement.

It was Lord Burydan who broke the silence first.

"We've just witnessed the first act of the final drama," he said. "It remains for us now to render Cornelius and Baruch incapable of doing any more harm, and inflicting upon them the punishment they merit. I give you my word of honor that I shall not fail in that task!"

18. MASKS OFF!

I. A Planned Marriage

For some time, the only topic of conversation among the "Five Hundred" constituting the financial aristocracy of America, had been the installation in New York of Señora Carmen Hernandez. The young woman, who would become, on the death of her mother, the possessor of a fortune of more than a billion and a half, had left Buenos Aires, where the family owned estates as vast as several French départements, and had bought one of the most luxurious town houses on Fifth Avenue.

Fifth Avenue, for which only certain streets in the Plaine-de-Monceau and the Champs-Élysées can provide any standard for comparison, is inhabited entirely by billionaires, and consists of a series of palaces and town houses surrounded by gardens, some of which cost fortunes. To live on Fifth Avenue is already proof of vast wealth.

The house that Señora Carmen had chosen was an exact replica of a Spanish Renaissance Palace, whose model could be found on one of the most picturesque streets of the ancient city of Cordova.

It was thought, not without reason, that Doña Carmen had selected, from among so many marvelous residences, the one that made the most advantageous frame for her beauty. Carmen offered, in all its splendor, a type specimen of the Castilian race, which was not mingled in her with the slightest drop of any foreign blood. Her skin was very pale, her hair so black that it had a blue metallic sheen in the shade. She had features of an admirable purity of design, and her adorers never failed to compare her eyes, whose gaze was both fulgurant and dominating, to beautiful diamonds in a dark velvet case.

Hr feet arched and her hands small and delicate, Carmen had a body of sculptural beauty. Her bosom as beautiful without exaggeration, and her hips harmoniously developed; when walking, she had the muscular rhythm "that reveals a goddess in every movement."

In addition, Carmen Hernandez was as intelligent, generous and honest as she was beautiful. The most indifferent individuals became her devoted friends, even her adorers as soon as they had seen her, as soon as she had smiled or pronounced a few words.

In spite of their billions, the Five Hundred did not offer many examples of similar perfection; young women who were sullen and ugly, spiteful and vulgar, were not rare among them. Thus, the arrival of Señora Carmen in the drawing rooms of Fifth Avenue had the effect of some quasi-celestial apparition.

In America, people are, above all, practical. They began by ascertaining the exact extent of the charming señora's fortune and situation, and what they learned was that she was the only daughter of Pablo Hernandez, one of the richest landowners in the Argentine Republic. He had doubled his fortune by setting up cotton-mills at the most opportune moment. It was the billionaire Fred Jorgell, then the owner of the Cotton Trust, who had provided his raw materials.

Pablo Hernandez had died about three years before in tragic and mysterious circumstances. He had been on his way to Jorgell City alone, in an automobile, in order to put a considerable payment into Fred Jorgell's own hands, when he had been murdered by malefactors who remained unidentified. His cadaver had been found some distance from the city, near a marshy stream, a few yards from the automobile, from which the unfortunate fellow must have descended in order to carry out a minor repair.

The banknotes had disappeared, but, extraordinarily enough, the body bore no trace of any wound, save for a slight contusion—an imperceptible black patch—behind the ear. The murderers were never found.

Other crimes had occurred thereafter, in the same circumstances, without the mystery being clarified, but it was repeated in whispers that the murders that had desolated Jorgell City has ceased abruptly as soon as Baruch Jorgell, the billionaire's son, had left the city to go to Europe, where he had soon acquired a bloody celebrity by treacherously murdering his host and benefactor, Monsieur de Maubreuil.

On the death of her husband, Doña Juana Hernandez, aided by a few trusted servants, had continued to administer his estates and factories with a great deal of activity and intelligence. When the Trust had passed from the hands of Fred Jorgell into those of William Dorgan, she had continued to buy from the latter, every year, quantities of cotton that were measured in millions of bales.

She had been grief-stricken to learn of William Dorgan's death in the Rochester Bridge catastrophe. She knew the dead man's two heirs,

Harry and Joe Dorgan. She was pained to see a legal battle engaged between them that was to result in striping the engineer Harry of his possession and transferring almost all of the property in the Trust to Joe and his two associates, Cornelius and Fritz Kramm.

Joe Dorgan—or, rather, Baruch, to whom the diabolic artistry of Cornelius had given his victim's features—was determined not to lose such an important client, so he multiplied his visits to Señora Juana. Harry Dorgan, who was running the Lightning Steamship Company on behalf of his father-in-law, was by no means so assiduous. He only made a few widely-spaced visits, and the two proud Spaniards—the daughter as well as the mother—were somewhat resentful of the young man's negligence.

Baruch cleverly took advantage of the situation. He gained the good graces of the old lady entirely, and one evening, declared to her that he was passionately smitten with Doña Carmen and solicited the honor of becoming her husband.

Doña Juana only raised objections for form's sake.

"You love my daughter," she said, with an entirely Spanish frankness. "I don't know whether she loves you, but I believe that you're capable of making her happy."

"My entire life," the suitor murmured, "will be devoted to making your adorable daughter happy!"

"And of course," replied Doña Juana, who had spoken a trifle freely, "you believe that, for her part, will bring you a sum of happiness far superior to the one you are promising her? What woman is more capable of rendering a husband happy?"

"I know," Baruch murmured gallantly, "that I'm unworthy of a person as perfect in every respect as Doña Carmen."

"Enough compliments!" the old lady exclaimed, abruptly, to whom a suspicion of a gray moustache gave a hint of virility. "I've already told you that from the viewpoint of moral qualities and affection, I believe you to be worthy of becoming my daughter's husband. You're intelligent and energetic and I believe you to be honest. But there's one question, about which it's necessary to speak."

"The question of money?"

"Yes, Señor, and let's settle it right away, in order not to have to come back to it."

"In that matter," Baruch replied, with perfect assurance, "I believe that we can come to a rapid understanding."

"You're involved in a lawsuit with your brother?"

"Of course—but I'm certain of winning the case. Anyone will tell you that, even if I were to lose—which is improbable—I'd still have sufficient millions of dollars..."

"That's good. In that case, my notary will get in touch with your solicitor tomorrow, and as soon as I'm convinced of that important point, you'll be officially authorized to pay court to Carmen."

"My only desire is to conclude the formalities as quickly as possible," the young man said, in a detached voice. "But that's not, in my opinion, the most important question."

"What do you mean?"

"Does Doña Carmen have some sympathy for me. That's what preoccupies me more than anything else. She doesn't love me, I know, but I'm worried that she might be antipathetic."

The old Spaniard smiled thinly. "I believe that I can affirm," she murmured, "that Carmen has no prejudice against you. I can say, without overstepping my prerogative, that you are one of those who are sympathetic to her."

"I shall do the impossible," cried Baruch, with a gesture of emotional determination, "to conquer the Señora's affection entirely!"

The place where this conversation took place was a little summer drawing room furnished with bamboo chairs, cluttered with green plants, which overlooked the magnificent garden of the palace through a large bay window,

"Here comes Carmen now," said Doña Juana, amiably, pointing at the young woman, who was advancing insouciantly along a broad pathway bordered by magnolias. "I'll leave you alone. If you fear that Carmen has any prejudices against you, it's up to you to dissipate them. But above all, not a word about our plans!"

And, putting her finger to her lips with a malicious smile, the old lady disappeared just as Carmen came into the summer-house, strolling absent-mindedly. At the sight of the young man she started in surprise. Her cheeks were covered by a bright blush. "I don't know you were here, Master Joe," she murmured.

The young man kissed her the charming little hand that the señora held out to him respectfully. "I hope that my visit isn't disturbing you," he said.

"Not at all, my dear sir. It's always with great pleasure that my mother and I see you."

The conversation continued in that vein for some time, alimented by the commonplaces of social politeness. Baruch spoke negligently about the millions that he would soon acquire. He said a few words about the latest theatrical productions, the reception given the previous week by a member of the Five Hundred—the Rockefellers—and at which, by virtue of a eccentricity that everyone thought exquisitely tasteful, dinner had been served by tame apes admirable dressed and of a size ingeniously adapted to the dishes that they were charged with bringing. Thus, an orangutan had been charged with the roast, a gorilla had brought the salmon, a macaque the vegetables, a capuchin monkey the entremets and a marmoset the desserts.

"What about the coffee?" Carmen asked, laughing wholeheartedly.

"That was a negro boy."

"It must have been a charming dinner, but I think people must be very desirous of being talked about to take pleasure in such feasts."

"Bah! It's necessary to give original feasts. When you're married, it will be necessary for you to have your receptions too."

"Oh, there's plenty of time to think about that," Carmen murmured, blushing imperceptibly.

She looked Joe in the face. Their eyes met. They had read one another's thoughts.

With a tender gesture, Baruch took hold of Carmen's hand; she did not withdraw it.

"Listen, Señora," he said, "I'm frankness personified, and I can't hide from you any longer that I have the profoundest admiration for you, and the most entire devotion..."

"Is this a declaration?" the Señora replied, withdrawing her hand. Then, suddenly assuming a serious expression, she continued: "You said just now Mr. Dorgan, that you were frankness personified. I have the pretention of being just as frank as you can be, and you shall know my opinion of marriage in a few words. I will only accept the spouse that my mother selects for me."

"On condition, of course, that he pleases you."

"Oh, my mother would never marry me off against my will. She would be desolate if she caused me any pain. For my part, you understand, I would never take a husband who displeased my mother."

"Señora," the young man murmured, with a tremor in his voice, "what would your decision be if Señora Juana had agreed to my request?"

"I don't know," the young woman murmured, surprised by that unexpected question. "I've never thought about such a thing."

The conversation, which was taking on a very intimate appearance, was abruptly interrupted by the entrance of a domestic who was carrying a visiting card covered in fine handwriting on a silver-plated tray.

The young billionaire was burning to know the name of the inopportune visitor, but, in spite of his curiosity, he could not make out what was written on the card.

After glancing at it, Carmen had risen to her feet precipitately.

"Excuse me, Mr. Dorgan," she said. "I'll leave you for a few minutes. If you're not in a hurry, wait for me to return. The piano and the albums in the drawing room will assist you to be patient. There are also dry Havanas in the little ebony sideboard.

As light and nimble as a fairy, Carmen had already disappeared, without waiting for her admirer's response.

Baruch was enchanted. In his mind's eye, he could already see himself in control of Doña Hernandez' regal fortune.

"All's going well," he murmured. "This time, I believe that I'll attain my objective without too much difficulty."

Nonchalantly, he took a golden cigar from the ebony sideboard, split it with a stroke of his fingernail and lit it, extending himself voluptuously in a rocking chair. He abandoned himself to exceedingly pleasant thoughts, swathed in a cloud of smoke, without noticing the passage of time.

An hour went by, and Doña Carmen had not yet returned.

If Baruch had been able to guess who the visitors were for whom Doña Carmen had left him, he would certainly have been less comfortable. The message written on the visiting card handed to the young woman was:

Lord Astor Burydan and Madame Andrée Paganot, née de Maubreuil, recall themselves to the memory of Doña Carmen Hernandez, and beg her to accord them a few minutes of conversation, concerning an extremely serious matter.

Carmen knew Lord Astor and Andrée, whom she had met on various occasions in the drawing rooms of the Five Hundred. She therefore hastened to grant their request.

She had thought at first that it was merely a mundane matter, but as soon as Lord Burydan had pronounced a few words, the young woman understood that what they had to say to her was of exceptional gravity.

When she finally rejoined Baruch, her features still expressed a violent emotion and her beautiful velvet eyes were reddened by tears, but she made an effort not to let any of these disturbances show. It was with a smiling face and a perfect calm, at least in appearance, that she went back into the small drawing room.

If Baruch had been more observant—or, rather, if he had not been misled by the conviction of success—he would have noticed that the young woman's words and manner had neither the same insouciance not the same frankness as before. A secret constraint was detectable in her slightest gestures and most insignificant remarks.

"Excuse me for having kept you waiting," she said. "I could not liberate myself sooner from an inopportune visit. Now, however, I'm all yours."

"Please don't apologize, Señora."

"You must have been bored."

"No matter. You're here, you're forgiven..." He added, boldly "Would it please you, Señora, to resume the conversation at the point at which it was interrupted?"

"What was it that we were talking about?" she murmured, with a feigned distraction.

"Don't you remember that it was the question of marriage?"

"That's true," said Carmen, with an abrupt gesture.

"I was saying," Baruch went on, "that you would make me the happiest of men, Señora, by consenting to grant me your hand."

Carmen blushed and paled alternately. It was under terrible constraint that she replied: "Indeed, Mr. Dorgan—and I explained to you that I would only accept a husband if it were agreed with my mother..."

"I believe," murmured Baruch, with a well-feigned emotion, "that I have every chance of obtaining Doña Juana's consent."

"I shall do what my mother says..." she said, lowering her eyes. With an inflection hat seemed strange to Baruch, she added: "Certainly, I'm not in love with anyone—but I confess that I would immediately accord my hand to the man who succeeded in discovering my father's murderer and avenging his death."

Baruch had gone pale. "I know," he stammered, with great effort, "that Señor Pablo Hernandez perished in a mysterious fashion in Jorgell

City. Believe, Señora, that I will do everything possible to be agreeable to you and to discover the murderers. If I don't succeed, no one can."

Carmen had recovered all her calm and amiability. "I see, Mr. Dorgan," she said, smiling, "that we understand one another perfectly. Don't forget that the most important thing of all is to obtain the consent of Doña Juana."

She extended her hand to Baruch, who deposited a long and respectful kiss thereon.

The bandit withdrew with joy in his heart. He could not see any serious obstacle to his marriage to the charming Spaniard. He was even surprised not to have encountered more difficulties.

Initially vaguely worried by what the young woman had said about Pablo Hernandez' murder, he was quickly reassured.

Carmen is like all young women, he told himself. *She would like to marry the avenger of her father's murder. It's a romantic declaration that has a fine effect. But the death of the old textile merchant is already ancient history. It's been shelved, forgotten; it's improbable that it will ever surface again. I'll make a few enquiries for form's sake; I'll offer rewards; Carmen will be impressed by my zeal. But nothing can be done about the impossible; it will soon be perceived that the murderers are undetectable, and no more thought will be given to it. I have Doña Juana's consent; all will be well. Within three months, I'll be the husband of the most charming woman in America—and I'll be the richest man in America.*

A week later, the Union's newspaper reported, in tentative terms, the imminent marriage of the beautiful Carmen to the celebrated young director of the cotton and corn Trust.

II. A Rescue

A large automobile, massive in form and hermetically sealed, had departed the previous day from the manor house that Lord Burydan possessed in the environs of Winnipeg in Canada.

On that clear spring morning it was going along the bank of the Red River, which irrigates the state of Minnesota on the Canadian border.

In any other country than the United States, where everyone has the principle of not meddling in his neighbors affairs, that vehicle would have attracted the attention of the curious for more than one reason. It was only illuminated by two small windows of frosted glass with internal bars. One might have thought it a veritable prison on wheels. At any rate, in spite of its solidity and weight, it was equipped with a very powerful engine, and it could easily reach a speed of a hundred and twenty kilometers an hour on occasion.

Three people occupied that mysterious vehicle. One, who was never seen, was, according to the other two, an invalid afflicted by insanity, who was being taken to the state of New York, where he would be interned in a sanitarium. That was what his guardians had affirmed when they crossed the Canadian border.

The Yankee customs officers, more suspicious than those of any other country in the world, had demanded to see the invalid. They had been shown, sprawling in the back of the vehicle, a thin and pale individual whose arm as surrounded by an apparatus and who seemed to be plunged in a coma-like unconsciousness. The customs men had had no further doubts hereafter.

"Anyway," one of the drivers had added—a man of gigantic stature who answered to the name of Goliath—"we're obliged to so take many precautions because our invalid, Mr. Slug, is subject to violent fits of rage."

All that seemed quite plausible.

The vigilance of the two guardians with regard to their prisoner was such that they never permitted him to get out of the vehicle, even to take his meals. When they stopped—which was always at some isolated inn—Goliath went to eat first, leaving his companion, Bob Horwett, on sentry duty. Then it was the turn of the latter, in such a fashion that Slug was never alone for a moment.

Perhaps the precaution was superfluous, for the poor devil seemed to be in such a lamentable state that it would have been difficult for him to free himself. Without relaxing their surveillance, Goliath and Bob Horwett had ended up becoming completely tranquil with regard to the possibility of an escape on the part of their prisoner.

That morning, charmed by the beauty of the weather, they had both climbed into the front seat after having carefully locked Slug in his rolling prison. They were taking pleasure in gazing at the banks of the Red River, bordered by poplars, alders, willows and tall osiers that were just coming into bud.

In the nearby forest, the rhythmic noise of a woodcutter's ax could be heard, and that solitary region had something simultaneously wild and placid about it that rested the eyes and the mind.

"Say," said Goliath, suddenly, taking an enormous gold-plated chronometer—a gift from Lord Burydan—out of his pocket, "it's nearly eleven and I can see a small house over there that might be a tavern."

"It certainly is," said Bob Horwett. "I can see the sign from here."

"In that case, we'll stop there for lunch. The keen river air is making me hungry."

"Me too. And we might go a long way before finding anywhere else as nice..."

A few minutes later the automobile stopped in front of the tavern, a pretty wooden building newly painted red and green, and well-varnished, like one of those doll's houses that are given to children on their birthday.

There was an arbor in front of the door, presently deprived of its foliage of hops and cobaeas, but from which one had a magnificent view of the river.

"This will suit us admirably," said Goliath, summoning the innkeeper with a thump of his fist that almost split the table.

"There are people in here already," said Bob Horwett, pointing to two men at the other end of the arbor costumed as tourists, sitting in front of a bottle of whisky.

"Bah! Day-trippers!"

"For once," Bob Horvet proposed, "we might eat together. Slug won't fly away."

"Agreed. There's nothing as disagreeable as eating alone. Besides which, I'll watch the vehicle while we eat."

The landlord, a jovial Scotsman, had come over.

Now, then," said Goliath, thumping himself mightily on the chest, which sounded hollow. "What do you have in your larder? I warn you that I have a serious appetite."

"One only has to look at you to be convinced of that," the host replied, facetiously. "It's certainly not by eating grasshoppers that you acquired such biceps. Don't worry; my larder is well-furnished."

"Tell us briefly what it contains."

"Nothing but good things, sirs. God salmon from the Red River, good Canadian bear hams, good roast beef from the prairies of Minnesota. Not to mention smoked eels, tomatoes from San Francisco and other trivia."

"I can see that we understand one another," Goliath said. "Serve us right away."

"But what should I bring you."

"The best of everything, and better," replied Bob Horwett. "We're not worried about the expense..."

"So serve us everything," Goliath put in, displaying a formidable row of teeth in a yawn. "I feel so hungry his morning that I could eat a whole sheep—as I once did, for a bet."

Delighted to be dealing with such good customers, the innkeeper hastened to set the table, which he flanked symmetrically with two pitchers of pale ale to the right and two bottles of Californian wine to the left. He was soon convinced that Goliath had not exaggerated in speaking about his appetite. It was a pleasure to watch him wipe the plates clean and cause sides of salmon and quarters of beef disappear as if they were being hurled into some abyss.

Without possessing his comrade's capacity for absorption, Bob Horwett demonstrated that he was what is commonly known as a good trencherman.

The innkeeper, who had once studied to be a teacher in Glasgow, was not far from thinking that he had the famous Gargantua at his table, along with his rival, the famous Gouliafre.[11]

He was not the only one to admire the appetite of the diners. The two tourists, sitting with their whisky at the other end of the arbor, were no less impressed, especially one of them, an old man with gray hair and blue-tinted spectacles, clad in a green flannel suit and a yachtsman's cap. He never took his eyes off Goliath and Bob Horwett.

---

[11] Gouliafre is not the name of a literary character but merely a trivial noun indicating a glutton; the author is improvising.

The latter ended up noticing the attention of which he was the object, and asked the landlord casually if he knew the two gentlemen.

"Not at all," the Scotsman replied. "but I think they're decent fellows. They've been here since yesterday, and they pay up promptly. The big motor-launch that you can see anchored over here behind the willows is theirs. They're hunting and fishing. They say that they plan to work their way up the Red River in stages to the lake."

Reassured by these words, Bob Horwett paid no further heed to the two strangers. At any rate, they both got up shortly thereafter and headed placidly toward the place where their boat was moored.

To reach it they had to go around the automobile, whose heavy mass separated them from Golith and Bob Horwett. At the moment when the yachtsmen went behind the vehicle—when, in consequence, they could not be seen by the diners—the man in the flannel seat leapt nimbly up on to the footboard and plunged an inquisitive glance through the barred window.

Immediately, he uttered an exclamation of surprise. "But it's Slug!" he cried. "I thought he was dead!"

"Who are you?" asked the prisoner, excitedly.

"Silence, in the name of the Lords!" said the stranger, putting a finger to his lips—and he continued on his way, leaving Slug in the most profound amazement.

Goliath and Bob Horwett had, of course, seen nothing of this little drama, which had unfolded a short distance from the table where they were eating lunch.

A few minutes later, the yachtsman, still followed by his companion—a vigorous sailor—came back from the motor-launch to the inn. He asked for writing materials, and appeared to absorb himself in drafting a long letter.

In reality, he had only written a note ten lines long, in handwriting so compact that the entire missive only occupied a tiny piece of paper.

Then, without attracting anyone's attention, he went toward the kitchen. One the massive table that occupied its center there was a tray on which the elements of a substantial but not luxurious meal were set.

A kitchen-boy was finishing laying out the necessary utensils.

The stranger approached him. "Who's this lunch for?" he asked, with an affable smile.

"Sir," the boy replied, "it's for an invalid who's travelling in the auto with the two men you've seen under the arbor."

"Are you going to take it to him?"

"No—the gentlemen insist on serving their friend themselves."

"Good," said the stranger, moving away with an indifferent expression.

As soon as the boy had turned away, however, the yachtsman came back and slipped the note he had just written, and had rolled up into the form of a tube about as long and thick as a match, into the bread, shoving it deeply enough into the roll for none of the paper to protrude. Then he left the kitchen stealthily and went back to sit down under the arbor.

Ten minutes later, Goliath got up to take Slug his lunch.

He opened the door of the automobile, deposited the tray on the bandit's knees, and locked him in, as usual.

Slug started eating with a hearty appetite, for, although he was putting on an appearance of being very ill, he had almost completely recovered from his shoulder-wound.

Suddenly, he felt resistance between his teeth, and pulled the folded note out of his mouth, having almost swallowed it. He unfolded it carefully, and when he had read it his face was radiant.

"I knew that the Lords wouldn't abandon me!" he exclaimed. "Now I'm sure that I won't remain a prisoner for long."

With his habitual prudence, Slug tore up the tint piece of paper, chewed it up into a ball and swallowed it.

Shortly thereafter, Goliath came back to collect the tray and the debris of his prisoner's meal. They did not take long to get back *en route* thereafter.

One of the spring showers that do not last long and are soon followed by sunshine had begun to fall. Goliath remained on the front seat while Bob Horwett retired to the interior of the vehicle and sat down beside Slug.

The automobile continued along the bank of the Red River. The countryside was absolutely deserted.

Suddenly, Slug, who had been on the alert since reading the note, heard three regularly-spaced blasts of a horn in the distance. He shivered. It was the signal for which the note he had received had told him to watch out.

Neither Goliath nor Bob Horwett paid any heed to the sounds of the horn coming from the motor-launch that had set off almost at the same time as he automobile, following a parallel course along the river.

Motionless in his corner, Slug held his breath, his heart palpitating with anxiety. Suddenly, a loud scream rang out. It was the sailor in the motor-launch, who had just fallen into the water and was shouting for help at the top of his voice.

Bob Horwett, who, as is well-known, held a world record for swimming, did not take time to reflect. He opened the door abruptly, closed it again negligently, shouting to Goliath to watch out, and ran to the bank opposite the place where the man had disappeared. Without even taking the time to undress, he dived in, and, swimming under the surface, set out in search of the man.

Slug had followed Bob Horwett with his eyes. At the precise moment when he dived into the water, the bandit opened the door, which had not been locked, and started running at top speed.

He had a significant advantage, because Goliath, by virtue of his enormous weight, was a mediocre runner.

The giant realized that immediately and, uttering a resounding oath, launched the automobile in pursuit of the fugitive, who was running straight for the river.

In the meantime, the motor-launch had moved closer to the shore. Slug leapt into it at the precise moment when the fake drowning victim hauled himself aboard.

The man whom Bob Horwett had so generously gone to help was an excellent swimmer. He had dived twice in order to elude his rescuer and, after having gone around the launch, had calmly climbed back aboard.

Immediately, the yachtsman, who was none other than Leonello, Dr. Cornelius' trusted servant and laboratory assistant, started the engine of the motor-launch, which sped away with all the velocity of which it was capable.

Bob Horwett, in despair at his imprudence, had understood too late the stratagem to which he had fallen victim. Furious and disappointed, he swam after the motor-launch for some time, but the men aboard fired revolver shots at him, which caused the water around him to crackle under a hail of bullets. With rage in his heart he was obliged to dive, beat a retreat, and finally return to the bank.

No less exasperated than his companion, Goliath fired revolver shots of his own after the launch, but the boat, favored by the rapid current, did not take long to disappear.

Two hours later, Slug and Leonello, leaving the launch in the charge of the sailor, disembarked opposite a railway station and bought tickets to New York, where they arrived the following day.

The old Italian took Slug to one of the houses secretly owned by the Red Hand, and then hastened to give a report on his mission to the sculptor of human flash.

He found Cornelius in his subterranean laboratory.

"Well, Leonello," asked the doctor, impatiently, "have you brought me good news?"

"There's good and there's bad. I couldn't get my hands on Joe Dorgan."

"Explain that," growled Cornelius, frowning. "That's a very regrettable failure on your part, which astonishes me. You know how important it is that we have the fake Baruch in our hands."

"It wasn't my fault, as you'll see. I went to Winnipeg, as you'd ordered me to, asked around for information, and learned right away that Lord Burydan and all of his friends, among whom was Bondonnat, had just left Canada to return to New York."

"Indeed—I've been notified of their arrival."

"I didn't take long to pick up Joe Dorgan's trail. For a long time he was cared for in a cottage inhabited by Noel Fless, the son of the old miser that Slug once tried unsuccessfully to rob. The local people called him the madman of the Blue House. They regarded him as an inoffensive idiot, absolutely incurable."

"That's reassuring," murmured Cornelius. "If Bondonnat, who's no fool, had taken it into his head to study him at close range, he might have been capable of curing him."

"It's impossible that anyone could suspect such a substitution."

"I think so too. Even so, I was wrong to let that Joe live. Baruch can't enjoy the identity he's usurped in peace until Joe has disappeared conclusively."

"There's still time. The amnesiac has left Noel Fless's cottage and no one could tell me what had become of him. Then I learned about a mysterious prisoner who was kept out of sight in Lord Burydan's manor house."

"That was Joe?"

"I thought so too, and took measures in consequence. When the captive was taken away in an auto by his two guards I followed their vehicle from stage to stage and seized the first opportunity to take a look inside the rolling prison. I expected to see Joe. You can imagine my surprise when I found myself in the presence of Slug, whom we thought dead and buried in the Florida swamp."

"It's necessary to get him out! Slug has been very faithful to the Red Hand. Furthermore, he's a resourceful man, and a man of action."

"I have got him out. Unfortunately, I don't have any information to give you with regard to Joe Dorgan."

Cornelius reflected momentarily. "We need to find out where he is, at all costs! I won't rest easy while he's still alive!"

"I assume that he's in New York, or somewhere nearby. I also think that it won't be difficult to find out where by following Lord Burydan and Bondonnat."

"In order to succeed, don't spare time or money. We've been too negligent with regard to Joe, and it's necessary to make up for lost time. Everything's going well. Baruch will soon enter into possession of William Dorgan's billions, and we'll get our hands on Fred Jorgell's too."

"How's that?"

"Isidora will inherit from her father, the engineer Harry from his wife, and Baruch from Harry. It only remains for the Red Hand to organize the schedule of the three individuals' decease."

"What a grandiose plan!" said Leonello, amazed.

"Grandiose? Yes, perhaps. But it only requires a trifle, a single overlooked detail, to reduce it to nothing. Start your search right away. It's necessary that Joe Dorgan is found before the end of the week."

III. Settling Accounts

Joe Dorgan had just spent the evening with Carmen Hernandez, whose officially recognized fiancé he had been for several weeks. The marriage, announced with great noise by the entire New York press, was to take place in three days, and no one was talking about anything except the marvelous gifts that the members of the Five Hundred had sent the young woman.

Baruch was swimming in joy. The future extended before him like a cloudless sky. He had definitely won the terrible game that he was playing. That very morning he had signed, in the office of Harry Dorgan's lawyer, the documents that would put him conclusively in possession of the cotton and corn Trust.

He could not see any shadow upon his happiness.

"Three more days!" he had said to Doña Carmen, on taking leave of her. "Those three days will seem very long to me!"

"I don't doubt it," the young woman had replied, with a strange smile. "But isn't it necessary, in all things, to be patient?" And, with a gesture worthy of a queen, the young woman had held out her hand to Baruch—who, as he did every evening, had deposited a kiss thereon that was both respectful and tender.

It was about ten o'clock in the evening. The young man climbed back into his automobile and did not take long to absorb himself in an agreeable meditation.

Carmen is charming, he thought. *A trifle proud, disdainful and cold, but I'll end up making her love me. I've succeeded in more difficult things than that. After all, she can remain as ceremonious as she likes, once I've got my hands on the dowry...*

He picked up the acoustic funnel that allowed him to speak to the chauffeur. "Stop at the entrance to Thirtieth Avenue," he said.

"Very good, sir," the man replied, obsequiously

And the automobile flew at top speed through the already deserted avenues.

A quarter of an hour later, Baruch got down and, after having ordered the chauffeur to wait for him, went along Thirtieth Avenue on foot, with his overcoat pulled up over his ears as if he were afraid of being recognized.

He went past the gate of the magnificent house inhabited by Dr. Cornelius, went around the high walls of the garden and found himself in a deserted back street bordered with tumbledown houses. He stopped in front of a wooden hut on the edge of a piece of waste ground surrounded by a fence, and rapped four times, regularly spaced.

A door opened and Baruch slipped silently into a ground for room illuminate tremulously by an oil lamp suspended from the ceiling. It was in this place that the divisions of booty took place that the Lords of the Red Hand made to their affiliates at regular intervals.[12]

As he entered, Baruch perceived Fritz and Cornelius sitting at a small table on which square pieces of paper were stacked bearing the signature of the Red Hand in one corner.

"Well?" asked Baruch, joyfully. "Is the division concluded?"

"It's just finished," Cornelius replied.

"I would have been present, as usual, but a loving fiancé has his duties..."

"Which we understand perfectly," murmured Fritz, in the same jovial tone. "You're entirely excused, my dear chap."

"We have no reason to stay any longer in this hovel, I believe," Baruch went on. "We can chat more comfortably elsewhere."

"That's what I thought," said Cornelius. "I've had a little supper set out in my laboratory. No one will disturb us there."

The three Lords of the Red Hand went out of the small house one by one and went along the street, presently deserted. They went into Cornelius' garden through a small door to which he had the key, and the elevator soon deposited them in the vestibule of the subterranean laboratory.

Cornelius opened a door. There was a dazzling light. Doubtless by reason of the solemnity of the circumstances, Cornelius had ordered magnificent preparations. The vast vaulted hall was lit by a hundred electric lamps, dissimulated by clusters of foliage and baskets of flowers. Half-dissected cadavers, and strange or frightful items apparatus were hidden from view by heavy drapes of orange velvet. Cornelius had only left in evidence one large display-case, in which there were wax statues colored with s much artistry that they gave the illusion of life.

---

[12] The reader might remember that when this location was previously featured, it was asserted that the Lords of the Red Hand had only rented it briefly, and never used the same location twice for their distributions—but circumstances have presumably changed since then.

In the center of the laboratory stood a table covered with silverware and rare crystal, decorated with sheaves of roses and orchids. Two dressers stood nearby, one laden with dusty bottles of the most celebrated vintages in the world, the other with pastries and magnificent fruits distributed on silver dishes.

Leonello was standing in a corner, making the final preparations.

"I hope," said Cornelius, "that you won't have too many complaints regarding my hospitality."

"It's well worthy of the Lords of the Red Hand," said Baruch, enthusiastically.

"Sit down, gentlemen. This evening is doubly solemn for us. It marks the coronation of one of the most audacious enterprises ever attempted!"

The three bandits sat down, and, while savoring the delicious dishes that Leonello served to them on plates sealed with silver lids, they began discussing the important business that had occasioned their meeting.

First of all, they drank to the engagement of the fortunate Baruch, the future husband of one of the most beautiful heiresses in New York, and perhaps the richest. Cornelius, with his somewhat caustic irony, did not fail to remind the fiancé about the circumstances surrounding the murder of Pablo Hernandez when Baruch had been living in Jorgell City. He also recalled how, kept under rigorous control by his father, Baruch had been reduced to filching his sister Isidora's jewels, and electrocuting passers-by in order to procure a few dollars to gamble at the Black Bean Club.

Baruch was so happy that evening that he was not annoyed by that evocation of a bloody past. "What does all that matter?" he exclaimed. "They're facts as far away from us, and as far beyond our control, as the history of the emperor Nero or the destruction of Babylon. Baruch no longer exists, thanks to the all-powerful science of Dr. Cornelius. There is no longer anyone before you but Joe Dorgan, who'll be the richest man in America in a matter of days, and is, at this very moment, perhaps the happiest. I declare to you now, my friends, that I don't have a shadow of remorse. I'm proud of the energy that has allowed me to accomplish deeds that would terrify the common run of mortals."

"You're no longer suffering, then, from those Saturday nightmares that used to frighten you so much?"

Baruch shrugged his shoulders. "Bah! I ended up by taming my nerves. My health is now as good as it's possible to be."

"To your health!" cried Fritz.

All three clinked their glasses, which were full of an old Lacrima Christi with golden gleams, and drank in silence.

The conversation continued in that vein until the end of the meal. It took on a more serious allure when Leonello had taken away the dessert and brought coffee, liqueurs and cigars.

"My friends," said Baruch, taking a notebook filled with figures out of his pocket, "it's time to talk about practical matters. As my dispatch this morning informed you, we're now in possession of the Cotton and Corn Trust. Thanks to the sage precautions we've taken. Harry has only received twenty million dollars of the paternal inheritance, while we each have a share in excess of twenty-five million. That sum is likely to double in a relatively short lapse of time because of the extension—automatic, so to speak—of the Trust, which ought at a particular moment to monopolize all of American production. These are the detailed figures, which you can check for yourselves."

First Cornelius and then Fritz, examined Baruch's notebook with meticulous attention, and found everything perfectly in order. By virtue of a scruple quite frequent among rogues of his stripe, Baruch had given proof in that division of a meticulous probity. His two accomplices congratulated him warmly, and all three of them, under the influence of the great wines and food of the highest quality, abandoned themselves to their ambitious dreams.

Baruch was dreaming about the Trust of Trusts, the universal sovereignty of money.

"The three of us," he proclaimed, "are equipped to tackle such a sublime enterprise. What king, what emperor, could ever possess such power? What grandiose dreams could we not realize with that lever in our hands? The most audacious and chimerical concepts would become easy to realize. To reach the planets, to burrow all the way to the center of the Earth, to render humans immortal—all that would become possible. Is not science the sovereign mistress?"

Cornelius threw a few drops of cold water on that enthusiasm. "In principle," he said, "none of that is impossible...but we'll talk about it later. For the moment, I think we have something better to do, which is to consolidate our situation, to render it entirely unassailable, and to avoid being talked about too much."

"In that context," Fritz said, abruptly, "do you have any news of Joe?"

It was Leonello who took it upon himself to reply. "At this moment," he said, "He's at the property that Harry Dorgan owns on Lake Ontario."

"Isn't that where the golden bust with the emerald eyes was?"

"Exactly. But the property is so well-guarded that there's no means of getting into it. As I've explained to the doctor, I don't believe we have anything to fear from Lord Burydan and his friends. They're thwarted, and they have other things to think about than harming us."

"Of course," said Baruch. "I know that. The lawsuits that Harry Dorgan's Lightning Steamship Company have launched against me are going very badly; there's every chance that they'll go down and that the loss of the suit might lead to bankruptcy. On the other hand, I've learned that Bondonnat is about to return to France, taking Paganot and Ravenel with him. Once he's on his own, Harry isn't strong enough to sustain the struggle."

"I'm also going to start the process of dissolving the Red Hand," said Cornelius, abruptly. "The bandits comprising it up are dangerous allies. We need a completely new skin. Henceforth, we're honest billionaires; we mustn't have anything in common with the rabble."

The three bandits parted at a rather late hour. As he took his leave of the Kramm brothers at the little door at the main gate, Baruch reminded them that he was counting on them to be present at his marriage, which was to be unprecedentedly sumptuous even in the world of billionaires. They both assured him that they would be there. He gave them a final handshake and, with a cigar between his teeth, he strolled nonchalantly along Thirtieth Avenue.

His automobile was waiting for him where he had left it. After climbing into it, he lay down on the sumptuous cushions, his eyes half-closed, savoring the pleasure of being carried along at a rapid speed and allowing himself to drift into a reverie.

The Trust of Trusts! he thought. *I have to convince Cornelius. I need his science to bring such a magnificent project to fruition. What would all the Heads of State be in the presence of what would be the ultimate possessor of the magic metal, the gold that the alchemists called "the essence of the sun"? And when I've become the king of kings, the emperor of emperors, who will dare to reproach me for having sacrificed a few lives to the realization of such a grandiose idea?*

The speed of the automobile had increased further; it had become vertiginous. Baruch looked out of the window mechanically and did not recognize the place where he was. There were wooden hovels and waste ground: a miserable suburban landscape, lit by the moon's rays in a sinister fashion.

"Damn!" he muttered. "the chauffeur's drunk. This isn't the right road. Chauffeur!"

The only reply he received to his call was a sardonic snigger.

At the same time, two mechanisms were triggered with a dry click. Two think plates of sheet metal slid in their grooves, completely obscuring the glass in the windows. A profound darkness reigned in the vehicle's interior.

Baruch was caught like a rat in a trap. He shouted, stamped his feet and uttered threats without the slightest attention being paid to what he said. Seeing that everything he was doing was futile, the bandit became quiet. He understood that his own vehicle had been replaced by another, exactly similar in appearance. His chauffeur had doubtless been murdered, and he was a prisoner.

A prisoner of whom?

That was the agonizing mystery.

He hoped with all his heart that he had fallen into the hands of veritable malefactors. They way, he would get out of it at the cost of a ransom.

It can't be the police, though, he thought, trying to reassure himself. *If anything were to be attempted against me from that direction I'd have been warned. The Red Hand has devoted agents at Police Headquarters, as it has everywhere. Who knows? Perhaps it's one of Carmen's lovers, who is kidnapping me to prevent my marriage?*

Baruch delivered himself in that fashion, for several minutes, to all kinds of extravagant suspicious, but in the final analysis, he could only find one that seemed plausible.

The car that served as his prison was now moving at a more reasonable speed. Finally, it slowed down, and abruptly came to a halt.

Baruch experienced a momentary anguish. He wondered impatiently whether someone was going to take him out and finally explain to him what they wanted with him. He had his Browning in his hand, in case he was dealing with murderers, and was determined to sell his life dearly.

Suddenly, both side doors opened at the same time, and before he had time to use his weapon four men of Herculean stature grabbed his wrists, and tied him up.

"Where am I?" he cried. "Who are you? You're making a mistake. I'm the billionaire Joe Dorgan. If you're bandits, I'm ready to pay any ransom that you ask."

No one replied.

To reduce him to complete silence, however, one of the men gagged him with a handkerchief, while another blindfolded him. Then he was lifted off the ground and carried away like an inert mass.

Soon, by the sound that he perceived and the slight shock he experienced, he deduced that he had been placed in the cage of an elevator.

He heard the apparatus stop.

Brutally seized again, he was set on the ground. The blindfold and the gag were removed.

A door slammed noisily, and Baruch found himself in pitch darkness.

IV. The Saturday Nightmare

Baruch remained in the place where he had been set down for more than an hour without making the slightest movement.

He was so astounded, so stunned, that he could no longer think straight. The transition had been so abrupt between the pinnacle of triumph on which his imagination had placed him and that dark dungeon, that it was as if he had been thunderstruck.

In the disarray of his thoughts he got to the point of wondering whether it might not have been Cornelius and Fritz themselves who had set the trap for him, but it only required a moment's thought for him to realize that his accomplices had every interest in his entering into possession of the immense sums that he was about to acquire.

Gradually, he calmed down, understanding that in any circumstance so perilous to his life he would need all his self-composure, lucidity and intelligence.

Baruch was brave, and the idea that he was about to lose the game at the very moment when he thought he had won it restored all the spring to his energy. He needed to fight again? Well then, he would fight.

The conviction that he had powerful allies behind him, who, when they discovered the situation he was in, would hasten to his aid with the formidable means at their disposal, completed the recovery of his courage.

It would be shameful, he thought, *to abandon myself in a cowardly fashion to despair, when I still have so many cards to play, even in the state to which I've been reduced.*

The first use that Baruch made of his recovered energy was to free himself from his bonds. He observed with surprise that they were not extremely tight, either by virtue of negligence on the part of his captors or because they believed that he could not escape. With the aid of a series of torsions and movements of his wrists, he got rid of the cords binding him. After half an hour of effort, he had the satisfaction of recovering the complete liberty of his movements.

"Now we'll see," he murmured. "My hands are free."

He began striding back and forth in his cell in order to restore the circulation of his blood, and while marching, he searched. To this great disappointment, he did not find the Browning that he always carried with

276

him, or even his handkerchief. He had not been left with any object that might serve as a weapon or a means of corruption with regard to his guardians.

In the profound darkness in which he was plunged, he set about exploring the walls and floor of his cell. In spite of all his efforts he could not discover any evidence of a door or a window. The floor, the walls and even the ceiling of the square room in which he was imprisoned were uniformly covered in a thick padding, carefully quilted, like the cells in which insane people afflicted with suicidal mania are enclosed.

What alarmed Baruch even more was that he perceived that he had not been provided with anything to eat or drink. He wondered, shivering, whether he might be condemned to die of starvation, in the padded cell, from which no cry for help could be heard outside.

It was, however, necessary that breathable air was getting into the carefully sealed cage; it was doubtless only arriving through imperceptible openings, so well-hidden that it would be a waste of time searching for them.

Soon, he fell into a profound depression. He lay down full length, closed his eyes and tried to go to sleep or to think. As soon as he closed his eyes, however, he was obliged to open them again.

He suddenly remembered, fearfully, that it was the night of Saturday and Sunday, on which he had, for such a long time, been haunted by the most terrible nightmares.

That dread hastened the commencement of the very hallucination that he feared.

In the profound silence, in that pitch darkness, he heard the beating of his heart, sounding with great muffled thumps in his breast. It seemed to him then that voices were whispering in his ears. At the same time, the obscurity became animated by all sorts of grimacing faces, the aspect of which was incessantly modified and which fluttered and whirled around him.

At certain moments, it was as if they were thousands of fireflies endowed with a rapid vibratory movement. Then the luminous dots combined to form innumerable bloody hands, which all extended index-fingers to point at his face, as if to say: "That's him!"

"The Red Hand!" he stammered, terror-stricken.

It seemed to him that those hands, more numerous and more menacing with every passing minute, were leaping on to his shoulders, tugging at his hair, suspending themselves from the lapels of his jacket or moving slowly over his face. procuring him the same sensation as if he were being brushed by the wings of bats.

Baruch was terrified.

If I stay here much longer, he thought, *I'll surely go mad...*

He began trembling in all his limbs, thinking that the place where he was confined might be a padded cell in some Lunatic Asylum, from which he would never get out, and in which his reason would soon capsize.

Some hallucinations have the property of varying with the incessant rapidity of a kaleidoscope. The bloody hands that were whirling around him were succeeded by grimacing faces, which were staring at him with hideous smiles, among whom he recognized the physiognomies of some of his victims.

In the first rank he perceived Pablo Hernandez, who advanced linking arms with the chemist Gaston de Maubreuil. Both had cadaverously pale faces, but their eyes were radiant with an unsustainable glare of cruel fixity, and the contemplation of those gazes seemed so terrible to the murderer that he ended up losing consciousness.

A heavy sleep populated with bad dreams followed that faint.

When Baruch opened his eyes again, he had completely lost all notion of time and place; it required a enormous effort to succeed in recalling what had happened to him the night before, and where he was.

He had been woken up by the sound of distant music, the sounds of which, simultaneously soft and majestic, grew gradually louder until they reach an imposing thunderous rumble, with which light and airy songs were mingled, as if the celestial voices of a choir of archangels were mingling with the roar of a tempest.

Little by little, the rumors of the storm were overcome, and the song of delight and amour swelled up more expansively, rising toward the heavens.

At first, Baruch was lulled by that mysterious music, which seemed to him to be supernatural in its expression, as if in ecstasy.

He eventually realized that what he could hear was the sound of a powerful organ on which a great artist was playing improvisations of genius.

The character of the music was abruptly modified; it took on a quality that was suave, intimate and melancholy at the same time. There was something like tender promises whispered in low voices, timid confessions and confidences mingled with chaste caresses, kisses and smiles moistened by rapidly-wiped tears. There was all of that, and many other things, in the superhuman strains that were reaching Baruch's ears as if he were very close to the instrument that was producing them.

Suddenly, it seemed to him that the opaque darkness was illuminated by a tremulous, feeble and uncertain gleam, like a distant reflection, which appeared to be rising from the floor of his cell.

With an instinctive movement, he raised himself up, put his hand to his forehead, which was burning with fever, and moved unsteadily in the direction from which the light was coming.

Having traversed the cell, he saw a kind of judas-hole at his feet, which had abruptly opened in the floor, in the place of one of the sections of the padding, the tight latticework of which was letting through the glimmer that had attracted his attention.

Avidly, feverishly, Baruch lay down on his stomach, stuck his eyes to the grille and stared.

The spectacle that appeared before his eyes was such that the murderer's blood ran cold. His ears were ringing, and he thought for a moment that he was the victim of a further hallucination, but the clarity and the very reality of the scene he perceived, lit by hundreds of electric lamps, did not permit him to believe that it was a dream.

From his cell situated in the eaves, Baruch saw beneath him, as if in the depths of a gulf, the choir and principal nave of a Catholic chapel, glittering with gold and candlelight; the altar was ornamented with flowers and the azure smoke of incense-burners was rising in harmonious spirals between pillars draped with white satin and decorated with garlands of roses, lilies, white lilac and jasmine. In front of the altar, an archbishop with venerable white hair and a chasuble coruscating with gems was getting ready to give the nuptial blessing to a young man and a young woman who, at that moment, had their backs turned to Baruch.

A brilliant audience filled the chapel, and Baruch recognized, to his amazement, among the brightly-clad guests, Lord and Lady Burydan, Fred Jorgell, Harry Jorgell and Isidora, Monsieur Bondonnat, Frédrique and Andrée and their spouses, Oscar Tournesol, Regina, Agénor, and the Indian Kloum.

That stupor changed into a veritable horror when, in an old gentleman dressed with supreme elegance, who had been hidden until then behind a pillar, Baruch recognized, with no possibility of error, William Dorgan himself!

William Dorgan, whose death certificate had been duly issued!

William Dorgan, whose corpse Cornelius and Fritz had found underneath the wreckage of Rochester Bridge, and whose inheritance he, Baruch, had acquired, almost in its entirely, after a resounding victory in court over Harry Dorgan.

Baruch put his hand to his forehead, with a muffled plaint. He felt his reason capsizing in utter nightmare, utter implausibility.

He thought, momentarily, that he had been given one of those cerebral poison that, like hashish, have the power of deforming sensory perception.

He pinched himself until he bled. He rubbed his eyes, in order to be sure that he was not dreaming.

But no! Everything that he could see, everything that he could hear, was too intense in its reality to belong to the domain of dreams.

He could make out the slightest details of the costumes; he could count the sparkling pearls on the necks of the young women. The rumor of the organ-pipes was still humming in his ears, and the perfume of the incense rising to his nostrils.

Everything that he could see, therefore, had a perfectly tangible existence. Baruch wondered how all his enemies had come to be there, united as if for some express purpose, in that chapel.

He had not been able to perceive the face of the bride, but he trembled at its divination. He was afraid to know. At the moment when the young woman in the sumptuous dress of silver brocade garnished with pearls turned round for the ceremony of the ring, he closed his eyes in order not to see her face. Nevertheless, curiosity being the stronger force, he opened them again almost immediately.

He saw the proud Doña Carmen Hernandez, simultaneously smiling, ecstatic, blushing, exchanging the nuptial ring with Joe Dorgan.

Joe Dorgan himself, his face radiant with intelligence and health!

Baruch had the sensation of being a man falling over the edge of a precipice.

He uttered a cry of anguish, and fainted.

Dr. Cornelius was placidly occupied, working in his subterranean laboratory in the company of his assistant Leonello when his brother Fritz abruptly irrupted into it.

The art-dealer's face was pale and distraught. His disordered clothes and his sweat-drenched brow demonstrated that he had been run precipitately, without making use of his automobile. He collapsed rather than sat down in a chair beside his brother's.

"What's wrong?" asked Cornelius, surprised.

"All is lost!" stammered Fritz, in a strangle voice. "Baruch's been caught. Doña Carmen is married."

"What are you saying? You're crazy! What you're telling me is impossible."

"Baruch never got back to his house after our last meeting, and neither he nor his automobile have been seen since. No one knows what has become of him."

"Come on, you're not making sense. If Baruch's been arrested or has fled, Doña Carmen can't be married."

"That's the most terrible thing of all! She's married Joe Dorgan! Do you hear? The real Joe Dorgan! But that's not all. William Dorgan is alive!"

Cornelius was astounded. "I'm beginning to think seriously that you're insane. Calm down to begin with—don't panic. Above all, logic and precise facts."

"The facts are, alas, all too precise," Fritz murmured, dejectedly.

"William Dorgan can't be alive, since we were the ones who identified his body after the Rochester Bridge catastrophe."

"It wasn't him. William Dorgan, I've been told by one of our affiliates employed at the court, has applied for a rectification of his civil status. Picked up from the disaster site by his friends, he's been cared for until now in a sanitarium, and he has all the proofs necessary to establish the truth of his affirmations. The man buried in his stead was someone named Murray. The entire scaffolding of our plans is collapsing like a house of cards..."

"We've been rolled over like infants, like imbeciles, by Lord Burydan. I need to think about the best course to take. But first tell me the story of Doña Carmen's marriage."

"Nothing simpler. The young woman was in on the conspiracy. I've just learned—too late—that she's had several secret meetings with Lord Burydan and Andrée de Maubreuil. Andrée and Carmen, who both had the death of a father murdered by Baruch to avenge, understood one another marvelously. That's why they organized a comedy, of which we became the victims today."

281

"I understand now," said Cornelius, with muted exasperation, "why the Spaniard seemed so haughty and ceremonious with Baruch, and why she only granted him brief meetings."

"She granted longer ones to the veritable Joe, whom, it appears, Bondonnat has cured completely. She's known him for a long time, of course, for William Dorgan and Pablo Hernandez once has business ties. Convinced by Lord Burydan and Andrée, the Spaniard threw herself impetuously into the plot that would ensure her vengeance. As for Baruch, he's disappeared, and now we have to contend with both William Dorgan and the real Joe."

"And doubtless," Cornelius added, somberly, "with the Unites States police. It's a veritable catastrophe."

"For which you can blame tour own imprudence!" exclaimed Fritz angrily. "If you'd killed Joe Dorgan in the beginning, as I told you to, we wouldn't be in this mess."

"There's no point in quarreling. Your reproaches serve no purpose and have no significance. We have a better hand to play than you think. Our contracts with William Dorgan's Trust are perfectly legal. He'll have to go to court, and between now and then, many things might happen."

"But what if you're accused of having brought about the transformation of physiognomies?"

"It will be necessary to prove that it was me. The procedures I employed are known; I've explained them myself in various publications, which any physician could have read. Pull yourself together, my dear Fritz. The situation isn't desperate yet."

"I'm glad to see you so confident," the art dealer murmured, calming down somewhat. "But what do we have to do?"

"The most urgent thing is to get Baruch back, to find out what they've done with him. In reality, he's the only living proof they can invoke against us."

"I'll get busy with that. Slug will set out on campaign today, with a dozen of our most loyal affiliates. Believe me, though, our adversaries must be very confident of victory to have unmasked themselves as they have."

"It's precisely that confidence that will doom them. Once we've got Baruch back, I can affirm that I won't be embarrassed personally. It's fortunate, moreover, that you've warned me. I'll take advantage of the time that remains to us to dispose of certain compromising objects and documents. Believe me, Lord Burydan and his gang haven't yet won the battle, as they imagine."

"I'd like to believe that."

"One doesn't attack a man like me in this fashion. I'm famous! I'm rich! And I have the daggers of the Red Hand at my orders."

The two bandits spent three long hours taking the measures necessary for their defense. When Fritz Kramm left his brother, he had recovered almost all of his serenity—or, at least, all of his audacity.

When Baruch recovered consciousness, he was very surprised to find that he was no longer in the dark cell from which he had witnessed Doña Carmen's marriage. Someone had taken advantage of his unconsciousness to transport him to another prison. It was a whitewashed chamber lit by a narrow window fitted with strong iron bars and furnished with a camp bed, a stool and a table.

The murderer thought at first that he had finally been handed over to the law and that he was in one of the penitentiaries of New York State, but the sight of a vast park that he perceived through the panes of the window, even though the precaution had been taken of blurring them with whitewash, informed him that he was mistaken.

He sought in vain to figure out why his captors had transported him here. Everything that had happened to him since the commencement of his captivity was decidedly mysterious.

The real reason for his transfer was that it had been in Doña Carmen's palace—who, being Catholic, had had a chapel installed in one of the wings of her rich dwelling—that Baruch had been enabled to witness her marriage, but, after having inflicted that first punishment upon him, the young woman had wanted her father's murder to be handed over to the law without further delay. Lord Burydan had rapidly demonstrated to her, however, that that was impossible. The discovery of the truth would have caused a scandal of which Carmen and her husband would have been the first victims.

In addition, Lord Burydan and Fred Jorgell were insistent that Isidora, who knew nothing about these events, should remain in ignorance. The young woman still asked, from time to time, for news of her brother, and was continually told that his health was satisfactory, but that he would never recover his reason. She believed that he was still in Canada, and had many times made the resolution to go and see him, but her husband and his friends had always arranged things so that it was impossible for her to do so.

Very good and very generous, Doña Carmen had not wanted to cause Isidora any distress. Then, she had firmly declared to Lord Burydan that she wanted her father's death to be avenged, but that, on the other hand, she could not keep the vile blackguard in her house any longer, whose presence under her roof caused her an insurmountable disgust.

The matter was awkward. In order to resolve it, Lord Burydan had held a secret conference with William Dorgan, Fred Jorgell, Harry and Monsieur Bondonnat. The discussion was long and animated. Some were of the opinion that Baruch, whose true physiognomy had been rested, ought to be returned to the Lunatic Asylum; others wanted simply to get rid of the wretch with a bullet, as would be done with a rabid dog.

It was Fred Jorgell who had settled the matter. "My friends," he said, in a grave vice, "since I have the misfortune of being the monster's father, I alone have the right to punish him. I therefore request that my unworthy son be placed in my hands. You can count on me not to fail in my task as administrator of justice. Baruch will receive the punishment he deserves."

A profound silence greeted those words, which put an end to the discussion. No one opposed the inexorable old man's demand.

It was thus that Baruch had been transported to a property that Fred Jorgell owned in a suburb of New York—a property that comprised a park in the middle of which stood a villa, uninhabited for many years.

The murderer spent the rest of the day prey to an unspeakable anguish.

He wanted to know the truth at any price, to get out of the torturous indecision in which he was stranded.

At times, he had veritable fits of rage, on thinking that, while he was languishing between the four walls of a cell, his double Joe Dorgan was installed in his place and doubtless enjoying the tender prerogatives of a spouse with Doña Carmen.

"What am I now, then?" he cried, grinding his teeth. "I'm no longer Joe Dorgan, I'm no longer even the murderer Baruch! I no longer exist, save as a living ghost, who has no name or legal identity. I'm at the mercy of anyone who wants to kill me, since, socially speaking, I don't exist!"

Baruch was extracted from these afflicting reflections by the arrival of a jailer who brought him food.

In that man, who was colossal in dimension, he recognized the giant Goliath, whose description Slug had given him. From then on, there was no longer any doubt about his situation. It was obvious that he had fallen into the hands of Lord Burydan, from whom he could certainly expect no pity.

That discovery was a terrible blow. He would a thousand times rather have been in the hands of veritable bandits, or even the police. With bandits, he could have got out of it at the price of a ransom; with the police, he would have been reclaimed by the Red Hand, who had numerous powerful acquaintances among them. Such procedures could not be operated with men like Lord Burydan and Fred Jorgell, who could neither be seduced not tricked.

Baruch made all these reflections in a matter of seconds. He thought, however, that he might be able to obtain some information from his jailer.

"Who are you, my friend?" he asked him, in his mot affable tone.

Goliath's only response was to put his finger to his lips and roll his huge ferocious eyes, giving him to understand that he was forbidden to speak. There was definitely nothing to be done in that direction.

The giant had laid the table and set the prisoner's meal down upon it.

Baruch was hungry. In spite of his preoccupations, he ate with a considerable appetite, under the surveillance of his silent jailer, who did not take his eyes off him for a moment.

When the meal was finished, Goliath cleared the table and left.

Baruch noticed then that the door, massive and armored like that of a strong-room, was fitted with a spy-hole though which he could be observed at any time.

Prey to a somber despair, which his reflections only served to augment, the murderer threw himself on to his camp bed and tried to sleep, Exhausted by fatigue and emotion, he fell deeply asleep, and was very surprised, on opening his eyes again, to find that he had spent the entire night almost peacefully.

The sun was shining brightly through the panes of the narrow window. Baruch looked out for some time at the large trees of the park, and then walked back and forth in his cell, yawning. He was already feeling the first effects of the acute neurasthenia to which all those condemned to solitary confinement succumb sooner or later.

He had moments in which he wanted to be tried, condemned, and even executed, in order to escape that existence of inaction and terrible monotony. He had the painful sensation of being separated from the world of the living forever.

They don't dare kill me, he thought, clenching his fists in rage. *They're going to let me die of boredom in this hole, in order not to have a murder on their conscience. Oh, I'd a hundred times rather get it over with right away. These hypocrites are going to murder me slowly—a dagger-thrust would be preferable.*

That day seemed to Baruch to be interminable in its duration. He spent it lying on his bed or walking back and forth in his cell like a caged tiger. He was now convinced that his fate had been decided and that he would never leave his prison.

He was mistaken.

Toward the end of the afternoon, the door opened abruptly. Goliath came in, respectfully preceding an old gentleman whom Baruch recognized, with a shock, as his real father, Fred Jorgell.

They looked at one another silently for a few moments. In spite of all his insolence and audacity, Baruch was obliged to lower his eyes under the old man's severe stare.

"I thought I'd never see you again," said Fred Jorgell, in a glacial tone. "I thought, like everyone else, that after the first crimes you committed you'd lost your mind—and I was certainly glad of that. My friends were thus able to pretend, with some plausibility, that the murders in Jorgell City and the murder of Monsieur de Maubreuil were simply the results of a bloody dementia. I now know that you were perfectly sane, that you had never ceased to be intelligent and fully conscious of your actions."

His eyes lowered, Baruch listened to his father without saying a word, wondering where this preamble was heading.

"You escaped punishment the first time," the old man continued, and that for a crime more monstrous than the preceding ones. But once and for all, it's time to put an end to your exploits, and this time, neither the infernal science of Dr. Cornelius nor the daggers of the Red Hand will succeed in saving you."

The murderer experienced an impulse of revolt. His physiognomy took on a frightful expression of hatred and impotent rage. He clenched his fists, hurled himself at Fred Jorgell and tried to seize him by the throat.

Fortunately, Goliath was alert; a simple thrust of his formidable hand forced Bruch to sit down on his stool, and he was held in that position.

"I only regret one thing," cried the bandit, grinding his teeth hideously, "and that's not having killed you!"

"Silence, wretch!" said the old man. "I'm in a hurry to get this finished. I can no longer bear your odious presence."

"Yes, let's finish it! What do you want with me? Why have you come to torment me?"

"I thought that, coward as you are, you might still have had the courage to kill yourself. I'll leave you until tomorrow morning to make a decision on that subject. But if, by tomorrow morning, you haven't passed judgment on yourself, others will take care of it."

Baruch understood that all was lost. His pride vanished. He would have found himself, at that moment, perfectly satisfied with the prospect of being condemned to perpetual solitary confinement, even though he had preferred death to imprisonment not an hour before.

"Father!" he stammered, in a voice that was completely changed, "I'd like to see my sister Isidora again…the only person I've loved and has been good to me. Oh, you can't have told her what you intend to do. Isidora would have interceded on my behalf. What will she think, when she finds out that you've had the sorry courage to force me to die? Grant me life—just life! Mercy, Father, in Isidora's name!"

Baruch, whom Goliath had been unable to contain, had thrown himself at Fred Jorgell's feet.

"This cowardice is sickening," said the old man, in disgust. "I would have thought that a bandit of your sort would show more courage. These supplications are futile. I won't change my mind. You have until tomorrow morning to die."

Fred Jorgell had taken an elongated mahogany box from his pocket, which he set on the table. He left the room, followed by Goliath, without a word of farewell, without even looking at the wretch, who remained, with his head in his hands, slumped on the stool to which Goliath's powerful fist had, so to speak, nailed him down.

Baruch heard the lock and the bolts grate.

The door was locked again.

He got up, tottering on unsteady legs like a drunken man, picked up the mahogany box and opened it.

It contained a loaded revolver.

He took it and examined it carefully.

"It's a precision weapon," he said, with a bitter laugh. "A luxury weapon, worthy of being offered by a billionaire to his son."

He stood there for some time, his eyes fixed on the weapon's shiny nickel-plating, which seemed to have hypnotized him. Then, abruptly, he set it down on the table, went to the window and looked with avid curiosity at the sky, where the last rays of the setting sun were fading away by the minute.

"Tomorrow," he murmured, in a somber voice, "the sun won't rise again for me."

He threw himself on his bed, closing his eyes in order to stop thinking. When he reopened them again, his room was dark. Only the revolver was glinting in the gloom.

"Well, no!" the murderer exclaimed, hoarsely. "I won't obey that order to commit suicide; I'll fight to the end. My father—he's the cause of all my troubles—can kill me with his own hand, if he has the heart to do it. I'll defend myself, with the very weapon that they tried to make into an instrument of my torture. I'll kill the first person who opens my door tomorrow. I'll fight until the end!"

That moment of revolt did not last long. Baruch reflected that men as intelligent as Lord Burydan and Fred Jorgell must have taken precautions against any attempt at resistance.

"What point is there in trying to fight?" he murmured. "They'll see right away that I'm not dead. To perish of a bullet in the head or to die of hunger and boredom between these four walls—which is preferable? Better to finish it right away. No hope remains of my being rescued."

The bandit got up, took the revolver in a feverish hand and returned to lie down on his camp-bed again. With his finger on the weapon's trigger, he reflected.

All the scenes that had unfolded in the course of his tumultuous existence presented themselves one after another to his gaze. In his mind's eye, with a singular clarity, he saw actions and gestures that he thought he had completely forgotten.

He understood now that he was alone, that the passionate struggles of his active life had only served to distract him from his thoughts, and that he was condemned to live in the sole company of his terrible memories, to live night and day in the society of his victims.

"Decidedly," he sighed, "the eternal sleep of death is preferable to all those nightmares!"

He held the revolver firmly, this time, and put it to his temple.

Just as he was about to press the trigger, however, he seemed to hear a strange noise above his head.

What was that?

He sat up with a start and cocked his ear.

The noise had stopped.

"Bah!" he said. "What does it matter?"

At the very moment when he pronounced those words, a small fragment of plaster fell away from the ceiling and landed on his face.

The same scratching noises had resumed.

This time, Baruch put the revolver in his pocket and got up, prey to a great agitation. He was no longer thinking about the suicide that he had so firmly resolved to commit a few moments before.

Another piece of plaster came away from the ceiling, and then a third. Someone was now hammering with mighty blows, and Baruch was profoundly astonished that Goliath had not yet been attracted by the noise. The prisoner's heart was palpitating with hope. At the same time, however, Baruch trembled at the thought that Goliath might intervene.

"If that brute has the misfortune to come and disturb us," he muttered, "I'll kill him like a dog. My father definitely had a god idea in making me a gift of this revolver."

An enormous fragment of the ceiling fell away; a beam of light penetrated through the gaping hole that had just opened up, and Baruch saw the energetic face of Slug appear. He was armed with a hatchet, thanks to which he had hacked a passage through the ceiling.

Baruch thought that he would go mad with joy. He was tottering, as if gripped by a kind of drunkenness.

"Is that you, my brave Slug?"

"Yes, Milord," replied the bandit, respectfully. "I've received orders to liberate you."

"But you're making too much noise, wretch!" Baruch could not help saying. "I'm surprised that Goliath isn't here already. A little more prudence, damn it!"

Slug let out a loud burst of laughter. "Don't worry about the worthy Goliath," he said, jovially. "He's sleeping so profoundly—along with his colleagues who were mountain guard in the grounds—that I believe it would be exceedingly difficult to wake them up."

"You killed them?"

"No, Milord. They're merely asleep. I've brought with me, to make sure of the success of the expedition, ten of our most experienced Knights of Chloroform. At present, the jailers are all solidly bound and gagged. The Lords forbade us to do them any harm."

Baruch recognized Cornelius' prudence in that order. "The Lords were right," he said. "But tell me where I am."

"Simply in a suburb of New York, and I have a car here that will take you wherever you wish."

"Well, all right! But no more needless talk—I'm in a hurry to be out of here."

Baruch climbed up on to the stool, which he had set on the table, and with Slug's help he passed through the hole excavated in the ceiling and found himself in a grain-loft, from which it was easy for the two bandits to reach the grounds by means of a ladder. The same ladder also enabled them to scale the boundary wall. Finally, Baruch had the satisfaction of finding himself in an automobile—the phantom automobile itself—which, driven by Slug, departed at top speed in the direction of New York, the lights of which formed a kind of misty glow on the horizon.

Baruch experienced an immense satisfaction on finding himself so miraculously saved, after having been brushed by the wings of death, so to speak. He breathed in the fresh night air delightedly, swearing privately not to fall so stupidly into enemy hands again.

"Free!" he exclaimed, with a sort of intoxication. "I'm free! So I have a chance to take my revenge! They've been stupid to let me escape; they didn't get me, but I won't fail to get them!"

In conformity with the order he had received, Slug dropped Baruch at the end of Thirtieth Avenue, and after having asked courteously whether he needed anything, he got back into the car and disappeared.

Baruch was only a short distance from the house inhabited by Dr. Cornelius. He went there immediately, sure that he was expected.

The little door to the garden had been left open for him. He went in, after making sure that no one had followed him, and headed for the house, a few windows of which were still lit.

He did not encounter any servant on his way. The vestibule, the drawing room and the other ground floor rooms into which he went successively were deserted. One might have thought that the house had been abandoned, but Baruch knew its secrets. He went straight to the elevator. A few minutes later, he knocked on the door of the subterranean laboratory.

It was Cornelius who came to open it. They shook hands effusively.

"My dear Baruch," said the doctor, "I'm delighted to see you at liberty. I just heard, scarcely half an hour ago, about your successful escape."

"What!" murmured Baruch, surprised. "You already knew?"

"Yes. One of my affiliates telephoned me as soon as you were out of your prison."

"I owe you my deepest thanks for your intervention. Slug arrived just in time. He appeared to me like a celestial messenger at the very moment that I was putting the barrel of a revolver to my temple."

Cornelius frowned. "You wanted to commit suicide?" he said, with sudden suspicion.

"*Wanted* isn't the right word. I was being obliged to commit suicide." Briefly, Baruch told Cornelius about his adventures the previous day.

While talking they had gone into the laboratory, where Fritz and Leonello were. Baruch also brought them up to date with his captivity and escape. While he was talking, he gaze wandered around distractedly. He observed that a considerable quantity of apparatus and many of the colored moldings that had garnished the walls and display cases had disappeared.

"It seems to me," he said, "that things have changed here."

"Yes," Fritz replied. "We've been obliged to take a few precautions, to destroy certain compromising items, because it wouldn't be surprising if the police were to carry out a search here."

Fritz, in his turn, brought Baruch up to date with what he did not know, and made him understand the gravity of the situation.

All three remained silent for some time, as if no one wanted to state his opinion first.

"What are we going to do?" asked the agitated Baruch, finally.

"There's only one thing left for you to do," Cornelius replied. "That's to get away as quickly as possible Tonight—this instant. And you have to go a long way, until we've repaired the check that we've just suffered."

Baruch was utterly dejected.

"I would never have believed," he said, "that such a complete catastrophe could happen. It's the collapse of all our plans! For myself, though, I don't believe that the check is reparable."

"You're wrong," said Cornelius, hypocritically. "Our adversaries aren't immortal. Trains derail, steamers sink, houses blow up. It would only require one such accident to restore our fortunes. I've won more difficult games."

"You're giving me a little hope," Baruch murmured, bleakly. "I'll do whatever you say."

"Everything's been arranged for your flight. In an hour, you'll be aboard a steamer whose captain is one of ours, and who is setting sail for the Antilles."

"But you'll need money," said Fritz, with a bizarre smile. "Here's a wad of banknotes to take care of your most pressing needs. You'll get more as soon as you arrive in Havana."

"I'll accept the banknotes," said Baruch, taking the wallet that Fritz held out to him. "I'd be grateful if you could give me something to drink as well. My throat's dry and I'm dying of thirst."

At a gesture from Cornelius, Leonello brought three glasses and went to fetch a bottle of extra-dry from the ice-bucket where it was cooling.

Fritz and Cornelius drank a toast to wish their accomplice *bon voyage*. Baruch got up and made ready to leave.

"Leonello will take you to the steamer in my car," said Cornelius. "He won't leave you until you're safely aboard. *Adieu*, then, my dear Baruch, and *bon voyage!*"

The three bandits exchanged a final cordial handshake. Baruch headed for the laboratory door, followed by Leonello, who had courteously stood aside to let him go first.

As the Italian was about to enter the vestibule he turned and exchanged a rapid glance with Dr. Cornelius.

Baruch was already going into the elevator. At the precise moment when, turning his back to Leonello, he lowered his head in order to step into the glass-sided cage, the Italian, with a lightning-fast movement, struck him at the base of the skull with a sharp stiletto.

The thrust was delivered with a precision and sureness of which a professional assassin would have been proud. The sharp point of the weapon had attained the spinal cord at the location that the ancient anatomists had called "the vital knot," the slightest lesion in which causes instant death.

Baruch collapsed like an inert mass on to the seat of the elevator. He had died without uttering a sound.

Leonello wiped the scarcely-reddened stiletto on the dead man's clothing and went back into the laboratory.

"It's already done?" said Fritz, surprised.

"Yes, Master," the Italian replied, with perfect calm.

"Now," said Cornelius, "it's necessary, without losing a moment, to carry the cadaver to the electric furnace and fire it up with as powerful a current as our accumulators can furnish. In half an hour, there'll be nothing left but a handful of ash."

Leonello immediately loaded the warm cadaver on to his shoulders and deposited it inside the electric furnace."

"That's curious," murmured Fritz, becoming suddenly thoughtful. "Baruch died in almost the same conditions as the French chemist, Monsieur de Maubreuil, whom he once murdered."

"Don't you believe in Providence?" said the sculptor of human flesh, sarcastically. "I do. That must be what has permitted us to get rid of Baruch so easily, who could only have compromised us and from whom we've extracted all possible utility."

"One way or another, he wouldn't have been any inconvenience," said Fritz, "since he would have blown his own brains out tonight. If I'd known that beforehand, I certainly wouldn't have put Slug to the trouble of rescuing him."

"The disappearance puts me entirely at ease. Let Lord Burydan and his band dare to lay any charge against me! It'll be impossible for them to prove a single one of their accusations. Baruch was a living piece of evidence, and now nothing remains of him."

"What's even better," said Fritz, with a smile of satisfaction, "is that we've got our share of the Corn and Cotton Trust."

"Not forgetting that we still have a large quantity of Monsieur de Maubreuil's diamonds..." Cornelius interrupted himself abruptly. For a few moments he had been darting anxious glances at the electric furnace. "What's that animal Leonello doing?" he muttered. "We should already be feeling the heat of the oven. Has the current been interrupted somehow? That really would be bad luck."

The sculptor of human flesh got to his feet and headed toward the furnace.

Scarcely had he turned away than Fritz took a little bottle from his pocket and tipped a few drops of its contents into Cornelius' glass, which was still half-full following Baruch's departure. Then he put the stopper back in the bottle, briskly made it disappear, and got up to go and join his brother, simulating a great interest in the accident that had befallen the electricity.

"What are we going to do if there's no current? Will we be obliged to dissolve the body in acid?"

"We won't have that difficulty," sniggered Cornelius. "The current's working perfectly again. In a minute, the temperature inside the furnace will surpass two thousand degrees.

"Where has Leonello gone?"

"He's gone to fetch me a monkey wrench."

The Italian did indeed return, a moment later, twisted a wire and tightened a bolt—and the metal doors did not take long to become incandescent, in spite of the asbestos with which they were lined. A violent heat forced the three bandits to withdraw to the far end of the room.

"The radiation of that furnace is unbearable," said Cornelius, in the most natural tone possible. "Simply by spending a few minutes in its vicinity, I can feel my throat drying out. I'm going to have a drink."

"Me too!"

Fritz and Cornelius went back to the table. Leonello finished filling up the glasses, which were half-empty, and poured one for himself. All three drank the sparkling liquid to the last drop.

"It seems to me," said Cornelius, in a singular tone, "that this wine has an odd taste."

"I don't think so," Fritz replied, blushing slightly.

"Would you to see me poisoned?" added the doctor, in a stone of stinging mockery. "You'd certainly have the right to say that there's a Providence then. Not to mention that I'd leave a rather substantial inheritance...."

"Why talk about that?" murmured Fritz, embarrassed.

"Bah! It's necessary to talk about something. But what's the matter? It seems to me that you're very pale."

"It's nothing," stammered the art dealer, who was beginning to feel ill. "I have a headache..."

"If it's nothing, so much the better. To get back to my joke, I was saying that I'd leave you a very considerable inheritance, my dear Fritz. So, let's suppose that my dear Fritz were to say to himself one morning that he's waited for his legacy long enough, that Dr. Cornelius is a compromising relative, and that it really would be a stroke of luck if the aforesaid Cornelius happened to die suddenly..."

"No such thought ever crossed my mind!" protested Fritz, whose face had taken on a livid pallor. "Don't say things like that..."

"I'm joking. Let me continue my little story. The death of his excellent brother Cornelius has, therefore, become something of an obsession with Fritz, and, as the proverb says, 'it's the opportunity that makes the thief.' One day, when the two brothers are quietly sharing a glass of champagne, Fritz takes advantage of Cornelius turning his back to put poison in his glass..."

"Mercy! Mercy!" stammered Fritz, beginning to feel something like a red hot iron burning his entrails.

Cornelius continued, in a perfectly tranquil manner: "Fortunately for him, Cornelius, over whom the Providence we were talking about just now is watching, has seen his dear Fritz's rapid gesture in the Venetian glass. What does Cornelius do? He whispers a word in the ear of his faithful Leonello. The latter goes to the other side of the laboratory on the pretext of fetching a monkey wrench, and switches the glasses, with the result..."

During this explanation, Leonello had disappeared. Fritz was writhing in his chair. The effect of the poison was so rapid that his face was already dappled with large red botches.

"Mercy, Cornelius!" he repeated, in a heartrending voice, throwing the bottle he had employed on to the table. "You must have the antidote!" he added.

"I have it," said Cornelius coldly.

"Give it to me! You can still save me!"

"No."

"I beg you…!"

"No. You've betrayed me; you'll die."

Fritz no longer had the strength to speak. He was uttering inarticulate groans, waving his supplicant hands in Cornelius' direction. The latter was looking at him with an inflexible smile.

Suddenly, Fritz beat the air with his hands and fell to the ground. His entire body was agitated by violent spasms. Then, abruptly, he became motionless.

The poison had done it work.

Cornelius shouted: "Leonello! It's necessary to carry this body to the furnace, like the other."

Leonello appeared almost immediately, but his face was distraught. "Master!" he said. "We've waited too long! The house is surrounded. The street is blocked by a cordon of policemen, and the garden is full of detectives."

"We need to get out, quickly! We still have a few minutes in hand. Open the iron door while I get Fritz's papers."

A minute later, the two bandits went into a secret exit that led away from the laboratory. They carefully closed the armored door that gave access to it behind them.

Scarcely had they vanished when fifty detectives, revolvers in hand, irrupted into the laboratory.

At that very moment, however, a terrible quake shook the ground. A jet of flame enveloped the house, launching fragments of stone, wooden beams and fiery debris in all directions.

The laboratory of the sculptor of human flesh had just blown up.

VI. Epilogue

The news of the explosion of Dr. Cornelius Kramm's laboratory caused a profound reverberation throughout America. In certain devout milieux, both Protestant and Catholic, it was affirmed that the Devil in person, mounted on a fiery steed, had come to carry away the sculptor of human flesh, still alive, to Hell.

In addition, the rumor had spread that Cornelius and Fritz were the ultimate chiefs, the so-called Lords, of the Red Hand, and that discovery caused a considerable motion in New York society,

For three days, a cordon of policemen surrounded the ruins of the house, and detectives, assisted by a gang of laborers, explored the rubble.

Several cadavers were found, disfigured to varying degrees. That of Fritz Kramm was the first that could be identified; another, discovered in an electric furnace and badly charred, was absolutely unrecognizable. It was supposed, with some plausibility, that it was that of Leonello, who, knowing too much about his master's secrets, must have been murdered by him. Only Lord Burydan and Fred Jorgell, who were shown the body, were able to recognize Baruch, but they kept the secret to themselves, and the name of Monsieur de Maubreuil's murderer was not even mentioned in the course of the investigation that was launched to attempt to determine the cause of the explosion, in which more than fifty policemen had lost their lives.

Some of the senior officials at Police Headquarters knew the truth, but Isidora, to whom no one wanted to cause any unnecessary chagrin, never suspected the fashion in which her wretched brother had died. It was only several months later that a letter from Canada informed her that the madman of the Blue House had died quietly without having recovered his reason.

When the clearance was completed, Cornelius' cadaver was found, frightfully mutilated but—according to the detectives—sufficiently recognizable.

One fact that caused much astonishment, however, was that no trace was found, either in the ruins of the house or in the banks, of the considerable sums in banknotes and gold that Cornelius had possessed, as was public knowledge. It was supposed that the doctor had been warned in advance of the threat of arrest, and had put his money in a safe place, confiding it to one of the affiliates of the Red Hand.

As for Fritz's fortune, it had an unexpected destination. There was a will in the possession of a New York notary, duly drawn up and certified, in which Cornelius, Fritz and Joe Dorgan had bequeathed to one another everything that they possessed. It was, therefore, the true Joe Dorgan, Carmen's husband, who entered into possession of the vast storehouses filled with paintings and *objets d'art*.

Of that suspect fortune, the young billionaire only wanted to keep a few paintings of little value and the diamonds originating from the theft committed in Monsieur de Maubreuil's home, some of which had neither been cut nor sold.

That will, which Fritz and Cornelius had imposed on their accomplice Baruch, had the consequence of making Joe the sole owner of the Corn and Cotton Trust. He hastened to divide the capital derived from that inheritable equally with his brother, the engineer Harry.

At one time, certain newspapers, probably with the intention of blackmail, insinuated that Joe Dorgan had been on such good terms with the two brothers that he must have been their accomplice, but the senior officials at New York Police headquarters, well aware of Baruch's true identity, quickly reduced the expert blackmailers to silence.

Rid of its financial adversaries, the Lightning Steamship Company entered into an era of prosperity such as it had never known, and it soon merged with the Corn and Cotton Trust, in which Lord Burydan had a considerable shareholding.

Fred Jorgell and William Dorgan, who had become inseparable, had abandoned the running of the two Trusts to Joe and Harry. The latter would have been delighted to keep Antoine Paganot and Roger Ravenel with them, at princely salaries, being fully appreciative of their merits, but after so many adventures, the two young men and their wives, Andrée and Frédérique, wanted to return to France. Monsieur Bondonnat was also determined to reclaim his laboratory and his magnificent gardens in Brittany.

The Frenchmen stayed with their friends in New York for another month, and then embarked on the *Ariel*, which Lord Burydan commanded in person during the crossing from New York to Brest.

When they parted from Isidora and Regina, Andrée and Frédérique made them promise to come and see them in France at the first favorable opportunity.

The American kept their promise six months later, on the occasion of a family celebration that reunited all of the illustrious Prosper Bondonnat's friends in the property at Kérity-sur-Mer. At an interval of a week, Andrée and Frédérique had become mothers; Andrée's daughter was named Frédérique, and Frédérique's son Prosper, as his grandfather had wished.

The baptismal feast lasted a week, and gave rise to rejoicing the memory of which has not been lost in that part of Brittany. Monsieur Bondonnat, who had just won a Nobel prize following the publication of his fine book *The Consciousness of Vegetables*, was able to see united around his table almost all of these who had taken part, at close range or at a distance, in his fantastic adventures.

First of all there were Harry Dorgan and Isidora, who had wanted to hold little Frédérique Paganot over the baptismal font, while Joe Dorgan and Carmen were the godparents of Monsieur Bondonnat's grandson.

William Dorgan and Fred Jorgell had also come, glad to see once again the old friend whose science and abnegation had rendered them such great services. The two billionaires were laden with gifts that would have made the genies of the Arabian Nights and the princesses of fairy tales seem stingy by comparison.

Mr. Bombridge, who was in the process of becoming a billionaire, thanks to his selective breeding of an exceptionally tasty giant edible snail, was absorbed by the concerns of his business; in his stead he had delegated for daughter, the lovely Regina, and his son-in-law Oscar Tournesol.

It was with the most profound emotion that the former hunchback set foot on the soil of his native land and saw his friends and benefactors, Monsieur Bondonnat and his family, again. He was also very happy to see his old comrade Kloum, who had come with Lord Burydan, the Cossack Rapopoff, now a laboratory assistant, and the young Oceanian woman Hatouara, who had left the school in Paris where she as completing her studies to attend the baptism. It was an equally great pleasure for him to renew his acquaintance with Lord Burydan, who was accompanied by the indispensable Agénor.

Since his marriage, the eccentric had ceased to occupy the attention of the humorous papers of the two worlds. On the other hand, he was completely cured of his neurasthenia, and it was to the charming Lady

Ellenor, the lady of the scabious flowers, that he attributed—not without reason—all the merit of that cure.

Monsieur Bondonnat had been careful not to forget Lorenza and her husband, the painter Grivard, in his invitations. The latter had commenced a superb portrait of the old scientist a few weeks earlier. Everyone admired the beauty of the healer of pearls, whose health, temporarily compromised by the privations she had endured during her captivity among the Buddhists, was more flourishing than ever.

The dog Pistolet, as one might imagine, also played his part in the celebrations, and, if he had not been an animal almost as reasonable and as sober as a human, he would certainly have died of indigestion, so many sugary treats of every sort was he offered.

The week that the festivities lasted went by with the rapidity of a dream. It was with a genuine chagrin that Monsieur Bondonnat's guests finally thought of separating from their friends.

On the eve of the departure, the old scientist and the two billionaires found themselves alone on one of the terraces of the villa's magnificent garden. The flower-beds were embalming the air. The sky was scintillating with thousands of stars. They could hear in the distance, the murmurous song of the sea against the rocks.

The three old men remained silent for some time, lending an ear to the laughter and joyful voices that were escaping from the illuminated windows of the villa.

"Well," said Monsieur Bondonnat, suddenly, "what about the Red Hand?"

"Completely annihilated," Fred Jorgell replied. "The American government finally decided to take energetic measures. More than ten thousand arrests have been made. Police Headquarters has been purified. All the detectives who belonged, intimately or distantly, to the association, have been sacked. Only one of the bandits we knew has been able to evade all research, and that's Slug."

"What can have become of him?"

"It's supposed that he's withdrawn to the remote regions of the Mexican frontier, where bandits still exist. The last time I heard mention of him is when he attempted to pillage the hacienda of San Bernardino, where Dorypha and her husband still live. The tramps encountered a resistance on that occasion that they hadn't expected. Three of them were killed and Slug was seriously wounded."

"And our friends at the Blue House?" asked Monsieur Bondonnat.

"I'm the one who can give you news of them," said William Dorgan. "They're very happy. Baron Skinflint, who did last month, left them a princely fortune. After his death, a treasure of nearly a million dollars in gold and banknotes was discovered in a carefully armored cellar."

"I hope that they'll make better use of it than the baronet," said the old scientist, with a smile. Then, he passed almost abruptly on to another idea. "I often think about the mysterious Dr. Cornelius," he murmured, "who took his secrets with him when he died. His physiognomy is unforgettable, so far as I'm concerned."

"Do you believe that he's dead?" asked Fred Jorgell.

"His body was found," said William Dorgan

"Was it really his? You know better than anyone, Monsieur Bondonnat, that the sculptor of human flesh excelled in the art of faking anatomical specimens. On the Island of Hanged Men there was a bandit who offered an exact resemblance to Cornelius, who was never found. Might it not be the bandit's cadaver that was exhumed from the rubble? That's what I've often wondered, with a certain perplexity."

"But how could he have escaped?" asked William Dorgan.

"I can't be sure, but when the terrain was cleared, a tunnel communicating with Cornelius' laboratory was found, sealed by an iron door, which ended in an old sewer. If he did escape, perhaps that's the exit he used."

"What supports that hypothesis," said Monsieur Bondonnat, after a moment's reflection, "is that the enormous sums he had at his disposal disappeared with him."

"Look," said Fred Jorgell, taking from his pocket a crumpled newspaper. "This is an issue of the *Sydney Times*. It contains a portrait of a certain Dr. Malbrough, who, in spite of his side-whiskers, bears an astonishing resemblance to Cornelius. The strangest thing is that in a matter of months, he's built quite a reputation in Australia thanks to his surgical feats, which resemble in a singular fashion those that Cornelius once achieved."

"Perhaps it's just a simple coincidence," murmured Bondonnat, pensively.

"Who will ever be able to say?" exclaimed Fred Jorgell, getting to his feet,

No one answered that remark. The three old men went back in silence to the villa, filled with noise and animation by the merriment of the guests.

www.ingramcontent.com/pod-product-compliance
Lightning Source LLC
Chambersburg PA
CBHW030346020726
47493CB00003B/704